SHATTERED TO DEATH

SHATTERED TO DEATH

A KENZIE KIRSCH MEDICAL THRILLER
BOOK NINE

P.D. WORKMAN

ISBN: 9781774686232 (KDP Paperback)
ISBN: 9781774686249 (KDP Hardcover)
ISBN: 9781774686256 (Large Print)
ISBN: 9781774686263 (Lulu Paperback)
ISBN: 9781774686270 (ePub)
ISBN: 9781774686287 (Accessible Audio)

ALSO BY P.D. WORKMAN

FIND MORE BOOKS AT PDWORKMAN.COM

MYSTERY/SUSPENSE:

Zachary Goldman Mysteries

Private Investigator

She Wore Mourning

His Hands Were Quiet

She Was Dying Anyway

He Was Walking Alone

They Thought He was Safe

He Was Not There

Her Work Was Everything

She Told a Lie

He Never Forgot

She Was At Risk

He Drowned in Memory

Their Walls Were Empty

They Came for Him

They Sought Vengeance

She Was Their Target

His Fear Was Real

Kenzie Kirsch Medical Thrillers

Unlawful Harvest

Doctored Death

Dosed to Death

Gentle Angel

Rushin' Death

Posed for Death

Death of a Corpse

Endowed with Death (Coming Soon)

Shattered to Death (Coming Soon)

Captured in Death (Coming Soon)

AND MORE AT PDWORKMAN.COM

That those who are broken
may be mended

1

Kenzie was just dropping off to sleep when her phone rang, making both her and Zachary jump.

Zachary instantly sat up and reached for his phone, even though it wasn't his ringtone. He pulled back after touching it, realizing by then that it wasn't his phone that was ringing. It took longer for Kenzie to rouse herself to some semblance of logical thought and to reach for her phone. Her phone was usually on silent mode so that it would not disturb Zachary at night. In theory, Kenzie would awaken to the phone's vibration on the side table and be able to silence it and leave the bedroom to take the call without waking Zachary. In reality, he was usually the one who awoke to the vibration and had to shake Kenzie awake to see whether it was an important call.

But tonight, she was on call and had turned the ringer on and set her volume to high so she couldn't miss a call-out. Dr. Wiltshire had attended two calls in person the night before, so it was his turn to sleep while Kenzie dealt with any calls.

It wasn't like a call-out was an emergency. It could wait a couple of hours if she didn't answer the phone immediately. It wasn't like her patients were going anywhere or would be more dead when she got there.

She liked to get to a scene as early as possible to take temperature readings and talk about the circumstances with the person who had discovered the body and any other witnesses. While most calls that the ME's office got were routine, she wanted to be on top of it if it were a potential homicide, when details like an accurate time of death could become very important. A whole case could hinge on who was or wasn't around during the relevant window.

Kenzie blinked hard and picked up her phone. "Medical Examiner's Office," she answered, after confirming that the call had been routed through the ME's office line.

"We need the medical examiner to attend a scene." The voice on the other end was male. Calm and official. But there was something in the tone of his voice that alerted Kenzie that he was nervous or excited. A slight change in pitch? His breaths coming faster than she would have expected. She couldn't put her finger on precisely what made him sound young and inexperienced, despite the definite adult timbre of his voice.

"Can I get the details?" Kenzie asked. "Address and what happened?"

It wasn't a law enforcement officer; she was pretty sure of that. They had their own particular official tone. Much more forceful and confident. Expectation, but also a hint of the routine, of a resignation that the ME might not get there for several hours and they would be left standing around the body waiting for someone to show up.

"Persons Residential Care," the voice on the other end of the phone informed her, following up with the address. He didn't answer the "What happened?"

"Got it," Kenzie agreed. "Can you tell me the circumstances of the death? I'd like to know whether I can get by with the death kit I have with me or whether I need to pick up additional equipment from the office."

"Well… I don't know. He just died."

"He just died?" Kenzie repeated. "In a medical facility?"

"Yes. I don't know what happened. Someone should come."

"I'll be there. No sign of violence? What was the patient in care for?"

"Psychiatric."

His answers were not particularly helpful and, from the muffled sounds in the background, Kenzie assumed that he was covering the mouthpiece and speaking to someone else, or someone else was talking to him and he didn't want Kenzie to hear everything being said.

"I'll be there shortly," she promised.

He hung up without any thanks or goodbye.

"Everything okay?" Zachary demanded as soon as Kenzie lowered her phone. He ran a hand over his dark buzz-cut and blinked.

"Sure. Just got a call-out." She shrugged. "We both knew it could happen."

"People ought to pick a more convenient time to die," Zachary suggested playfully.

"They should," Kenzie agreed with a smile. She sighed and got out of bed, putting her phone back on the side table while she stripped off her pajamas and quickly pulled on clothes more appropriate for a scene of death attendance.

"Murder?" Zachary asked.

"No. Medical facility." She didn't tell him anything more than that. Not like she could; so far, she was completely in the dark about what had happened.

Kenzie glanced out the window. *In the dark* was right. The sun had been down for hours. People *did* choose inconvenient times to die.

"I could drive you," Zachary suggested. He had done that once or twice before, especially if he thought she was too tired to drive or needed him there for another reason.

But there was no need for him to be around in this case. No indication that it was anything other than a patient dying in his sleep. It was not an uncommon occurrence in a psychiatric facility.

"No, you stay home and get your sleep," Kenzie told Zachary, even though she knew there was no way he would sleep while she was gone. He would get up and work on his laptop or watch TV. Or just pace. "I don't know how long I will be, but I'm fine. No need for both of us to be out."

"I'd be happy to come along…"

"Not necessary. Thanks for the offer, though."

Zachary sighed. Kenzie knew that he would have preferred to go with her, but she didn't know how long she would be and didn't want him sitting around in the car waiting for her to finish her routine tasks at the scene.

Though it wasn't like he minded spending time sitting in the car. In fact, he chose to sit in it for hours on end when he was on a surveillance job. That was the life of a PI, sometimes. More often than not, he was assigned to keep an eye on someone to learn their schedule, where they worked, whether they were having an affair, or whether they were able to do more than they had told their insurance company after an accident. People actually lied to their insurance companies. Who would have guessed?

"Sorry," she told him. "I doubt I'll be too long. I should be back tonight."

"You'd better be. I don't like you stepping out on me for these stiffs."

Kenzie grinned. She finished getting dressed and ducked into the bathroom to check her hair and try to tame the wild, dark curls into something more professional. She put on a coating of her trademark red lipstick, though she knew no one but she would appreciate it, considering the circumstances. She picked up her phone and handbag as she walked back through the bedroom and got on her way.

2

enzie knew generally where Persons was, but hadn't been there before. Or she might have attended there once as a medical student, but couldn't remember much about it. Maybe when she was writing a paper and needed to interview someone? It was several years in the past, and the sleepless nights of medical school had blurred the memories.

She gave her baby, a beautiful, cherry-red convertible, time to warm up before backing out of the garage and getting on the road. She was soon outside the town limits, getting away from the glaring streetlights and sparse traffic. It took a few minutes for her eyes to adjust to the dark of the country road, and then she could see stars sprinkled across the black canvas of the night, thousands of twinkling pinpricks, and a sliver of a bright moon.

She had that awake-alert feeling that she got when she was taking care of an emergency when she would normally have been sleeping. She remembered the early morning starts to vacations when she had been young, sometimes having to go to the airport in the wee hours to catch an international flight. Sleeping with her head resting on her mother's shoulder while they sat in the chairs of the waiting area for boarding to begin. But not sleeping. Staring at the dark windows and watching the preparations covertly, looking as though she were asleep, but with an alertness running through her body, her brain primed to take everything in.

The care facility was not far away. Just away from the hustle and bustle of the town. Somewhere quiet for people to recover. To take a break from their stressful, pressured lives and regenerate, get healthy before returning to the homes and families waiting for them.

Kenzie pulled into the parking lot and couldn't identify any particular parking space that she should take. It was quiet; just a few cars from the night staff were there. And a long black hearse backed into one of the staff stalls near the doors. Kenzie pulled up to the big double doors and shut off the engine.

A security guard walked out to meet her as she grabbed her death kit and walked toward the doors. He held up his hand to stop her and send her back. "I'm sorry. You can't park there. And it turns out your services are not needed. You were called in error. Just a mistake."

Kenzie frowned at him. "I'm sorry?"

"You're from the ME's office, right? I'm sorry. You aren't actually supposed to be here."

"I was called about a death."

"Yes, that was wrong. You shouldn't have been. Someone who didn't know proper procedures…"

Kenzie shook her head, brushing aside his hand as he reached out to block her and send her back.

"I'm sorry, but once I am called to a scene, I have to attend."

"But you weren't supposed to be."

"Actually, I was. The ME's office is required to attend any deaths occurring at a psychiatric facility."

"There's no need." He blocked her more aggressively.

Kenzie looked him in the eye. "Look. I've told you that I'm required by law to attend. There's nothing I can do about it. There's nothing you can do to change my mind. I can call the cops to get them to remove you so I can get to the scene. Is that what I need to do?"

He hesitated, wavering.

"Events have been set into motion," Kenzie reiterated. "I need to follow a certain procedure. Will you let me in, or do I have to call for backup?"

He lowered his hand slowly. "Well, I don't see why you have to be so stubborn about it…"

"It's the procedure I have to follow. If it's just an unattended death, someone who died in his sleep, then my time here will be very short. I'll be in and out with no fuss or bother. But you can't stop me from attending, or there will be consequences. You don't want to get arrested for impeding an investigation, do you?"

"You're not even the police," the guard grumbled, but he stepped back and grudgingly let Kenzie pass.

Kenzie preceded him into the building, but she did not have any idea where to find the body once she got there. She looked around. There was no one waiting inside to escort her to her patient. The security guard trailed her in.

"Can you point me in the right direction?" Kenzie asked. "Or should I just wander around looking for a body?"

"Down the hall and to the right," he grumbled. Then he apparently decided he should do more than just give her directions. "I'll show you."

Once they were down the first hallway, Kenzie could hear voices. Casual, routine voices, doctors or nurses talking to each other as they completed their duties. The security guard led her around another corner, and then she could see where people were gathered in the hall, pulled in by the specter of death.

There were a couple of young men in dress pants and white shirts wheeling a gurney into a patient's room. Kenzie hadn't seen an ambulance nearby. And ambulance attendants did not wear white shirts.

But she *had* seen a hearse.

"Excuse me!" Kenzie hurried forward as the two men bent over in the cramped space, preparing to lift the body onto the gurney. "Don't touch that body. Get back."

They stopped and looked at her, frowning. A doctor standing outside the room, gray hair and a dark mustache, prominent creases between his eyes, turned to her.

"Who are you?"

"Dr. Kenzie Kirsch. Assistant to the Medical Examiner."

"What are you doing here?"

Kenzie motioned to the body on the floor. "Looking after him."

"You're not needed here. This is a doctor-attended death. No need for the medical examiner to be involved."

"Well, I was called, and I am required to be called for all deaths in a psychiatric facility. And you," Kenzie motioned again to the funeral home workers. "You can go. Leave me your card. I'll call you when we finish with the body."

The two men looked at each other, not sure what to do.

"You're not taking this body," Kenzie said firmly.

"Look, Dr. Kirsch," the doctor spoke to her again. "This is all just a misunderstanding. I'm sorry. You should not have been called. Just let the funeral home take care of the body, and you go home and get your sleep."

"I need to fulfill my obligations. There is a strict procedure to be followed. I'm sure you've seen it all before. It shouldn't take me too long."

There was no blood on the floor, no apparent injuries. The man had clearly not been shot or stabbed. Kenzie looked down at him, her mind already running through checklists. What she would need to see, what pictures she would take. What she would tell Carlos or whoever came from the office to transport the body, what she would tell death investigators if she needed someone else there to help collect evidence.

"This is ridiculous," the doctor complained.

"Well, it doesn't hurt you. It's just one extra step before the deceased is sent on to the funeral home. We make sure that there are no concerns, and then the family gets the body," Kenzie assured him. Of course, the doctor was old enough to know all of this anyway. He was obviously not inexperienced. He knew the way it all worked.

The doctor threw up his hands in frustration, defeated. "Fine. Do what you have to do. But it is over my objection. You don't need to be here. It is just a waste of time."

"Well, better a waste of time than having to exhume a body later on down the line!" Kenzie told him cheerfully.

The funeral home attendants backed off to let Kenzie do her examination. One of them hemmed and hawed for a minute, then handed her a business card, and he and his associate took their gurney and departed. The doctor shook his head.

"Everything would have been taken care of in five minutes. Now I'm going to still have a dead body here in two hours. Before long, we'll have patients getting up and finding one of their number dead on the floor."

Kenzie rolled her eyes as she performed the first checks on the body to ensure the patient was properly deceased. She would have the body out of there well before patients started getting up in the morning. Unless both of the ME office trucks broke down, and if that were the case, she knew of a hearse that could probably be pressed into service…

She rested her fingertips lightly on the man's arm. "How long has he been here, Dr….?"

He hesitated, then supplied his name. "Dr. Alvarez. He can't have been there for very long. He was asleep. Must have just gotten up… maybe he wasn't feeling well and went to get help, or something for indigestion, and just keeled over."

Kenzie shook her head. "He's in full rigor."

"That can't be right."

"How long did you wait before calling someone?"

"It takes a while for people to get here," he said cautiously. "Maybe… an hour?"

It had been less than an hour since Kenzie had been called, but she knew that it hadn't been Dr. Alvarez who had called her. He had an accent and an older voice. More of an attitude, almost a bullying manner. The man who had called her on the phone had been softer spoken, younger, probably not very experienced in dealing with unexpected deaths. And that someone had called her after Dr. Alvarez had called the funeral home.

"It's been more than an hour," Kenzie disagreed. "Full rigor. That takes a significant amount of time."

But something wasn't right, because the body was still quite warm to the touch. And it shouldn't be if he had been lying on the floor for long enough for full rigor set in. Kenzie took a couple of temperature readings, writing them down and noting the time and the stage of rigor mortis. When time of death indicators did not match the witness stories or each other, there was good reason to be careful. Measure everything twice. Note everything down with dates, times, and pictures. Interview all witnesses to get their stories before they started to change.

"He hasn't been lying there for hours," Alvarez objected.

Kenzie just shook her head. She knew he was wrong or lying to her. Or there was something very strange going on with her newest patient.

3

Kenzie continued to examine the body, a little bit at a time, head to toe, front and back. Much more carefully than she would typically inspect the body at the scene when there didn't appear to be any sign of illness or violence. She usually saved her detailed examination for the postmortem. But she didn't like what was happening at this scene already, which meant that she doubled down and did more than she had to.

The patient was a Black man, tall and thin, with the high cheekbones and very dark skin of a Nigerian. He was wearing what appeared to be institution-issued pajamas. Not the skimpy johnny worn at a hospital, open in the rear, but pants and a button-up shirt in matching lightweight blue-gray cotton. Such dark skin made it difficult to appreciate any bruises. She would have to use an alternative light source at the morgue, which would help make them a little more visible. She thought there might be bruising on the forearms and a swelling on the back of his head. There were no lacerations, nothing that appeared to be caused by a weapon. He could have hit his head anywhere. Falling out of bed. Looking for something that had fallen under a table and sitting up before he was clear of it. It might have happened before he was admitted to the facility.

"What can you tell me about the decedent?" she asked Dr. Alvarez. "Name, medical history?"

"This is Leander Isah. Bipolar. Began experiencing symptoms as an older teen. He has been in and out of institutions since then."

"Do you have his medication protocol?"

"It will be on the computer, of course."

"I would like to get a copy of that. And anything else you can provide about his treatment and medical history, when he was admitted, anything unusual that may have happened the last few days."

Alvarez looked at her silently, not agreeing or disagreeing. Kenzie wondered if he were going to be a problem. Or maybe she would be dealing with another doctor or the director of the facility.

"This was a natural death," Alvarez told her.

"It may have been," Kenzie said neutrally.

The frown lines between his brows deepened, as if Kenzie agreeing with him was more of a concern than her disagreeing.

Other people watched from doorways and the nursing station partway down the hall. Kenzie glanced up at the approach of a young man in blue scrubs. He was very handsome, very young. New on the job. He was trying to see or listen to what they were saying without being too obvious about it. Finding a reason to come a little farther down the hall to gather more intelligence about what was happening. Because he knew something, or just because he was interested in the gossip?

"Did you know Mr. Isah?" Kenzie asked him without raising her voice.

Alvarez looked perplexed at her question, then realized she was talking to someone else and turned his head to see. The nurse swallowed and looked at Alvarez before answering. Alvarez gave a curt nod to grant him permission to answer.

"I have treated him," he admitted.

"What was he on? Do you know his med protocol?"

The man scratched his neck, thinking about it, then shook his head. "I'm not sure. SSRIs. A mood stabilizer, but I don't remember which one. I think maybe... an antipsychotic? It will all be on the computer."

Kenzie nodded her agreement. "How about night meds? A sedative? Sleep aid?"

"Yes, most of them take a sleep aid."

Kenzie knew that when Zachary was admitted to the hospital psych ward, they usually insisted on his taking a sleep aid at night, even though he didn't like to. Sleep was essential to good mental health. And, she suspected, very important to the mental health of the nurses and other members of the staff, who liked things to be quiet and uneventful at night. It wasn't good if patients were up wandering around and getting involved in altercations.

"Did he wander at night? Was it unusual to see him out of bed?"

The nurse didn't say anything, looking again at Dr. Alvarez.

"What's your name?" Kenzie asked.

"Nurse Craig, ma'am."

"Nurse Craig. You were usually here at night?"

"Not always…" He looked around as if searching for a calendar or clock that would give him the answer. He looked back at Kenzie. "Uh… yeah, I guess I was usually here at night."

"And you knew Mr. Isah? He had been here before, or he had been here for long enough this time that you were familiar with him?"

"Yes."

"And did he usually get up and wander at night? Is it unusual that he was out of his bed?"

Nurse Craig cast one more look at Dr. Alvarez and then nodded. "Yes, I don't think I had seen him out of bed many times before. Maybe once. Not like some of the wanderers."

"How was he today? Were there any issues?"

A long silence. Kenzie busied herself with examining the body and didn't stare at Nurse Craig, but waited for him to decide to talk.

"He was agitated earlier. Earlier in the day."

"Over something in particular?"

"No. He was just… yelling a lot. Upset at the people around him. Acting like everyone was getting in his way."

"What is he normally like?"

"Very quiet."

"He doesn't yell?"

"No. Not like some of the patients."

Kenzie smiled and nodded. She remembered what it was like working in a hospital. People yelling for attention all the time. All her time being taken up by a few patients, and then she didn't have as much time for the quieter, more compliant patients. Time that they needed.

"Did something happen to upset him? Or had his meds been changed? Any change at all in health or care protocol the last few days?"

"Uh…" Craig looked at Alvarez. "You'd have to check with his doctors on any changes in their orders…"

"Anything?" Kenzie asked Alvarez, rather than arguing that the nurses probably knew all the patients' meds better than the doctors. The doctors would have to check his chart. The nurses would probably know at a glance if something had changed or was wrong.

"I'll have to look at his treatment protocol," Alvarez said vaguely. "Though I'm sure it had nothing to do with Mr. Isah's death."

"If you don't know what it was, how can you know if it had anything to do with his death?"

He favored her with a glare but didn't try to argue. Kenzie had dealt with doctors like him before. Big egos. Thought they were superior to everyone else and couldn't possibly make a mistake. Usually, it was the surgeons, but Kenzie was sure that psychiatrists were not immune.

"What do you know about what happened here today?" She asked Alvarez. "Rigor mortis says that Mr. Isah has been dead for some time."

As with the bruises, his complexion made it harder to see the livor mortis, where the blood in his body had settled due to gravity after his death. Kenzie could see faint shadows, but they were hard to make out and it would be easier with the ALS. She hadn't brought the portable light source with her in the death kit, not expecting to need it at a hospital death scene.

So she couldn't say for sure that his body had been moved after death, but she was pretty sure that it had. His positioning didn't feel right, though she had nothing to back it up yet. Her subconscious had noted something that hadn't yet made it to her conscious mind. She made a mental note to follow up on the livor mortis during the autopsy.

She stepped back from the body to take a few pictures, recording his position.

"Will *you* be doing the postmortem?" Alvarez asked, looking down his nose at Kenzie. "Or will that be handled by someone more senior?"

"I will be handling it," Kenzie said steadily. "So if there is anything that you want me to know before I start, you should tell me."

He pressed his lips together, sniffed, and shook his head.

Kenzie looked at Nurse Craig. "I want to talk to you alone. And anyone else who was involved in Mr. Isah's care."

"For a death by natural causes?" Alvarez challenged. "Why would you need to do that?"

"I need to make a full inquiry into anything that I believe needs investigation. And this case is starting off very strangely. You trying to keep me from the scene. The body being in full rigor but still warm. Your insistence that it was natural causes when we don't yet know anything of his meds or physical condition. He should have been asleep in his bed, not up. All of those things are setting off alarms for me."

"That's ridiculous."

He didn't say *what* was ridiculous or how Kenzie might have misinterpreted the circumstances. Just went straight for a complaint that her investigation was ridiculous. Nice.

4

Kenzie called Carlos and got him out of bed to come to the scene for transport. She didn't want to leave the body alone while she was conducting her interview with Nurse Craig and anyone else there who she might need to talk to. There was enough going on that was out of the ordinary that she didn't want to risk her death scene being "sanitized" by someone while she was out of sight. When Carlos got there, she took him to the side and explained as much as she could in whispers. He nodded seriously and didn't make any complaint about how boring it was to babysit a dead body while she interviewed the staff.

"Is there somewhere we could meet privately?" Kenzie asked Nurse Craig.

They both glanced at Alvarez for his objection, but he kept his mouth shut. Kenzie wanted to interview him too, but she had a feeling he wouldn't tell her any more than he already had. He would be a problem. She would just have to work around him. Hopefully, the doctors that were on during the day shift would be more helpful.

Nurse Craig led her to a family visit room and motioned to one of the soft chairs. He stood with his hand on the door, trying to decide whether to close it or to keep it open. He looked at Kenzie, brows raised.

"Closed," Kenzie suggested.

He gave a nod and closed the door. "Sorry, I don't mean to be stupid," he said, flushing a little. "Some women don't like to be shut alone in a room with a man... I didn't want to make you uncomfortable."

"Thank you, that was very thoughtful." Kenzie motioned for him to take the seat adjacent to her. She exhaled, took a deep breath, and let it out again. "Okay. This is all a bit of a mess, isn't it?"

He shrugged as he sat down, as if he didn't know what she was talking about.

"Information is being withheld. Evidence is being covered up or altered. I take it Dr. Alvarez has already told you to be careful of what you say, maybe to tell me a fake story to put me off the trail, but that wouldn't be a good idea. I would suggest that you *don't* do that."

"A fake story!" He tried, but failed, to sound outraged. It just came out as a weak, token protest. Kenzie was sure he wanted to share what had really happened. That's why he had been hanging around and had gotten close enough to involve himself in the conversation.

"I'm glad you're going to tell me the truth," Kenzie said. "That will make it much easier."

"Well, yeah. I wouldn't tell you a story."

"But you might neglect to tell me the full truth."

He grimaced. "I honestly don't know what happened here tonight. Like I said, Leander was agitated earlier. He was having a bad day. I don't know if it was a bad reaction to medication or something else. But whenever I saw him, he was upset, complaining, trying to get someone's attention to tell them his story. But nothing would settle him down. He wasn't normally like that."

"Has he had a recent med change?"

He hesitated for just a second, then dove into it. "He was in a drug trial."

"Oh. So he was on an experimental drug."

Craig nodded seriously. "An... experimental treatment," he agreed. "I don't know what drug or drugs were involved. They don't tell us. And they don't tell us who was participating, but it was pretty obvious which patients were in the trial."

"Because of their behavior?"

"Because their treatment schedules changed. Their meds, when they had therapy, which doctors were around for therapy at that time, stuff like that. I wasn't told which patients were on the drug and which were on a placebo… but it was obvious."

"Good? Bad?"

"I don't know."

Kenzie cocked her head. "You don't know?"

"Well… with therapy and medications, it can be hard to know, sometimes. Sometimes therapy… shakes something loose and, even though it makes the patient upset and unhappy for a few days, it was something that they needed to get out in the open and deal with. And sometimes quiet behavior just means… withdrawal. Shutting down. Deeper depression."

Kenzie nodded slowly. "You're right. That makes sense."

She thought about Zachary and his memories resurfacing when triggered by an adverse event. It made his life hell, and he complained about not being able to repress the memories as he used to, to just shove them down and forget about them again. Dr. B said that it was his brain's way of healing. Getting the memories out instead of keeping them inside to fester. It meant he was stronger and more equipped to deal with them now than he had been as a child or teenager. Even though Zachary would have preferred everything to go back to the way it was if he had a choice, it was better to heal. To deal with those memories in a positive, permanent way.

"So Isah was on this new experimental protocol. Changes to his meds and therapy schedule, who he was having therapy sessions with. Have I got that right?"

Craig nodded. He glanced toward the closed door to reassure himself that they could not be overheard by anyone. "This is private patient information, and we've also signed confidentiality agreements about any experimental studies that are going on. Even though I don't really know anything, I don't know if I should even be telling you that there *is* an experimental protocol."

"You are required by law to disclose information to me in the course of my investigation. It's not the same as when you have a living patient. Even then, if you knew that a patient was on a drug that had a negative interaction with another drug they were going to treat him with, you would be expected to disclose that information as early as possible."

Craig nodded slowly, but obviously was not entirely reassured.

"I appreciate that you have been eager to help," Kenzie told him. "I wish that everyone would be as helpful as you."

Rather than looking pleased at her compliment, Craig looked shamefaced. Kenzie tried to meet his eyes and figure out what was going on that he felt so embarrassed about, but he didn't look at her. He just stared down at the swirling, muted colors of the carpet.

"Did Isah have friends among the other patients? Anyone that he hung around with? Talked to?"

"No, not really. They all keep to themselves, mostly. They have group therapy meetings, but they don't… play cards together and that kind of thing, not really. People come and go, and some of them know each other from when they have been here before or at other institutions together. But no… really close friendships."

"Can you tell me what happened to Mr. Isah? How he died? How he was discovered?"

"I had other patients to deal with. Dr. Alvarez and the others were taking care of Leander."

"Dr. Alvarez and the others? What were they all doing?"

"I don't know. I wasn't there. I know he had been agitated, and… Dr. Alvarez was trying to calm him down. He had been violent toward the staff earlier, in the cafeteria, and they are very strict about that kind of thing here. A lot of places, they look the other way when patients are physically abusive of the staff, but at Persons… they don't tolerate it."

"How had Leander been violent?" Kenzie asked, adopting Craig's usage of the patient's first name.

"Just… pushing people away. Striking out. It wasn't… directed or angry. Just… you know how someone is when they don't want anyone to touch them. Defensive. Overstimulated."

"Sure." Kenzie nodded. "I can understand that. So what did they do about it if they have a low tolerance for any kind of staff abuse?

They threatened to have him transferred somewhere else, maybe? Kick him out of the program?"

"They called the cops." At Kenzie's look, Craig went on quickly, trying to fill in all the details before Kenzie could complain or express her disbelief. "I don't think they charged him with anything. It was a threat… showing him they were willing to act. And they have private security here, and they all kind of look alike, the actual police and the private cops. For someone like Leander… I don't think he knew the difference. He thought that the cops were always watching him. And if he didn't shape up, they would hurt him."

Kenzie nodded slowly.

"They could put him in jail for assault," Craig said. "But they wouldn't hurt him."

"But he hadn't had a good experience with police in the past," Kenzie guessed.

"He was from Africa. Who knows what kind of police force they had in the country he came from. Probably all corrupt. You hear that about them over there. And the police here… they're no picnic either. Not when you're a Black person with mental illness."

Kenzie could well imagine. She'd seen it on TV. Isah would be taken for a gang banger, an addict, a homeless person. The kind of person society did not want out in public, but were eager to put behind bars. The police would be conditioned to react to him as a violent offender rather than as a man needing help and extra patience and care.

5

S o what happened?" Kenzie asked. "When the police came? I take it that didn't help to settle him down."

"I don't know," Craig said, shaking his head. "I wasn't there when it happened. I was taking care of another patient. There was a ruckus. I knew something was going on. It was loud at first. But then he quieted down. I figured it probably took a needle to do it. He wasn't going to be quiet just because the police came. Probably made it worse."

"You think he was given a sedative?"

"Probably. They should have done that earlier rather than calling the police. There wasn't any way calling the police would make anything better."

"So, by the time you finished with your other patient, everything was quiet again?"

Craig nodded. His eyes skittered to the side.

"What did the other staff members say about it?"

"Nothing. Everyone was just quiet. The doctor said that he was asleep and to just leave him be, let him sleep it off."

"Was that Dr. Alvarez?"

"No, before he came on shift. Dr. Miller."

"So he didn't think that Leander needed any monitoring?"

"No. Said to just stay out of there."

"And you did?"

Craig looked at her, frowning. "I do what I'm told."

"Had Leander been sedated like that before?"

"Yes, sure… just the day before."

"And there hadn't been any complications? So you figured everything would be fine?"

"It seemed like everything was okay. He'd been okay before, and the doctor said not to disturb him, so I didn't."

"You don't have a policy about patients having to be monitored when they have been sedated? Every fifteen minutes or every hour?"

"Well… yeah. If the doctor doesn't say not to."

"But he said not to, so you didn't."

He shrugged uncomfortably. "I do what I'm told," he repeated.

"When did you know that something was wrong, then?"

"When…" He swallowed hard. "When Dr. Alvarez told me to call the funeral home."

"And you decided to call me."

His eyes didn't meet hers. "I just called the funeral home, like I was told. That's what we do when there is a death. The doctor decides if anyone needs to be notified, and the family says which funeral home they want to use, and we call them to pick him up."

Kenzie had known as soon as she heard Nurse Craig's voice that he had been the one who had called her.

"You wouldn't take it upon yourself to call the ME's office unless you thought something was wrong," she said.

"No," Craig agreed.

"It's a good thing you did call me. If there was something suspicious about his death, no one would ever have known. He would have been embalmed and buried or cremated without anyone ever looking into it."

"Seemed like… something that should be reported."

Kenzie nodded. "Any death in a psychiatric facility is supposed to go through the ME's office. And any death that is suspicious in any way."

"It wasn't really suspicious, though, was it?" Craig asked, his brow furrowing again. "I mean, patients do die. And when they're on as many meds as psychiatric patients are…"

"If it was a drug interaction, that should be investigated."

He shrugged. "I suppose. But there are a lot of deaths in hospitals that are not suspicious…"

Kenzie nodded. "Of course. But the laws regarding psychiatric facilities are stricter than those for a hospital. And you had a feeling about this one. And you should follow that feeling. I think you did the right thing, whether they agree or not."

He nodded slowly, but still looked unsure of whether she was right. He had stepped outside the bounds of what he had been told to do and was afraid he would lose his job over it. Afraid that he had gone too far and should have just kept his head down and listened.

"You did the right thing," Kenzie told him firmly.

"What do you think it was? You think it was a drug interaction?"

"I don't know. We'll do a tox screen. We'll need to know what drug trial they were doing. It could be a lot of things. Sometimes the cause remains unknown in a case like this. Sudden cardiac death."

"Excited delirium?" Craig asked.

Kenzie grimaced. "I won't attribute a death to excited delirium," she said. "There is enough controversy over whether that is really a thing or is just a way of covering up deaths in custody."

"You don't think it is real?"

Kenzie pursed her lips, considering her answer. She didn't want to step on anyone's toes. She didn't want to be accused of slandering anyone who had ever attributed a death to excited delirium or to say that it was just another way of saying that cops had been too violent with a detainee.

"I think that 'excited delirium' is unproven and has been applied much too broadly in the past. I think that there are actual physical reasons that someone dies in custody. Not just that the detainee was… overly excited or upset. I don't think there is a psychological state of excitement that kills someone without any other cause."

Craig didn't seem pleased by her answer. "But it does happen that way sometimes."

Kenzie shook her head, pressing her lips together. "I don't have the years of experience that Dr. Wiltshire has. I'll discuss it with him. Maybe he has seen cases where it is warranted. But the cases I have seen in medical school or the media… there has been a lot more going on than a patient just being overly excited or upset."

"I've seen it happen."

"Then maybe those cases should be reviewed by an ME as well. Have they been?"

He shook his head, clamming up.

Kenzie wondered just how many other cases there had been and if they had all been at Persons. Craig didn't look old enough to have worked at too many other places.

There was another nurse on duty. Michelle Hernandez seemed to be a very cheerful, bright-eyed young woman. Her oval face and black-framed glasses gave her an open and pleasant appearance. Kenzie wondered about two young nurses both being put on the night shift. It seemed like the presence of an older nurse would have been beneficial. The young nurses were equipped to handle most of the stuff they would see from one night to the next, when patients were mostly just sleeping. But occasionally, events such as Isah's death needed the steadying hand of a more mature, experienced nurse.

Hernandez seemed more curious than upset by the events of the night.

"So you're really a medical examiner?" she asked Kenzie eagerly. "Don't you get tired of dealing with bodies and wish you had a live patient now and then?"

Kenzie laughed. "I am an assistant to the medical examiner. And… no, I don't really wish that any of my patients were alive. That might be a little awkward, you know…" she teased.

Hernandez seemed not to follow her meaning for a moment, then giggled. "I didn't mean if any of the people you are supposed to autopsy were alive. I mean… don't you wish you had a real, live person to treat sometimes? Maybe a hybrid practice, where you see live patients for other things? I think… it would be really boring and depressing to only deal with dead bodies all the time."

"It isn't, actually. I find it quite interesting. I guess that I do get a little depressed by it sometimes… when a child is killed, or something else upsetting. But I try to distance myself from those things. Just view it as a puzzle that needs to be solved. I can't totally divorce my feelings from a case, but I try to look at each one as objectively as possible and not to take the stress home with me."

Would Zachary agree she didn't take her job stress home with her? Kenzie knew that she sometimes couldn't help it. Some cases *did* get to her. Or the outside pressures to make a certain finding or release her findings within a certain timeframe because of political issues.

But she had *tried* not to take the stress home with her, that was true. She hadn't said that she was always successful.

"I think I would find it really hard," Hernandez confided.

"Well, you might not be suited for pathology. If you picked your profession because you like to help people and be part of the healing process, then you're not going to find a lot of fulfillment in dealing with patients who are already deceased. But I got into it more because… I like to solve a puzzle and to dig down and find the truth. I'm more about… helping the survivors to accept what happened and seeing justice done."

Hernandez smiled sunnily, giving a nod of understanding. "That makes sense. It's more… like you're a cop than like a doctor."

Kenzie shrugged. "I am a doctor and not a cop… but yes, it is a lot more about solving crimes and protecting the public than any other job as a doctor. But not all the deaths that I investigate are homicides. There are plenty that are natural causes, accidental death, or suicide. And sometimes what I discover might help researchers to understand the processes that result in death… and maybe help to treat diseases in different ways in the future."

"That's so interesting."

Kenzie thought that they had exhausted the topic. Hernandez had been the one to introduce it, but she seemed to be done with it now. Kenzie readjusted her position, leaning toward Hernandez, trying to suggest by her body language that they were in this together, helping each other out. Kenzie was someone Hernandez could trust.

"How well did you know the patient who died tonight? Mr. Isah."

"Not real well. He hadn't been here for a long time. But I'm often on day shifts, so I probably knew him better than Anthony."

At Kenzie's puzzled look, she clarified. "Nurse Craig. Anthony."

"Ah. of course. He didn't mention his first name. So he's on nights more often, and you're on days more often? Or evenly split between the two?"

"I just take nights now and then. When I need a bit more money or pay rent, or someone calls out sick and they need someone to cover."

"I see. And how had Isah been? Have there been any changes in his behavior lately?"

Hernandez stared past Kenzie, thinking about it. "He's bipolar, so it is hard to say what is 'normal' in his case. Sometimes he is down, very quiet, in a depressive phase, and sometimes he is more..." She trailed off, searching for words.

"Happy? Outgoing?" Kenzie suggested.

"No... um... irritable. Intense. Maybe bordering on paranoia sometimes."

Kenzie nodded. "I see. And lately, he has been in a more manic state? More irritable and paranoid?"

"Yeah. Really... I haven't seen him that bad before. If I didn't know better, I would have thought he was off his meds. But he was still taking them. Sometimes a medication stops working without warning, and I think that might have been the case with Leander."

"You don't think that it was something they had added to his protocol? Maybe an experimental drug?"

"Oh... we're not told when they are put into those programs. We're not supposed to know. So that we can be more objective. If we are told that a patient is on a new drug, we might see symptoms or changes where there aren't any. Like the placebo effect."

"Anthony said that he thought Leander was part of the drug trial."

"Well... he might have been. I don't know for sure. But I hadn't seen him so agitated before."

Kenzie nodded. "I'll get his medical records, and we'll see what they show."

"I hope it isn't anything to do with the trial," Hernandez said, her face a picture of concern. "Research into effective treatments for psychiatric illnesses is so important. If it gets out that there was a death related to the trial..." She shook her head. "That would be really bad. We need the research."

"I hope it wasn't either," Kenzie agreed. "We'll just have to see what shows up in the postmortem."

6

There wasn't any point in staying around waiting for the other staff members to arrive. That was still several hours away. So Kenzie had Carlos take Mr. Isah to the morgue, and she headed home.

There was still a chance of several hours of sleep before she had to be at the office. Kenzie found herself pretty wired after the events at Persons. Still, she knew that if she didn't get a few hours of sleep, she would eventually hit a wall at work and not be able to get all the way through her day. So she returned home.

There were lights on in the house, so chances were that Zachary was still awake. He should have gone back to bed, but he rarely got more than a few hours of sleep and probably didn't think there would be any harm in waiting for Kenzie for a while to see if she got home in good time.

Still, Kenzie was quiet unlocking the door and stepping into the kitchen from the garage. It was possible Zachary had fallen asleep while working on something, leaving the lights on. She peeked into the living room, where she had seen the lamp on, and Zachary looked up from his laptop.

"Hey. How did it go?"

Kenzie divested her outer clothing and purse. "Hard to say. It was an interesting experience, I'll say that. I've never had anyone try to send me away from a scene before."

"Send you away?"

"Send me back… say that I wasn't needed."

Zachary looked comically puzzled. "Because… no one was dead?" he suggested.

"Oh, someone was dead. In fact, the funeral home got there ahead of me, and I had to chase them off. Another thing I've never had to do before."

"You *did* have an interesting night." He patted the couch next to him. "Come tell me about it."

Kenzie hesitated.

"Or did you want to go back to bed?" Zachary asked. "You probably need the sleep."

"Well, I do, but I'm too wired to sleep right away. Need some time to unwind first."

"Here? Or did you want to get changed? Stretch out in bed?"

"Yeah, bed would be nice," Kenzie admitted. She didn't want to wait until she was too tired to change and didn't want to lie down in bed with her work clothes on. She would need to shower and change in the morning anyway. She wasn't saving any time by already being dressed. She looked at the clock on the wall. It wasn't that late. She could still get a few hours in.

Zachary closed his laptop and stood up from the couch. "Let's go back to bed, then."

In a few minutes, they were cuddled together in bed. Kenzie knew she wouldn't fall asleep any time soon, but at least she was comfortable and in the right place. When the adrenaline wore off and her circadian rhythm reasserted itself, she could just drift off.

"So," Zachary prompted. "Why exactly did they try to chase you off? If there was a dead body, you couldn't just go home, could you? They can't just send it to the funeral home without your sign-off."

"Well, depending on the circumstances, they can. The ME's office doesn't investigate every single death in the state. Only the ones that we deem necessary. If someone dies under their doctor's care, and the doctor doesn't have any concerns, then he can sign the death certificate and the family is free to make all the necessary arrangements."

"Okay," Zachary was nodding. "Makes sense. Is that what happened? The doctor decided he just wanted to sign the death certificate himself?"

"Yes. Only, I had already been called to the scene. And the protocol says that once we've been called to a death, we have to follow through. They can't just change their minds and say they don't want us to look at it anymore."

"Then why did they?"

"It was an interesting case… It was one of the other staff members who thought that it should be looked at more carefully. So when the doctor told him to call the funeral home, he did, but first he called me."

"Sneaky," Zachary approved. "Good thing you got there before the funeral home had taken the body away."

"Well, I wouldn't have had to go far to find it again. They wouldn't have been able to have it cremated before I had an order to get it back again. But it's always better to examine the body in situ. See the scene. Anything else that is of note."

"Did the doctor know who had called you?"

"I'm not sure. The nurse who called didn't want me to say anything about it in front of the others. But they must have figured out what was happening because they knew who I was when I got there. The security guard tried to send me home and so did the doctor. Maybe they didn't know who had made the call, or the nurse pretended it was a mistake and he thought he was supposed to call me. I don't know. Everything is still pretty mixed up."

"Sounds like it. So what was this death? It was at a hospital?"

"Private psychiatric care."

He stiffened slightly. Usually if Zachary needed help during a depressive cycle, he went to the psych ward at the public hospital. But he had recently had an experience with a private hospital, and it had not been positive. Kenzie didn't think he would choose to go to a private psych hospital any time in the near future.

"Not that one," Kenzie assured him.

He let out a breath. "Good. Glad to hear that."

She could tell he was thinking it over. Whether she had ever been called out to that facility. Whether she ever would be. How close he had come to being the next body on the medical examiner's table. But they would probably have done the same as Persons. Called for the funeral home rather than the medical examiner. Or maybe even conveniently lost the body. Or arranged for the funeral home transporters to lose it. How many cases were slipping through the cracks because the doctors simply didn't want the medical examiner checking up on their work?

Any doctor could request that the medical examiner review a case. But they could also make cases that the medical examiner should have reviewed disappear.

"So can a doctor do that whenever he wants?" Zachary asked, his brain going down the same path as Kenzie's. "What's to stop him from bypassing the medical examiner on cases that should be going to you? Cases that are clearly malpractice or homicide?"

"There are certain cases that are mandated by law. The medical examiner must review them, and the doctor can't just sign the death certificate himself. Sudden deaths, unattended deaths, anything violent or the least bit suspicious—and deaths in a psychiatric facility. There is a list of cases that always have to go to the medical examiner."

"And what's to stop them from just calling the funeral home in those cases?"

Kenzie shrugged. "Medical ethics. If they *have* any. And I imagine if the funeral home director got suspicious or spoke up about cases coming to him that should be going through the medical examiner's office. I've never actually heard of it happening, so I'm not sure what the checks and balances are… they assume that doctors are professional and won't take the risk. But of course… you hear about doctors being accused of every other human frailty, so what is to stop them from breaching their professional ethics?"

"It could be quite a scam."

"Could be… but I don't think it is something that is happening all the time. I haven't heard about it before. I think I would have…

maybe gotten a memo to watch out for this or a warning that it was going on."

Zachary nodded. He rubbed Kenzie's back in soothing, slow circles. "Did it look like an interesting case? If the nurse thought it was something you needed to look into, it wasn't just a routine death."

"I don't know yet. No obvious sign of what he died from. We'll see what shows up when I have him on the table. It wasn't an obviously violent case. But he might have been in a drug trial, so I have to be concerned about whatever drug he was on and whether it could have contributed to his death. And there was police involvement earlier in the day."

"The police. Why?"

Kenzie spoke slowly, trying to figure out the best way to tell him about it. She was worried that it might be too close to a death that he had witnessed as a child in custody. Annie. The girl in the cell next to Zachary's. It burned her up just thinking of how he had been treated as a child and teenager. Being housed in isolation in the children's center because he could not comply with the rules. Imprisoned for being a kid with ADHD and PTSD that no one cared about.

"Kenz?"

"He'd been having trouble earlier. Agitated and violent. They had called the police to deal with him."

"Did they take him into custody?"

"No, doesn't sound like it. I think they ended up just leaving. But trying to deal with psychiatric patients by bullying and threatening them..." Kenzie shook her head.

"You can't bully someone into being neurotypical," Zachary contributed.

"No. That's exactly right. It's unfair and just not the right way to deal with people. I get it about holding people responsible for their own behavior, but when the person is clearly mentally ill and cannot comply with your rules... I think you need to find another way to deal with it. Calling the cops to deal with someone manic when you haven't tried every other possible solution..."

"They must have their own isolation rooms. Soft restraints. Something."

"Yeah. I didn't look around, but they seemed like they were fully equipped. They had their own security as well. And if he was unmanageable there, maybe they should have transferred him to the hospital. They could treat him there."

"You don't know how he died?"

Kenzie thought about it for a minute. "No. There are still too many possibilities. Without having conducted an autopsy, I can't really guess. It might have been medication, or heart disease, or an altercation earlier in the day. He could even have been in restraints and ended up hurting himself trying to escape."

7

At some point in the night, Kenzie had fallen asleep. She couldn't remember finishing her conversation with Zachary, so she had probably dropped off in the middle of it and slept soundly until her alarm went off in the morning. She turned it off and closed her eyes, falling quickly asleep again. She could go in a little late. Mr. Isah wasn't going to get any deader. Anything else that was waiting on her desk or computer could wait.

She had felt worn to the bone since Dr. Wiltshire had been gone. She tried not to take too much on, to keep to a reasonable schedule. It wouldn't do anyone any good if she burned out and couldn't do anything. Better to go slowly and fall a little behind for a while than to end up sick and unable to do anything or to face her work again.

She wasn't sure how much time had passed before Zachary was shaking her shoulder gently to wake her up.

"Kenzie. Sorry. Do you want to keep sleeping? I didn't know if I should wake you up. How long do you want to sleep?"

"Mmm." Kenzie stretched her muscles and rubbed her eyes. She wasn't ready to get up yet. And if she had to look at the time and answer his questions about when to get up, she would no longer be able to sleep.

"Your phone has been ringing," Zachary told her. "It's on silent."

"It's been ringing?"

"Yeah."

Kenzie swore under her breath. Who was so desperate to reach her? Why couldn't they wait until she was ready to get to the office and dig into her work? Did it really matter what time it was when she performed the autopsy?

She reached for the phone but couldn't find it. Zachary picked it up, detached the charge cord, and put it into her hand. Kenzie didn't recognize the number, but the same one was repeated several times.

With a groan, Kenzie pushed herself up into a sitting position. She rubbed her eyes and looked around. It was late but, as she had told herself earlier, she could start a little late after being out at a call the night before. She had that flexibility.

The number wasn't blocked, so it wasn't the governor or some other high-powered government official who wanted to know what was going on with a case. It wasn't Dr. Wiltshire; she knew his number, unless he'd had to change it for some reason. So who was harassing her so early and couldn't wait for her to get in?

Zachary put a glass of water on Kenzie's side table and left the room. He could be such a thoughtful guy when he wasn't distracted —or completely lost in his own world. Kenzie had a few swallows of water and cleared her throat before tapping the number to dial back her persistent caller.

He apparently recognized her number or had already added it to his contacts directory. He had a calm, pleasant tone, despite the fact that he had been calling her relentlessly. "Ah, Dr. Kirsch, thank you for getting back to me."

"I didn't check my voicemail. I just saw that you have been calling me. Who is this?"

"This is Dr. Cook."

Kenzie shook her head, the name not ringing any bells. "From Persons?" she guessed.

"Uh… no. I have been assigned to the Medical Examiner's Office. To assist while Dr. Wiltshire is healing."

"Oh! I wasn't told that someone had been assigned. I'm sorry. When will you be starting?"

"Today. That is, I would be… if I could. The office has not been opened, and I'm afraid I haven't yet been provided with keys."

"You're there now?"

"Yes."

Kenzie swore. "Sorry, like I said, I had no idea that you had even been assigned, let alone that you were starting today. I was out on a call late last night, so I slept in this morning." Kenzie ran her fingers through her curly hair, mussed and knotted from sleep. "I won't be able to get in for… about an hour. There's a coffee shop on the main floor of the building that is quite nice. Why don't you relax there for a while, and I'll meet you and give you the tour?"

"I have already discovered it and have been working on Wi-Fi. Although, of course, it has nothing to do with the Medical Examiner's Office. Just personal stuff."

"Okay. Hang out there, and I'll get in as quickly as possible."

After disconnecting, Kenzie got out of bed and went to look for Zachary.

"Would you believe that they got me a substitute pathologist without even telling me? And the guy's been waiting there since…" Kenzie looked at the call log on her phone. "Seven-thirty, the eager beaver. They had to do it on a day that I slept in, didn't they?"

"Of course," Zachary agreed. "So, are you heading straight in?"

"Not without a shower and coffee, I'm not. He's hanging out at Boys in Brew, so he's fine until I get there. He isn't just standing around waiting."

"Do you want me to get your toast and coffee? Or are you just going to get something at Brew?"

"I'll start with a coffee here… and pick something else up when I get there."

Zachary nodded. "I'll get it going."

He stood up right away, so Kenzie didn't have to worry about whether he would remember to get the coffee started or would get lost in his work and forget all about it. She could hear him setting up the machine for another carafe as she returned to her room.

. . .

Kenzie looked around Boys in Brew when she arrived. It was populated mainly by cops going on or off duty, with a few visitors or rougher-looking customers who had just been released from interviews or an overnight stay at the jail. In the corner was a young man with a button-up shirt and a lab jacket typing industriously on his laptop. He looked up from his work, apparently feeling her eyes on him, and smiled. He started to close his computer to prepare to join her. She waved him down.

"Just give me a minute to grab some breakfast. Do you want another coffee? A Danish or muffin?"

"Oh, I've had enough this morning. I didn't want to just freeload on the WIFI, so I've been working my way through more coffee and breakfast than I would normally have."

"Okay. I'll be with you in a minute. Finish what you were doing. No need to stop mid-sentence."

He raised the lid of his half-closed laptop again. Kenzie watched him while she waited in line and then waited for the barista to prepare her breakfast order.

Dr. Cook looked way too young and way too handsome to be a medical examiner or even just an assistant medical examiner. Kenzie had gone back to school several years after graduating, so she had been older than most of her classmates. She was used to doctors who looked younger than she was. But Dr. Cook seemed too young to even have a degree, let alone a doctorate. His hair was neatly styled, a little long on top and short in the back. His eyes were a clear blue that Kenzie suspected was boosted by a pair of colored contacts. Did anyone have such bright blue eyes naturally? He looked like he had walked off the set of *The Young and the Restless* rather than being an actual medical doctor.

The barista caught Kenzie's attention and handed her the breakfast order. Dr. Cook finished what he was doing and joined her.

"Sorry to keep you waiting," Kenzie apologized. "Like I said, I was out late to a scene last night and had no idea that you would be here this morning, or I would have arrived much earlier."

"No problem, doctor."

"Call me Kenzie."

He nodded, but didn't.

Kenzie led him to the security desk in front of the elevator, where he showed the guard his newly minted security pass and introduced himself.

"Did they give you a parking space?" Kenzie asked. "You can get in from the parking garage as well. You don't have to go all the way around."

"I don't think I'm senior enough to qualify for a parking space. I'm just temporary."

Kenzie shrugged. She didn't have any say in it. She knew that the parking garage was not full. There were plenty of spaces available. But how they were assigned was up to the police department and building management. Kenzie was just glad to have one herself. She wouldn't want to have to park her baby on the street.

"Are you new in Roxboro?" Kenzie asked Dr. Cook. "I don't think we've run into each other before."

"Yes, I'm out of Burlington. I've taken a long-term room at the hotel so that I'm not commuting back and forth. There's no point in wasting all that time and gas. I'll be here for a few weeks… however long it takes Dr. Wiltshire to get back on his feet. Or on his hands again. And then I'll head back to Burlington and see where they want to assign me next."

"Is that by choice? Or are you looking for something permanent?"

"I'm happy to be temping for a while. Figure out what I want to do. What I enjoy the most."

"And you're a pathologist?"

"Yes. I'm fully qualified for the position."

"Good. I didn't know how strict they are with their qualifications. If they would assign us someone from general practice or obstetrics or something. Officially, all that is required is to be a medical doctor."

"I've done my fair share of postmortems and death investigation reports."

"That's great." Kenzie was glad that she wouldn't have to train him. She still found herself in the position of apprenticing to Dr. Wiltshire, learning from him. While she had now done a few autopsies completely on her own, she preferred to have someone experienced she could ask questions of or bounce ideas off of.

"I'm here to assist you, not to cause you more work," Dr. Cook told her.

"Glad to hear it."

Kenzie gave him a quick tour of the office, past her reception desk at the outside of the suite where she answered phones and dealt with the public, to the meeting rooms, kitchen/breakroom, morgue, autopsy, and Dr. Wiltshire's office, from which she assumed Dr. Cook would be working until Dr. Wiltshire was back and fully functional. For the time being, Dr. Wiltshire was only coming in occasionally to consult with Kenzie and to sign off on various reports and documentation. Now that his hand was healing, he had dialed back on the painkillers and could focus longer than he had been initially. However, he still wasn't up to full days, even just doing paperwork.

"Okay." Dr. Cook put his laptop bag down in Dr. Wiltshire's office and hung his outer gear on the coat rack. "So where do you need me first? It looks like you have a fair bit of paperwork out there."

"It's not bad. I'm mostly caught up. An office like this goes through a *lot* of paper! I will want to do the Isah autopsy today. He is the body I was called in on last night. I want to make sure…" Kenzie trailed off, thinking about how to voice her concern. "I'm a little worried that there may be a problem at the private facility that he died at. Just a gut feeling…"

But it wasn't her gut. It was the fact that Nurse Craig had felt the need to go around his boss to bring the death to the attention of the medical examiner's office. It was the police involvement, experimental medications and protocols, and Isah's escalating violence. It was Dr. Alvarez's apparent attempt to cover up what had happened to Leander Isah and hurry the body to the funeral home without any examination.

But Dr. Cook didn't need to know all the details. She didn't want him to be biased by her feelings, but to approach the postmortem with the fresh eyes of an outsider. She shouldn't even have told him she had any concerns; that had just slipped out.

"Then we shall start with the autopsy," Dr. Cook agreed.

"If you can familiarize yourself with the morgue and get his body prepped for me, I'll just make sure there isn't anything urgent on voicemail or email."

Dr. Cook agreed and returned to the morgue, impressing Kenzie by not getting turned around. He acted like he knew exactly what he was doing.

8

When Kenzie was finished processing the emails and voicemails that had arrived overnight to ensure that there was nothing more urgent than the new arrival, she returned to the autopsy to find that Dr. Cook had taken care of everything as she had asked. He had retrieved the right body, which George had already processed and cleaned up. He had it waiting on the autopsy table Kenzie usually used, which was pre-set to the right height for her to work comfortably. Or as comfortably as possible. If she had a longer postmortem or several of them to do, she could get quite sore standing, reaching, cutting, and manipulating a body for that long. But that was just one of the things that a medical examiner had to be prepared for.

Leander Isah's clothing and the evidence bags containing any trace evidence collected for processing were arranged on the side counter should Kenzie need to examine anything more closely. The appropriate file was opened and on the computer screens, ready for her. Dr. Cook was clearly familiar with both the software and proper procedure, a time saver for Kenzie. She had been worried that she might have to walk him through everything, despite his being a pathologist and claiming that he had the experience necessary to do the job he had been assigned. When dealing with government bureaucracies, one never knew how much the people making the decisions on up the line understood what really happened in the ME's office and what their needs were.

"This all looks great, thank you," Kenzie told Dr. Cook.

"Is there anything else?"

"Nope, it looks like you've got everything ready. Dr. Wiltshire and I often work on separate postmortems at the same time so that we can consult each other on what we are doing. Mostly so that I can ask him questions or he can catch anything that I might miss or not be aware of. But I think we should do one together to start with. Then there are a couple of routine posts I haven't gotten to yet. We have a bit of a backlog because of Dr. Wiltshire's injury."

"That's why I'm here. You don't want me to start one of those while you do this one?"

"No. Let's do one together to get used to each other's processes."

Cook nodded his agreement. Kenzie washed up and donned the appropriate gloves and garb. Dr. Cook was ready to begin. Kenzie tapped the button on the floor for the recorder and announced the date and time, decedent's name and file number, and her own name. Cook announced his name, providing her with his first name, Jeffrey. She thought it suited him.

Kenzie began with the gross examination, talking to Dr. Cook as she began. A little self-conscious at first since it was the first time they had worked together.

"I didn't have an ALS at the death scene last night, so I want to use it today to identify any bruising. The victim has very dark skin, so it's hard to see any contusions under white light."

Dr. Cook murmured his agreement. Kenzie positioned the lights over the body and slowly worked her way down, head to toe, front and back.

"Victim has restraint bruises on the forearms. Some lighter bruises on the upper arms, possibly from being held down, but it is hard to tell for sure because they are faint." Kenzie measured and took pictures of the bruises. "Livor mortis in the chest makes it difficult to ascertain whether there is any peri-mortem bruising. When I arrived on the scene, the victim was on his back, but the livor mortis in the chest indicates he was prone, not supine, for some time after his death."

Kenzie paused in her examination of the body for bruises to tell Dr. Cook about the advanced rigor mortis, which suggested that the man had been dead for several hours before she had arrived, in contrast to the elevated body temperature, which indicated that death had been quite recent.

"Does that make any sense?"

Cook nodded slowly. "There have been some studies done… try a search for hyperthermia and rigor mortis or postmortem caloricity. It seems counterintuitive, but a high body temperature actually speeds rigor mortis and livor mortis. You would think that a warm body would develop rigor more slowly, that it would be something that only sets in as the body cools, but algor mortis—the cooling of the body—is not actually what causes the stiffening of the body or the settling of the blood. A higher body temperature *speeds* rigor. The full cycle of rigor mortis, from stiffening to release, can occur in just six hours instead of twenty-four." Cook lifted one of Isah's arms to demonstrate the rigor had already released.

"So what does that do to our time of death calculation?"

"Screws it up royally," Cook admitted. "Full rigor in three hours or less. It is impossible to tell anything from the body temperature if you don't know what temperature you are starting from. With such quick rigor, you know you are starting with a higher-than-normal temperature, but you don't know what that temperature was, so you don't have a starting point."

"So he had a fever."

Cook nodded. "Something raised his body temperature. Whether it was illness or something else, we don't yet know."

"We'll check for common viruses and white blood cell count," Kenzie determined, and gave the voice commands to add those tests to the appropriate section in the postmortem document on the monitor so she wouldn't forget them.

She looked at Cook. "Anything else? To do with the rigor mortis or hyperthermia?"

"Tox screens."

Kenzie nodded. They were already on the default checklist, so she didn't need to add them. Several drugs were known to raise body temperature. Maybe it was surprising that Kenzie hadn't encountered this problem before. How many drug addict autopsies had she done without realizing that a high body temperature could throw off all the Time of Death calculations?

"It's not particularly common," Cook told her, reading her face. "If you don't know that hyperthermia was present, you must work on the assumption that it was not."

"Right. Okay. Continuing with the contusions." Kenzie went on. No abdominal bruising. There was some faint bruising on the upper thighs and, when Kenzie rolled the body over, around the buttocks. Kenzie's eyes met Cook's. She dictated her findings to the computer, again taking pictures and measurements, and continued with the gross examination.

After reaching the victim's toes and the soles of his feet, Kenzie returned once more to his head where, at the scene, she had noticed a bump. She took pictures and measurements and probed the swelling with careful fingers.

"X-rays. We're going to want skull and chest at a minimum."

"Throat?" Cook suggested.

Kenzie looked back at Isah's throat, where she had found no bruising. She raised her brows at Cook, wondering what he had seen that she hadn't.

"The other bruises would indicate a pattern of restraint and assault. Even though we can't see anything on the throat, we should be extra careful to identify any hairline fractures to the hyoid or other structures. When death occurs very quickly from strangulation or blocking the blood flow to the brain, there may be very little bruising on the throat. TV would have you believe you will always have a ligature mark or finger bruises around the throat, but that is not the case. There may be no visible bruising. Especially in a patient with as much skin pigment as your victim."

Kenzie nodded. "Any other X-rays you would recommend?"

"Maybe knuckles, in case we have any boxer's fractures."

In case he had fought back against someone who had attacked him and broken his knuckles on their face.

"Okay."

Kenzie started to set up for the X-ray series that would be required and put on a lead apron. Rather than bother with the lead barrier himself, Dr. Cook left the autopsy and watched Kenzie from the observation room, getting a couple of bottles of water from the small fridge while he was there.

He returned once Kenzie was finished taking the X-rays, and they scrutinized each series on the monitors.

"No skull fracture," Kenzie observed. "I didn't think that the bump on the head was that serious."

"Might want to do more imaging to check for hematomas."

Kenzie nodded. It was still possible that there had been bleeding inside the brain, even without a skull fracture. The brain bounced around inside the skull, structures tearing, blood building up between the membranes, between the brain and the skull, or deeper within the brain. It didn't look like the head trauma was that bad, but even a whiplash with no impact could cause the brain to bounce around enough to start a bleed.

Kenzie magnified the X-rays of the throat several times, and they both searched it for any fractures on the hyoid bone, but it seemed to be undamaged.

"Here, though…" Kenzie turned to the chest series. Isah's sternum was clearly fractured, as were a couple of upper ribs. "CPR breaks?" she suggested to Cook.

"Possibly."

"But I don't see any bruising or swelling around them." Kenzie's brow furrowed as she looked at them as closely as possible.

"We can check more easily when you open him up."

Kenzie nodded.

There were no fresh fractures on the knuckles. But there were many bright white patches showing calcification from previous breaks.

"He must be a fighter," Kenzie suggested. But the man's very thin build did not suggest a street fighter or MMA fighter. He did not have the muscles she would expect on someone who fought professionally.

Cook shook his head. "I don't think so." He took over manipulating the images, zooming in and examining each finger individually. "These aren't boxer fractures."

"An old crush injury, maybe?" Cook was right; there were a lot of breaks, but they were not on or around the knuckles where she would expect them to be. But maybe something heavy had fallen on his hands. Or they had been slammed in a door. Perhaps a heavy garage door rather than a car or house door.

"No. I've seen something like this before in cases of torture. All of these individual breaks in every finger. In an accident, a crush, or single impact, there is an epicenter where there are more breaks, shattering, and then fewer breaks as you move outward from the impact. Not methodical breaks across each finger like this."

Kenzie shook her head slowly, fighting a brief moment of nausea at the idea of torture, of each finger being methodically broken individually. "Poor guy."

"Yes," Cook agreed. "Where did he come from?"

"I don't know for sure. I don't have all his history. One of the nurses said that he was from Africa and had experienced police violence over there. Still, he didn't say which country it was. Africa is a pretty big place."

"And they have some pretty brutal police forces. I don't know whether they do that or not," he nodded to the X-rays of Isah's hand, "but several countries are well known for their level of police violence."

9

Kenzie looked at the clock.

"I'm going to need to take a break before we continue. Clear my head, use the bathroom, check the mail. Make sure that Julie got down to cover the phones."

Cook nodded. "Sure. Half an hour? An hour?"

"Probably just half an hour."

"What can I do for you while you're working on that?"

"Uh... I guess familiarize yourself with the files on Dr. Wiltshire's desk. Most of them are just reports ready to be released, but I don't want to do that without someone else looking at them first. Catch any possible errors, let me know if you think there is something else that should have been checked or discussed. Just backstop me."

"Sure. I can do that. I'm going to get another coffee, even though I don't need one." He gave her a model-perfect smile. "Can I get you one?"

"I can do that—"

"You had more things on your list than I have on mine. I'll do the coffee."

Kenzie shrugged and shook her head, stopping herself from objecting further. She was used to being the one to get Dr. Wiltshire his coffee and see to all the other administrative duties. It seemed backward to have Dr. Cook, her senior in experience, doing it. But he was there to support her in whatever ways she needed help while Dr. Wiltshire was unavailable. So if he volunteered to make the coffee, then she should let him make it.

"Of course," she said finally. "That would be great."

"Good. I'll bring it to you at the front desk?"

"Yeah."

He nodded his agreement and began to strip off his gloves and other protective gear. Kenzie did the same and walked out to her desk to check on Julie and the mail.

She worked rapidly through the mail and the forms that had been submitted in her in basket while catching up with Julie and seeing how long she would be able to help. Julie worked on contract with several law enforcement agencies in the building, so her time was not all Kenzie's. She had been covering more hours since Dr. Wiltshire's accident, but couldn't be there all the time. Kenzie covered the phones some of the time and forwarded them to voicemail the rest of the time. People were used to dealing with electronic communications and could fill out most of the forms they needed online, so they didn't need someone in the reception area all the time.

Dr. Cook walked out with a couple of cups of coffee, gave one to Kenzie, and offered the other to Julie.

"We haven't met, so I'm not sure how you like it. I'm Dr. Cook."

Julie smiled and giggled, took the coffee from him, and then shook his hand. "Julie. Nice to meet you."

"Dr. Cook has been assigned to help us with the backlog created by Dr. Wiltshire's injury," Kenzie told Julie, even though she already knew this much.

Julie smiled and nodded, her eyes shining as she looked the young Dr. Cook over. When Dr. Cook went back to the kitchen to get his own coffee and retire to Dr. Wiltshire's office, Julie looked at Kenzie, her eyebrows up and bright eyes snapping with excitement.

"He is so cute! Why didn't you warn me?" She patted at her hair as if he'd caught her right after getting out of bed or the shower.

"I didn't know I needed to," Kenzie laughed. "Don't you have a boyfriend?"

"Well, technically…"

Kenzie knew that Julie was practically engaged to the guy. She chuckled. "I'm going to call him and tell him you're making eyes at the new doctor."

Julie snorted. "Yeah, let him know that he'd better up his game if he wants to keep me."

"Well, no making eyes at Dr. Cook and distracting him from his job. He's supposed to be reading reports and helping with autopsies, not chasing after the admin staff."

"Who's making eyes? I'm making *plans*."

Kenzie sipped her coffee and went back to the mail, chuckling.

Kenzie was glad she had taken a break as she returned to the autopsy with fresh eyes and a refreshed outlook. It could take an effort not to be swept into the misfortunes that had brought victims to her table. She tended to take some cases a little too personally. As if she had been responsible for letting the tragedy take place in the first place.

Now, she'd had a chance to distance herself again and was ready to proceed. She suited up again.

"Anything else you think we should check before opening him up?" she asked Dr. Cook.

"I'd take some swabs of bodily fluids before going any further. Always best to get what you can before beginning the internal examination and potentially causing contamination."

Kenzie agreed and began with the various swabs and fluids they would need to test before opening the thoracic cavity. Each sample was carefully labeled and double-checked before going on to the next one. Cook didn't make her feel like he was hovering over her, waiting impatiently for her to get done, so Kenzie felt comfortable taking her time to ensure everything was double and triple checked. Better to get it right the first time.

Eventually, they were ready to begin with the Y-incision.

"Would you like to?" Kenzie asked, gesturing to the body. "You must be getting bored just watching."

Not to mention that she was interested in seeing his technique and making sure he was just as capable of doing a postmortem as he seemed to be at everything else.

Dr. Cook raised one brow. "Are you sure? You're doing just fine yourself. You said you just wanted the supervision."

"No reason both of us can't work it together."

"As long as you don't think I'm interfering in your case…"

"No. I'd just as soon have you participate."

He nodded and picked up a scalpel. "Besides, then you get a chance to see what I'm made of."

"Well, that too," Kenzie admitted. "But you haven't done anything to make me think that you're not fully capable. I don't think you're going to break down or go into hysterics."

"Or throw up?"

Kenzie shrugged. "Everyone throws up sometime. Just don't do it on the body."

He grinned and proceeded with a very neat and professional Y-incision. They both examined the sternum and fractured ribs, bringing the camera in close and magnifying the area.

"There's no bleeding," Kenzie pointed out.

"None at all," Cook agreed. "I would say that the resuscitation attempt occurred quite some time after death."

Kenzie made a note of their findings. She resisted the impulse to sigh. How long had Mr. Isah's body lain undiscovered before someone had realized he was deceased and attempted to resuscitate him?

It at least matched up with Nurse Craig's claim that he was told to just leave Isah alone to sleep off the sedation. No one had checked on him. No one knew he had died until it was far too late to do anything about it.

But at least that pointed toward natural or accidental causes rather than homicide. No one had been in with him. It had, at least on initial examination, not been a violent death.

"Do you have his medical records?" Dr. Cook asked.

"Still waiting for the facility to send me what they have. There was the suggestion that he might be involved in an experimental treatment."

"Oh? What sort of treatment?"

"I'm not sure. The nurse said he didn't know anything, and the doctor was difficult. The staff wasn't supposed to know who was in the trial. But there had been changes in his daily schedule and some observable changes in behavior."

"Good or bad changes?"

"More agitated. Sensitive about people in close proximity. It sounds negative, but might actually be a positive sign."

"Right," Dr. Cook agreed.

He motioned for Kenzie to take over and, without discussion, they began the dissection of the organs, trading off every so often so that they both had the chance to participate.

"Organs are congested with blood," Cook noticed.

"Yeah. Asphyxiation, do you think?"

"No froth in the lungs. I would suggest sudden cardiac death, perhaps due to a reaction to a medication or allergy. Perhaps a congenital disorder. We can run DNA for known mutations. Long QT syndrome and others."

Kenzie wouldn't mind if it turned out to be a natural death. She could just send the body to the funeral home without having to involve the police or worry about whether the culprit would ever be brought to justice.

10

S o, how did everything turn out?" Zachary asked. "How is the substitute for Dr. Wiltshire?"

"He seems to be pretty good. I was worried at first about him being so young, but I don't think he's quite as young as he looks. Either that, or he was a prodigy and started medical school early. He has a good solid base, more experience than I have."

"Just a youngster?"

"Looks like some teen heartthrob."

"Oh, boy." Zachary put his hand over his heart and feigned concern. "Do I have reason to be jealous?"

"Yeah, I think you'd better be. Although Julie will probably get his phone number before me. She was pretty taken with him."

"Don't you already have his phone number?"

"Oh… that's right. I do. Well, then, you might have to settle for Julie, instead."

Zachary chuckled. "Well, I suppose if I have to settle for the younger woman… Wait, isn't she engaged?"

"Practically. But she said that she wants to keep her options open. I don't know if you could keep up with her, though, old man."

"I can barely keep up with you. I don't know how I would manage with anyone younger."

Kenzie laughed.

The screen on Zachary's phone flickered to life, and his eyes darted over to it.

"I'm going to change," Kenzie offered, "then we can get started on dinner."

"Sure."

But when Kenzie returned a few minutes later, Zachary's gaze was tightly focused on the phone in his hands, and he didn't even look up at her. Kenzie walked into the kitchen and started to bang around noisily, waiting for him to notice that she was back and could use some help getting dinner on the table. But there was no response from him.

She could march back into the living room, shake him out of his trance, and insist that he put away his phone and help her out. But that would result in their both being tense and upset and with Zachary making apologies, yet still distracted by his unfinished text conversation, making it difficult for him to get anything done or to engage with her at supper.

On the other hand, if she let him finish what he was doing on the phone then, even if he didn't help her prepare dinner, he would at least be able to hold a conversation with her while they ate. She could tell him a little about her autopsy, and he could tell her about whatever case he had spent most of his time on. They were each puzzle-solvers, interested in hearing about each other's investigations and trying to anticipate how things would turn out.

Unlike most of the people Kenzie knew, Zachary was not squeamish about autopsy discussions, even at the table. Even, occasionally, with pictures that would have turned most people off their feed. Maybe Zachary had spent so much of his time nauseated on his previous med cocktail that he had become accustomed to it.

She continued to work on dinner, and it was some time before Zachary wandered from the living room to the kitchen, his eyes still on his phone. Kenzie turned her body toward him and waited for him to say something.

"Kenz... It's Rhys."

Kenzie's stomach knotted. Rhys was a Black teen that Zachary had befriended during an investigation a couple of years earlier. A mostly non-speaking boy with lots of trauma in his past. He and Zachary shared some of the same sorrows and challenges. They had become friends despite the disparity in their ages.

He and Rhys communicated primarily through a messaging app on the phone since a spoken conversation was out of the question. Even Rhys's messages, communicated primarily in gifs and short phrases or single words, could be difficult to follow sometimes. Another puzzle-solving opportunity.

"Is he okay?" Kenzie asked, assuming from Zachary's tone that he was not. Something had to be wrong for him to use that cautious, concerned tone.

"He's been… the last few days, it has seemed like something was off. It just didn't feel right."

Kenzie nodded, encouraging him to go on.

"Then last night…"

Kenzie swallowed and waited. Then last night, what…? She hoped Zachary wasn't about to drop a bombshell about Rhys having committed suicide or something else equally horrible.

"Stanley Green saw him out at night, wandering. Alone in the dark."

Kenzie turned away for a moment to stir the pot and smooth out the expression on her face, then turned back to Zachary.

"He was okay, then? How did Stanley find him?"

Stanley was an old friend of Rhys's aunt. They had once expected to be married, but she had been abusive and Stanley had eventually withdrawn from her and her family, breaking things off. It wasn't until after her death that he had returned, deciding to be a male figure in Rhys's life, to try to fill a hole that had been left years before when Rhys's grandfather, who had been raising him, had been murdered.

"He was out on the streets near Stanley's house. I think… he must have gone to him for help. Wanted to talk to him. Or wanted some kind of help."

"What did he say? What did he want?"

"He didn't say. He was uncommunicative." Zachary held up his phone. Kenzie had assumed that it had been Rhys that he had been texting with, but she had been wrong. "They've been waiting most of the day in the emergency room, and he's just been admitted. But Vera and Stanley don't know what's wrong. Why he went looking for Stanley, and why he's stopped communicating altogether."

Kenzie's chest felt tight when she thought of Rhys shutting off the dribble of communication he had managed to keep going the last few years. It had been a challenging way for them all to live, but Rhys had seemed okay most of the time. He had seemed like a normal teenager, just one with communication problems. No teenager was completely happy. And Rhys had dealt with enough tragic and traumatic things that no one expected him to be happy and outgoing.

But losing that last bit of communication, having him go back to where he had been after his grandfather had been killed and everything in his life had been permanently changed, would be devastating for Vera, his grandmother. And for Zachary, who felt things deeply and had become very attached to his quiet young friend.

"I'm so sorry. Does Vera want you to go to the hospital?"

"No… I wouldn't be able to see him. And once she's finished with the admission, she'll go home. There's no point in her camping out at the hospital when she won't be able to see him."

"At her house, then? She probably wants to talk."

"It's Stanley who was texting me. I'm not sure what Vera will want. I'm sure Stanley will go there to keep her company…"

Kenzie looked helplessly at Zachary, unable to guess what he wanted from her.

"I just…" Zachary shook his head. "I don't know."

Kenzie opened her arms, and Zachary was immediately holding her, pressing himself against her, hanging on for dear life. Kenzie squeezed him, then just held him firmly, trying to communicate all her love and care to him. He was lost, struggling to find his way through this new challenge.

Zachary was sniffling, trying to hold back tears. Kenzie didn't tell him everything was fine or it would all turn out okay. That was unknowable. Rhys had lived a difficult life, and adolescence, with its hormones, bullies, and stresses, had been hard enough for Kenzie, raised by two loving parents and not dealing with the losses and abuse Rhys had suffered. His mental health was already tenuous, and something seemed to have put him over the edge.

Kenzie held on to Zachary. She pressed her cheek against his. "It's good that he was seeking help. That he was reaching out to Stanley. I think that's a good sign. A sign that he hasn't just cut himself off from the world. If his mutism has gotten worse, it's not necessarily because he chose not to communicate, but because whatever he wants to communicate is such a big deal for him."

Zachary nodded.

"He *wants* help, Zachary. He reached out to someone."

"Yeah." Zachary's voice was hoarse, almost breaking. "But why not me? What did he need? Why didn't he message one of us? He knows we'd do anything to help him."

"I don't know. Maybe it is something that he thinks Stanley can help him with better than you or me. Or Vera. You can offer him many things, but you're not a Black man, and maybe that's the perspective he needs right now. Or maybe... he feels like Stanley could protect him from something or give him some kind of opportunity that you and I can't."

"Do you think he'll be okay?"

"He's in the best place for him right now. You know the psych ward at the hospital. That's where you would want to go, isn't it? When you are having problems and know you need professional help, that's where you feel the most comfortable."

Zachary nodded. "Yeah. The staff is really good."

"You know they are. You've been there and experienced it. You know that they'll help him. They know what they're doing and are compassionate and professional."

"Yeah."

Of course, Zachary had also had a bad experience there with a nurse who wasn't so nice or professional. But Nurse Debbie was no longer there. She was behind bars for the crimes she had committed. Rhys wouldn't have to deal with her whispering lies in his ears.

"We can call later and see how he's doing. Vera can put you on his list so that the staff can talk to you. Once he's ready for visitors, we can go see him. You know it isn't the end of the world. He just needs to be somewhere safe right now."

Zachary cleared his throat. "He can't be out wandering the streets."

"Exactly. Even though he was trying to get help, that's not a safe way to get it. There are so many people who would take advantage of someone like him. I'm glad Stanley found him and that they took him to the hospital."

"Yeah."

Zachary finally pulled back from Kenzie. They both breathed, looking at each other, and then Zachary looked away, overwhelmed by the intensity of his emotions.

"I'll set the table."

Kenzie's first instinct was to tell him that he didn't need to do anything; she would take care of it and all he had to do was sit down and eat with her.

But it would be better if he had something to do to keep him busy. He was doing something with his hands and being helpful and productive. Sitting around in silent contemplation would not improve his outlook.

Kenzie turned back to the stove while he went to the cupboard and started to pull out the dishes to set the table.

He was back and forth between the table and cupboards too many times. It irritated Kenzie, but it wasn't Zachary's fault that he couldn't remember everything he needed the first time or that he might be intentionally dragging out the job so that it took as long as possible. She would have preferred that he went back into the living room and watched TV for a few minutes until dinner was ready, but that was what was best for her, not best for him. And he was the one who needed the support right now.

11

"You think Rhys will get better?" Zachary asked tentatively. Kenzie didn't answer right away, building time into her answer so that he would know she wasn't just responding off the cuff or brushing off his question as unimportant. It was a question that deserved due consideration and an answer that was thought out instead of just a programmed social response.

"I do think he'll get better," she said. "He has been doing pretty well this year. And he has lots of loving people in his circle that want to help him. He didn't try to harm himself. As far as we know, he hasn't been experiencing any new symptoms. This is probably… surfacing trauma that he hasn't dealt with yet. Something that he needs to have some counseling on. Maybe get a med change. Sometimes, a patient stops responding to a treatment. He's getting older, bigger, and is dealing with hormonal changes. I think they'll stabilize him fairly quickly, and he'll be able to go home."

Zachary adjusted and readjusted the table place settings. "Is that right?" he asked anxiously. "I know the forks are supposed to go on the left, but today, it just doesn't look right."

"Of course it doesn't look right," Kenzie told him slowly, "because it's left."

Zachary didn't respond for a minute, then looked at her in disbelief. "Are you teasing me?"

Kenzie shrugged and nodded. "I suppose I am."

"Don't you know that you're not supposed to tease someone when they are upset?"

"Why not?" Kenzie challenged. "It seems to me you could use a bit of cheering up. Something to laugh about."

He snorted. "I don't believe it. Do you have no social graces?"

But the corners of his mouth were turning up slightly now. His eyes took on a little life instead of being locked in that dark place Rhys's sudden decline had taken him.

"You're the kind of person who tells jokes at a funeral, aren't you?" he challenged.

"Or in the morgue. Yep. Sometimes, people can start out a little stiff. They need someone to loosen them up a bit."

He chuckled. "We should call you Morticia, like that woman on *The Addams Family*."

"I always did like her." Kenzie started to remove pots from the stove and to transfer them to serving bowls. "And the little girl. Wednesday. She's a blast."

Zachary blew out a breath, his shoulders lowering a bit as some of the tension released. "You know my favorite character?"

Kenzie looked at him, then back at her work. "That's easy. Thing."

"Have I told you that before? How did you know?"

"Because he can be anywhere, do anything without being tied down to a body or brain. He doesn't have to deal with unwanted emotions. Is practically invisible. But very… *handy*."

Zachary groaned. He took the serving bowls from her to put them on the table, and even remembered to get out serving spoons for them.

Kenzie kept an eye on Zachary throughout the evening. It was clear that he was still thinking about Rhys and wondering if everything would work out okay. But he tried to act as though his attention was on her and it was just a regular evening, with nothing on his mind.

She was torn between encouraging him to discuss it with her—to get it off his chest and be honest about his feelings—and trying to keep him distracted and not focused on it, worried that his own mood might spiral downward.

It was that time of year. She had already been watching him for any signs that he was entering his usual depressive cycle, which would culminate on Christmas Eve, the anniversary of the fire that had changed his life forever. It would start to manifest sometime during the fall, and ramp up from there. But maybe on his new med protocol, they would be able to manage it better this year, and it would not end with a stay in the hospital psych ward to keep him from harming himself. They could have a quiet Christmas Eve at home, enjoying a few simple traditions that did not include candles or trees, and on Christmas morning, the crisis would pass.

He had promised to tell her when he started to go down that tunnel again so she could support him. They could discuss with his doctors whether increasing his medication doses was warranted and the best way to get through it with as few problems as possible. But it was possible that he wouldn't recognize when the depression started. Or that he would choose not to tell her, unwilling to bring her down or admit his vulnerability.

She had seen some subtle changes in the last couple of weeks and was worried that the crisis with Rhys would bring his symptoms on in full force much sooner than they would if he didn't have to deal with the extra stress, focused on his friend's pain and trauma.

"You can stop looking at me like that," Zachary said, not turning his face to look at her. He must have seen her look in his direction in his peripheral vision. She didn't see how he could have.

Kenzie pretended she had been looking past him at something else or staring into space. She readjusted her head and her gaze slightly. "What? Oh, was I looking at you? I was just thinking…"

"I'm fine," he snapped. "I'm not the one who had to go to the hospital."

"No, you're not," Kenzie agreed. "I'm sorry if you're feeling stressed about it."

"I'm not. You don't need to worry."

"Okay," Kenzie agreed lightly. "No worries, then."

He did turn his head to look at her for a moment, searching her expression, then turned back toward the TV again. Kenzie tried to focus on what they were watching and not worry about him. He was far too attuned to her feelings and would know if she were brooding.

Kenzie's phone rang. She looked down at it and saw Walter's name on the screen. She stood up from the couch and flashed the screen at Zachary so he would know that it was a personal call and not a work call, then retreated to the bedroom so she could talk to him privately and without distractions. She swiped the call while she was in the hallway, then answered it after she closed the bedroom door.

"Hi, Dad."

She sat down on the bed and made herself comfortable.

"MacKenzie! I'm glad I reached you. How are you doing?"

"I'm good. How about you?"

"In the pink. I was hoping that you wouldn't be stuck in the morgue this late."

"No. It would have to be an emergency for me to be there now. Something really urgent because of political implications or a mass casualty event."

"You get called out to murder scenes sometimes."

"Yes. You're right. Or a call-out. But then I would be at the site, not at the morgue. So, how have you been keeping yourself?"

"Nothing unusual." He gave her a few details of bills he was lobbying for or against. Nothing that really interested Kenzie. It was hard for her to see the importance of many of the bills presented at the legislature. So many of them were unsuccessful because they had no merit. If she couldn't immediately see how one of them might impact her own life, it was difficult to be concerned. She wasn't like Walter, who would dig deep down to sort out the possible areas that a seemingly benign bill could impact in the future. He was the passionate lobbyist, and she kind of felt like he would address anything that was of any concern. so she didn't have to worry about it herself.

Even though she knew that they weren't always on the same page on important issues.

She still felt like he would do everything necessary to protect his family.

"But, enough of that," Walter wrapped up. "You're not interested in politics."

"It all sounds very interesting," Kenzie told him. It was important to support him and to show interest in what concerned him, even if she didn't see the point most of the time. He was important to her. Therefore, what he was concerned about was important to her, too. "What are your plans for Christmas this year? Are you going to be around?"

There was a pause.

Kenzie had been thinking about Zachary and how she would need to tailor their holiday season around his needs. And how that would change, depending on whether he was at home or hospitalized.

She hadn't been thinking about Walter's mysterious disappearance on Christmas Day the year before.

According to him, he had simply gone into hiding when a certain Russian oligarch had been looking for him. While he considered whether to support the Russian's cause as he had initially promised. Realizing that the man he was helping was a mobster responsible for all kinds of atrocities against his fellow human beings, Walter had initially backed out of the deal. Until the Russians had coerced his cooperation by kidnapping Kenzie.

She suspected that he had not been in hiding over Christmas, as he had said, but had actually been abducted himself. However, the Russians had been unable to gain his cooperation until they had pushed the right button by threatening Kenzie's health and safety.

"I just meant… I wondered whether you were going somewhere special, or spending some time at Mom's, or…"

"I like to keep things pretty quiet for Christmas, so I doubt I'll be jetting off to Paris or Hawaii," Walter said, his voice smooth and not showing any signs of distress over her question. "I will probably at least stop in to see Lisa on Christmas Day. We usually spend a little time together that day."

Kenzie made a noise of agreement. As a family, they hadn't done anything big for Christmas since the death of Kenzie's younger sister, Amanda. But her parents did usually spend the day together, even though they had been divorced for years. Kenzie was determined to be a better daughter and spend at least a few hours with the two of them this year. As long as Zachary's health would allow it.

"That sounds good. I hope I'll be able to stop in and see the two of you."

"Make sure your mother knows. You don't want her to be working at the soup kitchen or another function when you happen to drop in. Coordinate your schedules if you can."

"I'll give her a call," Kenzie agreed. "I don't know exactly what we'll be able to do, and if it will just be me or both of us, but..."

"How is Zachary?" Walter asked. "Is he worse? Is that why you're thinking about it?"

"No, he's doing pretty good. He's on a good med cocktail right now, but I know he could start having worsening symptoms any time in the next few weeks."

"It must be difficult to anticipate that."

"Yeah. I am trying not to think about it too much. We don't know what will happen. We know he will likely hit a depressive cycle, but maybe the meds will control it better this year. He hasn't had to be hospitalized every year, even when he hasn't been taking meds regularly. So as long as..." Kenzie trailed off, thinking about Rhys.

"What?" Walter asked after a moment when she didn't finish. "There is something?"

"No. Yes. It's just that today, one of his friends, a young man he has been trying to help, was admitted to the hospital. He's had some kind of episode... I don't know how long it will take him to get over the bump in the road. It could be quick and he's out in a few days with a med adjustment, or it could be something that takes a long time to address. And of course..."

"And of course, you're worried about how Zachary will react to it. Whether it will bring him down."

Kenzie nodded and sighed. "Yes. I shouldn't worry so much about outside influences. It's more about how he's been doing up until now, and how the meds are working. Things like Rhys having problems don't necessarily trigger depression in him. It's just that the depression is already there, and other things might aggravate it… But I'm talking out of school, because he says he is okay, and I shouldn't be second-guessing him. Zachary is good. We're both just dealing with something upsetting. We are resilient, and it doesn't directly affect us."

"It's hard seeing friends go through difficult times."

"Yes. And this kid had been through so much already. Lots of trauma when he was younger. He deserves a break."

"Maybe they'll sort him out at the hospital. He'll be able to deal with someone there who knows how to handle him better."

"Yes. Maybe. We have a lot of good doctors here, and I should assume that they will be successful and that he'll be back on his feet and better than ever."

"I hope they do. For his sake and for yours."

"And his family's. His grandmother cares for him, and she could really use a break, too. Can you imagine raising a teenager at this stage of your life?"

"Oof," Walter grunted. "That would be pretty difficult. At this age, I expect to be free to go where I want to go and do what I want to do. Not to have to keep track of a teenager and make sure he is safe and stays on track. Especially one who is mentally… vulnerable. I would be worried all the time, wouldn't you?"

Kenzie had to admit that she would be. She wasn't sure how people could raise children without going mad with worry. How could parents let them out the door, knowing what kind of crazies and influences were out there? How did they raise children to be emotionally resilient, independent, and savvy? How could they let their kids be themselves and explore the world without having a nervous breakdown?

"I think it would be really hard," she agreed. "I can't even imagine dealing with a teenager *now*. They have… so many needs."

Walter chuckled. "And when the time comes, you just step up and do what you can, knowing that you're going to make mistakes because you're not perfect, and neither are they. You're going to set rules they don't like, and argue, and have to discipline them. But they're also very rewarding." His voice was warm. "Teenagers can also be wonderful creatures, full of vitality and a fresh worldview. Passionate, fun-loving, and excited by the world around them."

"Really?" Kenzie thought back. She didn't think that she had been all those things. She had tried to follow her parents' rules and to help take care of Amanda when she was sick and to think about the future and how she was going to make her mark on the world when the time came and she was free of the constraints of parents. But she'd been so bogged down with responsibility and worry over Amanda, she hadn't really gotten on her own path until years later, after Amanda's death. Then, she had suddenly realized that she wasn't where she wanted to be in life. Things had to change.

"You were a serious kid," Walter admitted. "Maybe you didn't have as much fun as your classmates. You were too focused on Amanda's health and her future… whatever it was."

"And then I gave her my kidney and thought that was all I would ever have to do and I was free to go and do whatever I wanted to."

"And didn't know what it was you wanted to do."

Kenzie laughed. "How did you know that?"

"I watched you struggle. We both did. You'd had lots of responsibility in your life, right up to giving Amanda a piece of yourself. Then she was cured, as long as the kidney functioned, and you didn't really have any idea where you wanted to go. All those parties and social events were meaningless."

He had understood Kenzie much better than she had thought. She had felt that she was on her own and that no one saw what was going on with her. She thought that the struggle had all been in her own head and that she looked like every other young adult venturing into the world and finding herself amidst the parties and plays, the friendships and suddenly serious adult relationships.

And maybe her struggle had been invisible to the rest of the world, but it had not gone unnoticed by her parents.

"Well, thanks for being there, Dad. I always knew you guys supported me in whatever I decided to do."

No matter how much they disagreed on politics and causes, Kenzie had always known that her parents would do anything she asked.

12

Kenzie worked her way through the lab results that had appeared in her email inbox and various other pieces of correspondence, some of which required her action, and some which did not. It was hard to keep up with everything when she had an increased role in performing postmortems and managing the medical examiner's office. But with Dr. Cook there to take some of the overflow, she should be able to relax a little. Start taking her Sundays off again. Get home in good time for dinner instead of being late half the time and forced to rely on frozen dinners, leftovers, or takeout every day of the week. It wasn't good for her to be overworked and overfed. Both came with negative consequences.

Kenzie opened a report from the toxicology lab and read the bolded words several times before they sank in. She looked at the name and checked that everything was right.

"A drug trial, my foot!" Kenzie exclaimed as she entered Dr. Wiltshire's office, now temporarily Dr. Cook's office. "Look at that!"

She threw the printed copy of the initial toxicology screen down on the desk in front of Dr. Cook. He raised his brows and picked up the paper, wondering what she was blowing up about. He pursed his lips as he read the scant details.

"MDMA," he said.

"Methylenedioxymethamphetamine. MDMA. Freakin' ecstasy!" Kenzie blew up. "They gave him ecstasy!"

Dr. Cook made a calming motion with his hands. "MDMA has a long history of use in psychotherapy. It has been used off and on for decades."

"How does giving patients a rave drug, a psychedelic, count as therapy? How does that help anyone?"

"You're going to need to calm down before you talk to anyone at Persons about it. You need to approach it quietly and calmly, or they won't tell you anything. Have a seat."

He nodded toward the visitor chair that Kenzie usually sat in when she spoke with Dr. Wiltshire. She didn't feel like sitting. She felt like going out and punching someone in the nose. What were they doing, dosing psychiatric patients with ecstasy? They were causing more problems than they would ever solve. She forced herself to sit down and tried to listen to what Dr. Cook had to say.

There were, of course, legitimate uses for many drugs that were abused. Just look at fentanyl. It was causing terrible problems on the street. Yet it was a very effective painkiller at the proper doses and could help patients immensely.

But fentanyl was not ecstasy. It was an opiate. A painkiller. People might abuse it, but it was developed to treat pain and worked in cases where nothing else did.

"MDMA can be helpful in working with traumatized and defensive patients," Dr. Cook explained. "It helps to open people up so that they can talk about their feelings, about the traumas they have been through. There are indications that it could be a very effective way of treating PTSD if used wisely."

Kenzie thought about Isah's broken fingers. Every single digit broken in multiple places. Trauma? No one could deny that the man had been through a traumatic experience. Whatever torture he had endured before coming to the United States, whether at the hands of the police or some other faction, was enough to cause anyone long-lasting trauma symptoms.

She took a deep breath and tried to control her emotional reaction to the discovery. To hold off judgment until she fully understood from Dr. Cook exactly how MDMA might have been used legitimately in Isah's treatment.

"Okay. So how does that work? Is it approved? You can't just give your patients whatever you like. MDMA is a controlled substance."

"There are ongoing trials. The doctor would have to be part of one of those studies to use it legitimately."

"And is Persons in an approved clinical trial?"

He shrugged. "I assume that will be part of your investigation. If you want me to make some phone calls, I can find out. If you think that is the best use of my time."

Kenzie rubbed the center of her forehead. "I've heard of drug trials for marijuana. Of course it has some medical uses. And there were LSD trials years ago. I thought they had all proven that psychedelics are too dangerous and don't have any therapeutic value. All this nonsense about 'opening minds' ended up failing on all counts, damaging people further. Those trials were all shut down, the doctors who performed them disgraced."

Cook seemed unperturbed by any of this. Kenzie didn't understand why he wasn't just as upset as she was. Someone had overdosed their patient on MDMA. They had killed a man, and she and Cook were calmly discussing ancient drug trials.

"I don't know if that is a fair representation of the LSD studies," Cook said. "They weren't exactly discredited, but there was a lot of negativity surrounding them. And maybe too many people willing to experiment, whether they really had a psychiatric disorder that could be treated with lysergic acid or not. It was more the cultural view of LSD with the war on drugs than hallucinogenics not being effective in treatment."

Kenzie rolled her eyes. "You're younger than I am. It isn't exactly like you can remember that."

"No," he smiled. "I wrote a paper on it."

"Oh, really. Does that mean you are pro-hallucinogenic? You believe that it is an appropriate and effective treatment?"

"Some of the studies have been very positive. I have seen cases where LSD or MDMA has changed someone's life. It has been called miraculous. People who have suffered from anxiety or trauma for years, crippled by it, plagued with nightmares, flashbacks, and the inability to move forward in their lives. Suddenly, after a few treatment sessions, they can get out, to move past the fear. To start to live normal lives again."

"Are these controlled trials? Or off-the-books experiments?"

"There has been a plethora of both." He shrugged and smiled in agreement with Kenzie's cynicism. "With Nixon's War on Drugs, any use of LSD, mushrooms, or MDMA for treatment had to go underground. It wasn't tolerated. There is good reason to keep drugs off the street, not to let kids and addicts experiment with them, mix them, overdose, and get into trouble. The War on Drugs was a good thing. And a bad one. There are a lot of people suffering from trauma now who don't have to. They could be treated effectively if they knew about it and got into a program."

"So you think that they were treating Isah legitimately."

"I have no idea. Do you?"

"I know that the nurse said he was part of a trial therapy. And that his behavior had changed."

"So you said. If you believe that the MDMA had anything to do with his death, then you will need to investigate it further."

"You don't think it did?" Kenzie challenged.

She wondered briefly if she were overreacting. If she were jumping to conclusions. But there was a connection between ecstasy and hyperthermia. She knew that much. Isah did have MDMA in his system and her death scene observations had shown that he was hyperthermic. It didn't take a huge rise in body temperature to kill a person. There was a clear line from MDMA to death by hyperthermia.

"What else was in the tox screen?" He looked down at the paper she had thrown at him. "No LSD. No street drugs. Just MDMA."

"It's only a preliminary result. There is still more testing to be done. They roll any positive results to us as fast as they come in. We don't know yet what other drugs might have been in his system."

"Well, this will help guide you in pursuing other testing. Was the MDMA pure? Was it mixed with something else that might have caused a reaction? Was it part of a trial being held at Persons or smuggled in or passed to him by another patient? Did he take it on his own, believing that it would help? Was he trying to commit suicide?"

Many questions needed to be pursued before Kenzie jumped to conclusions about what had happened to Isah. Maybe the MDMA had been a contributing factor, but only one of several. Or maybe it had been the only factor, and the staff at Persons were being reckless in their experiments. There had certainly been indications that they were trying to cover something up. Maybe she had just found out why.

13

Kenzie sat down across from Paul Casey, the director of Persons.

"So, explain to me what you are here about today," Casey told Kenzie, frowning and looking around his messy desk as if the answer might be there. He was a large man, spending too much time sitting at a desk. His short dark hair framed his round face, gray at the temples, and he had a small mustache over his lip. His clothes were rumpled-looking even though it was early in the day. As if he had slept in the brown leather couch in his office the previous night instead of at home in bed.

"I'm following up on the death of Leander Isah."

"So you said."

"We are waiting for the medical records you were going to send us."

"It will be sent. I don't see any particular urgency, considering he is already dead."

"We need them to conduct our investigation properly."

"Yes. I'll get them over to you."

He looked at the door, like it was time for Kenzie to leave. But she was just getting started. "Mr. Casey—it is *mister*, not doctor?"

"Yes." He looked irritated by this inquiry. "I am not a medical doctor. I have some background in medicine, but I am an administrator, not someone with my boots on the ground. Do I need to have a doctorate to have this conversation?"

"No, I just want to know for sure who I'm talking to. We need certain things to ascertain how Mr. Isah died. I know it is inconvenient for you, and maybe you think we don't need these records, but we do. It is my responsibility to investigate deaths like his and to find out what happened."

"Deaths like this? Mr. Isah was ill. He was under the care of a medical doctor. It is my understanding that the medical examiner does not investigate cases where the deceased was under the care of a medical doctor."

"We can. If we are called in, or in certain other cases, such as a death at a prison or a mental institution."

"You can't tell me that you have to autopsy every person who dies in a mental institution."

"I'm saying that we have to investigate it, yes. There won't necessarily be an autopsy required for every case. Still, we need to see what the circumstances are, investigate, and decide whether we need to do a postmortem."

"Every death," he repeated.

"Have you had other deaths here that have not been reported?" Kenzie asked suspiciously. It certainly sounded like it.

"No." He closed his mouth and shook his head. "Leander's death was the first we've had to deal with. That is why I was not familiar with the requirement."

"There haven't been any other deaths at this institution?"

Casey was sweating. He wiped his forehead with a limp-looking sleeve. "We are a fairly new facility."

"Where did you work before this?"

"I was at a clinic in Burlington."

"In charge of it? Like here?"

"Yes. Well, there was someone else over my head, but I was mostly in charge of how things were run. I do have experience in the industry."

"And was that clinic a mental institution?"

"Why?"

Kenzie favored him with a glare. She was the investigator. He was the one who was supposed to be answering the questions. And she was starting to suspect that he was not telling the truth. Not a word of it.

"Was it or was it not?"

"It wasn't *just* a mental institution. We did family counseling. Other outpatient services. Whatever we needed to do to serve that community."

"What community? Burlington?"

"Yes, but… I meant serving families who were… concerned with mental health."

"Who had people in their families who were being treated."

"But it wasn't all inpatient. Plenty of work was being done for walk-ins, families of patients, the school system, and all those touch points in the community…"

"And housing mentally ill patients."

"Yes. That was one of our services as well."

"So it is a mental institution. And we should have been investigating any deaths there, too. Were there any deaths while you were there?"

"No. It's not that common. Our patients are generally not physically ill. If they were, they would be treated at a hospital or medical clinic somewhere."

Kenzie wrote down a few notes. She would need to follow up on Casey's history and see just how many patients had died at the institutions he had run. It was pretty hard to keep track of any statistics if the bodies never came through the medical examiner's office. If they were sending them all directly to funeral homes, saying that they had died of natural causes, how would the funeral homes know any differently? How would the medical examiner ever hear about them? How could they keep on top of any problems in the system?

But she didn't want to back Casey so far into a corner that he wouldn't answer any of her questions. She didn't want him dummying up and going to his lawyer for advice. So she didn't ask him the names of the other institutions he had been at lately. It would be easy enough to find his employment history through other means and find out where he had been. If she couldn't find it easily herself, she could ask the police to find out for her. Or even Zachary. It wouldn't be hard for a private investigator to find out.

"So, now you know," Kenzie said, giving Casey a reassuring smile. "When there is a death here, it's like a death in custody at the prison or police station; we need to review it just to make sure that everything is being run properly and there aren't any concerns. I'm sure you won't have any trouble complying with that rule in the future."

"Of course not," Casey assured her. "We run a tight ship here. We follow all relevant laws and ensure that our patients receive the top medical care they deserve."

"It's a very important service," Kenzie told him. "Mental health is one of my passions as well. One of the things that my family foundation is putting money into, and that I am interested in for personal reasons as well. I think we need to do a lot more for the mentally ill than we do. Providing services like you are here."

Casey puffed out his chest proudly. Kenzie had learned from her father that she could rarely go wrong by complimenting people, even if it was over the top. People drank it in, felt that they deserved it, even if it wasn't sincere. It was a lot easier to deal with people if you complimented them. Preferably more than once.

"I see this as one of the most vital services in the community," Casey told her. "We have done a lot to improve our physical health over the last hundred years. Figured out a lot of things about how the human body works and made a lot of advancements in treatment and in extending life expectancy by decades. But what have we done by way of treating the mentally ill? We might have moved away from barbaric shock treatments, straitjackets, and people locked away in institutions for the rest of their lives, kept away from the public where they might upset people. But where are we on curing schizophrenia? Or even just finding effective treatments? Where are the drugs that are *effective* against depression, bipolar, anxiety, dementia, autism, ADHD? That don't just mask it, shave the peaks and valleys, or slow the progression?"

"Or PTSD," Kenzie suggested. "That should be treatable. And so many people suffer from it. And children with complex PTSD. We know what causes it, why can't we reverse the process? Why can't we do anything for these people?"

Casey leaned forward in his seat, nodding eagerly. "The number of PTSD cases has skyrocketed with lockdowns, school shootings, and the child pornography trade on the internet. Abuse is rampant. Children and spouses have no safe place to go. And when they escape it... It isn't over. They still suffer for years and decades afterward. Can you imagine all the pain?"

Kenzie adjusted her body language to mirror his. "And when people have these symptoms, this problem in their lives, what do we give them? Antidepressants and various kinds of talk therapy? Why is there so little we can do?"

"Persons is at the forefront of treatment of PTSD," Casey told her. "There are some fresh new—and older, proven—therapies that can help. You would be amazed at some of the miraculous recoveries we have seen. I think that PTSD is the perfect condition for us to target. It isn't congenital. It isn't genetic. It isn't caused by a virus or bacteria and is not progressive. It has been caused by a discrete event or series of events, and should be reversible. And in fact, we have proven that it can be reversed. *Permanently* reversed."

"That's amazing. And this is just through talk therapy? Behavioral stuff or EMDR?"

"No. And not antidepressants, either. The cutting edge in trauma recovery is hallucinogens."

Kenzie raised her eyebrows in a parody of surprise, hoping she wasn't overdoing it. "Hallucinogens? What do they have to do with trauma?"

"All of those gurus in the sixties and seventies who preached using psychedelics to alter your consciousness and open your mind were absolutely right. These altered states of consciousness and removing fears and anxieties are vital to treating PTSD. Combining these drugs with exposure therapy and helping patients to be able to talk about their trauma is life changing. People who couldn't even put into words what had happened to them, or couldn't even recall it, are able to face their traumas and move on from them."

Kenzie nodded slowly. "That's amazing. I had no idea. So, do you use LSD? Mushrooms?"

"Both are possibilities, and we find that different things may work for different people. But LSD is tricky and is hard to get approval for. The drug of choice is known as MDMA, which you may know as—"

"Ecstasy," Kenzie filled in. "But isn't that dangerous?"

"In a clinical setting? No, everything is carefully controlled, and we start with very small doses. It would be dangerous for people to experiment with it on their own, especially getting MDMA off the street, cut with who-knows-what other garbage, if it even is really MDMA and not some substitute. But in a carefully controlled treatment program, it is one of the most important tools in our arsenal."

"Huh." Kenzie nodded, hoping she looked impressed. "Isn't it amazing how some of these old cures and treatments come back around again in slightly different forms? I've heard that mushrooms were used by indigenous tribes for their psychoactive properties."

"Absolutely. It can be very helpful to look at how certain illnesses were treated by shamans and healers in all different societies. The ancient oral traditions of these cultures are steeped with all kinds of knowledge that we can tap into. Modern man is not necessarily smarter than primitive man."

"So you're using these methods now? Here at Persons?"

He nodded, then his eyes flickered with the sudden consciousness that he should be cautious about what he told her. That their life-changing therapies could have something to do with Isah's death. Or that they might be blamed. He stilled and looked at her, trying to decide if he had already said too much or if she were really interested in his responses.

"With MDMA and psilocybin?" Kenzie persisted.

"We really can't divulge anything about our patients' treatment plans. That is highly confidential, as are any drug trials or new treatments."

"But I do need to know this information as it relates to Mr. Isah. You are required by law to provide the medical examiner's office with the information we require to investigate his death."

"We cannot disclose any details of drug trials. Including who the participants are or were. Breaking the study controls will mean the trials cannot be used."

"And if you need to start new ones, I'm sure you will. It was suggested to me by one of the staff members that Mr. Isah was a subject in one of these trials. His therapy schedule had changed, and his behavior had been altered. I understand he was increasingly violent toward the staff, and there was an altercation the day he died."

"I don't think anyone in this facility had enough information to determine whether Leander was in one of the experimental programs. And violence is not a common reaction to MDMA."

"Maybe not, but agitation, anxiety, and panic attacks are not unheard of."

"At higher doses," Casey dismissed. "Not in the controlled doses that we use in our trials."

"So you would have investigated any deviations from the norm, anything that was not a known side effect of MDMA and the treatment program you were using."

"All of the patients, their reactions, and the program itself are being carefully monitored. We have plenty of protections in place. It is of the utmost importance to us that our patients are treated safely and that if there are any problems, they are addressed immediately. We'll have a team meeting, go over any problems, and come up with solutions before it goes any further. We are a small, agile company. We can make the necessary adjustments quickly."

"Even to a trial protocol? There must be things that you cannot just change on the fly. Controls and procedures that are in place."

"Still, if we felt that a patient's health was in danger, either because they were on the protocol or because they were not, then we would address that. We won't put our patients' lives in danger."

Kenzie nodded sagely as if satisfied by this. She had a lot more questions to be answered, but it was probably time to get the police there to ask. They were the ones who were trained in interrogation and investigation procedures. As a representative of the medical examiner's office, Kenzie was authorized to ask questions that pertained to the postmortem and investigation into Leander Isah's death, but she needed to get the police involved before going too far afield. And she didn't want to take the chance of spooking Casey into destroying records or convincing other members of the staff to cover things up.

"It's good to see that you put such a high priority on patients' safety," Kenzie told Casey. "So many places now seem to put profit above everything else. But I know that you are not like that."

14

This is Dr. Richards," Casey introduced a blond woman in a lab jacket to Kenzie. "She was the doctor in charge of Leander's care. She can answer some of your more specific questions about his background and treatment. And I'll check the status of those records you needed."

Kenzie got the feeling that he was more likely to stall on giving her Isah's medical records and information on the trial protocols they were running and Isah's involvement in the program. She really hoped that he would not go so far as to destroy information. One reason that she needed to get the police involved as quickly as possible. Kenzie was the best person to ask the medical questions, but the cops could go in with a subpoena and a search warrant and get their hands on the information she needed.

"Thank you," she murmured. "That would be very helpful."

Casey left Kenzie with Dr. Richards, glad, Kenzie was sure, that he was quit of her, for a little while at least. He had not been happy having to deal with her questions. He would be even less pleased about the police when they arrived.

Kenzie turned her attention to Dr. Richards, who took Kenzie to a family visiting room where she could sit in a comfortable chair and sip a bottle of water while they pretended to be cordial to each other.

The first thing Kenzie had noticed about Dr. Richards was her mass of blond, curly hair. Sitting facing each other, Kenzie found the woman's face even more striking. She was beautiful, perhaps more believable as a model than in the role of doctor. Even, well-proportioned features, expertly applied makeup, and doll-like "bedroom eyes" that Kenzie was sure Richards used to her full advantage if she were ever pulled over by the cops for speeding or had to convince a store clerk to allow her to return a product that was not normally returnable.

And how did it affect her relationship with her patients? She would be alluring or threatening to men, depending on how secure they were. Or maybe both alluring and a threat at the same time. And women… Dr. Richards had probably been dealing with the jealousy of the women around her all her adult life.

She wasn't young like Dr. Cook. Older than Kenzie, perhaps heading toward fifty or even sixty. It was hard to tell with the makeup and the youthful curls arranged around her face. She had a lot of fine lines around her eyes and mouth. The hair was probably bleached and dyed, professionally highlighted to look sun-kissed. Kenzie was sure she did not get that much time out in the sun with a busy doctor's practice. A sweet floral scent floated around Kenzie when Dr. Richards sat down.

"So you are with the medical examiner's office," Dr. Richards said, sounding surprised and interested. "You are certainly not what I would have thought of on hearing your profession."

"You don't look particularly like a doctor in a mental institution either," Kenzie pointed out.

Richards laughed softly. "You know, I suppose you're right. We are both used to dealing with people's prejudices and preconceptions about what someone who lurks in the morgue or spends her days in the halls of the cuckoo's nest should look like. We've both kind of… broken the mold."

Kenzie had to admit, despite having to fight people's biases against women doctors and against their idea of what a woman in the medical profession or in the morgue should look like, that she had to fight the same biases in herself when she looked at Richards. Dr.

Richards wasn't the blocky-faced, bullying, sexless woman that might be portrayed on a TV show. Just as Kenzie was no Morticia Addams.

"Funny how we have certain expectations," Kenzie agreed.

"Amazing. Society expects that two women as attractive as you and I wouldn't have two brain cells to rub together, forget actually getting through medical school and having a successful practice." Richards raised her hands, palms up, and shrugged. "Yet here we are. Tell me about your job."

"What do you want to know?" Kenzie returned, surprised by the question. She was there to talk to Richards about her treatment of Leander Isah, but Richards was leading with Kenzie's role. "I investigate suspicious or sudden deaths. See whether there has been any foul play or if the death could have been prevented. As I was telling Mr. Casey, any death in a mental institution is treated the same as a death in custody in the prison or police station, so we are required to investigate Mr.—Leander's death. To nail down the cause and manner of death."

Richards was nodding. "Of course. I understand that. It sounds like a very interesting job."

"Most people find it pretty morbid, but I enjoy solving a puzzle, seeing how our bodies work—or don't work, as the case may be. Human bodies are much more resilient than we give them credit for. Many of us are walking around with genetic mutations or tumors that we will never know about, pain that we can't identify the source of, organs or blood vessels in the wrong locations..." Kenzie shook her head. "And yet we survive and thrive."

"Until we don't," Richards offered dryly.

"Yep. And then it is my job to identify which of those things—or some outside event—caused your death. It's fascinating work."

Richards leaned back in her chair, smiling and nodding. "So, tell me what you have discovered about our Leander. I was shocked to hear of his passing. I know he wasn't in the best of health, but I certainly didn't expect him to die."

"I am still investigating, which is why I am here looking for records and the opportunity to talk to you and anyone else involved in his care. I was quite surprised to discover that he had MDMA in his bloodstream."

Dr. Richards chuckled at this. "Most people don't know about the use of hallucinogenics in the treatment of mental health conditions. Or if they have heard about it, they believe it was abandoned back in the seventies. And, of course, it was for a time. Or went underground. When legitimate treatments are vilified, it can set medicine back by decades. But we are now in the position where people are more open to these methods of treatment again. I think that the use of medical marijuana has helped. People can see that something once considered a tool of the devil has many legitimate medical uses, from glaucoma to nausea, pain control, and anxiety. It makes them more open to the possibility that other chemicals they consider 'bad drugs' can be used for good."

"Like healing trauma victims."

"Exactly."

"What can you tell me about Mr. Isah and his treatment?"

"Well, we have to be careful there for several reasons. Of course there is doctor-patient confidentiality..."

"Which is not an issue any longer."

"And we have also all signed nondisclosure agreements with regard to certain treatment programs."

"Because they are experimental? Or for other reasons?"

"As we've just covered... society has certain negative opinions about some of the available treatments. Even if these are well-established ways to treat trauma patients and help remove inhibitions, they are looked at with a certain amount of skepticism. We have to be able to control the dialogue, to make sure that they are presented the right way so that people can understand how they are being used and how helpful they are."

"I don't see how that stops you from talking to me about the treatments Mr. Isah was receiving."

"Well, I might need to talk to our corporate attorney about whether I can do that under the terms of the NDA."

"The NDA can't tell you to do something illegal, and withholding vital information about a death from the medical examiner is a breach of the law."

Dr. Richards frowned, but she did not argue the point.

"What can I tell you about Leander…? He has had mental health issues for many years, with symptoms initially emerging when he was a teenager, which is pretty typical. He had a lot of negative encounters with doctors and law enforcement in his native country. They are not well-known for treating the mentally ill with any compassion or understanding. He came here as a refugee after proving torture and demonstrating his life was at risk. He's lucky he got in before they tightened up immigration. If he tried now… with his mental illness diagnoses, I don't think he would get in, no matter what shape he was in."

Kenzie shook her head. "How terrible."

"It was. And it is still something that happens all over the world. We are lucky here, and yet I'm sure you know that even in the most progressive countries, there is still a lot of prejudice against the mentally ill. Lots of abuse, people who target vulnerable populations. Many of our homeless are the mentally ill who simply have nowhere to go. Nowhere safe. Most of those on the streets will be incarcerated at some point. We opened the doors to release people from the asylums and pushed them into the prison system instead."

"Had Leander been incarcerated?"

"Nothing of any length. Mostly just the types of misdemeanors that the homeless and mentally ill are charged with—loitering, vagrancy, disturbing the peace, public intoxication or urination." She gave a little shrug. "Where are they supposed to go? What are they supposed to do?"

"And he could afford to come to Persons?" Kenzie asked, making a motion that encompassed the institution. "How did he get placement in a private institution?"

"He was able to access it through a grant. There are foundations and government programs that provide 'scholarships' for those who can't afford it to get better medical treatment than they would be able to access through the public hospitals. Or specific treatment programs that are not offered through the public system."

"I assume the government doesn't support or provide any hallucinogenic treatments."

"They will," Richards said with certainty. "The number of people suffering from PTSD and other trauma-related illnesses will make it impossible to ignore the fact that there is a solution out there. People will not allow the government to blithely push aside a treatment that is so effective for so many people. It may take time, but they will have to accept it sooner or later."

Kenzie suspected she was probably right. The population wasn't likely to accept it if word got out that hallucinogenics were more effective than any other treatment. People would be self-medicating. The government would be forced to step in and start regulating the industry and making sure it was available to more than just an elite few.

"How was Leander responding to the hallucinogenic program?"

Richards didn't answer at first, pondering the question. "I think he was doing very well here. I know we all hoped to see positive results very soon. The treatments were having an effect on him."

"Good or bad?"

"It can be very difficult to process trauma. Very tough on the sufferer. Painful, dealing with flashbacks and anxiety, feeling like you're right in the midst of it again. That's one reason we recommend hallucinogenics. It allows the person to get out of themselves, to dissociate from the negative feelings, and view the trauma from the outside. To get desensitized. But it is a process. Patients don't always have positive experiences to begin with. They are re-exposing themselves to a trauma, which stirs up many negative feelings. Leander was… not yet able to separate from those feelings."

"So it was making things worse for him."

"No." Richards shook her head. "That would be misconstruing what was happening with him. Even though he was dealing with negative emotions, he was progressing well. We would have been able to cure him. I'm sure of it."

15

Kenzie wasn't sure she had made any progress on the investigation into Isah's death. While she did have confirmation that he had been part of an MDMA treatment trial, she still didn't have his medical records and sensed that everyone at Persons was holding back information and doing everything they could to keep her from discovering what was actually going on in the place.

Was it just MDMA? There wasn't really any reason to cover that up if it was an approved trial. Maybe they had decided to use other hallucinogenics that were not on the books? LSD or a dangerous psychedelic like PCP? On the drive back to the morgue, she called the tox lab and asked them to look for any other hallucinogenics that might not be on their standard panel, just to be sure.

She hesitated about calling homicide, but knew that she would have to. Especially since the staff at Persons were not cooperating with her requests for information. Once she returned to the office, she called Dr. Wiltshire, hoping that discussing it with him would help clear up her conflicting feelings about it.

The phone rang several times, and she thought it would go to voicemail. He could be out doing something else. Or sleeping. She was glad he was weaning off the heavy painkillers he had been on when he first broke his hand and in the days leading up to and immediately following the surgery. She needed him to be awake and alert when she talked to him.

"Kenzie."

"Oh!" Kenzie was startled by Dr. Wiltshire's voice, when she had already decided that he wasn't going to answer and the call would go directly to voicemail. "Hello, doctor. It's good to hear your voice."

"And yours," he agreed warmly. "What can I do for you today? I hear you've got a substitute now so, hopefully, you can catch up on some of the things that have fallen behind."

"Yes, we got a Dr. Cook. Do you know him?"

"We've met. He's young. Devastatingly handsome?"

Kenzie couldn't help giggling at the description. "Well… yes. Glad I wasn't the only one who noticed. He seems to be competent."

"Top of his class all the way, from what I understand."

"Was he? Wow, good for him."

Kenzie had done well but had not been at the top of her class. Not very often, anyway.

"So, what can I do for you today, Kenzie? You have something you need me to sign off on?"

"No. Nothing that's ready to go yet and, once it is, Dr. Cook can do it. But… I don't know; I wanted to talk through a case with you and see what you think. I think I will have to call in homicide, but I was hoping to avoid that."

"Okay, tell me what you know."

Kenzie related what she knew about the private hospital trying to send the deceased directly to the funeral home without letting the medical examiner review the case first, about the various findings in the postmortem and the MDMA trial. And the facility's refusal or at least resistance to handing over the medical files she asked for.

"Hmm." Dr. Wiltshire cleared his throat. "Well, the resistance from the care center is certainly concerning. We should have all the details of how the deceased was treated before his death. There may be other things that we need to check before releasing the body."

"Yes. And I wonder about talking to some of the other patients about how the care is, what they are doing in this therapy, and so on? To ensure that everything is aboveboard and that they aren't fudging on the trial results or covering up if Isah's death was somehow related to the trials."

"Not a bad idea. Probably best to go in with a detective so that there are witnesses and someone is there to help you out if you experience more resistance from the staff."

"I should call them in." Kenzie wasn't really asking the question. She just wanted Dr. Wiltshire to confirm that was what she should be doing. She already knew it.

"Sooner is better than later. You don't want to wait until evidence has been destroyed, either inadvertently or intentionally. You have been at the facility twice now. They might decide it is time to take measures."

"That's what I was thinking, too." It would be stupid of the clinic, of course. They were better off cooperating with Kenzie and the police, even if something they had done had contributed to Leander's death. The destruction of medical records would be evidence of a guilty mind. As long as they didn't tamper with anything, they could keep saying they didn't believe that anything they had done had resulted in Leander's death. They could keep saying that they had made all the right choices and wouldn't have changed anything. But as soon as they started the coverup, they were shooting themselves in the foot.

"Give them a call," Dr. Wiltshire advised. "Read them in on all the results to date and your feelings about the resistance and the medical staff there. They know you're not someone to raise alarm bells for no reason."

"Okay," Kenzie agreed with a sigh. As much as she didn't want to, she knew that it was the right thing to do. She couldn't even explain why she was so uncertain about making the call that she knew needed to be made. Maybe it was because she knew how they would react to the hallucinogenic trials. Even worse than she had. And if the results were really as promising as the doctors said they were, Kenzie didn't want to take the chance that an investigation could get them shut down and a treatment that might be life-changing for people like Zachary and Rhys could be put out of their reach.

Dr. Cook was hanging around when Kenzie terminated the call with Dr. Wiltshire. He raised his brows at Kenzie.

"Everything okay?"

"Sure. I just wanted to run things by Dr. Wiltshire and to see what he thought about the Isah case."

"You called Dr. Wiltshire on that case?"

"Yes."

"I am the other doctor on that postmortem. Don't you think you should talk to me instead?"

"Oh..." Kenzie blew her breath out. "I didn't really think about that. Sorry, I'm not used to having you here yet."

Though Dr. Wiltshire hadn't suggested she take it back to Dr. Cook. He could have, but he had been willing to consult on the case instead.

"What did he say?"

"That I should go ahead and talk to the police, get them involved, so we can get the documents we need before they are potentially destroyed."

"You think that you need to bring them in?"

"Yes. I knew that I needed to... I hoped he would say no, that I'm just seeing shadows where there aren't any. But he didn't oblige."

Dr. Cook was quiet for a minute. He looked at Kenzie. "What do you think of your Dr. Wiltshire?"

"He's a great doctor. I've learned a lot from him. And he's very personable and compassionate, as well. I think those are important traits in a medical examiner."

"Otherwise, they come off like Igor?"

"Or Frankenstein. Yes. You don't want to come off as unfeeling or taking pleasure in other people's tragedy."

"And how about... his personal life? That doesn't impact his job?"

Kenzie frowned at him. "What do you mean, his personal life?"

"His... hobbies. What he does in his off hours."

"I don't really know anything about it. He's married, or at least jokes about his wife a lot. May or may not play golf." She shrugged. "He's here when he should be, puts in a lot of hours, He's pretty productive, runs this morgue efficiently."

She wasn't quite sure what Dr. Cook was talking about. Did he know something about Dr. Wiltshire's private life that Kenzie didn't?

Dr. Cook looked like he would walk away without any further comment.

"Hang on!" Kenzie insisted. "What are you talking about? You don't ask a question like that and then walk away! Spill."

He hesitated, half turned away from her. "I've heard rumors. They're probably not true. You're the one who knows him personally. That trumps things that I might have heard."

"You've heard what rumors?"

There was another pause before Cook decided to answer.

"I've heard that he gambles."

"Gambles? Really?" Kenzie shook her head. "I've never seen any sign of that."

"Then like I say, it's probably just unfounded rumor. People who are jealous and want to see him brought down a notch or two."

But Kenzie's mind was already off and running. Was that how Dr. Wiltshire's hand had gotten broken? He owed some bookie or loan shark a lot of money and it was a warning to pay up? It had been a pretty brutal warning, if that were the case, and could have permanently retired him. Dr. Wiltshire had needed a specialist to reconstruct his hand. Judging by the complexity of the external fixators, the damage had been very extensive. Was it all because he was behind on his debts?

She tried to think of whether there had been any other signs that Dr. Wiltshire might be a closet gambler, but couldn't think of any. He was never away from the morgue unexpectedly and hadn't shown any sign of sudden windfalls or financial difficulty. He didn't talk about sports, cards, or betting. He spoke of his wife and gave every indication that he just lived a quiet, uneventful life, doing yard work or playing golf when he was not working.

"I really can't see it," she affirmed. "I don't know who started that rumor, but I've worked with him for a few years, and I don't think he does. I really don't think he does."

Or maybe that was just what she wanted to believe.

16

When Kenzie arrived home, she could hear Zachary talking to someone on the phone, and he did not come to the garage entrance to the kitchen to greet her as he usually did. She took off her outdoor clothing quietly so as not to startle or disturb him, and stood in the kitchen, straining her ears to hear every word or nuance to figure out who it was. A client? Someone he was investigating or one of the resources that he used? One of his brothers or sisters? There were a lot of people that he emailed or talked to throughout the day. Still, he usually dealt with them earlier, not into the supper hour when Kenzie should be arriving home.

Zachary spoke quietly, just a few words here and there as he listened to the caller. But Kenzie had a pretty good idea who it was by the time he had finished. When he disconnected, she stood in the doorway to the living room, looking at him.

"Was that Vera?"

Rhys's grandmother. Zachary nodded. "Yeah, she wanted to give me a rundown on how he's doing. I wish I could be there..."

Kenzie nodded sympathetically. Zachary was used to being the one in the hospital, and it was probably frustrating that he had no control over the situation. It was in Vera's hands, and he couldn't even talk to Rhys unless she approved of it and ensured that Rhys had access to his phone or someone who could communicate his messages. And that assumed that Rhys wanted to communicate and was able to. Was his silence the previous day just an aberration? Caused by missing his medications or his body not responding to them the same way anymore? Or was it something more serious that would take longer to resolve?

"What did Vera have to say? How is he?"

"No change since they admitted him. He still isn't communicating. Very withdrawn. What could have caused such a drastic change? I don't understand it."

"We don't know. The doctors will investigate and try to counsel him, try to figure out what happened, if anything. It may be random... we just don't know. I assume since it has been a day, they have checked for anything emergent, like a stroke or seizure. It's not unusual to see sudden changes in teenagers. A lot is changing, physiologically."

"But they don't usually stop communicating."

"Well..." Kenzie couldn't help smiling. "Actually, a lot of parents complain about how their teens have stopped communicating. But that's more of a relationship thing, kids developing independence from their parents, focusing on peer group and their place in the new communities around them."

"They don't just stop talking altogether."

"No. Though Rhys didn't communicate that much before now. Maybe this is his brain's attempt to go to the next stage, moving away from dependence on his caregiver to more independence." Kenzie shook her head. "I don't think that's what it is. But it's something to think about."

"I'd like—" Zachary started, then stopped, shaking his head. Kenzie waited to see if he were going to finish his thought or reword it and, when he didn't, encouraged him gently.

"You'd like what?"

"You're busy. You've had a long day. It's not a good time to make last-minute plans."

"Sometimes life happens, and we have to adapt. No one was

expecting Rhys to crater like this. It's no different than if he was in an accident or came down with some physical ailment. We can't wait for a better time to deal with it. It's happening now. We adapt to it."

"Okay... I was just thinking... that we should get together with Stanley. I don't know why... whether it's because he needs support, or because I need to hear for myself what's been going on with Rhys, or just... because it's the only way I can feel closer to Rhys right now. I just feel like we should."

"Okay. You want to call him? Do you want to invite him here? Go out for dinner?"

"I'll call, I guess. You're okay with doing something if he agrees? It just seems like too much of an imposition on you."

"It's not. I want to do what I can to support Rhys too. And to support his support network. I don't know whether we can do anything that helps. But we can be there. We can ask."

Zachary nodded, but didn't make any immediate move to pick up his phone and make the call. Maybe he knew Stanley would still be at work and didn't want to bother him there, or perhaps he was just trying to process the conversation before taking the next step. Kenzie considered her next move.

"I think I'll change. You can let me know what he says."

Zachary didn't need the pressure of her hovering over him, waiting for him to make the call. She would normally shower and change into her jammies or start making supper, but if they were going out to dinner with Stanley or having him over, neither was really appropriate. So she would just give Zachary some room and change out of her work clothes and wait to see what was decided.

After changing, she pulled out her laptop, checked her email, and fiddled around without getting anything done. After a few minutes, Zachary tapped on the door, then opened it and peeked in. Kenzie nodded at him.

"He's agreed to go out for dinner," Zachary said. "Is that okay?"

"I said it was."

Arrangements were made and, an hour later, the three of them were sitting at the bar where Zachary had met with Stanley once before, back when he'd been working on the murder of Robin Salter.

Zachary looked around as if refamiliarizing himself with the place, and Stanley gave a little laugh.

"It was a pretty messed-up case," he said. "That family... not exactly the most functional one."

"No," Kenzie agreed. There had been a lot of big problems with Rhys's mother and aunt, and things had not ended well for either one of them. And Rhys was probably damaged forever by the traumas they had both inflicted on him.

Or maybe not. Maybe there was a chance that someday Rhys would be able to be treated with whatever therapy came out of the trials being conducted at Persons and in other psychiatric practices across the country and around the world. Maybe one day, it would be unimaginable to them that once upon a time, childhood trauma had been something people had been forced to carry around for the rest of their lives, whether they could deal with it or not.

"But you really stepped up," Zachary said. "You've been a real role model for Rhys. Someone that he looks up to and admires."

Stanley was embarrassed by the praise. He rolled his eyes and didn't address the compliment directly. "I really felt like he needed someone. And when he was younger... well, I thought we would be family. I would marry Robin, and even though Gloria didn't have a man in her life, I could be a positive male role model for Rhys as his uncle." He sighed and wiped his forehead, eyes far away. "Then I had to leave because of Robin's instability and abuse. But I always regretted that I couldn't fill a role in Rhys's life. I was glad to become a part of his life again after Robin died."

"Well, you've done well," Kenzie affirmed. "Like Zachary said."

Stanley sipped a bottle of beer, looking away from them and shrugging a little as if protesting that it was nothing.

"So tell us about last night, what happened with Rhys," Kenzie suggested.

Stanley nodded. He stared off into space. "There isn't much to tell. I think Zachary already knows the whole story. I had gone out for some pizza and, on my way home, I saw this boy on the street... and it looked like Rhys. I thought it couldn't be, but as I got closer, I got more and more sure, instead of realizing that it wasn't him, like I expected. So I pulled over and told him to get in. Took him home and asked him what had happened, what was wrong. I didn't expect any long explanation. You know how our Rhys is…"

They nodded in agreement, both having dealt with Rhys's communication difficulties in the past. Kenzie would have expected a few gestures, a gif or two on Rhys's phone, maybe a typed word or two. No actual speech, but they had all become accustomed to Rhys communicating in his own way.

"He didn't try to respond to me in any way. He had obeyed when I told him to get into the car and he came with me into my apartment, but he acted like he was in a fog, like he couldn't even understand what I was saying, let alone know how to communicate back to me. No gestures, no voice, no phone. Just… nothing. Like he wasn't even there."

"Dissociated?" Kenzie asked.

Stanley raised one hand palms-up in an "I don't know" gesture. "One of the doctors said something about a dissociative fugue, so maybe. But I thought those things were pretty quick. A few minutes, and it would pass."

"Well, no. A dissociative episode can be very quick, just a few seconds, so that people around you don't even notice. But a fugue state can last weeks, even months."

Zachary made a noise of protest. "Don't tell me that!"

"It doesn't mean that's what Rhys is experiencing or that it will last for very long. I'm just saying… that type of state *could* last a long time. But he's safe where he is. Everyone knows where he is and that he is safe. They'll keep him there until they can be sure he'll be safe when he's released."

"I don't think they've even diagnosed anything yet," Stanley said. "That's just one of the phrases they were throwing around. They said there were a lot of possibilities."

"Of course," Kenzie agreed. "It's too early to know for sure what has caused this or what the diagnosis or prognosis will be."

"How has he been the past few weeks?" Zachary asked. "I have talked to him a few times on the phone, but I haven't seen him face to face. Is this… something that has been coming for a while, or was it completely out of the blue?"

Stanley rubbed his chin. "I didn't see it coming. But… he has been having trouble in other areas. And he's been quite emotional. So… I guess I'm not surprised that something broke. But I don't really know what caused it."

17

Zachary scratched the back of his neck, looking at Kenzie and then back at Stanley. Kenzie tried to think of a way to help reduce his anxiety.

"I worry," Zachary said slowly. "I mean... he's had to deal with so much already, and he's been strong and been able to get through it. But there's still Luke, and I don't like the two of them being involved."

"But Luke has been fighting against the traffickers," Kenzie pointed out. "He's been working with Joss against them. He isn't working with them anymore."

"I know... and I gotta give him that. But he could always go back. I know it's a hard temptation to resist. The drugs and the lifestyle and doing what he knows. And even if he continues to fight the traffickers, what if they figured out his connection with Rhys and targeted him because of what Luke is doing? Or even if... they identified Rhys as a target another way? Through other kids at school who are in the business? Or because he's alone by himself wandering the streets?"

Kenzie put her hand over his on the table. "I know that there are a lot of hazards and things to worry about. But Rhys is safe right now. He's in a safe place. We need to focus on what's going on with him now rather than what could happen in the future. You are catastrophizing. Imagining the worst that could happen. And it's not even related to what's going on with him right now."

Zachary blinked at her and shook his head as if she had missed the whole point. "I *am* thinking about what's going on right now. Rhys is out on the street alone at night, looking for Stanley, and he's so traumatized he can't communicate? It's Tirza all over again."

The name didn't mean anything to Kenzie. She glanced at Stanley and saw the same blank expression on his face.

"Who's Tirza?" she asked.

Zachary made a noise of disgust, as if she should have known immediately. "The autistic girl at Summit who was snatched from school and trafficked. They let her go after a few days because her mother did a big media blitz, confronting the police for ignoring what she was telling them about Tirza and saying that she had just run off with some boy. But she insisted it was a kidnapping and made things too hot for the traffickers, so they dumped her. *She* was found wandering on the street. Unable to communicate with anyone because she was too traumatized and she normally uses an AAC to help her communicate."

Kenzie saw the parallel immediately. How similar the two cases were and his concern that Rhys might have escaped or been dumped by similar traffickers after a night of abuse. They both looked at Stanley. Rhys hadn't been able to communicate so, of course, Stanley couldn't answer their questions about what had happened to Rhys that night. And the doctors wouldn't tell them anything. But there might be other signs. Stanley might have guessed.

"Do you think… something like that might have happened to Rhys?" Kenzie asked Stanley. "I know there's no way for you to know, but did it look like he was just out walking on his own, or like something might have happened to him? Some violence…?"

Stanley shook his head slowly. "Well, I can't be sure, but… I mean, they wouldn't just dump him after a few hours, would they? I mean… he didn't look scuffed up or… torn clothing… anything like that. Physically, he seemed pretty much the same as ever. It was just…" Stanley swallowed. "He seemed so far gone." He licked dry lips and then took a swallow of beer. His eyes glittered, but he shed no tears.

Kenzie turned her attention back to Zachary, trying to take the pressure off of Stanley to let him recover. "I think Stanley would have been able to see the signs if he'd been kidnapped, assaulted, and trafficked. And I agree; I don't think that traffickers would just take him for a few hours and then dump him."

"There are plenty of other predators who would," Zachary argued.

Kenzie nodded, conceding the point. "But it didn't look like there had been any physical violence. So hopefully... that wasn't the problem." She sighed. "But I don't understand what he was doing out there, looking for Stanley. And why no one knew he was gone until Stanley saw him wandering the streets. He should have been at home. Vera wouldn't let him go out late like that."

"She doesn't always know where he is," Zachary said with a quick shake of his head. "There have been other times when he's shown up to see me, and I know she didn't allow it or know he was there. Sometimes, he takes off during school, and they must not do callouts when students miss classes. Or not every teacher takes attendance, and he knows which ones he can scam. At night... I didn't know he was going out at night, but he probably just waits until she's asleep, and she never knows he's gone. If Luke could sneak out on Joss, who's pretty savvy and, I would guess, doesn't sleep well, then it would be easy for Rhys to sneak out on an old woman who takes out her hearing aids for bed and might take a sleep aid."

Kenzie had to admit that there had been a few times when her parents hadn't known where she had been as a teenager, and would have been horrified if they had known. She hadn't been that wild, but she had tested the limits and experimented, like any child growing up and trying to separate from her parents and become independent. Zachary was right; it probably would not be hard to sneak out on Vera.

"And what happened? Where did he go? What did he do? Did something happen while he was out, so he went to find Stanley? Or did he sneak out because he needed to see Stanley?"

They both looked at him. Stanley's eyes were no longer filled with tears. He frowned and shook his head. "I wish I knew. I've never known him to do that before and, when we connected, he didn't communicate anything to me."

"What things did you normally talk about?" Zachary asked. "You were a father figure to him. Did he talk to you about school? Challenges he was going through? Complain about Vera's cooking?"

Stanley snorted. "He never complained about her cooking," he said with a forced laugh. "That boy might have been as skinny as a rail, but he sucked the food down like a vacuum cleaner."

Kenzie and Zachary both laughed. They had seen it too.

"Never really said much about school, either," Stanley continued. "If it was too hard, or he was being bullied by a student or harassed by a teacher. I remember how bad school was for me, and I was a big kid and could defend myself and speak just fine. I can only imagine what it was like for a kid like Rhys."

Zachary rubbed his eyes. Sitting beside him rather than across from him, Kenzie could see behind his hands rather than being blocked by them. She couldn't see much in profile, but she could see his grimace.

"Have a drink," she suggested, worried about flashbacks to his own painful school experiences.

Zachary picked up the glass of ice water before him and took a couple of swallows. He nodded at Kenzie. She took deep, measured breaths, hoping that he would match his breathing to hers and be able to stay in control of his emotions.

"What did you talk about, then?" Kenzie asked Stanley.

"I don't know. We hung out. Watched sports, did some guy stuff together. We didn't spend a lot of time talking. I asked him how he was, but we didn't discuss feelings or what was happening at school."

A safe relationship. Non-demanding.

"Did he talk about Luke and Aster?" Zachary asked. "Anything about what they had gone through?"

Stanley shook his head. "I only know of their existence by talking to you. Rhys never mentioned them."

And he hadn't gone to Luke. If something had happened to

trigger Rhys's episode, it had been something that had sent him to a father figure, not the boy he was attracted to.

"And Vera... she doesn't know about his interest in Luke?" Kenzie asked.

Stanley shook his head, but Zachary made a face that suggested he disagreed. "She hasn't said anything about it, and he hasn't told her," he said carefully, "but that isn't the same as not knowing."

"You think she knew?" Stanley said doubtfully. "I think she would have said something."

"She has said a couple of things that made me wonder. I think she has her suspicions, even if she isn't sure. She didn't want him to be bullied at school if people saw him and I out together..."

"Oh." He hadn't mentioned that to Kenzie before. She thought about it. "When did she say that? I didn't realize."

"It was way back... a year... almost two. With all the publicity after..." He cleared his throat. "After Teddy Archuro."

"That was before Rhys even met Luke, wasn't it?"

Zachary shrugged. "Yes. Vera's raised Rhys from the time he was a baby. She's probably had plenty of occasions to notice who he tends to be attracted to."

"But he hasn't told her? They haven't discussed it?"

"Not as far as I know. He has wanted it to be kept quiet from her. I've been careful not to allude to it. I've seen what can happen when kids are outed before they are ready or when their caregivers are unwilling to accept it. I don't want him to be kicked out and have to fend for himself."

"Vera wouldn't do that. She loves him too much."

"She's religious. She's quoted Bible verses to me before. When parents are wrestling between moral values they have spent a whole lifetime learning, and their children's choices... too often, their response is to split with the kid."

Zachary's intuitions about such things were usually pretty accurate, so Kenzie didn't argue. Maybe he was right and, if Vera were faced with a crisis, she would choose her religious beliefs over her grandson, though Kenzie had a hard time believing it.

"Do you think it might have leaked out at school?" Stanley asked. "Kids can be pretty good at picking these things up."

"It's possible," Zachary said. "They might have guessed, or he might have done something to give himself away. Maybe there is someone at school that he likes, and it has ended up causing problems. Only…"

Kenzie waited to hear what the counterargument was.

"Why would he go to Stanley?" Zachary said with a shrug. "If he'd never talked to you about it before," he looked at Stanley, "and you're not gay. Then why would he come to you to talk about it?"

Stanley shook his head. "I've tried to be careful of what I say around him. You know…" His cheeks and throat were turning a dusky red. "Not saying anything disparaging or using slang words for them. So maybe he knows that I'm a safe person. But…" He shook his head. "It isn't something we have ever gotten into. I hope he knows he could come to me about anything, but I'm not exactly the person most kids would choose to confess their deepest secrets and attractions to."

Kenzie looked at Zachary. "You're wondering why he didn't go to you?"

"Well, I guess," he admitted. "I'm trying not to be all egotistical about being the person Rhys would go to for help or to talk about it. I've helped him with other things in the past. I already know about him being attracted to Luke. We've talked about mental health issues. He knows that I have admitted myself to the hospital before. So why wouldn't he talk to me if he was having problems with bullying, being gay, or being depressed or having other health issues? Why Stanley instead?"

18

Kenzie could hear Zachary on the phone again as she got ready for bed. She had expected him to be tired and getting ready for bed too, but he seemed restless and wound up. He didn't usually make late phone calls unless it was urgent, and he didn't seem to have any particularly urgent cases.

She waited until she thought he was off the phone before entering the bedroom and potentially distracting him. She peeked around the door to make sure he was off.

"Sorry," Zachary apologized. He massaged his forehead tenderly. "I just... had to make sure."

Kenzie moved into the room. "Had to make sure of what?"

"I just called the hospital. Asked whether I could talk to Rhys."

Kenzie looked at the clock. "It's late. He'll be down for the night. They'll have him on a sleep aid to make sure that he takes the time he needs to recover."

"I know. He is. I mean, they wouldn't tell me that because of privacy, but of course he is. And even if he wasn't asleep, they probably wouldn't let him talk on the phone. And even if they let him, and I was on his approved caller list, he wouldn't be able to because he's not communicating right now. I was just hoping for... something. Just a bit of reassurance."

Kenzie nodded. "Did you get it?"

She fully expected the answer to be no.

"Actually…" Zachary gave a small smile. "Do you remember Nurse Val from when I was in?"

"Sure. I remember Nurse Val. Very nice lady. Helpful."

"Yeah. So I got her. And she said, 'You know we always take good care of you when you're here, Zachary. We give you something if your anxiety gets too bad, and we make sure someone is with you or checking on you every fifteen minutes if we have concerns. We always respect your privacy, but we let your family and friends know that you are okay and we are taking good care of you.'"

Kenzie breathed out. "So Rhys has been given something for his anxiety and they are keeping him under close supervision."

Zachary nodded. "Yeah. I just wanted to know that he was okay. And I shouldn't even have to ask because, like Nurse Val says, they've always taken good care of me there. I know they are professionals and I know what the routines and procedures are. I just needed to hear it."

In the morning, Kenzie got an early call from Detective Elena Garcia, who had apparently been assigned the Isah case.

"Dr. Kirsch, it's good to talk to you again. I'm going up to Persons and, from what I understand, you have been involved in this case from the start. Do you want to go with me? You can fill me in on all the details on the way there, and be around while I conduct a few interviews; let me know if you see anything I don't?"

Kenzie knew from a past case that Zachary had been involved in that Garcia took an unusual approach to her investigations and seemed to enjoy involving non-law enforcement officers, something that most of the detectives Kenzie knew wouldn't have even countenanced.

But it was to her advantage. This time, at least.

"Sure, I'd love to help out," Kenzie agreed. "I have already talked to a couple of people, though, so I probably shouldn't be around when you do it. They wouldn't want to talk in front of me in case something they said conflicted with what they had told me before."

"Right. I've read your interview notes and know who you've talked to and the broad strokes of those investigations. I think you're right, and I won't have you sit in on those re-interviews. But I'd like to talk to some patients over there and get a feel for what is happening. I don't like the idea of this drug trial. Certain drugs are restricted for a reason."

"I don't know what to think of the trial right now, to be honest. In concept, I can understand why they would want to do it and how success could change the whole landscape of how we treat these conditions. But there is also such a potential for misuse and abuse..."

"It's something that can only be used in hospitals, right?" Garcia asked.

"Mmm. I don't know what the guidelines are, but I don't think it is restricted to hospital use. I suspect that it could be used in an outpatient model too. Maybe not with take-home meds, but a doctor or nurse who would see to their administration and stick around for a few minutes to make sure that there was no reaction."

"I've seen what these drugs can do to people. You probably have too, on your table. Why they would mess around with them, I don't understand. It's too dangerous."

"We prescribe other drugs that are dangerous when taken as a recreational drug or used the wrong way. Amphetamines. Fentanyl. Ketamine. Digitalis."

"And the opiate epidemic should be warning enough for us."

Kenzie shrugged, almost dropping the phone from her shoulder. While she didn't agree with Garcia on this point, there was no point in arguing about it. That was outside of the scope of the case. And neither of their opinions would have any effect on whether opiates were deemed too dangerous to be used in a medical setting.

"What time do you want me there?"

"I could come pick you up now if that's convenient. Spend however long we need to at Persons, and then I can drop you back at home to get your car and go wherever else you need to."

"That doesn't make much sense if you're conducting interviews that I'm not attending. Either I end up hanging around with nothing to do while you do those interviews, or you have to run me home and then go back. I'll just meet you there."

"Okay, fair enough. I can be out there in about half an hour. What is your schedule like?"

"I could make it in about the same. After I have my coffee."

Garcia laughed. "Already had mine. Okay, I'll see you out there shortly."

Kenzie had not thought it possible that the staff at Persons could look at her with more disapproval than they had on the previous occasions. But they were clearly not happy about the police now being involved, as well as the intrusive medical examiner's office. Garcia waited impatiently for the person who would approve her talking to some of the patients and explain to her where the medical records were and why they hadn't been copied or released to the medical examiner's office yet.

The blond receptionist clearly had her nose out of joint and didn't want to let them talk to anyone, but Garcia pushed back pretty hard, and the woman was eventually cowed into calling Dr. Richards to ask what to do about the police investigation.

Dr. Richards entered the reception area, her forehead creased in consternation. She shook her head, her blond curls bouncing gently.

"I'm sorry, Detective, uh…?"

"Detective Elena Garcia," the detective announced crisply. "What exactly is the delay?"

"Er… what delay? I don't understand what you're doing here."

"We are here to continue with the investigation into Mr. Leander Isah's death."

"I'm sure the medical examiner's office will tell you that they have fully investigated that case and are about ready to issue their findings," Dr. Richards said, nodding in Kenzie's direction. "We have been fully cooperative. But we are now getting into the situation where your investigation is interfering with our operations and could compromise patient care."

Garcia looked at Kenzie, who shook her head. "We're still waiting on the medical records we requested several days ago."

Richards brushed these concerns away with a motion. "They're in the works. And you aren't going to find anything different from what we already told you. There really isn't any reason to get them other than the completeness of the records. You're barely even going to look at them."

"We have significant concerns about how this case has been handled thus far," Garcia said. "Dr. Kirsch's findings thus far are quite concerning."

"We have explained the treatment that Leander was undergoing. And his history. The traumas that he had suffered in the past necessitated quite intense treatment. And I'm sure Dr. Kirsch can tell you that those who have survived torture often suffer from significant physical and emotional impairments. They unfortunately have a significantly shortened lifespan."

"You're saying that it was the torture that caused Mr. Isah's death?"

"I'm not saying that. I'm just pointing out that it is not unusual for a patient with that sort of history to die... unexpectedly. It may have been a stroke or seizure, some kind of infection or old shrapnel still in his body..."

"I don't believe that any of that is the case," Kenzie said evenly.

"Still, torture has many physical and psychological effects. I can't be expected to tell them all to you now..."

"What would help," Kenzie said evenly, "would be his medical records."

Richards blew out her breath explosively. "They are in the works."

"They better be in my briefcase before I leave here today," Garcia told her.

The two women glared at each other, neither willing to back down. But Garcia had the law on her side, including a subpoena for the records. There wasn't much that Richards could do unless she wanted to end up in a jail cell for contempt. The longer she delayed, the better the chances were of her being incarcerated. Garcia did not want to give them any longer to destroy records.

"And you will note that we have also asked for all security video for the forty-eight hours before Mr. Isah's death. And it had better all be there. Missing time or cameras would be a problem."

"We need to protect our patients' privacy—"

"And we need to protect your patients from you. If all the proper safety protocols were followed, you should not have to worry about the recordings."

"What about the other patients?"

"What about them? You're afraid of their faces being on video? We're not going to send footage or patients' faces to the media, you know."

"Our patients frequently come from very wealthy and influential Vermont families. Even if your officers see their faces, happen to mention the names to their wives…"

"That will not happen."

"So you say. But how can I be sure of that?"

"You don't need to be sure. You only need to follow the law, which says that you must turn that information over to me."

19

They had finally been given a patient consultation room in which to interview a few of the patients in Isah's ward to see if they had seen or heard anything the night that Isah had died or in the days leading up to his death.

A woman was brought in, dressed in the blue scrubs that most of the patients wore. She had long dark hair, which hung in curtains around her face. She kept her head bowed and didn't look at them.

"What's your name?" Garcia asked gently, even though she had already been provided with it.

An easy question to get the woman started, to help her to share in a way that wasn't painful or threatening.

"Janice Martin." Her voice was low and subdued, almost too quiet to hear. Like she wanted to just fade away from them.

"Janice. My name is Detective El Garcia, and this is Dr. Kirsch. It's nice to meet you."

Janice nodded, but her eyes were far away and she didn't look at either of them.

"Do you know why we wanted to talk to you today, Janice?"

"Because of Leander."

"Yes, that's right. Your room is right next to Leander's, is that right?"

She nodded.

"So you see him coming and going, or if there are people coming and going to his room."

"Not all the time," Janice objected. "We aren't allowed to stay in our rooms all day."

"Oh, you're not?" Garcia leaned forward, looking interested. She had probably thought of it as a hospital where people stayed in bed all day. But that wasn't the way it worked in a psychiatric treatment center. People were encouraged to be up and around, socializing, participating in activities, group therapy, personal therapy, and so on.

"No," Janice shook her head. "You're not allowed to just withdraw from the world." She said it wistfully, as if that were exactly what she wanted to do.

"Oh, I see. They want to keep you... present," Garcia said. "An active participant."

Janice nodded, moving forward and back a little with the nods, like she was in a rocking chair. She put her feet up on the seat of the chair so that her knees were folded in front of her chest. She wrapped her arms around them, curling herself into a ball. Demonstrating very effectively how she wanted to just withdraw from the world.

"So did you see Leander the day before he died?"

"Yeah, I guess."

"Did you see when he went to bed?"

"I might not have been in my room then."

There was a period of silence while Garcia considered this answer. "Do you know when Leander went to bed?"

"I don't know when he went to sleep."

"Was he up and around during the afternoon before he died? He wasn't sick in bed?"

"No."

"No...?" Garcia prompted, realizing she had asked two questions and wasn't sure which one Janice intended to answer.

"He wasn't sick in bed."

"Good. So he was apparently feeling well enough during the day to participate in activities."

Janice's shoulders lifted and fell.

"Did he have therapy? What was his schedule, do you know?"

"Yes. He had therapy in the afternoon. With Dr. Miller."

"Good. He went to his appointment?"

"Yes. You have to. You can't say no."

"And when he got back from therapy, what did he do then?"

Janice stared down, not answering for a long time. Then finally she spoke again. "He wanted to go to his room."

They waited for more information. Kenzie studied Janice's pale face. It was difficult to read anything from her flat affect. Withdrawn, not wanting to engage with them or talk to them about Leander and whatever had happened the day he had died. Because she didn't know? Because it was too painful? Was she afraid?

"And did they let him go to his room?" Garcia asked.

"No, they said he wasn't allowed until bedtime, that he needed to do other things." Janice shook her head. "Write a letter. Socialize with other patients. Engage with the world." She let out a sigh. Obviously, she didn't like doing any of these things any more than Leander did. Or maybe she was projecting her feelings onto Leander.

"So what did Leander choose to do?"

"He didn't want to. He said he wanted to go to his room, kept trying to go back there. Sometimes after therapy… you just want to sleep. They should let you sleep. It's hard."

"What kind of therapy had Leander been doing?" Kenzie asked. "Do you know? Was he doing CBT? EMDR?"

Janice looked at Kenzie. "Are you a real doctor?"

Kenzie smiled. "I'm a pathologist, actually. Not a therapist. I don't know as much about psychotherapy as I should, but I know some of the therapies that are used. I understand that Leander was in a program for his PTSD."

Janice nodded but didn't offer any details.

"Was it to do with the drug therapy?" Kenzie prodded. "Had they given him the trial meds?"

Janice looked around uncomfortably, as if trying to find a way out of the room and away from their questions.

"What other patients do is none of your business," she told Kenzie flatly. "You keep your eyes on your own page and worry about the work you have to do. Everyone is entitled to privacy in their treatment program."

She was clearly repeating the words that had been told to her more than one time. The party line. Stay focused on your own therapy and don't worry about anyone else's.

"But you probably know more about other patients' therapy than they thought. One of the nurses said that he knew which patients were in the experimental program, because their therapy schedules had changed. And some of them, like Leander, were acting differently than they had been before."

Janice nodded her agreement.

"So you noticed the changes too?" Garcia asked.

Janice shrugged. "We all know everything," she said. "Everybody sees where everyone else goes. Everything they do. You can't help knowing."

"And what kind of therapy was Leander doing?"

"He was in the trial drug program."

"And do you think he was in the control group or getting the actual drug?"

"Getting the drug. If he was getting the placebo… he wouldn't have been like that. He wasn't like that before."

"Like what?"

"So… agitated. He was upset all the time. But especially after a session." Janice swallowed and licked her lips.

Kenzie glanced around reflexively for a mini fridge or somewhere she could fill a glass of water for Janice, but there didn't seem to be anything. They should have had something available. A lot of psychoactive meds caused dry mouth. Kenzie was quick to spot the signs and was always filling glasses of water or handing Zachary water bottles if she noticed he was swallowing or licking his lips a lot. Or moving his tongue around his mouth, trying to generate some saliva.

"They have two kinds of sessions," Janice explained, her voice small. Doing what she knew was forbidden and talking about someone else's treatment. "Sessions where he got the drug, and sessions that were just talk. They alternated."

"Ah." Garcia made a note of this. "And this session was drug or talk?"

"Drug."

"How could you tell the difference?"

"His eyes were different. Big pupils. And other things. Sweating and anxious. They say it makes you more social, makes you want to be around people more, and that it makes you feel good. But not everyone was like that. And it didn't last for a long time. You would be happy and fun for a while, and then... when it wore off, you feel sad or mad, and some people really paranoid. Leander was never very happy or social."

"What time was his therapy?"

Janice frowned, thinking about it. "I don't know what time... hmm... after breakfast, and then he wouldn't be back until after lunch."

Kenzie raised her brows. She looked at Garcia, making sure that she saw this was significant. "That's a long session."

Janice nodded.

"When you have a therapy session, is it that long?"

"No. Half an hour or an hour. But Leander was always gone for a long time."

"Was everyone who was doing the experimental therapy gone for that long?"

"No. Different lengths. Maybe there were different dosages or drugs..." She shook her head. "We weren't supposed to talk about it."

"I know," Kenzie agreed. "But this is an investigation into what the doctors were doing. And if something was going on that shouldn't have been, and Leander was hurt during the process, then you need to tell us so that we can find out what was going on and who was responsible."

"Leander just died," Janice said. "It wasn't anyone's fault. He had a bad heart."

"Is that what the doctors told you?"

"Yes."

"That he had a bad heart?"

"Yes."

That was interesting. Kenzie looked at Garcia to make sure she wrote this down. "We don't have his medical records yet. I guess that will be one of the notes in the file we receive."

Janice nodded her agreement. She looked around. "I shouldn't be here. I should be doing arts and crafts right now."

"That sounds interesting. Do you like arts and crafts?"

"Sure." Janice looked directly at Kenzie for the first time, getting a little more animated. "I've always liked to make things with my hands. I'm good at it."

"What are you working on right now? Or do you do something new each session?"

"I'm working on a sculpture. It's clay. We don't get marble or anything like that. It would be too expensive."

"I guess so. And pretty heavy, too. I don't know what it's like to work with marble, but I imagine it would be difficult."

"Yeah. So we only have clay, but it is versatile. I'm working on this bird… it is an eagle, on a branch, just lifting its wings to take off."

Maybe representing Janice's wish to be able to lift herself up and fly out of there, away from their negative feelings and able to feel the wind through her hair. Or feathers. Whatever the reason, it was the only thing that had brought light into Janice's eyes during the interview.

"That sounds awesome. Inspiring. I'd like to see it."

"Maybe before you go. I should go now, though. Or I'll miss my chance." Janice stood up.

"We were hoping to find out a little more about the timeline," Garcia objected, motioning for Janice to sit again. "Leander got out of his session after lunch, which still leaves several hours before lights-out time and when he was discovered. Can you tell us about what happened during that time?"

"No." Janice looked around restlessly. "He kept trying to go back to his room. They wouldn't let him. He… put his head down on one of the tables and went to sleep, but they wouldn't let him sleep. We're supposed to follow a proper sleep schedule. Sleeping at the wrong times can mess up your circadian rhythm. See? I even remembered what it is called this time."

"He was trying to go to sleep?" Kenzie asked. "I thought he was agitated."

Janice made an impatient sound. "He didn't want anyone near him. He wanted to be alone. He wanted them to stay away from him and he wanted to go to sleep."

"Oh, I see." Kenzie wasn't sure she did, but she could look up some information later. Zachary had more experience with mental health issues than she did. Maybe he could explain the seemingly opposite symptoms to her.

She remembered how he had been after the assault by Archuro. He had switched from being unable to sleep more than a few hours at night to sleeping all the time, throughout the day and night. It was his brain's way of trying to heal from the trauma. Pulling away from the world. Cocooning to protect himself. He had not wanted to talk to anyone about what had happened. Not to Kenzie, his therapist, or his foster father. He had avoided and canceled therapy sessions. Dr. B had probably been horrified to hear what he had been through, and that he had withdrawn and not talked to her about it when he needed to the most.

Maybe that was how Leander had felt. That even though he should have been talking to someone about the feelings that the treatment was stirring up, he only wanted to avoid the issue and hide from the world.

20

The next patient they had in was David Gentle. The man looked nothing like his name would have implied. He was of average height, but with the back and shoulders of an ox, easily the size of two men. He looked like someone who could eat Zachary for breakfast. From his face, he was not a gentle giant, either. He scowled at the police detective and medical examiner, not happy to be there, already looking bullish and resistant.

Kenzie found herself immediately checking for escape routes and contemplating how to defend herself if he exploded. The orderly who brought him in did not stay with him as Kenzie thought he might. Kenzie knew that Garcia was trained in handling criminals who might get violent, but that didn't make her feel much better. Garcia wasn't there with a gun, taser, and baton on her belt. She was in plain clothes and, trained or not, she was much smaller and lighter than Gentle. Kenzie wasn't sure how much help she would be in a fight.

"You are David Gentle?"

"Yeah."

"You were told why you were here?"

"You want to talk about Leander."

"Yes. I'm Detective Garcia, and this is Dr. Kirsch. How well did you know Leander?"

He looked around, restless, apparently not liking being enclosed by these four walls. "I didn't know him. I don't know anyone here that well. We're not here to make friends."

"But you got to know people while you were both staying here together," Kenzie suggested, knowing how it had worked with Zachary. "Even if they aren't the type of people you would normally have befriended, when you're housed together for a few weeks or months, you get to know the others. Their personalities and behaviors. And sometimes... things that you have in common."

He grunted and didn't agree or disagree with this assessment.

"So you learned things about Leander, even if you were not friends," Garcia agreed. "What kind of person he was, how he spent his day, what his schedule was."

He shrugged his massive shoulders. Kenzie thought he looked like a huge turtle trying to retract his head into his shell. He continued to scowl at them as if they had personally offended him by expecting him to come and talk to them.

"What did you think of Leander?" Garcia prodded.

"I thought he was weak," Gentle grunted. "Physically and mentally. Frail. Like a puff of wind would blow him over. He needed to toughen up. Parents don't do their kids any favors by protecting them from every bit of opposition. They need to learn how to stick up for themselves and face things that are hard." He blew his breath out in a hard puff, clearing his throat with an animalistic growl.

Kenzie thought of what she knew of Leander. Gentle was wrong about his having an easy life. Run-ins with the police in a country where they were not nearly as nice as in the US. Torture and his mental illness. He'd had a difficult time, at least from his teen years. Before that, who knew? Did he have both parents? Had they been victims or abusers? Kenzie had little doubt that he'd had to fend for himself from early on in life.

"Did you talk with him very much?" Garcia inquired.

"No, we didn't talk. I told you he wasn't my friend."

"Can you tell me where you might have seen him during the twenty-four hours before he died?" Garcia suggested. "Can you tell me what his schedule was, when he was in his room, and when he was occupied with therapy?"

"What am I, his social secretary?" Gentle slapped his hand down on the table. Not hard, trying to intimidate them, but impatient. "This is ridiculous. I don't know anything about him."

"Was he in his room the whole time?"

"No. We weren't allowed to be in our rooms the whole day."

"So you weren't in your room the whole time either."

"No." He favored Garcia with a glare that said he thought she was an idiot for asking when he had just said they weren't allowed to stay in their rooms.

"So if you were not both in your rooms all day, you must have seen each other at some point."

"Maybe." He rolled his eyes.

"Did you take meals with him?"

Gentle considered the question. "Suppose so. I don't think he was there for lunch."

"Why not?"

"In therapy."

"Is that normal? To miss meals because of therapy?"

"If it's a long session." He shook his head and looked over their heads. "Sometimes they went long."

"Were you doing the same kind of therapy as Leander was?"

He eyed Garcia. "I don't know. I guess we were all doing pretty much the same thing."

"Were you both in the experimental program?"

His face tightened, jaw muscles clenching. Kenzie could practically hear his teeth grinding together.

"It's none of my business what else anyone else is doing."

"Are you in the experimental program?"

He looked around as if hoping to find a way to avoid the question. He looked back at Garcia. "Yes."

"What do you think of the program?" Kenzie asked gently, hoping that a less adversarial approach might help Gentle to relax and give them something useful.

"I don't know," he said after considering for a moment. "Sometimes it is good and sometimes not."

"What is good about it?"

"It... changes the way I feel." He shook his head, brows drawn down in concentration. "It... calms me down. Opens me up." He rubbed his hands on his pants, drying sweaty palms or trying to calm himself down without the drugs. "It's... different."

"So it lets you talk about yourself? Your feelings and things that might have happened in the past?"

He shook his head, mouth tightening.

"It can be hard to talk about the past," Kenzie prompted, watching his face for any changes. She didn't want to provoke him, but to nail down what was going on in those sessions as best she could. A man like Gentle could be very difficult to reach. He had so many layers of protection. His physical mass and strength, his intelligence, his anger, and other emotional barriers.

"Who *wants* to talk about the past?" he snapped. "The past is the past. I don't know why all of you psych types always want to talk about the past. It isn't like you can change it."

"No," Kenzie agreed. "But it can still affect how we think and act in the present, and sometimes that needs to be changed."

"What do you know about it?" he demanded. "Nothin' ever happened to you."

"I don't know what happened to you. I grew up in a pretty nice family, good circumstances. But my sister died, and that was really hard. And I have had... things happen to me as an adult that were... very difficult and upsetting."

"Maybe you should take some of their drugs and see if it helps you."

Kenzie nodded. "Maybe I should. Do you think it would help?"

"I would leave here. If it wasn't for the drugs."

"But if you leave, you can't be part of the program anymore."

"Yeah, that's right. It's good. I think... it's good to be able to turn the defensive part of your brain off. Sometimes. And then... just be open."

"But you said there were parts of the program you didn't like, too," Garcia said. "You said you didn't really know what you thought about it."

He looked at her, maybe a little less angry now, thinking about being opened up in therapy, about how good it was to be able to talk about his traumas in an open, nondefensive way.

"There are things I don't like. Things I don't remember."

Alarm bells rang in Kenzie's head. She leaned toward Gentle, studying his face.

"What things that you don't remember?" Garcia prodded.

"A lot of things. I remember the drugs opening me up... being away from my body. Looking at things in a way I never did before. But... sometimes it can be for hours, and I don't remember all of that. I only remember... a few minutes. And then... it's hours later, and I don't know what happened. Where I was, what I did." He shook his head. "Things happened that I don't remember."

Kenzie nodded slowly. She had heard that MDMA could leave memory blanks. And maybe that was a good part of the therapy, not bad. He couldn't remember if he'd had a traumatic session. He could get the memories out in the open, but not have to suffer from reliving them. But there were problems with the memory gaps, too. Things could happen when someone was in a suggestible state. It made him vulnerable. And if he couldn't remember it afterward to make an accusation, then there could be abuses going on that were never brought to light.

"It's good to feel different sometimes," Gentle said, "Not so... raw and angry. Being able to get out of my head sometimes is good. It's... hard in there."

"Yeah, I can imagine," Garcia acknowledged.

"But then there are times..." It took some time for Gentle to think about his answer and string the words together to describe what he wanted to say. "Sometimes you don't get that good feeling. Sometimes... it can be really bad. Really... freaky."

"A bad trip?" Garcia asked.

"Yeah. Yeah, I guess you could put it that way. I don't know, I never took illegal drugs, you know. Maybe that's what it's like. But I would see things, feel things, the whole world out of kilter. Like you were on a different planet or in a different time. And bad things happened. Really awful, terrible things."

"Like what?"

"I don't know. I could see things happening to me. Other doctors, experiments. And bugs and snakes. I knew those weren't real, but they were…" He shuddered. "I never knew whether it was going to be good or bad. I want to stay and have the good sessions, the ones that open me up, but the bad trips and then other times that I can't remember… I don't want that. No one would want that."

21

The interview with David Gentle had gone better than Kenzie had expected, but it was still a big relief when he walked out of the room and she could breathe freely again. Garcia eyed Kenzie as she took a long drink of water.

"That was an interesting one."

"Yeah. I was a little worried about him."

"I could see that. You don't trust me to handle it?"

"Of course I do... but he was a big guy. Obviously very strong. And you..."

"Not as big or muscular. But I assure you, I could have handled things if he had gotten violent."

Kenzie still had her doubts about that, but she kept them to herself. "I'm sure you could have. But society has trained us to believe that women are weaker... potential prey to men like him. So it is a conditioned reaction, no matter what I believe logically."

Garcia nodded. "I get that."

The final patient that they were to interview arrived with the orderly. A woman, slim, with dark, slightly tangled hair. Her face was closer in shade to Garcia's than Kenzie's, but she couldn't be sure whether the patient was Hispanic as well, or just tanned. She had a permanently wrinkled brow and bags under her eyes like she hadn't slept in days. Kenzie was sure the facility would have given her a sleep aid if she weren't sleeping well. Sleep was vital for good mental health.

The orderly had her sit down and, instead of leaving the room, just retreated to the door, shut it, and stood there like they were in a prison. Kenzie looked at him and then at Garcia to see what she thought of this.

"Is there a reason you need to stay with her?" Garcia challenged.

"She could be a danger to herself or others."

Garcia and Kenzie looked at the woman, who seemed so far away that it was hard to imagine she could be a danger to anyone.

"Hi," Garcia said, getting closer to the patient and trying to meet her eyes. "I'm Detective Garcia. What was your name?"

The woman didn't answer. Did she speak? Was she even aware of their existence or the questions posed to her? It was hard to imagine that she could be a very good witness to anything. She would have no idea when Isah had been in his room. She might not even know who he was.

Garcia opened her mouth to try again when the woman said faintly, "Cara."

"Cara? What's your last name?"

She didn't enlighten them on that point, even though Garcia gave her an extra long time to answer.

"Can you tell us her last name?" Garcia asked the orderly.

"Anderson."

"Cara Anderson." Garcia wrote it down in her notepad. "Thank you for your assistance. And is she… does she talk? I mean, there's no point in me trying to interview her if she isn't even verbal. Is there a better way to communicate with her?"

"She can talk," the orderly told her, but offered no other advice.

"Cara." Garcia continued to try to make eye contact with the woman who was obviously having none of it. "How are you today?"

Maybe it was Paul Casey's idea of a joke. Giving them a patient to interview who clearly could not be interviewed. The woman was practically catatonic.

Kenzie's mind wandered to Rhys, and she wondered if he were making any progress. Had they changed around his medications?

Increased the dosages? Was his anxiety being addressed through therapy? From what Nurse Val had said, he was being closely monitored,
someone either staying with him or checking in again every fifteen
minutes. That suggested they were pretty concerned with him and
taking the necessary precautions. But how long would it go on? They
wouldn't keep someone in his room for days on end.

Cara's eyes flicked over to Garcia after a few minutes. "Who are
you?"

"I'm Detective Garcia. And this is Kenzie Kirsch."

Cara's eyes did not move to Kenzie.

"Do you know why we are here, Cara?"

"Why am I here," Cara countered.

"Well… to help you with the problems that you've been having,"
Garcia offered vaguely. "They take good care of you here, don't they?"

"I need to go."

"Go where?"

Cara looked around the room, frowning. "I am not supposed to
be here."

"You are being treated. This is the right place for you to be. And I
am here to interview you about what happened to Leander. You know
Leander, right?"

"Leander." Cara looked around, but he wasn't there. She gave no
sign of whether she was upset or disappointed by this or preferred not
to have him there. But Kenzie thought there was a slight lift in her
voice. Someone who liked Leander. Maybe that was why Paul Casey
had picked her out to interview with them.

"Is Leander your friend?" Garcia asked.

"I'm not sure." Cara swallowed and looked around. She started to
rise from her chair, then sat back down again. "Is he here? He was
hurt."

"Yes, he was hurt," Garcia agreed. "Did you see how he got hurt?"

Cara shook her head. "He was very upset. He was telling them to
leave him alone. He wanted to go to his room. They wouldn't let
him."

"Yes, that's what Janice said too."

"They should just leave him alone. They shouldn't hurt him."

"Do you think someone hurt him?"

"He was on the floor." Her eyes were big and round.

Had she seen him after he had died? Or even before?

"Do you know what time he was on the floor?" Garcia prompted.

"No." Cara's head shook back and forth.

"Do you know what day it was? Was it the day he died?"

"They should leave him alone. He wasn't hurting anyone. Why do they act like he is when he just wants to be left alone?"

"Why did they say?"

Cara sat quietly, thinking about it.

"Was there a reason they wouldn't leave him alone?" Garcia tried again.

Cara rubbed the deep creases between her eyebrows. "It's so hard to remember."

"Are you on the experimental therapy too?"

A slight shake of her head, but Kenzie wasn't sure whether it had been intended as an answer or was just a random movement.

"Cara? Do they have you on the drug for the experimental program?" Garcia persisted.

"No!" Cara's voice was suddenly loud, accusatory. "That's not my program!"

They were all riveted on her, waiting to see if she were going to escalate. Maybe the orderly was right and she could be dangerous, and he hadn't just come to watch the entertainment of their trying to talk to a non-communicative patient. Cara didn't stand up or get confrontational. She didn't appear to be angry. Maybe just erratic. The occasional burst of pique, and then it was instantly gone again.

"How did Leander feel about the experimental drugs?" Garcia asked. "Did he like it?"

"No." Cara picked at the fabric of her hospital clothes. "He wanted out. He didn't want to take it."

Garcia looked at Kenzie questioningly. Kenzie studied Cara. "If Leander didn't want to take it, then why was he still in the program?"

Cara stared up at the ceiling. "He wasn't allowed to decide."

"If a patient doesn't want treatment, he is allowed to refuse," Kenzie pointed out.

"No. We can't." Cara looked at Kenzie for the first time and shook her head. "You're a doctor. You know that."

"Why aren't you allowed to refuse?"

"Someone else says so."

"Who says?"

She shrugged. "Whoever. Your mother. Brother. Doctor." Her shoulders lifted again. "Whoever."

Kenzie looked over at Garcia. "My best guess is someone holding medical power of attorney. If a patient is judged not to be competent to make their own medical decisions."

"That makes sense. These people are—" Garcia looked at Cara and reworded. "These patients may not be capable of making those kinds of decisions for themselves."

"But if he wanted out of the program, they should have taken him out. He was the one who knew what it was doing to him. Why was he kept in the program?"

"I guess we'll find that out when we get his medical files. Who made medical decisions on his behalf and what they had to say about it. I can understand that sometimes patients might need treatments they don't want, but… it seems to me that with an experimental program, there are more risks. More reasons to avoid the treatment until it has been fully approved and deemed safe. Let someone else be the guinea pig."

Kenzie nodded. "If things were not going well for him, and all the accounts we've had so far are that he was reacting negatively to the therapy, then why didn't they pull him out when he asked them to? It seems like the right thing to do."

Garcia nodded. "But if they really believed in the program and thought that it was doing him good… maybe they could see benefits that the other patients and Mr. Isah himself did not."

"Maybe," Kenzie agreed. It was hard to know what anyone was thinking or feeling. Leander might have objected to all forms of treatment. He might have just wanted to go home. And he couldn't. He still had to be treated. He wasn't ready for the outside world yet.

"They shouldn't have hurt him," Cara repeated. "They shouldn't have put him down on the floor."

22

The video recordings Garcia had demanded and Isah's medical records were in a box ready for them when they were finished interviewing the witnesses. Garcia looked through the box doubtfully. "This is all of the video recorded in the forty-eight hours before Mr. Isah's death?"

The earnest receptionist raised her hands in a pleading gesture. "That was what I was given. I'm sure it's everything that you asked for. I don't have any way of knowing personally if that is all of the video or not."

"And are these all of Mr. Isah's medical records? History, current treatment protocol, everything?"

"Yes, that's everything."

Garcia showed the files to Kenzie. "They seem pretty slim to me."

"Everything is digital. We've printed out everything we can, and it's all in there."

"You have digital records that are not printed?"

"I don't know. We printed everything…"

"Everything you *could.*"

"Yes."

"What about the stuff you couldn't print? Where is it?"

"It's… in the system."

"Why don't you copy it onto a USB drive for Dr. Kirsch."

"I... don't think I can do that."

"We've subpoenaed all of the information."

"I know. But I don't think... I don't think the system allows you to make a USB copy. They don't want people taking information off the system. Just walking off with it."

"There must be a way to make a backup copy."

"I guess."

"Your system is backed up every day, isn't it?"

"Yes."

"Then make us a backup."

"I don't know how to do that. We'd have to get one of the techs in to do it. I've got no idea how."

Garcia rolled her eyes at Kenzie. Kenzie shook her head.

"Get your tech guys in here," Garcia told the woman sharply. "I will be back for the backup tomorrow. It better be ready."

"I'll... I'll courier it to you," the receptionist squeaked helpfully.

"Good. Then I won't have to come back here again. Because I'm not going to be happy if I have to come back here."

She nodded vigorously. "I completely understand that. I'll get it together. I promise. I'll find out how to do it."

Garcia nodded. She lugged the box full of recordings and files out with her. Kenzie laughed as they left the building. "I thought that poor woman was going to wet her pants. You weren't very nice to her."

"I'm done being nice. I'm nice the first time I ask for something. You keep stringing me along, and I'm not going to put up with it for long."

"I guess that's how you get things done."

Garcia nodded. She grabbed the bundle of files from the box before putting it into her car. "I will give those to you. Review them and fill me in on anything I need to know. So far... I don't necessarily like what these people are doing, but it doesn't seem to be anything criminal or that directly caused Mr. Isah's death. But I'm not the one who is qualified to make that judgment. I look forward to hearing from you."

"Thanks." Kenzie took the files from her. She thought that Garcia was right; the files did seem a little light. They might cover the basics, but Kenzie suspected that there was a lot more information the hospital could have given them about Mr. Isah.

She headed back to the office to read through them and find out what more she could.

Kenzie looked up from the files, her eyes sore and gritty, to see who was calling her on her cell phone. She was ready to close her eyes and take a break so, when she saw that it was Lisa Cole Kirsch, she picked up the phone and swiped to answer the call.

"Hi, Mom."

"MacKenzie. How are you doing, dear? I'm sorry for calling you in the middle of the workday. I know you are probably swamped right now..."

"No, it's okay. I need a short break. How are you?"

"I am just fine. Enjoying the lovely autumn weather. I don't like the winter, but when the leaves start changing color, there is nowhere I would rather be than Vermont."

"A lot of people would agree with you. It is very nice right now."

The autumn weather could be wet and miserable, so Kenzie, too, had been enjoying the fact that it hadn't yet turned. She should spend more time outside. Zachary had made a goal to spend more time outside getting some exercise and fresh air and pursuing his photography hobby—a change from taking pictures of adulterous couples, accident reconstructions, and insurance scammers—and he had done very well at following through and getting more sun and exercise during the year. Which was a pretty big accomplishment for someone with ADHD, whose natural inclination would have been to put it off or forget about it.

"And Zachary, how is he?"

"He's doing pretty well. I was just thinking about how much he's been enjoying the weather this year. He's been spending a lot of time outside, and I should be following his example."

"We should *all* be following his example," Lisa agreed with a laugh. "Good for him. And his mental health? I would imagine it has improved with being outside more."

"He's had a pretty good year. It's that time now, though… As it gets closer to winter, I worry about him. The days are already getting shorter, and I'm sure he's thinking about Christmas and how he's going to manage it this year, even if they haven't started talking about it on TV yet."

"I hope he has a better time of it this year. He was in the hospital for a long time last year."

"Yes, he was. But they got him stabilized on this new med protocol, and it's been pretty good all year. So, fingers crossed that it continues to hold out and we don't have to make any big adjustments. And that if he does spend time in the hospital this year, it won't be as long. He doesn't have to be hospitalized every year so, hopefully, this will be one of his better years."

"I certainly hope so," Lisa agreed.

Hopefully, it would be better for all of them. They had all been through the wringer the previous year, even if it wasn't something they wanted to discuss.

"And Walter was telling me about your young friend…?" Lisa suggested. "That has just been admitted?"

"Yes." Kenzie sighed. She hadn't heard an update on Rhys's condition yet and hoped he was doing all right. "Rhys. He's had a pretty tough time in life. I don't know whether the trauma has resurfaced for some reason, or something new is going on, bullying or hormones maybe, but he is having a difficult time. I'm hoping his stay won't be long, that they can deal with these new issues."

"Rhys. That isn't a very common name. What's his last name?"

"Salter. Do you know him?" Kenzie couldn't imagine Lisa would have had the opportunity to run into Rhys anywhere. It was just idle curiosity, or she knew someone else by the same name and wanted to make sure that it wasn't him.

"Salter. No. I don't think I know anyone by that name."

Kenzie was glad this was not followed by, "Wasn't that the name of the woman who was murdered?" She didn't want to have to explain that.

"Well, I certainly hope he gets the help he needs," Lisa continued. "I am increasingly convinced that we need to put more time and money into these issues. There are so many people who are suffering so badly from mental illness. You don't know it until you start looking around, asking questions, and really listening to the answers."

"Mental illness does need more attention," Kenzie agreed. "It's not a very sexy cause, but people desperately need the funding. Depression kills just as many people as some of the other causes you campaign for. We can't ignore it just because we can't see it as easily as a wheelchair or dialysis machine."

"You know that we are now," Lisa said. "The foundation is putting a lot more money into mental illness in the last couple of years. It has really come to the forefront now. We can't ignore it."

"Yeah. Thanks." Kenzie always choked up a little when Lisa started talking about how much money the Kirsch family foundation was putting toward mental illness campaigns. She knew it was because of Zachary, and she loved her parents for caring enough about Kenzie and her partner's happiness to make such significant changes to their funding.

"I have sent you some documents to be signed. Have you had a chance to look at them yet?"

"No, I'm sorry, Mom. Things have been crazy, and I am behind where I should be. I know I promised to pay more attention to it, so I'll get to it as soon as I can. With Dr. Wiltshire breaking his hand, things have been a little crazy lately. Can you get a second signature from someone else this time?"

"Of course. But do try to stay on top of your emails. And read through the new funding requests. We need to keep things moving forward. There are a lot of people who need that money a lot more than we do, you know."

Kenzie smiled. "I know, Mom. We just have to keep giving it away."

Lisa laughed. "We'll do our best."

23

More than one person had asked Kenzie about Zachary's mental health recently. Kenzie could not escape the fact that his depression was not going to just go away. The usual seasonal depression was bound to hit him any time now. The last couple of years, it had hit earlier, so she knew they were living on borrowed time.

With the worry over Rhys's hospitalization, Zachary was bound to be worrying and thinking about his own mental health.

She didn't ask him how he was doing. He had promised to tell her about any major downturns. She knew that the year before, he had kept her informed about how he was feeling, even though he'd been disappointed with himself and had not wanted to let her know how much he was struggling. She didn't want to make things more stressful by hovering over him, waiting for something to happen.

But it was already on her mind and, when she woke up a couple of hours after lying down to find Zachary's side of the bed empty, she felt a familiar tightness in her stomach. That feeling of dread that his health had taken a turn for the worst, and he had begun the descent. She feared not just for his happiness, but for his life. He had attempted suicide in the past, and his behavior the previous year, when he started having suicidal thoughts again, had been very scary.

Kenzie got out of bed. She pulled on her housecoat, slid her feet into her slippers, and shuffled out to the living room.

If Zachary were working at his computer, that was a good sign. As long as he wasn't watching some horrible video over and over again, trying to solve a murder case. And if he had started to work on his computer and then fallen asleep on the couch while he worked, that was a good sign, because it meant that he had fallen asleep spontaneously instead of having to take a sleep aid or sit up awake all through the night because his brain just wouldn't shut down or he was worried that he would never wake up.

But he wasn't in the living room working at his laptop or slumped over asleep. He was pacing.

Kenzie caught him as he paced from the kitchen into the living room, then turned around to go back. He saw her and stopped.

"Hey," Kenzie said softly. "How are you doing?"

"Oh. Just restless. Sorry, I didn't mean to wake you up."

"You didn't wake me up. I just woke up on my own and you weren't there. So I thought I would check on you."

"You should go back to sleep. You have work in the morning."

"So do you. What's up? Are you worried about something?"

He tried to stay where he was, but eventually gave in and paced back into the kitchen.

"I don't know. Just restless, really. My brain is going, but... it's jumping from one thing to another. As soon as I tell it to stop thinking about one thing and try to switch to something else... then it starts grinding away on something else. I really just want it to stop."

"But there's no off switch."

They had talked about it before. Kenzie knew how frustrated he got with his brain and his inability to just shut off when he wanted to. Kenzie knew that it was hard enough for her to let go of a problem and relax for the evening or night so that she could sleep, but it was much worse for Zachary. Kenzie could usually do a bit of meditation or get a few minutes of exercise, think about something else that she enjoyed, and her brain would usually settle down enough to relax for the evening and sleep at night. But the same was not true for Zachary. When his brain got in a rut, it *really* got in a rut, and he could be going over the same argument in his head or fighting the same obsession for days without relief.

"Maybe it's time to take something to help you sleep," she suggested.

Not a hard push. A hard push, and Zachary would get upset about her trying to force him to do what she thought was right. It was his body and brain, not hers, and she wasn't his doctor. It was up to him to decide whether to take something to help him sleep, and he would resist it for as long as he could. All Kenzie could do was to make the suggestion. If he were unable to sleep for several days, he would probably end up in the hospital again. But she couldn't jump directly to that just because he was having one restless night.

"It's pretty late to take anything tonight," Zachary said, marching restlessly across the room, back and forth. "If I take something now, I won't be able to get up before noon."

An exaggeration, but Kenzie understood his concern. There was a point at which it became inadvisable to take anything, because he needed to be able to get up and get back to work in the morning. He had to take high doses of strong medication for it to work, and they always made him groggy and made getting up and getting his brain operating again difficult.

"You slept last night?" she checked.

"Yes, I did. This is the first night I've been up... and I'll probably still get an hour or two in." Zachary looked at his spot on the couch as if wishing he had already fallen asleep there. "I just need to wait... until my body is tired enough to tell my brain to shut off..."

"Are you worrying about Rhys?"

He stopped momentarily and looked at her, then resumed pacing. "Yes."

"I'm worried about him too. I hope that we'll hear he's doing better soon."

Zachary nodded jerkily. "Poor kid. I just want to be there to help him through this, and that's the one thing I can't do. I can't be there with him when he's in the hospital."

"I know. It's hard."

He looked at her and nodded, acknowledging that she knew what it was like to have a loved one in the psych ward and not to be able to do anything for him.

"I left a message for Vera during the day, but she hasn't gotten back to me. I don't know if that means that things have gotten worse, and she doesn't want to tell me."

"It probably just means that she's spending a lot of time at the hospital, and then going to bed as soon as she gets home."

He considered that, his steps slowing a little. "Yeah. Maybe."

"She needs more sleep than you do, especially going through a stressful time like this. She's probably sleeping ten hours a day. Between that and meals and visiting at the hospital…"

"If she's visiting. If she's allowed to see him."

"She's his guardian. They can't stop her from seeing him."

"The psych ward has rules…"

"I know. But she can insist."

"She wouldn't. If they told her not to, she wouldn't go. And what if Rhys didn't want to see her?"

"Why wouldn't he? He loves his grandma."

"I know, but… it's different when you're feeling so bad, and you don't want anyone to see you like that and don't want to have to talk about how you're feeling. And I'm okay with talking, normally. I don't have the trouble with communicating that Rhys does. It might just seem too hard."

Kenzie sighed. "I supposed so. But I hope not. I hope he's okay with her just visiting and talking to him or holding his hand."

Zachary stopped pacing and closed his eyes briefly, maybe picturing it, trying to see how that felt. He nodded, letting out his breath in a long, controlled stream. Maybe that image helped. He could picture Rhys being comforted and in a safe place, sleeping tonight and having someone there to take care of him and his grandma visiting again in the morning to see him through the dark tunnel.

Kenzie took a step toward Zachary and brought her hands apart, offering a hug. Zachary took a step toward her. They both closed the distance and held each other for a few minutes.

"Come back to bed?" Kenzie suggested.

"I'm too restless. I'll keep you awake."

"Just come and cuddle for a few minutes, then. I need you."

She thought he needed the physical comfort more than she did, but if she said *he* needed it, he would just resist. If she said that she needed him, it was different. He would do whatever he could to comfort her and fulfill her needs.

"Okay," he agreed, as she knew he would. "But I don't know how long I'll stay. I might leave as soon as you're asleep. If I can't lie still, I don't want to disrupt your sleep."

Kenzie nodded. She took him by the hand and led him back to the bedroom.

24

One of Kenzie's problems with Dr. Cook substituting for Dr. Wiltshire was the time he arrived at the office. Not because he started late, but the opposite. He was there too early. With Dr. Wiltshire, she had time to get to the office and work her way through the voicemails and emails that had arrived overnight to make sure that there wasn't anything urgent that needed to be taken care of and to get the majority of the reports printed and digital filing done. And then there was checking on any bodies that had arrived overnight to make sure that everything had been checked in properly, assigned a file number, and assigned a position in the queue. And she needed to check which funeral homes were planning to transport the bodies they were finished with.

But Dr. Cook arrived too early and messed up the workflow. Sometimes, he had reviewed the voicemails in the main mailbox before she got there, which was irritating. With Dr. Wiltshire, she just passed on any messages that he needed to deal with. She handled the rest and made sure that everything was logged and filed. She didn't like Dr. Cook changing things around, even though, of course, he was entitled to and, as Dr. Wiltshire's substitute, he was really her superior rather than her helper, even if that was how he chose to frame it. She couldn't order him around or tell him to stop trying to be helpful.

"Dr. Kirsch," Cook sounded grave, and Kenzie wondered what was going on. "I'm glad you're here. If you could come to my office…"

Kenzie motioned to her desk. "I have a lot of stuff to clear first thing."

"I've taken care of it. Please come with me."

Kenzie did, of course, once she had removed her outer clothing and stowed it away.

"Is something wrong?" she asked as she sat in the visitor chair in front of Dr. Wiltshire's—or Dr. Cook's—desk.

"I picked up a disturbing voicemail this morning. Let me play it for you."

"We get crank calls sometimes," Kenzie told him. "Stupid kids fooling around, people who are worried about zombies or mentally ill people who think they are dead."

Dr. Cook looked at her for a moment, mouth open, then shook his head. He picked up Dr. Wiltshire's desk phone and put it on speaker while he dialed into the voicemail box and then accessed it. He played a saved message.

"Why don't you just stay in your office and do your job there?" A flat computer voice read. "Stay where you belong instead of trying to stop good people from doing good things. Just do your damn autopsies and stay out of everyone else's business. Your friends will benefit by you staying out of the way. You do your job and let us do ours."

Kenzie closed her eyes. It was too early in the day to be dealing with voicemail threats.

"Uh…" She rubbed the orbital bones around her eyes, looking for something to say. "Yeah, sometimes we get stuff like that. It's just people blowing off steam. It isn't anything."

"Do you know who this is?"

"Someone at Persons, I would guess." At his questioning look, she clarified. "Persons Residential Care. That's where Leander Isah was."

"And why would they be making telephone threats?"

"Because they don't like the fact that they are being investigated in the context of his death. Whether or not they have done anything to endanger Isah or any other patients, I can't tell you why, but they have been resistant from the beginning, from the minute I showed up there for the scene review. It's been challenging to get the records that we needed from them. It took Detective Garcia going there with a subpoena yesterday before they finally released anything. And even then, the files seem a little... light. Sanitized."

"How do you know it is them?"

"I guess I don't for sure. The police will have to check the incoming line and see where the call came from. But that's the only one that I'm doing anything on outside of the office. So if they want me to stay in the office and not investigate elsewhere, that is the case they are talking about."

Cook nodded. He steepled his hands together and thought about it. "We'll need to bring the police in on it."

"Detective Garcia is already on the case. I'll let her know. And we can send her a copy of the voicemail. Not that it will help, since they used text-to-speech to synthesize the voice."

"Sounds that way," he agreed. "But as you say, they may be able to trace where the call came from. We might get lucky with it pointing directly back to Persons."

"Not that it is such a big deal. It's certainly not the first irate call we've gotten from someone we were investigating."

"Hmm." He didn't seem willing to let it go. "What did that mean? Your friends will benefit by you staying away?"

"I... don't know," Kenzie admitted. "Just blowing smoke, I would guess. I don't have any friends involved in the case. Maybe they're talking about the patients we interviewed yesterday. Calling them my friends would be a stretch, but you know how people talk sometimes. Doctors' offices, especially therapists, use the 'royal we' when talking to patients. I could see them referring to the patients as friends to make it sound more supportive and less clinical."

"Your friends will benefit by you staying away," Cook repeated, trying it out. His tone was skeptical, but he nodded. "It could be, but why *your* friends instead of *our* friends?"

"Because I spent time with them yesterday... so now they're my friends too."

"Do you really think so?"

Kenzie shrugged. "I have no clue. It was just an idea."

"You have friends who are in psychiatric care? Who might benefit from the types of programs that Persons is running?"

Kenzie's stomach tightened. "Oh..."

Cook studied her face. "So you do. Who?"

"Well... my partner, for one. He is okay right now, but he has been hospitalized for... psychiatric care in the past. And... a boy that we know. A teenager. He was just admitted to the hospital. He's having some kind of crisis. Both of them have very traumatic pasts... the type of thing that Persons is treating with this MDMA program of theirs."

Cook nodded slowly. "So... maybe if you backed off, they could help you with those friends. Seeing that they got treatment. This new, experimental treatment that isn't available anywhere else."

"Maybe that is what they were talking about. Though I don't know that. It's as good a theory as any. And I don't see how they would know anything about Zachary or... either of them. They would have to be guessing that I am close to someone who had mental illness and could benefit from their program or the type of program they are doing."

"Considering the statistics, everyone has a friend who could benefit from psychiatric care."

"I guess so," Kenzie admitted. "It's a pretty good bet that everyone knows someone who is struggling with their mental health. Although something like PTSD is not quite as common as just depression or anxiety."

Cook waved a hand. "Still pretty common in today's world. With kids going through lock-down drills at school and war and terrorist threats, human trafficking, child abuse... I'm sure you probably have other friends with it that you haven't even thought of yet."

"I guess."

"Okay. I'll pass this on to the police."

"I have Detective Garcia's information, and I can just email it to her."

"Make sure you do it right away. Don't sit on it."

Kenzie nodded. "Sure. Thanks for taking it seriously. We've had threats before and... it can be disconcerting."

"I'm sure nothing will come of it. They didn't exactly threaten to come after you and your family. They just said they're doing important work and don't want you to interfere with it. But I want to be sure it is handled."

"Yeah, I agree, better safe than sorry."

Kenzie stood up, not sure whether she had been dismissed yet.

"Your partner," Cook said, "what's going on there?"

Kenzie hesitated. "What do you mean?"

"I mean... well, I wouldn't ask for any private medical information, of course, but... how is his health? Is this something that concerns you?"

"I told you, he's good right now." Kenzie wavered. "Well... I mean, he had a bad night. Worrying about our other friend that I mentioned. But overall, he's doing okay right now."

If it weren't the beginning of his depressive cycle. Kenzie was braced for it. For how thin and gaunt he would get. The loss of him from her life, as his thoughts and attention were turned inward, leaving her on the outside, all by herself.

"I hope," she added honestly. Zachary promoted openness about his mental illness, trying to be a part of the solution in overcoming the stigma. "He will hit a depressive cycle sometime in the next few weeks. That is his usual pattern. Then he will improve again after Christmas."

"That's pretty exact."

"Like I said, he had a lot of childhood trauma. Beginning with a fire on Christmas Eve. Or rather, culminating with a fire on Christmas Eve. So he has a connection with that date. It isn't exactly Seasonal Affective Disorder because it isn't triggered by the change in the weather or the days getting shorter. It is cyclical, but because of his history."

"I see. And he's had this for how long?" He held up his hand, stopping Kenzie from answering. "This is personal. I'm sorry. I shouldn't be asking. I was only curious, but it is none of my business and he isn't even here to say whether you can talk to me about it or not. I'm sorry."

"No, it's okay. He has said before that he wants to be open and transparent about it and that the more people talk about mental illness, the more normalized it can become. He was ten at the time. So this has been going on for many years."

"Good grief. It's depressing just to think about it. The poor guy."

Kenzie nodded. "And until now, I would have said that it will likely be a pattern that continues for years to come. We're doing our best with medications and therapy, but PTSD can be pretty hard to overcome, and it's become so ingrained."

"But hallucinogen-mediated trauma therapy might offer some relief."

Kenzie shrugged. "It could," she admitted. "I haven't discussed it with him but, as you can imagine, I have been thinking about it."

"Well, maybe things will work out well for Persons. And if not, they are not the only place offering this treatment. There will be other opportunities to get into it."

25

K enzie called Detective Garcia about the voicemail and forwarded a copy to her by email.

"It's really nothing," she told the detective, "I'm sure you get much worse threats all the time. I'd put money on it being someone at Persons. And, of course, someone we talked to, which is why they used the computer voice. It was someone whose voice we would have recognized."

"Undoubtedly," Garcia agreed crisply, her accent stronger for that one word. "I'll make some waves. They can't threaten law enforcement and get away with it. I don't suppose you've had a chance to review the medical records yet, have you?"

"I've been through them once. I'll need to study them carefully at least one more time. Make sure that I pick up everything I can. But on the surface, there isn't anything that points to cause of death. No matter what they told Janice Martin, he did not have a bad heart."

"Oh, let me write that down." Garcia shuffled papers for a moment, and then Kenzie could hear computer keys being tapped. Garcia had pretty good speed. "Okay, got it. Anything else in the medical records that I should know about?"

"I'm not sure the files are complete. Like you said, they were pretty slim. Some abbreviated stuff on his medical history. They wanted to ensure that we got the stuff on torture because people who have been tortured have shorter lifespans and, sometimes, we never really know what killed them. We don't know enough about how the body works to understand all the ways that torture can damage it. There may be stuff right down past the cellular level that we don't understand. The way that neurons communicate with each other. Mitochondrial function. Remapping the brain."

"But you know for sure that there is stuff missing? Or you're guessing that there must be?"

"Well, for one thing, there are no consents."

"What kind of consents?"

"Consents to treatment. Especially for the experimental program. That kind of thing usually involves all kinds of paperwork—waivers, consents, long lists of the potential risks. They don't want to get sued if things don't go well. They need informed consent. And I don't see it anywhere."

"Would that be something that Isah had signed? Or his guardian?"

"Hard to say. If it was me, I'd get both. Was he competent? Was he not competent? I'd want to get his signature to prove that he consented to it, and to get his medical attorney's signature to make sure that they approved it. There are a lot of ethical problems with experimenting on people with serious psychiatric illnesses."

She could tell Garcia was thinking this through. "Because you have to experiment and test it out on psychiatric patients to find something that works, but if they have serious issues, how can they consent to it?"

"Exactly," Kenzie agreed. "We have a bad history of experimenting on people without their permission or guardians' informed consent, so we need to cover all our bases. But it is still an ethically gray area. Psychiatric patients, children, pregnant women, the elderly. They are all vulnerable populations. We want to have the proper medications to treat them, but we don't want to experiment on them. Or we do, but we're not allowed."

"Not speaking for yourself, of course," Garcia said dryly.

"None of my patients need to give consent. They're all dead. About as safe as you can get."

Garcia laughed.

"Although, we do try to respect things like last wishes, religious constraints, that sort of thing. If we know of a prohibition, we'll try to work around it if we can."

"So even after they're dead, you still have to deal with the nut jobs."

"Uh…"

Kenzie wasn't sure how to approach Garcia calling religious people nut jobs. Garcia hadn't meant it that way, she was sure. She was thinking of the more extreme cases that sometimes made the news, with people shrieking to the cameras about their religious rights being violated.

"Okay, not nut jobs," Garcia said irritably, understanding Kenzie's silence. "I just mean… hysterical families. People who are always threatening to sue. They are so… reactionary and don't really think things through."

"There can be issues," Kenzie said. "We do our best to respect people's beliefs, but we can't always do things the way they would like." She'd had more than one experience with a crazed relative who thought she wasn't handling things as she should. Or crazed members of the public. Things *could* get a little crazy sometimes.

"So, consents are one thing you are missing," Garcia said, reminding her where they had segued from. "Anything else?"

"Well, the receptionist talked about the electronic assets that she hadn't been able to give us. There should be recordings of the sessions. From what I see of the protocols on the paperwork we have, all the sessions were supposed to be video recorded. And there is nothing like that in what I got. Not even photographs or audio recordings. So that's going to be a big thing if we want to see just what they were up to. If we can watch a recording of how Isah reacted during his session that day, what kind of shape he was in and if he was agitated like the witnesses suggest…"

"They recorded all the sessions? Isn't that a breach of privacy?"

"Not if the patient knew they were being taped, and it was for clinical purposes. It's a good record for the people running the drug trials. Provides you with a lot more information than just a page of written notes."

"I told them I would go back today. So I definitely will. That will be the mother lode."

Kenzie nodded her agreement. "Yeah. It will be very helpful to see what he looked like that last day. Skin color, respiration, what his emotional state was. All of that."

"And if he was being restrained," Garcia suggested.

"Yes. It would be helpful to know that, too."

"I have a couple of other questions," Garcia said. "If you have a few minutes to humor me."

Kenzie looked at the system time on her computer. She would probably advance the Isah case more by answering Garcia's question than anything else she could do. "Yeah, sure."

"First, talking about consent and competence and all of that…"

"Uh-huh."

"Our interviews yesterday."

"Yeah?" Kenzie started to think about where Garcia was going on this before she got around to asking the question. They had interviewed psych patients. They would not be reliable witnesses if ever called to testify in court. But they had gone into the interviews knowing that. Knowing they were not interviewing experts, but people who might be able to give them a small insight here and there into the life or the mind of Leander Isah.

"Obviously, they are not good witnesses," Garcia confirmed. "But if we had to use something that one of them said, we could, right? I mean, just because they are psychiatric patients, that doesn't mean that they don't know when someone enters or leaves their room. They can tell time or know that it was after lunch or before supper, or that everyone had just been given their meds."

"I guess, yes. It would be up to you to figure out how much to ask them and how to present it to the jury. Because they will be seen as… well, crazy."

"Fair enough," Garcia agreed. "How about the drugs?"

"The drugs?" Kenzie echoed. She thought about each of the

patients they had interviewed. Janice, David, and Cara. They had all seemed to be coherent and anchored to the present. They seemed to understand what she was talking about. But they were on psychoactive drugs. And possibly hallucinogenics. Kenzie blew out her breath through pursed lips, whistling slightly. "Well... I hadn't really thought about that."

"Cara Anderson was definitely high," Garcia said. "Did you see her eyes? I think she had just come from therapy. Should we even have been interviewing her in that state? As far as I could tell, they all knew what was going on. But that Cara, she was pretty far gone."

"I don't think it was all the effects of the drugs, but yes, I think it would be hard to separate the effects of the drugs and her psychosis and to say that she knew what she was talking about when she said this or that."

"She said Isah did not want to be in the drug trials. That he wanted out."

"Maybe you can find someone else who will say the same thing. From a more... stable perspective."

Garcia sighed. "That's what I was afraid of. There aren't going to be a lot of people who can verify that statement. And most of the people who can, who would be good witnesses, are the people who don't want to talk to us."

"The doctors rather than the patients."

"*They* are not going to tell us that Isah wanted out of the drug trials," Garcia said flatly.

Kenzie grimaced. "Yeah, it might be hard to find anyone who will say that on the record."

"The second question," Garcia said, "is even less pleasant than that one."

26

K enzie took a deep breath and held it for a moment.

"Okay. What do you want to ask me?"

"I've been doing some research on these MDMA trials. I know some stuff about it from dealing with raves and kids on X."

"Uh-huh?"

"The kids think that rave drugs are harmless, that nothing will come of them taking them. They're just good fun. Get a good buzz or have an out-of-body experience, and the next day, you're back to school or work with no adverse effects. But I know the stuff can kill you."

"Yeah," Kenzie nodded. "If you get too much and your body overheats... it can cook you alive. Your brain can't operate at those temperatures." Her mind went to Isah's hyperthermic state when he had died.

"Ecstasy also makes the users... well, more sexually outgoing," Garcia said delicately.

Kenzie cleared her throat. "Yes. Increased libido and sensitivity are associated with MDMA. Though it also causes sexual dysfunction."

"One thing that I found was that a number of these trials had been shut down or disqualified because the supposed therapists running them were taking advantage of their patients'… sexual openness."

Kenzie tried to hold back her disgust that someone who claimed to be a medical practitioner trying to heal someone would do something so reprehensible. She sipped her water, trying to swallow the lump in her throat.

"Unfortunately… I did find evidence in the autopsy that Mr. Isah had been sexually active. There was bruising that would indicate that it was either rough or non-consensual." She had another swallow of water. "We took swabs and sent them for analysis. But there was no semen present. If his assailant was a male, he was wearing a condom."

"When were you going to tell me that little tidbit?"

"When I release my findings. Along with everything else."

"But you didn't think it was worth mentioning before this? As part of my investigation into Persons, for example?"

"I didn't get the lab reports until this morning. Until then, I was hoping that it would not be a dead end. That I would be able to give you more information than just that he appeared to have been assaulted sometime in the days before his death. I was really hoping there would be DNA."

"No such luck," Garcia said philosophically, as if she had been expecting this all along. And maybe she had. That would have made it only too easy. Only Isah's rapist had not necessarily had anything to do with his death. It definitely meant that Persons had to be thoroughly investigated by the proper authorities. But the two incidents did not necessarily tie together, other than by the fact that Isah had been the victim in both cases. "Okay. So that's a dead end. We'll inform the feds and have them start an investigation into the possibility of a sexual predator operating around vulnerable people at Persons."

"That was your last question?" Kenzie asked.

"That's it. For now. I'll head over there later today and get a copy of the electronic assets, which hopefully includes the recordings of the therapy sessions."

. . .

"I got a call back from Vera today," Zachary offered during dinner that evening.

Kenzie breathed a sigh of relief to hear that, especially since Zachary's voice was upbeat rather than depressed or flat. "That's good to hear. Has she been spending a lot of time at the hospital?"

"I'm not sure how many hours she has spent there. They're going to put Rhys into a different facility, one that is better for treating kids with trauma issues."

"That's good news! Is it inpatient or outpatient?"

"Inpatient. At least in the beginning. They'll also have transition programs to help return him to outpatient care once he's shown an improvement."

Kenzie nodded. "I didn't think the city had anything like that. How did Vera say he was doing?"

"She was… worn out. He's not good. It's been an emotional few days for her. It was completely unexpected. She was blindsided. But they're keeping a close watch on him, doing everything they can to get him the help he needs."

"Were there any signs that something was going on at school? Bullying or abuse of any kind?"

"It sounds like there might have been something," Zachary admitted. "They'll need to investigate it more carefully… dig into it when he's able to talk again. Or… communicate, anyway. When he can tell them what was going on with school."

Kenzie remembered Cara Anderson, her eyes so far away, in the same room as Kenzie and yet Kenzie hadn't even been sure that Cara knew she was there until she had finally started answering their questions. It was heartbreaking to think of Rhys like that. He had blossomed so much in the time that they had known him, growing into a prankster who loved to tease Zachary, especially about his relationship with Kenzie, and who Kenzie knew cared deeply about his friends. What had happened to make him withdraw so completely?

"What did Vera know about school?" Kenzie asked. "Had Rhys's grades dropped?"

"She said that there had been some fights at school. Nothing big, just… some scuffles. School locker room. Cafeteria. Not actually during classes. Of course." Zachary chewed vigorously to get his salad down. Kenzie knew he didn't enjoy it. He tried to eat whatever she served, but vegetables were always a challenge. "Who would do something in front of a teacher? Nothing blatant, anyway. Maybe a little verbal abuse. Maybe touching or poking him when the teacher was turned around. But they wouldn't be able to beat him up or do anything too obvious. Not right in class."

"And Vera didn't know what those scuffles were about?"

"No. When the school administrators brought them up, they suggested it was just horseplay. Friends getting too into it, not knowing when to stop or when someone's feelings were hurt."

Kenzie rolled her eyes. "Am I glad that I'm not in school anymore. Teenagers are vicious creatures."

"Yes, they are," Zachary agreed. "The biggest incident, I guess, was when he blew up at the resource room teacher when she was trying to help him with something. That got an immediate call home to grandma and one-day suspension."

"What happened? And what did Rhys tell Vera? Did he have any explanation?"

"According to the school, to the resource room teacher, he had been stubborn, angry. In a mood. She noticed that something was bothering him before anything actually happened. She tried to distract him from whatever it was with the work rather than demanding to know what was going on."

"Sounds reasonable," Kenzie approved. She picked up a carrot stick and munched it while Zachary continued with the description.

"She had him working on math, which is one of his better subjects. She put her hand on his shoulder to check his work, and he blew up."

Kenzie held her breath. "Physically? Verbally?"

"Jumped up, knocked her away from him, and shouted at her not to touch him." Zachary sounded sympathetic rather than judging of this behavior. Kenzie wondered, though, what had triggered Rhys's violent reaction. He had undoubtedly been in the resource room and dealt with the resource teacher many times. It sounded like she knew him well, and he would have been used to her presence and the way that she worked, the way she would lay her hand on his shoulder when she was ready to look at his work. So what had triggered the reaction this time? Was he off his meds or on something illicit? Steroids to build up his muscles or alcohol intended to help him to relax and loosen up?

"What explanation did Rhys give? To the teacher or Vera?"

"The teacher thought she had just startled him. She said it wasn't his fault. When Vera tried to talk to Rhys about it, he just kept pushing her away." Zachary caught Kenzie's look. "Emotionally. Not physically. He would wave her off and shake his head and growl at her. Go to his room and shut the door. Signaling that he wanted space and didn't want to talk about it."

Kenzie picked at her salad. While she enjoyed it more than Zachary did, she still wasn't really big on green salads herself. Even though she knew she needed them.

"I hit a teacher once," Zachary offered.

"You did? Why? What happened?"

She couldn't imagine Zachary hitting anyone without being heavily provoked. He was the victim of abuse. Not the perpetrator.

"It was when I was first in foster care," Zachary said, mulling it over. "I think… I was still with the Petersons. Mr. Peterson and his wife, Lilith. Back before." He shrugged expressively.

Back before Lilith had become aware of Lorne's affair with Patrick Parker, and they had immediately been disqualified as foster parents. The Petersons had been the first family Zachary had gone to in foster care. Straight from the hospital, Kenzie assumed, though he didn't talk much about that time and she wasn't sure what rehab and care he had been through during that time.

"I fell asleep in class," Zachary explained. He rubbed his forehead, trying to remember the details. "I think… that was when I'd had a reaction to my meds and ended up in the hospital, and then I still had to go to school, even though I'd been awake half the night. So I fell asleep. And the teacher… smacked my desk with the ruler to wake me up. I guess I just reacted. Thought I was being attacked and defended myself before I was even awake." He swallowed and shook his head. "I remember how I felt. The horror when I realized that I had punched her, right in the stomach. I thought they were going to kill me. I thought that they would lock me up and throw away the key. I knew you weren't allowed to hit adults. Especially teachers. I ran... and hid..."

"You were ten?"

Zachary nodded. "I think so. Maybe just turned eleven, I don't remember. That's when Mrs. Peterson said I couldn't live with them anymore." Zachary poked at the food that remained on his plate, his face clearly reflecting the pain and sorrow he had felt when he learned he was being moved from the home. "She figured if I would attack a grown woman, that she and the other children in the home were not safe. It didn't matter that I didn't mean to do it. I could just as easily make a mistake and hit one of the other kids."

Kenzie reached across the table to pat his hand. "You never would."

"I never hit any kid in my family. Unless they hit me first and I had to defend myself."

"You had the right to defend yourself. And it wasn't your fault that you hit the teacher, either. She should have known better than to do something like that. I remember the crack it would make when a teacher smacked a ruler down on a desk. It was like a gunshot. Meant to frighten and intimidate."

Zachary frowned. "You think she meant to scare me?"

"Why else would she do that? If all she wanted to do was to wake you up, she could say your name or nudge your shoulder. She wanted to scare the pants off you and to humiliate you in front of the rest of the class."

He considered this. "I don't know about that. Do you really think so?"

"Would you ever do something like that to a kid? To Mason, maybe?" Mason was Tyrrell's son, Zachary's nephew, a kid who kept his parents hopping with a raging case of ADHD. He very much reminded Zachary of himself as a child. Kenzie knew how hard Mason was on his parents. Not because he was a bad kid or tried to upset them, but because he just couldn't moderate his behavior and was constantly getting into things that he shouldn't or doing things he should have known better than to do. And he was also a very sensitive little boy who would cry over his daddy not showing up for a visit or being shouted at when he stepped over the line, as he invariably did multiple times a day.

Zachary shook his head immediately. "I would never do something like that to Mason. He can't help the way he is and, if he was sick and fell asleep, I'd just let him be."

"And if you had to wake him up, you wouldn't do it like that, would you?"

"Well, no. But I understand Mason. I know what it's like to be in his head. Most people… don't know what it's like. They think he's just being bad, acting out, trying to get attention. So they get frustrated, and when they see a way to call him out on his behavior, to try to teach him a lesson…" Understanding flooded into Zachary's features as he connected this to his teacher's behavior when she had woken him up. "It was. It was a way to get the better of me, call me out in front of my friends."

Kenzie nodded. "Yeah. It was."

"Well, the joke's on her," he said flatly.

"Oh, how is the joke on her?"

"Because I didn't have any friends."

Kenzie shook her head. She didn't laugh. It was tragic, not funny. "You must have had a few."

"I was only there for a few weeks. I think… maybe there was one kid who liked me. And we weren't friends. He just… needed someone to stand by him."

That sounded like a story for another day. She didn't want to focus too much on Zachary's stories from the past. They were likely to make him depressed, and she didn't want that. She wanted to keep his spirits up as much as possible.

"So where was it that Rhys got transferred to?" she asked. "The place that has this program for traumatized kids?"

"I wrote it down," Zachary offered. He had known that she would ask. And maybe hoped to be able to see Rhys before too long if the program would allow it. He pulled out his phone and tapped and scrolled to find it. "Here it is. Persons Residential Care."

27

Kenzie stared at Zachary in shock.

"What?" she demanded, aware that her voice was screeching. "They're transferring him to Persons?"

Zachary nodded, his eyes wide as he took in her reaction. "Yeah. What—what's wrong? You know them?"

"I'm investigating a case involving them right now!"

"Investigating a case..." Zachary repeated. "You mean that there was a death there."

Kenzie nodded. She looked around, trying to figure out what to do. Who to call. How to make sure that this didn't happen. "Yes, there was, and there's no way I want Rhys going there."

"But it sounded like... Vera said that... I thought this was a really good opportunity. She was going on about the program, how there isn't anything like it in the state and Rhys was lucky to get into it. She's really excited about it. They told her that it could really help him. They've had miraculous results."

Kenzie shook her head. "No, no, no. We don't want him getting into that program. You don't. Trust me."

"Well... what are we going to do? They've already started the process." Zachary touched his phone to wake up the display and looked at the time. "He's probably there now, just getting settled."

"We have to put a stop to it. She doesn't have to go ahead with it, even if she's already signed all the paperwork. She can withdraw her consent at any time."

Zachary nodded. "Okay. Then we need to get her on the phone." He tapped the screen again, unlocked it this time, and tapped to find Vera's number and call her back. He put it on speakerphone as it started to ring.

Kenzie held her breath, unable to believe the coincidence. Vulnerable Rhys going to Persons? Being put into the hands of a predator? At least she knew what was going on. At least she was in a position to put a stop to the process before Rhys got hurt. If she hadn't known… She shuddered at the thought of them all supporting Vera and telling her that she was doing the right thing, with Rhys suffering abuse at the hands of his therapists, drugged and confused about what was going on.

The phone had rung quite a few times before Vera picked it up. "Hello?"

"Vera, it's Zachary. And I have Kenzie here with me."

"Oh, thank you for calling. It's nice that you're concerned with Rhys and how he is doing. I already told you everything… We're just in the middle of things right now, so…"

"Vera," Kenzie interrupted, "you can't put Rhys into that program."

There was silence for a moment, and Kenzie thought Vera had already hung up. "He's already been approved for the program," Vera said, her tone confused. "I don't know what you mean."

"It's not right for him." Kenzie didn't want to say too much and tell Vera that there had been a death at the institution or that she believed there might be abuse taking place in the sessions or after the sessions were over, while the patient was still under the influence of the drugs. She didn't want to get sued for anything she said to Vera. "There are… some questions about the program and whether it might be harmful to the patients. I really don't think you want to put Rhys into it."

"We've already talked to the doctors about it. They gave me a list of possible risks, but I don't think there is anything to worry about. The benefits far outweigh any of the risks that they talked about."

"I doubt they have been open with you about all the risks. What did they tell you about the program? What are they going to do?"

"It's the only one in the state that's open to minors," Vera said promptly. "If I want to get him into one, it has to be this one, because otherwise he has to wait until he's an adult. And we don't want to wait until he's an adult. We need to work on this now. Try to reach him... to get him back on track again."

"What kind of therapy is it?" Kenzie pressed.

"There is... a drug-mediated therapy," Vera said, talking slowly in order to remember and recite what she had been told. "That just helps him to relax so that he can be open to what the therapist is saying, and be able to talk to them. Or communicate with them. You know."

"That drug—" Kenzie started.

"And there were some other therapies that they do. I don't remember all the initials. Different kinds of behavioral therapies. I think he has done some of them before. It seemed like they helped for a while, so maybe he just needs a 'refresher.' They're always finding new things, you know, ways to make it work better, and they say they are at the cutting edge. They can do a lot more for him now than they could when he was little. They were very positive and said that they were sure they would be able to help him."

"The drug they are using is not approved," Kenzie told her. "There could be side effects. Or other problems. Conflicts with the meds he's already on or a preexisting condition..."

"They said that. But they said they would be doing a full review of what he is on now and a physical, to make sure there was nothing to worry about. They said that was a risk that they could limit. They're doing really good work, Kenzie. They had a lot of success stories that they were telling me about. Kids who hadn't improved with anything else, but they were cured with this new therapy."

"It isn't safe," Kenzie repeated. "There are a lot of questions and concerns. I don't want Rhys to be put into that program. It is too dangerous."

"He's already all signed up," Vera said firmly. "I appreciate your concern, Kenzie, but it isn't up to you. It is up to me."

"I know, but you haven't been given all the information. They're sugar-coating it for you. Telling you all the good possibilities without telling you what damage you could be doing. Is the drug MDMA? Is that what they're doing?"

"It was a very long name," Vera said. "I don't recall. They said it is a very safe drug. It was developed in 1912, and has been safely used since then."

"Do you know what this is? Have you ever heard of ecstasy?"

"Yes. I know that a lot of legitimate drugs get used as street drugs," Vera told her in a clipped tone. "People sell painkillers and amphetamines and a lot of other legitimate drugs on the streets. That doesn't make them bad. They said it isn't addictive, and it will be strictly controlled. They won't make any mistakes. They know how much is safe to use for a teenager like Rhys."

"It hasn't been approved for psychiatric use, only for testing. If you want Rhys to take this therapy, you should at least wait until it is approved," Kenzie said desperately.

"If I wait, then we will miss this window of opportunity. It could be years before the authorities get around to recognizing it as a legitimate treatment. Rhys needs something now, Kenzie. You haven't seen him. He can't wait. We need to bring him back now, before he falls deeper into this… this hole."

"If I could tell you more about the dangers, I would," Kenzie said. "Maybe you could look it up online and get an idea of what some of the other risks are. Don't rely on them to tell you everything, because they won't. It's really not a safe therapy."

"I trust the doctors who are running it. They seem to be very experienced with it and very competent. I'm sure they know what they are doing and that Rhys isn't at any risk."

"Which doctor is running the program?"

"A Dr. Richards. She is really a lovely woman. We had a long talk, and she told me all about her experience and that she would personally be in charge of Rhys's case. She said she was so impressed with

Rhys and the work that he's done so far, and she wanted to help him to succeed in life. If she can get him talking again..."

"There isn't any guarantee that this program will do that—"

"I know there is no guarantee. But if we could get Rhys back, if there is any possibility of getting the old Rhys back... Do you know what I would give to be able to have a conversation with him again? Not just gestures and phone pictures and some written words, but an actual spoken conversation...?"

They had really preyed on Vera. Kenzie thought that the chances of getting Rhys talking normally again were slim to none. It had been years since the initial trauma. Nothing that they had done thus far had been able to bring the old Rhys back. Kenzie remembered the pictures of the grinning, happy boy in Vera's photo album. Rhys before his grandfather had been killed. That carefree boy was gone for good. No amount of therapy could take away the memories of what had happened to him and the troubles he had gone through since. But Dr. Richards had worked away on Vera, promising results that far outstripped what they were likely to accomplish with the hallucinogenic therapy. There was no guarantee that the treatment would work. And every possibility that it could result in abuse and further damage. Or even result in his death.

"Vera. You could lose him. You might never get that little boy back, but you have Rhys now, and if this messes him up worse or kills him..."

"I've already lost him," Vera told her. "You haven't seen him, Kenzie. You don't know what it's like. He's gone to a place where I can't reach him. He won't talk to me or even look at me. I don't know if he can even hear me. He needs this, Kenzie. Don't try to talk me out of it."

Kenzie opened her mouth, looking for something to say. Then the call ended on Zachary's screen and the display dimmed.

She looked at Zachary. He shook his head.

"How do I convince her?" Kenzie asked. "They can't put him into that program."

"It sounds like it's too late. I don't think you're going to be able to convince her."

28

Neither of them slept very well that night. Kenzie didn't know what to do. She kept going over the conversation in her mind, but couldn't come to a conclusion as to what she could have said or done differently. She needed to see Vera face to face. To talk to her more openly about what had happened at Persons. But she knew that if she did, she would be opening herself up to a lawsuit. Even if she were vindicated, there would still be a black spot next to her name, and who knew if she would be able to continue in her position in the medical examiner's office? If it came out that she had given Vera confidential information while trying to convince her to take Rhys out of the MDMA therapy, Kenzie couldn't see her employment continuing for long.

She was sitting with a cup of coffee in the morning before work. She was up too early because she hadn't been able to go back to sleep. She'd only gotten a couple of restless hours in, if that. She was barely functioning. She couldn't face her usual toast and marmalade for breakfast, so she would be running on caffeine and adrenaline. And by the afternoon, that would be gone, and she would be crashing.

She considered calling Dr. Cook and telling him she would not be in. It was a Saturday, and she wasn't required to work, though she usually put in a few hours anyway. But she didn't want to take the chance of messing up because she wasn't properly focused. Her work required great accuracy and attention. She couldn't afford for results to be misfiled or to miss an important clue in a postmortem, allowing a killer to go free.

Her phone rang. It was Dr. Wiltshire. Kenzie was surprised. She picked it up and swiped to accept the call.

"Kenzie," Dr. Wiltshire's voice sounded strange. "You're on the morning news."

"What?" Kenzie went into the living room, where Zachary was sitting with his computer. She turned on the TV. "Why would I be on the news?"

She couldn't think of anything she had done recently that could have made interesting news. Her work was interesting, but most people were not interested in pathology. Those who did had CSI on TV, which was much faster paced than anything Kenzie worked on. And it wasn't like she had talked to any reporters or was working on anything high profile.

"It's looping," Dr. Wiltshire said. "They'll rerun your segment in just a few seconds."

The "up next" banner running along the bottom of the screen said, "Medical Examiner investigates violent death in Persons Residential Care."

"I never talked to anyone about the investigation," Kenzie told Dr. Wiltshire. Though he should have known that without her saying so. They had worked together long enough for him to know that she wouldn't go babbling about a case to the press.

The segment began. Zachary looked up from his computer as the reporter announced that the medical examiner's office was investigating a death that had taken place in a private psychiatric clinic the previous Monday. A picture of Leander Isah was shown. Not one that Kenzie had ever seen. He looked younger in it by perhaps ten years. Were they trying to make him more appealing to the public by presenting him as younger than he was? To outrage viewers even more? Or had it been that long since he had seen his family, and that was the best picture they had of him?

The reporter gave some background context for Persons and Isah himself, talking about the torture he had endured as a young man and his immigration to America. Pulling at those heartstrings. Getting them invested. Everyone watching already knew it was a death investigation, but they were prepared to be shocked and outraged even with that foreknowledge.

"Mr. Isah came to this country hoping for a better life. He was admitted to Persons Residential Care with the promise that they could improve his life and help him move on from those things that had happened to him as a young man. His stay at the home was sponsored by an anonymous donor. He could not have afforded it himself and neither could his family or friends. They were all hopeful that this was the opportunity they had all been praying for. A chance to get better."

Kenzie was too angry to grieve Leander's passing. She had done that privately already. She was angry at whoever was making a big show of a family's private grief in the media, trying to profit from it. She was angry at Persons for putting Isah in danger and offering therapies that hadn't been properly tested. Angry at the anonymous donor who had made it possible for him to live there and receive the treatments that had contributed to his death. She was angry at everybody involved. It wasn't fair that he had to go through it.

After feeding the audience a little more schmaltz about Isah and his situation, the reporter continued with the story.

"We have received exclusive footage from the final night of Mr. Isah's life. Let's have a look at that."

The reporter turned to look over her shoulder at what was probably a blank green screen as the channel rolled the footage of Persons Residential Care behind her and then switched to full screen.

No sound accompanied the video, and it had that jerky quality that Kenzie knew meant it was from a surveillance camera that used a lower frame rate to limit the file size. She saw Isah sitting in an area with tables and chairs. The dining room during mealtimes. Multipurpose room when meals were not being served. Patients could play games, put together puzzles, or visit with friends or family members. Similar to the setup that Kenzie had seen when visiting Zachary in the hospital psych ward. Isah was sitting with his head down on the table. The other patients they had interviewed had said that he was tired and wanted to go back to his room. He'd had a very long session.

A very long drug session, Janice had told them. The session had probably included both the administration of the MDMA and talk therapy. Then that was alternated with sessions that were just talk, without any drugs. Patients would have to learn to communicate and experience their feelings and memories without the drug too. To integrate with the rest of the world without a hallucinogen.

An orderly walked up to Isah and slapped him on the back. Encouraging him to get up and not fall asleep at the table, Kenzie assumed. Isah startled, throwing his arms out in alarm. The camera caught the orderly's profile as he laughed at this response. He punched Isah in the shoulder. Probably not hard. Just another encouragement to get up and engage with the rest of the residents. He wasn't allowed to go to sleep, it would mess up his circadian rhythm and make it harder to sleep at night. Though Kenzie assumed Isah would be given a sleeping pill if needed. The psych ward was pretty free with them. They wanted the patients to be able to get the sleep that they needed. It made things easier on the night staff, and patients who had slept well would be better behaved during the day. Sleepless patients were not stable.

When Isah did not get up, the orderly stepped away at first. No need to get into a fight over it, Kenzie assumed. One of the doctors or nurses might have an easier time convincing him he needed to get up.

But the orderly returned with a helper. They stood there, just a few feet apart. Both orderlies talking animatedly with Isah, while he tried to shut them out and put his head back down again. They got in his face. They poked and prodded him. The bigger of the two hauled him to his feet. Kenzie was struck by how thin and frail Isah seemed. She had noted his height and weight during the autopsy, of course. He was underweight. But she hadn't really thought that much of it because Zachary often lost a considerable amount of weight during his depressive cycle, which he then had to gain back when he was feeling like himself again. And the men from some of those African countries were very slim. Isah's forehead gleamed with sweat and his clothes looked limp and damp.

Isah fought back against the two orderlies. Several doctors and nurses hurried in and tried to break up the skirmish. The lack of sound to go with the video made it seem like it was happening in a vacuum. A void that swallowed up every noise.

They all latched on to Isah. Two people, then five, then Kenzie wasn't sure anymore. She could no longer see Isah as he was swarmed. He struggled as the staff held on to every limb. They took him to the floor and pinned him down. Kenzie held her breath, watching them, waiting for them to jab a needle into him or haul him off to an isolation room to calm him down.

When they finally backed off, satisfied that he was cooperating or that they had punished him enough, Kenzie expected him to remain there, motionless. She'd seen enough videos on the news of just that thing in recent months. Police detaining criminals and holding them down for too long. Squeezing every last breath out of them.

But Isah moved sluggishly when they backed off. The two original orderlies lifted him to his feet. Isah was breathing heavily. He staggered like a drunk, but was clearly alive as they took him out of the camera's range. Kenzie breathed a sigh of relief. She knew that he still ended up dying, of course, but she was glad not to have to witness his death herself.

The altercation matched what the witnesses had said, but that wasn't the end of it. Nurse Craig had told her that they had called the police because Isah had fought back, which had then caused another skirmish. Only then had Isah been sedated and been allowed to go to sleep, never to waken again.

"Within hours, Leander Isah was dead," the reporter announced solemnly. "The medical examiner's investigation began at the scene on Friday night. Why have her findings not been issued yet? It seems pretty clear from this video that Isah was injured during this altercation and that those injuries led to his death. But where is the medical examiner in all of this?" They showed Kenzie's professional headshot. The one that used to be on the ME's website, before it had attracted too much unwanted attention.

"I hate it when they show that picture," Kenzie grumbled to no one in particular. There was a reason that it wasn't on the website anymore. They didn't want the weirdos and psychos to be able to track her down so easily.

The reporter went on about Kenzie being unable to be reached for comment and Dr. Cook announcing that they had nothing to say about a death still under investigation, and that the ME's report would be issued in due course.

A non-story. Meant to get a lot of people angry and demanding answers. But of course they would not be satisfied with what she put in her report. Not when the reporter had said that Isah was injured. They would be more interested in making up conspiracy stories to explain what they and the reporter had decided were the real facts of the case.

Of course, in this case, they might be right. The clinic was going to a lot of trouble to cover up what had happened to Leander. Missing consents, video of the session, and treatment notes. Kenzie was glad that the footage had been leaked. Too much was being kept quiet. It was too easy to silence the vulnerable patients. Even if they were able to tell the truth, the staff would just say that they were lying.

"Where did they get the video footage?" Dr. Wiltshire asked.

Kenzie shook her head slowly. "I don't know. That's the first I've seen of it. Detective Garcia got the surveillance video yesterday, so I guess it came from her office."

"You're saying that the police leaked it?"

Kenzie stiffened at his tone. "I'm not *accusing* anyone. I'm just answering your question. I haven't seen the video before. I don't know how I could have leaked it if it was never even in my possession."

"There is going to be a big stink over this. The police and our bosses do not like stuff like this getting out. Especially on an active case."

"No," Kenzie agreed evenly.

"This is not the first thing we've had leak from the medical examiner's office."

"I don't know how I or anyone else in our office could have leaked something that we never possessed in the first place. You'll have to talk to the police department, see what they did with it. It must be someone from their office. Like I said, I don't even have that footage. Pretty hard for me to send it to anyone."

"They did mention you by name. They know you are working on the case."

"Since that's my job, it's pretty obvious. Dozens of people could have told them you were off on medical leave and I was the only one doing autopsies."

Dr. Wiltshire sighed. "You're right," he said. "I'm sorry, I'm not even there, and I'm acting like I know what's going on. I guess maybe I feel guilty for not being on top of everything. Though you know I wasn't always on top of everything when I was there…"

"I don't think that's fair," Kenzie said. "You always seemed to have things under control. No one can do everything. I can't keep up with everything with you gone. Dr. Cook and I are doing what we can to keep up, but it's not like having you there. It's going to be a long, hard haul with you gone. Are they giving you any idea when you will be able to do procedures again?"

"The bones are healing as they should, but it isn't a quick process, especially at my age. And then I imagine I'll need to do a lot of dexterity exercises before I feel ready to jump back into it."

"Well, at least if you slip, the patients aren't going to complain."

He chuckled. "No. So, what should I know about this case? Things do not look good after seeing that video."

Kenzie agreed and brought him up to speed with what she knew.

29

It was a while before Kenzie got off the phone with Dr. Wiltshire. She had retreated to her bedroom so that she was out of Zachary's way and not revealing any confidential information. When she finally disconnected from the call and returned to the kitchen, looking for something to eat, Zachary closed his laptop and joined her.

"Vera called."

"Oh." Kenzie was cautious, assuming the worst. "What's up? Is Rhys okay?"

He nodded, but his eyes were grave. "No change, I don't think. But Vera saw the coverage about Persons this morning and is a *little* upset about it."

Kenzie let out one bleak bark of laughter. "*Now* she's concerned about it."

"She didn't know why you were trying to discourage her from the program before. Now she knows it was because you are investigating a homicide there."

Kenzie nodded. "Right. So does that mean she's pulling Rhys from the program?"

"No."

Kenzie looked at him. Zachary didn't say anything while he got himself a yogurt cup from the fridge. He sat down, removed the top, then got up again to get a spoon from the drawer. He looked at Kenzie.

"Vera's not going to pull Rhys from the MDMA program?"

"No. She's upset, but not enough to pull him out. She said that one patient dying doesn't mean the whole place is rotten and that it wasn't anything to do with the MDMA program. It was obviously because of them piling on and restraining Isah like they did. Not anything to do with the drug. She still thinks that the trauma therapy is worth the risk. The chances of Rhys improving, maybe going back to normal, versus the chances that something could happen to him and he could die like Isah… she thinks it is worth the risk. The chances of something happening to him like that is so remote… she doesn't think it is even worth considering."

"So she's upset about it happening at the facility that Rhys is going to, but she doesn't think that there is any danger to Rhys."

Zachary nodded. "Yes."

"Oh…" Kenzie ran her fingers through her hair, trying to decide how to handle this. Vera wasn't asking her to do anything. It wasn't Kenzie's responsibility. But she and Zachary felt very close to Rhys, and she couldn't just let it go without going to bat for him at least one more time. "I want to do *something!* Is there any way we could go see him? Are they allowing visitors?"

"There's nothing that says we can't try."

Kenzie studied him, trying to read his face. "Yeah? Does that mean you're okay with going over there? Even if the chances are low that we will be able to see him?"

"Of course."

His response was so quick and certain that Kenzie had to laugh. "Well, okay. I guess I know how you feel about it." She wanted to ask a second time to make sure that he really, really understood that it might just be a wasted trip, but Zachary wasn't a child. He understood the time it would take to drive out there, jump through the bureaucratic hoops, and then drive back home again. He knew the time it would take out of his schedule and that their chances of doing anything productive were slim. Chances were, they wouldn't see Rhys, no one would tell them how he was doing, and they would be run out on a rail, wasting several hours of the day. "Okay," Kenzie said again. "Let's go, then."

Zachary indicated his yogurt cup. "Breakfast."

"You can eat it in the car."

"No, *you* need to eat something for breakfast. I'll be done by the time you're ready to go out the door."

That *was* why Kenzie had returned to the kitchen. It was late for her to eat breakfast, and her body was waking up and telling her to do something about it. If she didn't grab something at home before they went out, she would end up buying a donut or something equally unhealthy on the way there.

"Grab me a granola bar. I'll eat on the way too."

Zachary raised his brows at this suggestion. He knew how adamant she was about not eating in her car. But just this once... Kenzie had the uneasy feeling that she should not wait. She should get over to Persons as soon as possible.

"I'm just going to get my purse. Grab me a granola bar," Kenzie repeated.

Zachary stood up to obey, and Kenzie retrieved her purse from the bedroom. She put on her outdoor gear and shoved the granola bar into a pocket before getting her shoes on. Once in the car, she let the engine run to heat the car a bit before leaving. She pulled the granola bar out and started to remove the wrapper. She became aware of how much the wrapper was crinkling and looked over at Zachary. The grimace on his face told her that it was, in fact, triggering his misophonia. She tried to remove the wrapper quickly to reduce the time he had to listen to the noise, which meant that she spilled greasy crumbs into her lap. And onto the car's upholstery.

"Argh. Going to have to get it detailed," she complained, brushing the crumbs away the best she could. She didn't have a plate for the granola bar. Now that it was out of the protective sleeve and catch-all wrapper, she would get more crumbs on her clothing and car as she ate.

But she would need to vacuum it out anyway. Whether she had to vacuum out a sprinkling of crumbs or half a granola bar's worth, it would be pretty much the same amount of effort. She put the car into reverse and backed out of the garage.

"They're not going to let us see him," Kenzie said with certainty when they were halfway there. Leaving the city streets behind, driving through the countryside to the facility, which felt both isolated and close by at the same time. "They haven't been at all cooperative with my investigation of Mr. Isah's death, and they're certainly not going to be any happier after seeing that video leaked to the public. Especially with my name all over it as if I were the one who had released it."

"They must know that they gave it to El—Detective Garcia, not you."

"Sure, but they'll assume she gave it to me."

"Nothing you can do about what they think. I know they might not let us in. We talked about that."

Usually, he was the one who obsessed over a problem. Kenzie felt like someone else had taken over her brain and she could not control how it was working—or not working—anymore. She wanted to argue with Zachary, to explain to him how she was sure that they would not be able to see Rhys. To argue him to the ground about it.

But she was the one who didn't want to be disappointed. She wanted to see Rhys and to know that he was okay. That the facility hadn't just eaten him whole. That he was being treated with kindness and respect, not shoved around and abused the way that Leander had been. There were too many similarities between the two. Maybe they were just superficial—both very slim, black men. Both had dealt with terrible traumas and been institutionalized in the past. Both wanted desperately to be free of the trauma and the ways that it had held them back in their lives.

She had not been able to save Leander. He had died before she had even met him. It was her responsibility to reveal the cause and manner of his death, to bring the truth to light.

And she had to do what she could to save Rhys from harm and further trauma.

She hadn't told Zachary or Vera about the sexual abuse. She

couldn't bring herself to. They knew that Rhys was vulnerable. Zachary had brought it up many times before in connection with Luke's history of trafficking young men and women. They all knew that when a person was unable to speak up, it made them a target. Like Tirza. The perfect victim was one who couldn't point the finger at his abuser.

Kenzie managed to keep quiet and not raise her doubts again before they got to Persons.

There were several media vans parked just outside the property, reporters and their equipment, hoping to find a way in. Being kept outside the property line because it was a private clinic. Kenzie drove in through the open gate with a guard standing next to it, eyeballing all the cars. She found a visitor parking space and eased her baby into it.

At the front desk, Kenzie didn't speak, but let Zachary take the lead. She hid partially behind him while he told the receptionist confidently that he was there to see Rhys Salter.

The receptionist looked at him with an uncertain expression. They probably discouraged visitors, even if they didn't outright ban them. The woman tapped Rhys's name into the system and read what appeared on her screen.

"Rhys has just arrived. The program doesn't usually allow any visitors in the first couple of weeks."

"His grandma asked us to check in. To make sure that everything is okay and he is settled in."

"If there were any problems, she would have been informed."

Zachary nodded and waited. She made a gesture as if expecting him to leave, but he didn't.

"Is he in a therapy session right now?" he asked and, when she opened her mouth to answer that he was, so Zachary would have to leave, he quickly inserted, "I'll wait until he's done."

"We don't have the space for visitors to wait here for hours."

Zachary looked at the small grouping of chairs. "Oh, this is just fine. We'll stay here until he's ready."

She was trying to be polite, but Zachary didn't seem to be getting the message. "You can't wait here," she said flatly.

Zachary motioned Kenzie over to the chairs, and they both sat down. Kenzie looked at Zachary speculatively. "Do you really think you can get us in?"

He nodded, keeping an eye on the woman as he talked to Kenzie in a low tone. "If she'd made a big deal, a scene, or just called security, then I wouldn't be as sure. But they're trying to avoid the appearance of anything improper. After the media attention this morning, they need to look squeaky clean. And there are going to be a lot of people in today to check up on their loved ones."

"They need to reassure everyone that everything is fine and the death of Mr. Isah was just a one-off."

"And the assault," Zachary reminded her. "If it was just a death, it wouldn't be as big of a deal. People do die in hospitals and psychiatric care. But the assault is what frightens people. He wasn't doing anything except sitting at a table with his head down, and they attacked him for no reason."

"Well, they had their reasons. But they won't get very far with people telling them that Isah wasn't allowed to just rest after a therapy session. He had to be involved in socializing with others or taking part in other activities. Intervening with him physically—and so violently—is over the top. People will not just accept it."

"You hope not." Zachary's eyes were far away. "But I didn't think they would accept shocking autistic kids for behaving like they had autism, either."

Kenzie had to concede the point. Zachary had believed that exposing what was going on at Summit would have enraged people so much that the place would be shut down, or, at the very least, would be prevented from using electrical shocks in their therapy any longer. But the public did not rise up against them and insist that they be shut down. A couple of years later, they were still operating.

Dread crawled in Kenzie's gut. Surely she wouldn't run into the same problems with Persons. Surely, the public wouldn't accept that it was okay to use drugs and other practices that could result in the patients' deaths in their desperate search for a cure.

30

The receptionist kept throwing glances in Zachary's and Kenzie's direction, and Kenzie knew that she was anxious about having to deal with them. She didn't like them sitting in her waiting area, patiently waiting for something she couldn't grant them. She wanted them out of there, someone else's responsibility.

Eventually, Dr. Richards entered the reception area and looked around. Kenzie nudged Zachary. He looked up, and his eyes widened at the sight of the white-jacketed, golden-haired bombshell. He looked at Kenzie.

"The lovely Dr. Richards," Kenzie murmured.

"Wow."

At Kenzie's reproving look, he fumbled for a better response.

"I mean… how does she have enough time to put that much care into her hair and makeup when she's working as a doctor?" Zachary said. "I mean… granted, this is a private clinic, but they still keep their staff busy, don't they?"

Kenzie chuckled. "Good save. Looks like she's coming over here."

Dr. Richards looked at Kenzie for a moment before deciding to approach her. She looked hesitant. Not what she wanted to be doing.

"Uh, Dr. Kirsch, isn't it?" she asked. "You're the one who wanted to see Rhys Salter?"

"Yes. Zachary and I." Kenzie nodded at him. "We are close friends and I'm sure you can understand that after the publicity this morning... we had some concerns."

"Well, of course, everything in the media has been blown out of proportion." Dr. Richards hesitated, then tilted her head slightly to indicate they should join her somewhere more private. Kenzie and Zachary stood and followed her. She led them to a meeting room, not her office, and motioned for them to sit.

"I'm sorry. I'm sure you understand that things are a little disrupted here this morning. We are not used to dealing with so many inquiries and requests to see patients." She waited for Zachary and Kenzie to make themselves comfortable, though that was impossible in the cheap, hard-seated stacking chairs. "As I say, the media is really blowing this situation out of proportion. You already know, Dr. Kirsch, that the footage you saw on the TV this morning had nothing to do with Mr. Isah's death. He was alive and well following that incident where he was... safely restrained. He went back to his room and was perfectly fine."

"And then he died."

"Yes... But I'm sure you already know that his death had nothing to do with that minor scuffle. Really..." she rolled her eyes, "it looked much worse than it was. People expect trouble these days, after seeing so many police actions go awry, that is where their minds immediately go. But our staff are well trained in proper restraint and de-escalation. What you saw was really nothing. There was no risk of Mr. Isah being hurt."

"Well, that isn't what we are here for," Kenzie told her. "We're here to see Rhys. He was just transferred yesterday, and we would like to see that he is settled and has everything he needs. We want to see him and talk to him."

"There's no need to take on such a confrontational tone," Dr. Richards said repressively.

Kenzie would show her what a confrontational tone really sounded like if she continued to stall and block them from seeing Rhys. Kenzie forced a smile and a light tone. "Good. Are you going to bring Rhys in here, or will we be going to his room?"

She and Dr. Richards stared at each other, a showdown. Kenzie was not someone who would be put off by an administrator mouthing meaningless reassurances. Nor was she going to back down because of Dr. Richards's physical appearance. She was there for one thing, and that was perfectly reasonable. Zachary had already assured her that if they pushed, the hospital would give in rather than having to face any more negative publicity.

Eventually, Dr. Richards took a deep breath and let it out again. "It would probably cause the least disruption if I take you to him," she relented. "I would ask that you just speak with him briefly to satisfy yourself that he is in good condition and then leave quietly so we can continue treating him. I don't want him to get agitated, which he may do if he has visitors. It is difficult for him to be here, leaving everyone he loves on the outside, and we don't want to remind him about what he is missing. We want him to be comfortable and rested so that he will not be resistant when we begin his therapy."

"What therapy are you planning? Are you talking about giving him MDMA?"

Richards's lips pressed tightly together, drawing a thin, flat line that was not particularly flattering. "Since you are a doctor, I know you understand doctor-patient confidentiality. You are not Rhys's guardians. Even if you were, there are certain things that I would not be able to tell you, to preserve his confidentiality and his trust in me."

"You are not prevented from talking to his grandma about what therapy he is undergoing. In fact, you would be negligent in not giving her all the details about any therapy he was undergoing."

"Nevertheless…" Dr. Richards stared steadily at Kenzie. "You are not his guardian. Mrs. Salter has been informed about what therapies Rhys will be undergoing. If she has not communicated those to you, it is not up to me to tell you anything about them."

"You are doing hallucinogenic therapy. That's what she said."

Dr. Richards shrugged, still giving nothing away. If Kenzie were just guessing, then Richards would not be tricked into telling her.

"When are you starting?" Kenzie asked, hoping that they would be able to push it off as much as possible. "I assume you'll wait until he has been here long enough to establish a relationship of trust. It wouldn't be good to jump into something scary like that without first ensuring he could trust you not to do anything detrimental to his health."

No comment from Dr. Richards.

Kenzie shook her head, exasperated. "Okay. Let's go see Rhys." She stood up.

Zachary scooted his chair back noisily and stood as well. Dr. Richards nodded and led them out of the room. "Again, I would ask you to keep this brief and low-key. It is not the time for a long, involved meeting. You don't want to make Rhys homesick."

Kenzie didn't make any promises.

Dr. Richards didn't push it further. Maybe she recognized that she had already done as much damage control as possible. Now, she needed to shut up and let the visit progress. She needed things to seem as routine as possible so that Kenzie didn't overreact and report to the media that there were even bigger problems at Persons than she had initially thought.

She led them into the wing where Kenzie had initially attended when she had found Mr. Isah on the floor that first day. It was a sobering thought, and Kenzie grew even more tense about the visit to Rhys. What if they found him motionless on the floor or on his bed? Or hanging from a light fixture?

31

S he needn't have been so worried. When they arrived in Rhys's small, bare room, they found him lying on his side on the bed, facing the doorway. At first, Kenzie thought he was asleep, but his eyes were not closed. He stared out at the empty hallway dully, and did not look at all interested when Kenzie and Zachary appeared there. She was used to him being animated and interested whenever she saw him. He was always friendly, teasing Zachary, giving them a few big smiles, even if the rest of the time, his face fell into a long, hangdog frown. He was not a happy boy, but he could still enjoy a visit from his friends.

But this time, he did not. Kenzie wondered whether he was even aware of their entering the room and greeting him.

They both said hello, and, not receiving any response from him, turned their gazes toward Richards, who had stationed herself inside the door and appeared to intend to stay there.

"We would like some privacy," Kenzie said firmly.

"I need to make sure that everything is going well..." Richards countered.

"You didn't have anyone in the room before we came. Now, there is someone here visiting with and supervising him. You don't need to be here, eavesdropping on our conversation."

"I am here for Rhys's protection. You are not his guardians. It would not be wise for me to leave you alone with him without knowing your intentions."

"You know our intentions. To talk to him and make sure that he is okay. And I'm not going to do that with you hovering over us. If you aren't sure if it would be okay with his guardian, then you can call her."

Richards didn't move.

"Do you need her number?" Zachary asked politely, pulling his phone out.

"I do not," Richards snapped. She withdrew from the room, leaving them alone there. The door to the cell-like room was still open, with staff walking by occasionally to keep an eye on things and ensure that all residents were well and safe.

Zachary moved over to the bed, in front of Kenzie. She held back her irritation at her view of Rhys being cut off. But it was really Zachary who was Rhys's friend, not Kenzie, so it was appropriate that he should be the one to move closer and try to engage with Rhys. There were no visitor chairs in the room. No furniture other than the bed, and a little closet alcove that was empty. Rhys did not have any personal items there. No phone, no change of clothing, no pictures.

Zachary crouched on the floor in front of Rhys, about an arm's reach away.

"Hey, Rhys. It's Zachary. How's it going?"

He waited for what seemed like a long time. The seconds drew out with no response. Rhys didn't acknowledge his presence and didn't answer him. He was much like Cara had been at first, acting as if he were completely oblivious to their presence, even with Zachary right there in front of his face.

"I guess you're having a pretty tough time," Zachary said quietly. "Vera said that you've been having some trouble at school. Maybe dealing with some teasing or bullying? It's so tough to be a teenager. You feel like you can't be in control of anything in your life. And when things go wrong... there's nothing you can do about it. You can feel so helpless and hopeless."

He paused again. He shifted his position, moving from a crouch on his feet to kneeling in front of Rhys. Not very comfortable on the hard floor.

"Vera said that you had trouble with the resource room teacher too," Zachary offered. "Did she do something to you? Was she giving you a hard time?" He paused. "Was she bullying you or touching you?"

Something in Rhys's face shifted infinitesimally. Kenzie couldn't have said what exactly it was. She still couldn't tell if Rhys were actually seeing Zachary or not. His attitude didn't change. He didn't answer Zachary, but he had reacted, however tiny that reaction had been.

"Teachers do that sometimes," Zachary said, watching Rhys closely. "Even though they know they're not supposed to. It's not your fault if she did. Any more than it would be your fault if she hit you."

No movement, no response.

"How are you feeling about being here?" Zachary put his hand on the bed. He didn't touch Rhys. The gesture seemed to be one of solidarity and comfort, even though he didn't make contact. "I know how hard it is to admit that you need help. To have to go to the hospital or another place like this to get treatment. It feels like a failure, even if everyone tells you that it isn't, that it was something outside of your control." Zachary rubbed his temple. "I always feel like... I should be able to control what goes on in my own head. How can I not be responsible for what happens in my own head? But they're right. It isn't something that I can control. All I can do is try to get help when I need it. Let someone else in."

He knelt there, staring at Rhys for a few minutes in silence. A staff member walked by in the hallway, looking in at them and then continuing on his way.

"Did they tell you about the therapy they're going to do here?"

Kenzie could feel Rhys listening to Zachary now, attentive to every word. Nothing had changed in his position or in his face that Kenzie could tell. She could just feel that he was listening to Zachary. She no longer had any question about whether he could see them and knew that they were there.

"It's something called hallucinogenic mediated therapy," Zachary told Rhys. "Do you know about the LSD trials they did back in the seventies? Well, it's sort of like that, except with a different drug, MDMA. They use it to put your mind in a more receptive state. To open you up to new experiences and make it easier to talk about your feelings and what happened in the past."

Zachary broke eye contact with Rhys for a moment to look at Kenzie. She wasn't sure whether he was hoping that she would jump in at this juncture to talk to him about the therapy process he was facing. But there wasn't much more Kenzie could tell Rhys about it than Zachary had already said. She hadn't been through one of the sessions herself. Hopefully, Garcia had gotten the videos of the therapy sessions with the other patients at Persons, and Kenzie would get a chance to review a few of them. Then she would have a better idea about what to tell Rhys about it. By then, he might have already gone through a session or two. She wished she could shorten the process and prepare him for it now.

Rhys's hand moved, and he caught Zachary by the wrist. Zachary immediately looked back into Rhys's face, smiling reassuringly.

"Hey, bud. I'm still here. I'm not going anywhere."

He didn't say anything, just looking at Rhys. Kenzie breathed, waiting to see whether Rhys would say a word or make a gesture to let them know what he was thinking. He was good at finding nonverbal ways to communicate what he wanted to tell them. But she didn't see his phone anywhere in the room. Had they taken it away from him? Stored it somewhere safe so that it couldn't be taken from his room? Or was it at home with Vera?

"It's okay," Zachary assured him. "This is probably pretty scary, isn't it?"

No sound or further movement from Rhys. Kenzie believed he understood what Zachary was saying to him.

At the very least, Rhys had reached out to make physical contact.

"You went to Stanley Green," Zachary said, eyes intent on Rhys. He shifted his position again, to sit on the floor, slightly below Rhys's level, relieving his knees. But he didn't appear to be comfortable in this position either. Kenzie doubted whether the bare floor felt very good on Zachary's tailbone, which he had broken, not for the first time, the previous year. While he appeared to have healed up from that accident without any significant effects, Kenzie did see that flash of pain every now and then when he sat down the wrong way or had been sitting for too long in a hard chair. He changed his hand position to squeeze Rhys's hand for a moment, then let it go again. "Did you go to Stanley for help? Were you having a problem that you thought he could help with? Or you just didn't know where to go for help?"

Rhys didn't give any sign of why he had gone to Stanley. Or if maybe he had just been in that part of town and it had been a coincidence that Stanley had seen him out walking. It seemed too much of a stretch that it might have just been a coincidence. He had to have been going to Stanley for something.

"Did something happen, Rhys?" Zachary gazed into Rhys's eyes. Trying to read him without any verbal communication. "Did someone hurt you? Kidnap you or abuse you…?" Zachary's eyes again went to Kenzie. This time, probably to make sure he hadn't managed to trigger her by mentioning kidnapping. The word still made Kenzie's heart race and her gut clench, but she was stressed already and didn't think that her response to the word was significant enough for Zachary to see it.

Rhys pulled his hand back from Zachary. They weren't touching, and it was a definite withdrawal. Zachary looked back at him.

"It's okay," he reassured the boy. "Whatever happened, it's okay. We'll help you get through it. Okay? I'm not going to force you to talk about it. You know that. I can wait. Handle it however you want to. But you're safe here. You're safe here from whatever might have happened to you out there."

You're safe here.

Kenzie wished she could be sure Zachary was right. She wanted to reassure Rhys that everything was okay and that he would be safe at Persons and could take his time to tell his own story. But she had her doubts about just how safe it was.

32

Eventually, Zachary was all talked out. He wasn't getting any more information from Rhys about what had happened to him and why he had been out wandering in the streets so late at night. And why he had lost his ability or will to communicate. Kenzie felt worn out just from watching the interplay between Zachary and Rhys, looking for the tiniest indications of what Rhys was thinking or feeling. She was sure that it must have been even more exhausting for Zachary, and probably for Rhys, too, who seemed to be tired now, at the brink of sleep. His eyes kept blinking, slower and slower, glazing over in the pauses between Zachary's comments. Eventually, they both knew that it was time to go.

The staff had been keeping an eye on them and, when they exited Rhys's room, an orderly or male nurse hustled over.

"All done? I'm not sure how you can have such a long visit with someone who does not want to communicate!"

Zachary looked at him. "What makes you think that Rhys doesn't want to communicate?"

His name tag gave his name as John. He rolled his eyes. "Well, the fact that he doesn't try. No words, signs, writing, nothing. He's just completely blocking everyone out."

Zachary shook his head. "Maybe he's blocking *you* out."

"Everyone else, too," John insisted. "You're nothing special. I know he didn't say a word to you while you were in there. If you're going to try to tell me that he was communicating with you telepathically, you're just as disturbed as he is."

"I am," Zachary confirmed. "Maybe even more so."

John looked momentarily confused, his brows drawing together. He looked at Zachary to see whether he was serious, then looked over at Kenzie, waiting for her to laugh or to give him some sign as to whether Zachary was teasing. Kenzie shrugged her shoulders, not bothering to give him any information.

"Would you mind showing us around a little?" Kenzie asked. "I was going to get a tour the last time I was here, but we ended up going too long with our interviews and had to get home."

"Uh, I haven't been authorized to do that."

"I'm not asking about anything confidential or private. Just… the arts and crafts room, where the MDMA or talk therapy are held, if they aren't in use right now. Any common areas, I'm not asking for trade secrets."

John looked around for one of the doctors or administrators who could tell him whether this was kosher, but there didn't seem to be anyone senior around to tell him. Kenzie gave him her most charming smile.

"Oh, come on, John. Are you telling me that the arts and crafts room is a secret? That there is something there I can't be allowed to see?"

His neck was a little red. Kenzie cajoled, pleased to see that she was having an effect on him. "Please? I would really like to see some of the other areas. It doesn't have to be anything to do with any studies or treatment options. You must tour prospective patients or families through here from time to time, as they are considering whether it is where they want their loved one to be admitted."

He shrugged uncomfortably. "Well, yes."

"Then I don't see the problem in giving us the tour. As you know, our loved one, Rhys Salter, has just been admitted. And if you want more reason, maybe Zachary here would consider Persons the next time he needs a med review or supervision."

John looked at Zachary, brows down, then back at Kenzie, not quite believing what she was saying. He knew that she was just trying to get him to give them a tour and didn't think that she was serious about Zachary, even though she said it in a perfectly serious tone. People didn't talk about their mental illness that way, or about their potential need to be hospitalized for it again in the future.

"Uh, what…?"

"I have seasonal depression," Zachary said. "Some years, I end up needing to be admitted for a few weeks. Or longer, if there is a change made to my cocktail or something that needs more intense therapy."

"You do?"

Zachary nodded. He raised his brows. The orderly cocked his head, brows drawing down, and shook his head slightly. "No…"

"I sometimes need extra support," Zachary said. "Isn't that what you're here for?"

"Of course." He nodded his agreement. Then he gave a shrug. "Fine, I'll take you around, but it will be a short tour. There's a lot going on today, what with…" He didn't finish.

"The media attention this morning?" Kenzie asked.

"Yeah." He rolled his eyes. "I don't know what that chick at the ME's office is doing, leaking that video to the press. Just what does she think she's going to accomplish? All she's going to do is ensure that there are fewer options available for people who really need them."

Zachary looked at Kenzie, smothering a laugh.

"Maybe it wasn't the ME's office," Kenzie said.

"It was." He was sure of himself. "She's been making all kinds of trouble here, coming around, interviewing people, making a pest of herself. Got everybody wound up over it."

"You think she's intentionally making trouble?"

He considered for a minute, then grimaced. "I don't know. I mean… I can see how it looks bad, but sometimes, the only way to get a patient under control is to intervene physically. I don't mean like that was normal, what you see on the recording, but you can't hear what's going on, you can't see what happened the rest of the day. The guy was trouble. He was all over the place, unpredictable. He needed to be shown that there are consequences. You can't just diss the staff and refuse to cooperate and think that everybody is going to serve you hand and foot. We're not here to make the patients happy. We're here to make them better."

Kenzie nodded as if this all made perfect sense to her.

John looked at Zachary. "Like I said, that's not usual. It isn't like we go around beating up patients or physically restraining people who aren't doing anything. You wouldn't be like that. You would be cooperative and understand that sometimes there are rules that you don't like, or you have to wait, or that it takes time to get meds adjusted. You wouldn't be like that."

Zachary nodded. "He was causing a lot of trouble?"

"He'd be like that, quiet, looking like he wasn't going to be a problem for anyone, and wait until everyone's attention was somewhere else. And then he'd suddenly explode, causing all kinds of trouble. It was deliberate. You couldn't leave him alone, couldn't assume that because he was quiet, he was going to stay that way. All it would take was one patient going over to talk to him, someone getting into his space, and he would go ballistic. You can't tell from the video how crazy he would get. Everybody had to help get him under control right away, or we wouldn't be able to."

They walked in silence for a couple of minutes. John led them into a room that was clearly the arts room. Shelves lined with half-finished sculptures and tools, vertically filed portfolios and paintings, easels, paints, jars of paintbrushes, with some textiles work at the far side of the room, away from the paints.

"Oh, this is cool." Kenzie walked around the room, looking at the works in progress. "It's always so neat to see what everybody is working on. Did you ever do anything like this?" she asked Zachary. "Were you ever anywhere they had an art therapy program?"

He shrugged. "When I was a teenager, I remember a couple of programs. But nothing like that in the city psych ward. They just don't have the funding. If they try to kick off an arts program, it's just like... pencils and reams of copy paper. As cheap as possible. Pretty hard to get inspired with anything like that."

"Yeah, that would be hard."

"I'm not artistic," he confessed. "My drawings are just about as good as my handwriting."

Which was to say, unrecognizable to anyone but him. Unless he really spent the time and attention on it, like he did when filling out a form. But the personal notes he made to himself in his notebooks were dauntingly messy.

"You can be artistic in other ways. You have your photography."

"That's not really... well, yeah, I guess it is. Some of the stuff I see other photographers putting on display is very artistic, so I guess it *can* be artistic..."

"Yours is, too. I love having a peek at what you are looking at when you show it to Lorne. You never show it to me because you don't think it's good or that I would be interested, but I am. I think your photography is really good."

He blushed. Kenzie laughed. They headed for the door to exit the art room. Kenzie glanced down at a garbage can she passed, with the remains of a broken sculpture in it. It looked like it had been really detailed, and she stopped to look at the feather pattern on a wing and to try to reconstruct the sculpture in her mind. A bird lifting its wings to take flight, or alighting on a fence post. She took a couple more steps before she heard Janice Martin's voice in her head.

An eagle, on a branch, just lifting up its wings to take off.

She stopped and looked at the sculpture in the garbage again. Had Janice's sculpture been broken accidentally? Had someone done it on purpose? Did she know about it?

Kenzie got an uneasy feeling, dread creeping up on her again.

33

"W hat is it?" Zachary asked, instantly zeroing in on Kenzie and the worry that must have been written all over her face. "Are you okay?"

"Yeah. It's just..." Kenzie couldn't tear herself away from the broken sculpture and the worried anticipation making her heart race and her breathing quick and shallow. She looked at the orderly. "John... where is Janice Martin? Can you take me to her room?"

He scowled and shook his head. "No. I told you we can't be bothering the patients. I agreed to show you some of the common areas and, if she is out doing something, you can see her, but—"

"I need to see her. Now."

"You can't," he said flatly. "Now, let's stop with all the demands. It's time for you to go. We have too much else to do to be worrying about your questions. Okay? Enough is enough."

"I want to see Dr. Richards."

He widened his eyes at her. "I just told you—"

"Get her for me. Have her paged. Something. I need to talk to her."

"Dr. Richards is very busy." He looked at his wristwatch. "She'll be starting a session soon and will be tied up for a couple of hours—"

Kenzie looked around. She started trying random doors, knowing that they were not in the housing wing, but intent on causing enough disruption that he would have to listen to her and call one of the doctors or security.

"Ma'am," John said in exasperation, trying to stop her. But Zachary stepped in between them and, while he was far from being an imposing figure, he was like the short basketball guard who was *always* in your face. The orderly could not get past him to deal with Kenzie unless he really got physical, and he didn't want to do that. Not after the media leak that morning. "Ma'am!"

"Get me one of the doctors," Kenzie insisted. "I need to see Janice Martin. If I don't see her, I will call the police."

"The police? For what? We aren't required to show you anything or anyone."

Kenzie pulled out her Medical Examiner's Office badge. "You see that? I'm law enforcement. And you need to show me Janice Martin's room or let me talk to someone over your head in administration. Have you got that?"

He looked at the badge, confused and stunned. "What the...?"

She pressed it toward him. "Medical Examiner's Office. And you know I have an active investigation going on here. So you need to listen to what I'm telling you."

"But you..." His neck and face flushed a deep red, remembering how he had mocked her and called her out, not realizing who he was talking to.

Kenzie waved this away. "I don't care what you said about me. I already knew what people were saying. It was on the morning news. Janice Martin's room. Now."

He shook his head and staggered away from them, not saying whether he was taking her where she had asked him to or back to an administration office. She followed him anyway. Either one would help. They turned into the housing wing, and he started to work his way down the hall, sticking his head into the doorways of the rooms that stood open to see which was which. There were no nameplates outside the doors, probably for privacy purposes, so a staff member had to either remember each occupant or look inside to see who was there. John was clearly flustered. He probably knew which one was hers when he wasn't.

"Here," he motioned to a closed door, "she's probably having a nap or is out at a therapy appointment."

With complete disregard for the patient's privacy, Kenzie grabbed the door handle and pushed the door open. The door stuck and there was resistance as she pushed it open. On the other side, with part of a sheet looped around a corner of the door, Janice hung.

34

John shouted a curse when he realized why Kenzie had to put her shoulder to the door to get it open. He shoved her to the side while he tried to reach up to unhook the loop of the sheet and get Janice down. Zachary grabbed Janice by the legs and lifted her, muscles straining with the effort. Kenzie did the best she could to help the two of them get her down and, once Janice's body was on the floor, Kenzie immediately took charge, checking for a pulse and starting chest compressions.

"Get help," she told John. He darted out to the hall and raised the alarm, calling out code words to get the attention of any nearby staff. An alarm rang. Too late for Janice, Kenzie knew. She kept up the chest compressions, knowing how unlikely it was that she'd be able to bring the woman back. She didn't have any equipment with her. No epinephrine. No heart monitor. Not even a stethoscope. But the woman was still warm, and Kenzie kept at it so she could at least tell Janice's family that she had done everything she could.

Zachary stood back, white-faced, staring down at Janice's body and Kenzie in her fruitless labor.

John returned to the room with others. Too many people for the tiny room. They squeezed through the half-closed door to gawk at Kenzie and make unproductive recommendations.

"We've called an ambulance," John said. "They won't take long to get here, even though we're outside the city. We're actually pretty close to the fire station."

"It's too late," Kenzie told him.

He stared at her blankly. "But you're doing CPR."

"It's too late. It's not going to do anything. By the time they get here…" Kenzie trailed off, looking down at Janice Martin's red face and the bruises around her neck where the sheet had been tied. She sat back on her heels, stopping the compressions.

"Aren't you required to continue until the EMTs get here?" Zachary asked. "I thought that once you had started, you had to keep it up until…"

Kenzie shook her head. "I'm calling it. I'm a doctor. I declare someone dead or confirm death every time I go to a scene." She looked at her watch and pulled out her phone. She started a voice recording and, announcing the date and her name, started dictating to the phone. After making her initial observations, she turned off the recording. "I need everyone out of the room. You need to clear out until any forensic evidence has been gathered. I'll call in a couple of death investigators to help me out and arrange for transport."

"What's going on?" A woman's voice cut above the babel of the onlookers, and Dr. Richards forced her way in as others were exiting. She looked down at Kenzie and at Janice's body, and her face turned gray. She swore and stepped back as if she had been slapped. "Janice! No!"

Kenzie nodded. "She was hanging when we opened the door. I'm sorry. It's too late for us to do anything for her."

Dr. Richards sank down to sit on the bed, swearing. Kenzie nodded to her and spoke to Zachary. "Can you help the doctor out? She looks a little faint. But she shouldn't be touching anything in here, potentially contaminating the scene. Just out into the hallway. She can wait there."

Zachary nodded. He took Dr. Richards by the arm and coaxed her up and then out of the room, murmuring to her.

Kenzie called the staff from the medical examiner's office who would be needed, then turned her attention to who else would need to be involved. She dialed Detective Garcia's number.

"Dr. Kirsch," Garcia read the caller ID before answering her phone. "Nice to hear from you. Did you call to discuss that impromptu press release with the video this morning?"

"What?" Kenzie was momentarily distracted from her purpose for calling. "How could I have been the one to leak that video? I didn't even have it."

"Nice try. I sent it to you. You might think that it was something the public should be informed about, but we have to follow certain protocols, and doing what you did to leak it like that could cause damage to our case. I know that you want to know as badly as I do what happened to Mr. Isah and see that the perpetrators are brought to justice, so—"

"I didn't get the video," Kenzie said flatly. "When did you send it?"

"Last night." computer keys tapped briefly. "And... I do have a read receipt, so obviously, you opened it."

"Obviously *someone* opened it," Kenzie corrected. "I didn't. I haven't even looked at my email from yesterday yet."

There was a pause as Garcia considered this. She apparently decided she couldn't prove who had opened the email and read it. "Who else would have had access to it? Assuming that it was not someone who hacked your email system."

"Well... Dr. Wiltshire is not in the office. He has remote access to his own email, but I don't know whether he would be able to figure out how to retrieve mine. It is the main department email, so I assume he has all those details. All the lab work comes back to that address, so I guess he could if he needed to retrieve something while he was away. The substitute ME, Dr. Cook. Julie, who handles phones and such when I'm away sometimes. She temps for others in the building. I don't know if you use her?"

"Julie? Sure, I know who she is. I can't imagine her trying something like that. She'd lose all the clients she temps for."

"Yeah. I don't know. I don't think anyone else in the office can access it easily. And I don't leave the computer turned on if Julie and I are away, so no one like the cleaners or death investigators who are there after hours."

"That's a fair number of people who could access it."

"Yeah. And I imagine anyone on your end could access it, too."

Garcia made a growling sound and swore in Spanish under her breath. Kenzie didn't really want to know what she was saying. She was not happy, that was for sure.

"When I find out who leaked it, heads are going to roll," Garcia threatened. "Things like this could really mess up a case."

"At least your name wasn't attached to it. The reporter didn't say that I was the one who leaked the video, but they certainly talked like I was, mentioning that I was the one at the ME's office investigating the death."

"They certainly left people with the impression that the video came from you," Garcia admitted. "I figured it had too, since you were the person I sent it to."

"The only person?"

"No, of course not. I shared it with others who are involved in some way with the investigation. And I saved it to the electronic workspace on our servers so that anyone involved in the investigation can access it."

"That's a lot of people who could have accessed it."

"Yes, it is. And who knows how many of them would be outraged enough to leak it to the press to influence public opinion." Garcia sighed.

"So... I didn't call you because of the video."

"No?" The snap re-entered Garcia's voice. "What's up?"

"I'm at Persons right now—"

"What the hell are you doing there again? I thought you were going to stay away from the place. You've been threatened once already. You shouldn't be there talking to anyone without a police escort to keep an eye on things and attest to anything the witnesses say."

"I was here to see a friend. But while I was here... there's been another death."

"What?"

"Janice Martin, one of the patients you and I talked to."

"She's dead? What happened?"

"You should come over, or send someone from your team. It appears to be suicide."

"I was planning a nice quiet catch-up day today," Garcia grumbled. "What did she have to go and do that for? Why today?"

"Sorry. Wasn't in my plans either."

"I'll be over soon. Don't do anything until I get there."

"I've called my office, so they'll be here shortly too. Help with collecting any evidence and processing the scene."

"What happened? What did she do?"

"Hanged."

"Okay. I'll be there as soon as I can."

35

When Garcia arrived, Kenzie walked her through what had happened, as far as she knew.

"You remember the sculpture she talked about making? The one she was so proud of? When I saw it in the art room garbage, I just had a feeling. I knew that she wouldn't throw it out unless…"

"Unless she was despondent and never planning to come back."

"Yeah. So I insisted on looking in on her. But I was pretty sure…"

"It was a good call."

Garcia looked at the body and swore under her breath. "Two deaths in a facility this size in a week. That's gotta be a record."

"I doubt it. Sometimes, one death can trigger another, especially in someone already having suicidal ideations. And deaths in a facility like this… I have to say, they're not rare. You take a lot of people who are depressed or bipolar, having breaks with reality, or tortured with traumatic memories, and you can imagine… they're not the most stable population."

"But while they're here, they are supposed to be monitored, aren't they? Someone is supposed to be checking on them regularly. Janice said herself that the patients aren't allowed to just stay in their rooms all day. They have to be out where there are other people around."

Garcia glared at the door, still only partially open because of Janice's body on the floor behind it. "Why do they even have doors? Wouldn't it make more sense to have rooms with no doors? So that the people who are supposed to be supervising them can see what is going on? I mean, how do you stop this?" Garcia gestured. "How do you stop people from finding new ways to kill themselves?"

"People have the right to privacy, I guess. They aren't in prison. They need to be able to change and sleep in private. They lose a lot of autonomy in a place like this, and what little they have left is precious." Kenzie pressed her lips shut, thinking about Zachary. How much more she knew about how a place like Persons operated and how it felt to live there from her talks with him about his experiences, when he was willing to share them.

Garcia nodded. "And any death in a psychiatric facility must be reported, right? So you would know how often people die here and from what."

"Well, you would think so. That's the law. But when I first came here to review Isah's death scene, a funeral home was already trying to collect the body. They seem to be in the habit of just calling the funeral home instead of the medical examiner's office. They are required by law to report it to us, but they haven't been. In some jurisdictions, anyone who dies within two days of being released from a mental facility is supposed to be reported, but how many of those do you think get reported?"

"I'm guessing not very many?"

"From what I was able to find—zero are reported under that statute. A few are reported as homicides or suspicious because of the circumstances, but none are investigated or tracked just because they were psychiatric patients who were released too soon."

"Wouldn't it be obvious if they were suicides?"

"Some suicides are obvious. Like this." Kenzie pointed to Janice's body. "But what about suicide by cop or by provoking someone else to harm them? Or the person who steps into traffic or falls from a mountain trail? Or a drowning victim? They might be classified as accidental or undetermined, but if they aren't connected with a psychiatric history…"

"I guess." Garcia thought about this. "So is it just Persons that is not reporting deaths, or all of these types of facilities?"

"Vermont law says that all deaths in mental institutions must be reported, but the psych ward in a public hospital would be a gray area, and that's probably where most of the deaths are. They probably make a judgment call. And there are only a few other psychiatric facilities like this. I don't know what their practices are. I did some calling around to the funeral homes to find out how many pick-ups they have made from Persons in the last year..."

"And?" Garcia looked at Kenzie expectantly.

"There are a lot more than you would anticipate. I would say it is... concerning."

Garcia did not appear to be happy about this. She rubbed her forehead. "Tell me I don't have to open a homicide file for each one."

"You'll have to look at them on an individual basis. I only have a rough list so far. I'll have to take it to Dr. Wiltshire and find out what he wants to do. What *do* we do? Exhume every one of them? What about the ones that have been cremated or shipped out of state? I would assume that at least half are natural or accidental. That's a lot of time to spend on cases that aren't going to lead anywhere."

"But then you wouldn't know how many were related to these drug-induced therapy sessions. The drugs alone can kill them, let alone the effects they might have on a person's mental health. I mean, we're talking about something that's supposed to make them *better,* but I know there has been trouble with some antidepressants that actually make people suicidal when they weren't before."

"Most of those warnings are attached to SSRIs," Kenzie advised. "But while I was waiting for you, I did look up MDMA and suicide."

"And?"

Kenzie hesitated. Garcia put her hands on her hips and gave Kenzie a stern look.

"These are just raw numbers. I haven't dug down into the analysis, and it was a study of teens using recreational drugs, not a study on people in MDMA therapy."

"Okay. Caveat noted. What did you find?"

"The rates of suicide in kids who use MDMA is twice as high as those who use other drugs and not MDMA."

Garcia whistled. "That sounds significant."

"And the rate of suicide is nine times higher in kids using MDMA than that of kids who are not using any recreational drugs."

"Nine times?" Garcia stared at her. "So, you take a kid with no history of drug abuse, and you put them on MDMA for this trauma therapy; you think that kid is now nine times as likely to commit suicide as he would have been?"

Kenzie looked for a way around it. She thought about Rhys. *Nine times more likely to commit suicide after using MDMA?*

She couldn't let that go. She had to call Vera about it again, even if Vera was angry at her for sticking her nose somewhere it wasn't wanted.

She nodded at Garcia. "Like I said, I haven't analyzed the study or its results. But the raw numbers… yes, that's what it looks like."

Garcia looked down at Janice's body. "These people are playing with fire. No, with Semtex!" She swore.

"Those stats wouldn't necessarily carry through to a clinical setting," Kenzie said cautiously. "Where they're using carefully controlled doses, staying with the patient while they are feeling the effects of the drug, and monitoring them carefully afterward, the rates shouldn't be that high. There have been very promising results in using MDMA to treat PTSD."

"I'm beginning to wonder if that's just pumped-up advertising copy. How do you know they aren't just seeing the placebo effect? Or making it up?"

Kenzie shrugged helplessly. She couldn't exactly argue against being paranoid about the results and seriously considering just how much they were being manipulated. They were dealing with two deaths. She had an idea of how many more deaths had not been reported, and it was mind-boggling.

36

enzie had planned to follow Janice's body to the morgue to start on the autopsy immediately. But when she stepped out into the hallway and saw Zachary's face, she changed her mind. It would make little difference to Janice's family whether she did the autopsy Saturday afternoon or Monday morning. But it would definitely make a difference to Zachary.

And to Kenzie herself, if she were honest. She knew she was running on adrenaline, and it wasn't a good idea to perform any medical procedure, even an autopsy, in that state. She didn't want to miss anything or make any mistakes. She didn't know whether Dr. Cook would want to come in to supervise or assist in an autopsy on a Saturday when there was no need for it to be done that quickly. Kenzie hadn't slept the night before; she'd had an emotionally draining visit with Rhys, and then she'd had to deal with discovering Janice's suicide, her initial attempt at CPR, and all the emotional fallout that came from her discussion with Detective Garcia about the other Persons deaths and suicides connected with MDMA use.

"Are you going to the morgue?" Zachary asked, anticipating Kenzie's plans.

She squeezed his arm. "No. Let's go home."

Zachary raised his brows. "Really? Are you sure?"

Kenzie nodded. "Yeah. It isn't urgent. We know what happened. I don't have a big backlog. I can do it Monday."

"If you're sure," he said doubtfully. "Isn't there going to be a big backlash from the media? They're camped out outside. They see the ambulance, police cars, and ME's van; they'll figure out that there was another death and will want details."

"The ambulance left again right away since there wasn't anything for them to do. I had them bring the unmarked van for transport." Kenzie nodded to Carlos. "Can you transport without parading the gurney past the media out there?"

Carlos nodded. "Yeah. We're parked in back, and there is a loading bay. Won't be a problem."

"Good. And Detective Garcia won't have come in a marked car. If we're lucky, the reporters won't have anything to report. Nothing to tip them off to there being another death. And if there is…" Kenzie sighed and shrugged. "If they figure it out and write headlines about it… then what? I can't control what they write. I'm not the one who leaked the video. I didn't have anything to do with that."

Zachary paused to consider the situation before nodding his agreement. "Works for me," he agreed. "I just wanted to make sure that it was what you wanted to do and it wasn't… because of me."

Kenzie guessed she hadn't masked her reaction to Zachary's state very well. "It's not just you."

Kenzie was concerned about him, though. Zachary was quiet on the way home. He didn't ask her questions about Janice's death or anything she had discovered or discussed with Detective Garcia when he had been out of the room. He didn't mention the visit with Rhys or his concerns about the boy's fragile mental health. Kenzie could think of little else. She could only imagine how Zachary's obsessive brain was managing it.

She watched him for clues as to how to help when they arrived home. Zachary paced back and forth through the house, apparently unable to settle down in front of the computer or TV, where he normally would have been on a Saturday afternoon when he took time off to relax.

"Do you want to do something together?" Kenzie suggested. "Or... have a shower or go for a walk?"

Zachary looked at her, continuing to pace. "I don't know. I have all this heat building up inside me. I don't want to explode. I want to do something with it. But there's nothing to do."

"Maybe a nice brisk walk? Try to burn off the energy that way?"

"Maybe," he agreed, but didn't make any immediate move to do so.

"Do you want to talk to Dr. Boyle?"

He immediately scowled. "There's nothing wrong with me. I'm fine, Kenzie. It was just an intense morning."

"I know it was. For me too. I didn't say anything was wrong or that you were going off the rails. I just thought you might want someone to talk to about it. You can talk to me, but if you want to talk to someone else, someone outside of it, you could try Dr. Boyle." Kenzie looked at the time. "Or your OA group meets in an hour. You could go to a session there."

"This isn't anything to do with obsessive behavior."

"Not exactly, no. But it might be what you need to keep from slipping into that territory." She didn't suggest he might be heading toward a covert visit to Bridget's house. He hadn't done that since the Godfrey case had been resolved. But there were other obsessive behaviors that could get worse if they were the only way to calm his brain. "I think the group is open to discussing anything that might be stressing you out. Get it off your chest and out into the open."

"I don't need a meeting." His tone was resentful, and Kenzie didn't pursue it. She hadn't intended to make him feel worse. She had meant to be helpful. Apparently, she had failed at that.

"Okay. I think I will decompress watching cat videos on my computer." Kenzie motioned toward the bedroom, where she would curl up with her computer and a glass of wine. "So I'm interruptible if you decide you want to do something. Go out or watch a movie or chat. Whatever you want. If you don't want to, that's okay too. I shouldn't make suggestions when you didn't ask for them."

Zachary's shoulders relaxed a little. "No, it's okay. I don't know what I want myself. I'm just all wound up. I'll figure it out."

Kenzie stopped herself from suggesting that he might want to take one of his antianxiety pills. He was aware of his options and could decide for himself.

37

Kenzie and Zachary managed to fumble their way through the weekend without stepping on each other's toes too much. Sunday was better than Saturday, with a quick trip to see the Petersons' for family dinner. The highway driving and seeing his family always helped Zachary to de-stress. He and Lorne Peterson exchanged their recent photography, heads together for a couple of hours while Kenzie and Patrick Parker drifted on to other topics. Nothing about work. Lorne and Pat did not have the same appreciation for postmortem procedures as Zachary did. Few people did. And Kenzie didn't want to bring up anything that would stress Zachary out more. She didn't make any mention of Rhys or the cases at Persons. She was sure that Lorne and Pat would have seen the leaked video from the previous day, but they also had enough experience with Zachary not to bring up institutional living or violence, leaving it to him to bring up if he wanted to talk about it.

On her way to the medical examiner's office on Monday, Kenzie was thinking about the leaked video. Had it come from someone at the office? Or from the police department? She certainly hoped that it was the police department, where there were a lot more suspects to choose from and she didn't have to think that it might be someone she worked closely with.

"You want to get to the Martin autopsy right away?" Dr. Cook asked on her arrival, as he brought her out a fresh cup of coffee.

Kenzie accepted it gratefully. "Yeah. As soon as we can. But I need to clear the weekend's email first, check for messages, and ensure everything is organized for the week."

"I've already been through most of it. Nothing too pressing. We might as well get to the autopsy before the media starts to ask questions about a second death at Persons. You know it won't take them long."

Kenzie tried to keep her expression neutral and not show Cook how irritated she was that he had been trying to do her job instead of sticking to his own. He was just trying to help. He thought he was doing a good job by clearing the decks before they started. Had he been the one who opened the video email from Garcia and leaked it to the press? Or left it up on his computer so that someone else saw it and decided to act on it?

She also needed to work on her report on the Isah case. She had most of the information that she needed, but she had wanted to watch the video recordings from Persons before finishing her report to make sure that there wasn't anything else that she hadn't been aware of.

Now that she had seen the altercation before Isah's death, she had to consider how that fit into the situation. And there would be more video from Garcia that Kenzie hadn't watched yet. Whoever had leaked the video to the media had only released the most upsetting one, but it wasn't the only video that was available. Other angles and other segments taken before and after that might provide more context and information about what had happened to Isah. She particularly wanted to see what happened after the staff had dogpiled onto Isah and then led him off. Then what…? He had been alive after being restrained, but had something that happened during that episode caused another problem that Kenzie hadn't noticed in the initial autopsy? And what had happened when they had called the police in, and then had to sedate him? She might need to go over the postmortem once more after watching the rest of the video recordings. Just to make sure she hadn't missed anything.

"Dr. Kirsch?"

Kenzie looked at Dr. Cook. "I would like to get both out on the table. Janice Martin and Leander Isah. If we have both up simultaneously, we may notice similarities that we wouldn't otherwise."

"Good idea. Do you want me to prep while you ensure everything else is covered?"

"Uh, sure. Just don't get started without me."

"I won't."

He was a good guy. Bright, respectful, and a good worker. But Kenzie was still uneasy about him. She didn't like having his fingerprints all over everything. Particularly not in the domains that had been solely her purview. Dr. Wiltshire had always expected Kenzie to take responsibility for the general emails, voicemails, service requests, filing, and other administrative work. She had her own procedures and didn't like someone else messing with them. That was how things got missed or misfiled.

She shook off her misgivings and put her nose to the grindstone. She wouldn't get anything done by worrying about what Dr. Cook, who was supposed to be her superior, was doing. Kenzie sat down at her computer with the fresh cup of coffee and went through what had accumulated over the weekend.

She even checked the archived and deleted emails before moving on, making sure that Dr. Cook had not deleted anything from the main inbox without telling her, thinking that she would be grateful for his taking charge of it.

Once she was satisfied that Dr. Cook was correct and nothing needed her urgent attention, she joined him in the autopsy. The two bodies were laid out on the tables, everything in order for Kenzie to start.

"Let's just do a quick refresher on Isah first," Kenzie suggested. She brought up his file on the computer and skimmed through the notes, transcribed recordings, imaging, and lab reports that had come back so far. She pulled back the drape and glanced over the work that she had done on Mr. Isah. Had she missed anything? Was there anything she needed to look at now that she knew about the violent restraint? She reviewed the bruising that she had already recorded.

She had noted restraint bruises on his arms already. And there was the cracked sternum. Evidence that someone had tried to perform CPR, or had he been hurt in the skirmish?

Kenzie searched for the word *sternum* in her notes and reviewed what she and Dr. Cook had earlier concluded. There was no swelling, bleeding, or bruising around the broken sternum and ribs. He had already been dead when it was fractured. Just as Janice had been when Kenzie had started CPR on her. No blood flow.

"Okay." Kenzie nodded. "Let's start with Janice, then. That is, Miss Martin."

She tapped the record button on the floor with her foot and dictated the usual setup information. Patient name and file number, date, Kenzie's and Dr. Cook's names. Kenzie began with the gross examination. She dictated Janice's vital information. Age, height, weight. She took pictures of the bruises left on her neck. Then she stopped and looked at Dr. Cook.

"We have a problem."

38

Elena Garcia sat down in the observation room. She looked at Kenzie, Dr. Cook, and the two bodies before looking up at the monitors.

"Okay, Dr. Kirsch. I wasn't expecting a call from you so quickly. And it looks like you haven't even started Janice Martin's autopsy yet. Is there something on Mr. Isah's autopsy that has come to light now that you've had a chance to examine the videos?"

"So far, the only video I've watched is the one shown on the news. Was there anything else I should be aware of?"

Garcia shrugged. "Nothing too worrisome. Mr. Isah was still alive after the altercation with the staff. If he was injured in that encounter, I'm sure you'll tell me about it."

"No. Nothing that we could see. I'll review the additional video later. How about his therapy sessions? Anything unusual there? An allergic reaction to the drugs that may have worsened over the next few hours?"

"I'm going to be picking it up this afternoon. I'll let you know when I've got it. Maybe we can find a more secure way to transfer it to you. Since we seem to have a security problem."

Kenzie nodded. "Yeah. Password protect and tell me separately. You can text it to me."

"Sounds like a plan. Anything else I should be watching for when I review them? A reaction to the drugs that seems concerning? Agitation or excitement? Anything going on that hasn't been disclosed."

"That's about it. Do you have the full experimental protocol so that you know what was supposed to happen? Anything on the doses they were using? What if someone wanted out of the trial? Reasons for withdrawal? What government guidelines did they have to work within?"

"I still don't have the full documentation."

"It should be on the file of every person involved in the trial," Kenzie said irritably, shaking her head. "Okay. Let me know when you get a copy."

Garcia indicated the monitors. "So what are we seeing here. Why haven't you started the autopsy?"

"The first step in a postmortem—after we have collected any trace evidence and prepared the body—is the gross examination."

Garcia nodded her understanding.

"What do you see?" Kenzie asked, falling into Dr. Wiltshire's usual Socratic method.

Garcia looked at the monitors as if there might be some small, hidden thing she should pick up on, but shook her head. "I see the bruises on her neck, from hanging. Red flushed face and swollen features."

"Focus on the bruises on her neck."

Garcia looked at the monitors. "Okay…"

Kenzie moved Janice's head this way and that, allowing Garcia to see the bruising all the way around.

"How would you describe the location of the bruising?"

"Around her neck."

"More specifically?"

Garcia struggled. "In a ring around her neck?"

"Yes." Kenzie nodded. "Now, when someone is hung, where is the force of the ligature? How does the ligature lie against the throat?"

Garcia opened her mouth, staring at the monitors. "Gravity pulls the body down, so most of the force is at the front of the neck, with little pressure on the back. And the ligature would be positioned upward?" She ended the suggestion with her tone going up in a question.

"Exactly," Kenzie agreed. "A bruise like this, on the same level all the way around the neck, with no break in the bruising at the back of the neck and no upward angle, suggests strangulation by a second party rather than hanging."

"And then hanged to make it look like suicide rather than homicide."

Kenzie nodded. "This was homicide, not suicide."

"You're sure?"

Kenzie looked at Dr. Cook. She still needed to do some further routine tests and to write her report, but it was clear that Janice Martin had been strangled. He nodded his agreement.

"Yes," Kenzie told Garcia. "This bruise is not consistent with hanging. Someone killed her and then hanged her after death."

"Pretty bold to be able to do that right in the middle of the day in a psychiatric institution where the patients are supposed to be closely monitored."

"Very bold," Kenzie agreed. "Or a conspiracy. He might have had someone watching his back, looking out for any witnesses."

"Right. And a murder after Mr. Isah's death...? What *is* your finding in Mr. Isah's death?"

"I'm still gathering information. It isn't quite as obvious as this." Kenzie pointed at the bruises.

"So that's it, you're not going to actually do an autopsy on Martin?"

"You don't always need to do a full dissection to find cause of death. In fact, we avoid doing a full dissection unless we absolutely need to. I'll do a few non-invasive tests. Some blood, hair, and tissue samples. Just to get a clearer picture of the state of her health prior to death. But I can tell you it wasn't a poisoning."

Garcia laughed tersely. "Fair enough. Well, I'll leave you to it, then. We will question the appropriate parties at Persons and I'll get you the session videos and testing protocol, if I get them today."

. . .

"What did you think of Dr. Richards?" Kenzie asked Zachary as they ate supper. She saw the confusion flash across his face and realized the question had come out of nowhere. "Sorry. I was just thinking."

What she had been thinking of was who might have been involved in a conspiracy to silence Janice Martin and ensure that she couldn't tell them anything more about Isah or the experiments going on at Persons. Of course Dr. Richards had to be one of the suspects. She was very involved with the therapy and with Janice. She had been the first staff member to respond to the orderly's shout for help, which meant she had been nearby. Maybe waiting for the alarm to be raised.

"If someone was murdered, rather than having committed suicide," Kenzie suggested to Zachary, making it a theoretical question rather than telling him anything directly about the case.

His eyes were bright and interested, and he watched her closely for more information.

"And if you had to look at other people in the institution who might have been involved... what do you think of someone like Dr. Richards. She could have been involved, but... she doesn't seem like the type, if you know what I mean."

"Because she's female?" Zachary suggested.

"No... well, maybe partly. But I've dealt with female killers before. I know they exist."

Zachary sipped his water, looking at her, his eyes thoughtful. "We have been programmed to believe that beautiful women are good and wholesome. That someone who acts pleasantly and smiles is good, and someone who is ugly, rough, dirty, or talks rudely or in a way that suggests he is uneducated is bad or dangerous."

As much as Kenzie wanted to deny it, she really couldn't. That was the way the world seemed to work. It was reinforced on TV shows and movies, by women in positions of power who were compelled to portray themselves as beautiful, young, professional women, despite how old and craggy their male counterparts were allowed to be.

Kenzie's own initial reaction to Dr. Richards's beauty was telling. She had difficulty believing that such a beautiful woman could be a doctor. Doctors had to work at all hours of the day, sometimes for incredibly long periods. Young doctors had to work a lot harder and longer than older doctors. They looked tired and careworn. Not bright and fresh and beautiful, looking like they had just come from a hair salon. Dr. Richards seemed like too much of a bombshell to be taken seriously.

Even though Kenzie had known a bombshell or two who had been incredibly successful professional women.

"So when I think of someone like Dr. Richards and my instinct is that it couldn't possibly be her, you think that's just my reaction to her looks, and not a gut instinct based on what I've learned about her over the past week."

Zachary shrugged widely, smiling. "I can't tell you which it is. But it sounds like you know."

Kenzie speared a few beans and ate them.

"And what is *your* gut instinct about someone like Dr. Richards?" she asked Zachary, interested in hearing his perspective. He'd solved his share of murders and dealt with his share of murderers of all persuasions.

Zachary rubbed the back of his neck. "Well…" he rubbed his arms as if trying to scrub something off of them. "I think of a young blond woman who had me completely fooled. Until the… err… *shocking* revelation that she was a sadist who had been deeply involved in several criminal enterprises and had been a participant in the murder."

Kenzie remembered the aide at the special needs school who had turned out to be an abuser. She nodded, remembering how innocent the woman had been able to portray herself as. A victim, even. She had been very good at manipulating people. An expert.

Was Dr. Richards another master manipulator? Someone who used her beauty and apparent youth to influence those around her?

"She's probably perfectly innocent," Zachary said, "but I happen to be a little leery of beautiful blonds working at institutions where they could do great harm."

39

Kenzie had tried several times to reach Vera on the phone to talk to her about Rhys and his admission to Persons. But when she tried in the evening, Vera was probably already settling into bed and not interested in taking any calls. During the day, she had likely spent a good amount of time at Persons, visiting with Rhys and staying close to make sure he was okay. Though she hadn't been there when Kenzie and Zachary had visited on Saturday.

Maybe she was just avoiding Kenzie and didn't want to talk to her. She wasn't under any obligation to, after all, and if she didn't like what Kenzie was saying, why answer the phone?

But Kenzie hoped that she was just busy.

She decided to try calling Vera from the office before taking her lunch break, hoping it would be a better time. Or that Vera would give in and answer Kenzie because she kept calling. Even if it were just to tell her to back off and leave her alone.

"Hello?"

Kenzie was glad to hear Vera's voice. She didn't sound like she knew who was calling, so maybe she hadn't looked at her caller ID before answering the phone. Kenzie put as much warmth into her voice as she could.

"Hi, Vera. It's Kenzie."

"Oh, yes. I'm sorry. You left me a message before, but my voicemail isn't working... Rhys always helped me to retrieve the messages and I can't figure out how to do it without him. I guess this old dog better learn some new tricks." She sighed. "I can't rely on him to do everything for me."

"I'm sorry about that. I didn't want to pester you with phone calls, but I didn't realize you were having problems picking up messages."

"It isn't anything you have to worry about. How have you been? I saw on the visitor log that you and Zachary were by to visit Rhys. You don't know how much I appreciate it. He doesn't have a lot of friends or outside support, and I know how hard it is to visit him now while he is... so unresponsive."

"We're glad to do it. We want to make sure he is okay." Kenzie made a mental note that she and Zachary should go by to see Rhys again, to ensure they visited him at least once a week while he was away from home. Vera needed all the support she could get, and it had to be lonely and frustrating to be the only one visiting Rhys. "Has there been any change? How is he today?"

"About the same. He will have his first treatment this afternoon. They are hoping that he'll be more responsive after that."

Kenzie swallowed. She hated the thought of Rhys doing the MDMA therapy when Persons had already demonstrated that they were, at the very least, having problems with the follow-up supervision required afterward. While it might be a legitimate therapy when handled correctly, she wasn't confident in their ability to keep Rhys safe.

"I wanted to talk to you about that. Do you think you could put off the drug therapy for a day or two while considering the risks? Or maybe get him transferred? I don't know if you heard that there has been another death over there?"

She wasn't sure how Vera could have missed it, but anything was possible. They surely wouldn't be advertising it over at Persons. If Vera didn't listen to the news on a regular basis, it could have escaped her notice.

"I heard about that," Vera admitted. "A suicide. Terribly tragic.

But they said that is what happens when you don't catch someone in time. They need to start the therapy early, and not wait so long. I don't want to put off Rhys's treatment, Kenzie. I don't want him to end up like that poor girl."

"It wasn't waiting too long that killed her," Kenzie assured Vera. "I can tell you that with authority. It had nothing to do with her waiting too long for drug therapy. If that's what they're telling you, it's just a pressure tactic."

"You know that he needs something. We can't just let him sit there like he is now. He is so lost in his world that half the time he doesn't even know if there's someone in the same room. I can't bear to see him drifting away like this. It hurts too much."

Kenzie's chest ached at the thought of Rhys sitting there day after day, for almost a week now, without any progress. Without any sign that he wanted to speak or was trying to reach out to them. Withdrawn inside himself.

"I want him back too. I want a therapy that will change things and bring him back to us. But this experimental treatment is not the answer. And Persons... I would rather he was anywhere right now instead of Persons."

There was silence from Vera for a few breaths. "Why do you say that?" Vera asked finally. "It was a godsend that we were able to get Rhys into this program. I don't understand why you are so against it."

"I can't say a lot about it. But I really don't like him being there. I think if you could get him transferred back to the hospital..."

"The hospital can't do anything for him," Vera snapped. "They already said as much. They have no idea what to do for Rhys. And how many years have they had the chance to figure it out and help him? He was there for months when he was a little boy, and that is no place for a child. The juvenile place they put him in after that was no better. You don't know what it's like, Kenzie, but I've already been through all the other options."

Vera was desperate to find the one thing that would turn things around for Rhys. But Kenzie didn't think Persons was the answer. Not with the deaths that she was aware of. Not just Isah and Martin, but the other names Kenzie had collected when she had made calls to the funeral homes in town. They had a problem.

"I know you wouldn't intentionally put him in danger…"

"Of course not. This is the best place for him, Kenzie, and I won't turn around and put him back into the hospital psych ward. That may be the best place for Zachary when he has his depression, but it is not the place for a boy like Rhys. He's better off at home than there, and I can't look after his needs. I'm an old woman and I'm tired. I've raised my family. I love Rhys dearly, but he's more than I can handle when he is this sick."

"I know. And… we would be happy to help in any way we can. With time, finances, whatever we can provide."

"I'm not asking for charity. We got a grant for him to be admitted to Persons, where the trauma therapy program is. And he needs trauma therapy. In all the time since my poor Clarence was killed, Rhys hasn't had anyone who has really been able to help him to understand and accept what happened." There were sniffles from Vera, which caused a lump in Kenzie's own throat. "He's never talked about what happened that day. What he saw. What Robin did. I thought… that it would be best if he just forgot and that he would be able to go on and have a normal life. You don't remember things that happened to you so young. We kept it quiet for so long, that trying to bring it up now and get him to talk about it… he just can't. We ruined it. We failed him."

"You did what you thought was best for Rhys," Kenzie assured Vera. Though she wasn't sure that was actually true. Vera had done what she thought was best for her daughter, not her grandson. She had tried to protect her from the consequences of her actions. To cover it up, bury it. Rhys had been the victim of that cover-up as much as he had as the sole witness of the murder.

"We've been given one more chance to fix it," Vera insisted. "This is our one chance at a therapy that isn't offered anywhere else, that might address the old trauma. They have so many stories of the patients it has worked for. Miraculous recoveries."

Maybe too miraculous. Kenzie was suspicious of any strong sell tactics from Persons or any other institution. Why were they pushing it so hard?

A private institution like Persons was sometimes set up for charitable reasons or because the owner really believed in what they were doing and wanted to provide a service that just wasn't being offered in public institutions. But that wasn't the vibe she got from Persons. They hadn't professed their faith in the MDMA treatment program and how they believed they were going to change the face of trauma treatment around the world. They had hidden it, pretended that it wasn't happening.

They were in it for the profit. The fact that there were even grants available for the program meant that there was big money behind it. A big pharma company, maybe, hoping to patent a new form of MDMA or a better delivery system. Or an institution that was packaging the entire program to sell it to hospitals and treatment centers all across the country and around the world.

"I know that they have told you a lot of great success stories," Kenzie told Vera. "But you don't even know if those are legitimate stories. And it worries me that they are pushing it so hard. I want Rhys to be treated just as much as you do, but with a legitimate, proven therapy. With something that I know has been tested and proven effective."

"They say that it has been. But they need more patients to provide the numbers. They've been able to prove it in cases that were not as serious, but they need participants like Rhys, who were more severely affected. And especially because he's so young. They don't get a lot of teenagers in a study like this, and they need to prove that it is effective for teens and young people too. They need kids like him in the study if it is going to be used to help them."

That sounded closer to the truth of why they were funding Rhys's treatment and pushing so hard for Vera to put him through the MDMA program. Rhys was a goldmine as a test subject, checking all the boxes for teen patients, severe psychiatric illness, serious childhood trauma, and minority race. They wanted to be able to say that it had been tested on all those demographics.

"They want him for their own purposes," Kenzie told Vera. "They don't care about him as much as they do about selling their system or their product."

"But they can't use him to sell it if it isn't successful," Vera pointed out. "They need good results. It's just as important to them that it be successful as it is to me."

"They'll twist the results to show whatever they want. It doesn't matter whether one individual succeeds or fails. It's the numbers they need. And your permission to put Rhys's face on their literature. A token young Black man."

Silence from Vera. Kenzie had probably pushed it too far. She had offended Vera with her suggestion, and she wouldn't listen to any other arguments.

"I did give them permission to use Rhys's picture," Vera conceded eventually. "They were so convincing. So passionate. And Rhys needs this so badly."

"I know. But I think it is too dangerous. Especially at Persons Residential Care."

40

Kenzie needed to get away from her desk to clear her head. She was bad about working through her lunch hour most days, relying on the sorry vending machine sandwiches down the hallway, which was not a healthy choice. She knew she needed to get up and move around when she had been sitting all morning, but she usually excused herself because sometimes she was standing for an autopsy, so her job wasn't *all* sitting. And the sandwiches… if they were not unhealthy for her body, they definitely were for her emotional state. She needed something that would make her feel alive. Thick brown bread and stuffed full of sprouts, tomatoes, and other veggies. She headed for *It's a Wrap*, a sandwich shop that did some really nice wraps, rolls, and regular sandwiches. They would satisfy her need for something that looked virtuous but tasted good too.

Her phone buzzed in her pocket, and Kenzie pulled it out, thinking it was a text message, probably from Zachary. They sometimes touched base over lunch if things were not too busy. Kenzie liked to know what Zachary was working on and that he was in good spirits. Especially as it was getting later in the fall and she was starting to see what she thought might be warning signs that he had started to slide back into depression.

But it wasn't a text message. It was a voicemail, left by Detective Garcia while Kenzie had been on the phone with Vera. She remembered now that she had seen the call ring through and had meant to call Garcia back when she got through with the call with Vera. But she had been so out of sorts when she had finished the call that she hadn't done it immediately and it had slipped her mind.

Why couldn't Vera just trust Kenzie enough to take Rhys out of Persons? She knew what Kenzie's job was. Kenzie had mentioned the deaths at Persons, so Vera knew that Kenzie was investigating them, even if she hadn't seen the leaked video of Isah's altercation with the staff. Vera knew that Kenzie was looking into one or both deaths at persons, so why didn't she just *listen* when Kenzie told her that there was a problem and Persons was a bad place for Rhys to be? That the MDMA program was too risky to bet Rhys's life on.

On the other hand, Kenzie had to admit that she could see Vera's point. What kind of quality of life did Rhys have if they did nothing? He had no life right now. All he did was stare at the wall. And even if he recovered from this episode and returned to the way he had been before showing up on the street in some kind of fugue, what kind of a life was that? If he had been given the choice of staying the way that he was or the possibility of dealing with his traumatic past and being able to speak to communicate like the rest of the kids he went to school with, wouldn't he have taken it, even knowing that there were risks?

Maybe he would be willing to take the chance of having a reaction to the drug, resulting in permanent physical disability or death, but what about the rest? What if it made his traumatic memories worse? Introduced flashbacks and bad trips? What about the risk of abuse by one of the therapists? Would he really choose to be exposed to possible predators while in a drug-induced, vulnerable state?

She couldn't see him agreeing to all the risks. But Vera was his guardian, and she was allowed to make that choice, to put him into a situation that could be dangerous to him physically, emotionally, and psychologically. Kenzie shook her head, scowling, and stepped forward to cross the street.

"Careful!" a bystander warned sharply, grabbing Kenzie's arm.

Kenzie froze, and a heavy dump truck went barreling by in front of her.

Kenzie put her hand over her heart. "Whew! Thanks!"

"I could see he wasn't going to stop," a tall man with silver-framed glasses said, peering at her as if to make sure she really was unharmed. "The light was red when he went through, but you have to watch. Don't be looking at your phone while you're crossing the street."

Kenzie looked down and saw that the phone was still in her hand, though she had not listened to the message from Detective Garcia.

"I wasn't, actually, but I was distracted by my thoughts. Thank you for grabbing me!" She laughed. "I don't normally thank strangers for grabbing me in the street, but in this case, I'll make an exception."

He laughed as well, and they crossed the street together now that it was safe.

"Can I buy you lunch?" the man asked.

Kenzie shook her head. "I should be buying you lunch, to tell the truth! As a thank you for saving my life. But actually... I'm just going to grab something quick and then get back to the morgue."

He gave her a confused look. Kenzie laughed.

"I work there," she explained. "I promise I'm not a zombie."

"Well..." he feigned relief at this, wiping his brow. "I'm glad to hear that. Maybe I could call you sometime...?"

Kenzie shook her head. As grateful as she was that this man had kept her from being flattened by a dump truck, she wasn't interested in pursuing any kind of relationship with him, even if it was just friendship.

"Umm... I'm sorry, no. I'm not interested. I'm... in a relationship."

"And that keeps you from talking to people?"

"Sorry," Kenzie brushed him off again. She looked around and decided to change her destination. The way the man's body was positioned, he was almost certainly going to *It's a Wrap* himself, and Kenzie didn't want to have to prolong the discussion any longer. "Thank you again. I've got to run."

She turned and walked the other way down the street. The man stood there, scowling after her. Kenzie grimaced to herself and hoped that she wouldn't run into him anywhere else in the next few days. Some people just didn't understand the word "no," and she didn't want to keep bumping into him. She would go back to vending machine sandwiches for the next few days, until she had given it enough time that she wouldn't be worried about his looking for her on the street.

She rounded a corner and found a hole-in-the-wall burger joint she had never been to. Crossing her fingers that the food there would at least be edible, Kenzie entered. It was a nice, clean, open cafe. Dark after being out in the bright sunshine outside but, after she blinked a few times, her eyes adjusted so that she could read the chalk menu board. They did not have a wide selection. Kenzie smiled at the woman behind the counter. A young woman, her hair pulled back and secured in a ponytail.

"A single burger and fries."

"You want a drink to make that a meal?"

"Uh, sure." Kenzie looked around. "Fountain drinks?"

"Over there." The woman pointed. "Self-service." She handed Kenzie a cup. "You go ahead and get the drink while I grab you a burger."

There were people there ahead of Kenzie, chatting and picking up their orders, and people coming in behind her. It seemed like the place was popular. That was a good sign.

The burgers looked and smelled fantastic. So much for getting an ultra-healthy sandwich for lunch. But Kenzie had barely escaped death. What was one burger now and then? She needed the iron in the beef anyway.

With the burger and fries in a bag and the cup all clutched in one hand, Kenzie remembered again about the message from Detective Garcia as she headed back toward the office. She used her other hand to dig out the phone. She thumbed through her screens again to find the voicemail, then pressed play and held it to her ear.

"Dr. Kirsch," Garcia's words were clipped. She sounded somehow more Hispanic on the phone. Or maybe it was the urgency in her tone. "I have received the therapy videos from Persons. Well, not everything, obviously, but I have video of Isah's latest sessions, and you are going to want to view them."

Kenzie stopped at the corner and waited for the light to change to allow her to cross safely. This time, she *was* paying attention to her phone when her attention should be on the traffic. She pulled it away slightly while she looked around, then put it up to her ear again.

"I'll send you an email with a link," Garcia promised on the voicemail. "But they will be password protected."

There was a hand on Kenzie's shoulder. She pulled away sharply while listening to the end of the message, irritated, knowing immediately that it would be the same man, getting after her for not paying attention to the traffic and putting herself in danger yet again.

"The password is—"

Before Kenzie could finish turning to glare at the man for daring to touch her again, it was too late. A second hand landed on her back, and both shoved suddenly and violently.

Kenzie was not braced for such a thing, and even if she had been, it was a hard, strong shove. She had an instant to register that it couldn't be the man who had held her back before, but she was staggering away from him, trying to stay on her feet. The momentum of his shove took her off the curb and out into the street. Kenzie knew the light hadn't changed yet and tried desperately to stop herself and get out of the traffic lane.

There was a scream, the screech of tires from more than one vehicle, and an impact.

41

Zachary was focused on the insurance reconstruction case to see what needed to be done, shutting everything else out. He knew his phone had buzzed a few times, but he ignored it.

The phone started to ring. Not just the vibration that he was expecting with the sound being switched off. A ring that meant that someone on his important caller list was calling through his do-not-disturb function. And yet, it wasn't one of the programmed sounds that would tell him who it was. Zachary looked over at it.

Blocked caller ID.

He rolled his eyes. Who was trying to reach him? For his phone to be ringing, the caller had to have dialed him two or three times in a row, not allowing any time in between. The behavior of someone who really needed to reach him and was going to keep trying until he got through.

He picked it up and swiped the onscreen slider to answer the call. "Zachary here."

"Zachary, thank goodness I finally got through to you!"

Zachary took only an instant to identify the voice. "Mario?"

Mario Bowman had helped him out in the past, and Zachary counted him as a real friend. A cop who knew how to make things happen, who could be counted on if Zachary needed help getting through to the right person on a case, who knew how to grease the wheels so that things happened.

"Yeah. You had your phone turned off, or what? Never mind. It's Kenzie. She's been in an accident."

Zachary's grip tightened on the phone. "What?"

"Motor vehicle versus pedestrian. Get over to the hospital."

"I will." Zachary swallowed. "Is she okay?"

"I don't know many details yet. She's injured. Rushed to the hospital in an ambulance. Cops on the scene are still getting the story. But I wasn't about to wait until they actually have something to say."

"Okay, thanks, Mario. I owe you."

"Are you driving yourself? Maybe you should take a taxi, Zach. I don't want you to be in an accident too."

"No, I'll be fine." Zachary wasn't going to wait around for someone to pick him up. He needed to be with Kenzie. He couldn't wait one minute. He disconnected the call and put his phone in his pocket.

He was hyperfocused on the drive, weaving his way through traffic and taking shortcuts through alleys, every little thing that could shave a second off the trip. He tried not to think of anything that Mario had said, but the words kept ringing through his head. *Rushed to the hospital. Vehicle versus pedestrian.* It was bad. A pedestrian had no protection from a car. A ton of metal racing toward an unprotected human at sixty miles an hour.

It was bad. Would she even be alive when he got to the hospital? Would she be in surgery? Would they take him off to a private room to break the news to him, confessing that she had died or that they didn't know if she were going to make it?

He didn't know how he would manage without her. What had started as a casual date and friendly relationship had developed into something far more for him.

He had known he loved Kenzie but didn't realize how much until that moment. How could he possibly live without her now? They had been weaving their lives together, fixing all the problems, building up their communication, learning about each other a little more each day.

He didn't know if he could live without her.

He pulled into one of the empty stalls designated for the emergency room. He ran into the hospital, seeing and hearing nothing around him until he reached the inquiries desk.

"Kenzie Kirsch," he said urgently, "she was coming in by ambulance. Is she here? Is she okay?"

The woman gave him a tolerant smile. She moved slowly, ridiculously slowly, like she was putting on an act for a comedy skit. Zachary wanted to shout at her to hurry up.

"Please," he said urgently as she typed something into his computer. "Kenzie Kirsch. K-I-R-S-C-H."

"I think I know how to spell *Kirsch*, considering we have a whole wing named that."

Zachary opened his mouth, and nothing came out. Despite his urgency to discover what had happened to Kenzie, he was stunned by this information. He knew that the Kirsch family foundation was very generous with its donations, and that they were primarily in the area of medical research because of the fact that Amanda had died from kidney disease, which they hoped to find a cure for. And he knew they had recently been giving more money in mental-illness-related causes too.

But he had no idea that a wing of the hospital was named after them. Was that a new development, or had it happened years ago and Kenzie had just never mentioned it?

"Kenzie. MacKenzie, actually, but she goes by Kenzie."

"If you'll sit in the chairs over there," she motioned toward the waiting area, "someone will come talk to you."

"Is she okay? Is she alive?" Zachary was immediately panicked that she hadn't told him anything about Kenzie's condition. Was that because it was too late? Over and over again, his brain replayed a scene of a grave-looking doctor breaking the news that Kenzie had already passed.

"Someone will talk to you," she repeated firmly.

Zachary stood looking at her, waiting for more information. She looked back at him, not giving in. Eventually, Zachary dragged himself over to the waiting room chairs. But he couldn't sit down. He paced back and forth, his guts tied in knots. He was falling to pieces. He knew he should be strong for Kenzie, but he didn't even know if she were still alive.

"Sir, you need to sit down." A Black security guard stepped in front of him, blocking his path. Zachary looked at the broad chest and broader gut, the high-vis X that made him look like a crossing guard, and the utility belt with a walkie-talkie jammed into a holster. He turned around and paced back the other way. The security guard followed him, persistent. "Sir. Sir! You need to sit down if you're going to wait in here. You're disrupting the other patients and visitors."

Zachary looked around at the people who were waiting in the chairs. Most were ignoring him while they tapped on their phones. A few were watching with keen interest. But he didn't see anyone who was alarmed by the fact that he was pacing.

"Disrupting them? I'll sit down when someone lets me know how my girlfriend is doing. She was hit by a car! I don't know if she is even alive!"

"I'm sorry to hear that, sir, but you need to respect the others who are using the waiting room the way it is intended." He rested his hand on his walkie-talkie, as if he might have to call someone, and that would show Zachary.

"There's nothing that says I can't pace. I'm not taking up any extra chairs, so there's room for everyone to sit down."

"*I* say you can't pace," the power-hungry security guard said in a tough tone. Who did he think he was, Dirty Harry? "Now you can sit down, or you can leave. I don't think you want to be arrested, do you?"

"Arrested for pacing?"

"For trespassing, after I kick you out," he said with a satisfied smirk.

"*I can hear him out there!*"

Zachary turned his head as a familiar voice emerged from one of the curtained examination areas.

"*Just go get him.*"

"Kenzie!" Zachary bolted toward the voice. "Kenzie?"

The guard chased after him, grabbing at his sleeve and missing, too out of shape to keep up with Zachary's sudden footrace.

"Where are you? Kenzie?" Zachary pulled open a couple of empty curtained areas before a doctor or nurse in green scrubs opened one of the curtains and stuck his head out.

"Are you Zachary?"

He dashed over to the cubicle. "Kenzie?" He pushed through the curtain and found Kenzie sitting on a bed. She was wearing her regular clothes, not a hospital gown. He didn't see any blood. No IV or bandages. She looked just like she did every day when she got home from work. Maybe a little frazzled, but she was often that way after work too.

42

Kenzie looked at Zachary and shook her head. "Look what the cat dragged in."

Zachary's wild eyes met hers, confused. "What?"

"You look like someone dragged you out of bed and roughed you up. What was going on out there? You fighting with security?"

"Nobody would say what had happened to you. They said I had to wait. The guard said I couldn't pace and had to sit down in a chair or he would kick me out. What's *wrong* with people?"

He got close enough to take her hands in his and look her over, eyes searching for any injuries. "Mario said you got hit by a car."

"Yeah, I did." Kenzie indicated the tear in the knee of her pants. "Scraped my knee. It hit the brakes before it hit me. It was mostly stopped. I think I fell because of the push, not the car."

"The push?"

"Someone pushed me. I stumbled onto the road." Kenzie shook her head. "I was off-balance and couldn't stop. There were cars, people screaming. I think I hit my knees before the car's bumper hit me. It happened so fast, and I hit my head."

Kenzie probed in her curly hair for the tender bump. "It's not bad. Just a small contusion. They want to do an x-ray, but you know they won't find anything in there, right?"

Zachary didn't smile at the joke. He was still confused and off-balance. Kenzie could understand the sentiments.

"I'm okay, Zach. I promise. I blacked out for an instant when I hit my head. That's why they insisted that I come in to get checked out. Otherwise, I would just have gone back to the office. But it couldn't have been more than a few seconds. It didn't seem like any time passed for me. I hit my head and then I was opening my eyes, getting up." Kenzie looked at the doctor who had come to talk to her before she'd heard Zachary arguing with the guard in the waiting area. "You don't think it's anything serious, do you?" She said it in a tone that told him what the answer was supposed to be. She wasn't asking whether she might have any serious damage. She was telling him to confirm to Zachary that she was just fine. Because she was.

"People get knocked on the head all the time," the doctor assured Zachary. "Nine times out of ten, it's nothing. They are told to go home and get some rest for a few days. We'll do some imaging to ensure there is no skull fracture, no blood pooling inside or significant swelling. Then I'm sure we'll be sending Dr. Kirsch home with you."

Zachary nodded, his eyes searching the doctor's face for the truth of the matter.

"Were you asleep?" the doctor asked sympathetically.

Zachary looked baffled by the question. He shook his head, then looked at himself. He seemed to realize for the first time that his feet were bare. He tugged at his pants with a drawstring waist. Not pajamas, but something he wore around the house when he didn't have to go out anywhere and just wanted to be comfortable. He ran his fingers over his head to pat down the hair that was standing straight up. He kept it cut very short so that it was low maintenance, and Kenzie had never seen it all sticking out like a porcupine before.

"Oh." Zachary started to get red. "No, but I just ran out of the house. I didn't think about anything. I just had to get here. They said Kenzie was hit by a car, and I thought the worst…"

She could only imagine how bad he'd thought it was. He was a master catastrophizer, an expert at jumping directly to the worst possible outcome. He'd thought Kenzie's next stop would be her own autopsy table.

"I'm okay," she reassured him. "More embarrassed than anything. People must have thought I was crazy, jumping out into the street in the middle of traffic like that. But somebody…" She frowned, trying to remember each second leading up to the accident. "Somebody pushed me. Intentionally."

"They pushed you?" Zachary repeated. He didn't say it in a tone of disbelief, like the cop who had first responded to the scene had. He immediately believed that was exactly what happened and was trying to work it all out. "It wasn't just someone who bumped into you? Did you see who it was?"

"No. I was just… There was a hand on my shoulder and then my back, and they shoved with both hands. Not an accident," Kenzie told the doctor, who was listening with diagnostic interest. *Concussion? Paranoia? Was Kenzie someone who normally told tall tales or made everything bigger than it was? Or was it a symptom?*

Zachary could read the physician just as well as Kenzie. He shook his head. "If she says she was pushed, then she was pushed."

"There was probably a crowd. People get jostled. For someone to push you out into the street like that… they had to know that you could be killed. I can't see anyone taking that chance."

Zachary's and Kenzie's eyes met as they both tried to work through the problem of who would want to kill her. Kenzie looked away. It wasn't something they could discuss in front of the doctor. She had already said enough to make him suspicious about her mental state. That wouldn't do. She wanted to go home for the night, not to have to stay at the hospital for observation. She hoped that Zachary would understand why she wasn't pursuing it.

"So once I get the x-rays done, I'll be able to go home," she told him.

The doctor didn't immediately nod, as she hoped he would. He motioned for Zachary to move back from Kenzie, which he did. Then he shone his light in Kenzie's eyes and ran her through a basic neurological check and asked her about her symptoms. "Any dizziness? Double vision?"

"No." Kenzie poked at the bump on her head again. "Just a throbbing headache."

"Yeah. Follow my finger with your eyes. Any nausea?"

"No. In fact, I'm starving." Kenzie looked around her. She was still feeling a little shaken and out of sorts. She knew what had happened, but there had been so much confusion at the scene of the accident, she wasn't sure who she had talked to or what had been done. "I had gone out to get lunch... but I don't know what happened to it."

At the doctor's questioning look, she explained further.

"I was holding my lunch when I... got hit. I don't know what happened to it. So I didn't get a chance to eat."

"Oh." He chuckled. "Well, why don't you have your partner go down to the cafeteria to get you something while we finish this examination." His eyes turned to Zachary. "Now that you know she's all right."

Zachary nodded, confirming that he wouldn't cause any further disruption. He looked again at his bare feet and pants and patted at the pockets, which were suspiciously limp. "I don't think I brought my wallet," he said, getting red. "I just flew out of the house without thinking about anything."

Kenzie smiled reassuringly. "You can probably tap your phone. If you're worried about it, my purse is around here somewhere..."

The doctor indicated it under the edge of the bed, but didn't pick it up. Zachary retrieved it so that Kenzie didn't have to bend over, and handed it to her. Kenzie unzipped the closure, chuckling to herself about the doctor's and Zachary's reluctance to touch it themselves. Was it memories of their mothers insisting on handbag privacy that made men afraid to touch a woman's purse or to open it? Or was it the possible risk of seeing or touching a feminine product? It was funny to see this unusual respect for a patient's or partner's privacy in action.

Kenzie found her wallet and pulled out her bank card, which she handed to Zachary. "There you go."

"What did you want me to get for you?"

"You know what I like. I did have a burger. Though I meant to get a healthier sandwich when I went out. But..." Kenzie trailed off. She didn't want to tell Zachary in front of the doctor about the man who had stopped her from stepping into traffic and then wanted to go out with her. Had he been the one who had pushed her? A complete stranger who she had spurned? Or was it just a random act by someone else? Or was it something more sinister?

Zachary looked at her with concern, waiting for her to finish her sentence. Kenzie shook her head. "I'll tell you about it later. But just... anything, really. I'm starving. I would take anything."

He nodded his agreement. "Okay. I'll try not to be too long."

43

It took too long to get home after the accident. Everything at the hospital always seemed to take much longer than it should. Kenzie knew she was impatient to get home, which skewed her sense of time and how long it was taking. Still, it really was ridiculous to have to wait for hours for an x-ray to be reviewed when they had the imaging almost immediately. And Kenzie knew all the post-concussion protocol. She shouldn't have to wait for the doctor to tell her everything she should and shouldn't do during the next few days.

She was as patient as possible, but Zachary was a bulldog, harassing the nurses and staff to keep things moving forward. If it had been for himself, she knew he would have been quiet and compliant and would never complain about the service he was receiving. But it was different when it was something to do with Kenzie. He was willing to step up and be a pain in the neck so they would get rid of him as soon as possible. Was that something he had learned while he'd been with Bridget? Or had he always been that way, used to looking after his younger siblings and ensuring that their needs were provided for or, later, for the other children in foster care with him whose needs might be ignored or neglected?

When it was time to go home and Kenzie had finally been

completely checked out and taken to the door in a wheelchair, they ran into another small snag.

"You don't have your wallet," Kenzie remembered. "I should drive."

"I can drive without it once."

"If you get pulled over, you could be in big trouble for driving without a license."

"I have a license."

"But you have to have it with you."

"It wouldn't make that much of a difference. And I'm not going to get pulled over. I'll drive slow."

"I should do it, just to be sure," Kenzie told him firmly, expecting him to give in.

"You shouldn't be driving."

"They didn't say I couldn't drive."

"They said that you have a mild concussion. You're not supposed to drive when you're concussed."

"And you know this from personal experience?" Kenzie challenged.

"Yes."

"And did it stop you from driving?"

Zachary opened his mouth and didn't answer, looking trapped. A red flush crept up his throat and into his ears and face. "Well, you would have told me not to," he pointed out lamely.

Which, of course, was completely true. She wouldn't have let him drive concussed. Kenzie rolled her eyes, which wasn't the best choice given how her head was already feeling. "Okay, fine," she conceded. "But you have to be careful. I don't want you getting a bunch of tickets and fines because you don't have your wallet with you."

"When was the last time you saw me get pulled over?"

Despite the way Zachary drove, fast and often reckless, in Kenzie's opinion, she had never known him to get pulled over by the police. He seemed to have been touched by the good luck fairy and got away with it.

"Drive slowly," she insisted.

Zachary nodded. He offered his hand to Kenzie as she stood up from the wheelchair. She waved him off. "I'm fine. I really am. It's nothing more than a headache."

"You need to take care of yourself."

"I am."

He took her by the arm anyway, and they walked more slowly than they normally would to Zachary's car, which he'd had to move a few hours earlier out of the emergency room space to a space in a more distant parking lot. Zachary had offered to drive around to the door to pick Kenzie up, but she had declined. It wouldn't hurt her to get a little exercise and fresh air to clear her head. She pretended they were just out for a stroll together on a date. Maybe in a park or somewhere romantic. It took a bit of imagination, but Kenzie had learned from Dr. Boyle to reframe experiences and get what pleasure she could out of them. Better to enjoy the positive than to focus on the negatives.

"So, tell me what happened," Zachary told Kenzie once she was settled on the couch with a small bowl of ice cream, which he insisted would make her feel better. She hadn't objected. That was the kind of medical care she could buy into.

She shrugged uncomfortably at his question. "It's a bit mixed up. I mean, I remember everything that happened, but I'm not sure what it all means."

He nodded. "Just go through what you remember and we'll try to sort it out. It's like that sometimes with accidents, everything can get jumbled."

Kenzie related her walk to the burger joint, including the man who had prevented her from crossing the street when the dump truck ran the red, and how he had persisted in trying to get to know her better.

"Do you think that's who pushed you?" Zachary asked. "He was irritated because he'd saved you from the traffic and then you didn't respond to his advances, so he pushes you out into traffic to let fate have its way with you?"

"It makes a twisted kind of sense. But I don't think so. I don't think it's anything to do with him. I just…" She frowned and shook her head, trying to remember each thought and perception separately and in sequence. "I remember thinking just as I was pushed that it *wasn't* him. I don't know if I saw him or if I realized that the hands were too high or low or the wrong size. I don't remember what it was."

Zachary nodded. "Maybe you caught a glimpse of his face or clothing. Something that told you it wasn't him. Did you have an idea of who it *was*? Did you recognize it as being someone else? Even just a flash of recognition?"

"No… I don't think so. But I don't know. It all happened so fast."

"Was it a man?"

Kenzie pursed her lips and closed her eyes, trying to picture it and to remember each instant before she had gone staggering out into traffic. And after that. She turned to see who had pushed her.

"I think so. I'm pretty sure it was. But what does that tell me? That doesn't get me any closer to identifying who it was or why someone would do that."

"Have you had any threats lately?"

"No." Kenzie frowned, thinking about it. "Well… maybe."

"Maybe?" Zachary raised his brows, studying her.

"Well… there was a sort of a threat left on the medical examiner's office main phone number. But it didn't use my name and didn't threaten anything; just said… to mind my own business or something along those lines. That my friends would benefit from me keeping quiet."

Zachary looked as mystified by this as Kenzie had been when Dr. Cook had played the message for her. What was it supposed to mean?

"Was it… a foreign accent? Someone who spoke English as a second language?" Zachary suggested.

"No. I mean, I have no way of knowing. It was a computerized voice. Text-to-speech. So they could have any kind of accent or be any gender. There's no way to know."

"Right. It just sounds backward. They should say that if you want to protect your family from harm, you'll listen to them, but instead, they say if you want your family to benefit…?"

Kenzie nodded. "Dr. Cook and I wondered if they might be referring to Rhys and to you."

Zachary looked at her blankly, shaking his head slightly in confusion.

"As people who might have need of psychiatric services."

"Because you think this message was from…"

"Well, with what's going on right now, we just assumed it was coming from someone at Persons. Because of the timing. I had just been out there and, if someone was upset by my investigation…"

"Ah…" Zachary nodded, filling in the blanks. "Okay. You go to Persons and get the body of the man who died there."

"Isah."

"Isah. And then you go back to interview people about what happened leading up to his death."

Kenzie nodded her agreement. "Talked to some of the staff and the patients, tried to figure out what exactly had happened leading up to Isah's death."

"And that was when you got the call?"

Kenzie nodded. "That night, I think."

"So you think that whoever left that message might have been the person who pushed you into traffic?"

Kenzie appreciated that he didn't say "the person you think pushed you into traffic" or "who allegedly pushed you into traffic." He believed her from the start without any concrete evidence.

"I don't know. Honestly, like I said, there wasn't any threat of violence in the phone call, so I don't think so. But there's no way to know for sure."

"How did the person who left that message know you had friends who might need psychiatric care?"

"Dr. Cook asked about that too. I don't know. It isn't like Vermont is a big state. You hear things about other people, know things about them because you happened to work at the same place together or go to the same restaurant or any of those sorts of things. Or maybe they just assumed that I had friends who needed psychiatric care. I mean… doesn't everyone?"

"More or less," Zachary admitted. "We don't always know what services our friends have need of, but mental health challenges are so prevalent…"

"Yeah, that's kind of what I thought. Not that someone knew about you specifically, but knew that I would know someone who needed services."

"Did you talk to anyone at Persons about me or Rhys?"

Kenzie shook her head. She didn't think she had, but it was hard to remember what had happened on what days. Even without a concussion, it was easy for the days to run together and get muddled. "No. At least, I don't think so."

"Your instinct says it was someone at Persons, so you are probably right about that. Did you let the police know?"

"Yes. I informed Detective Garcia. So she went with me the next time and we stuck together."

"What was her assessment of… the threat level?"

"Neither of us took it very seriously."

"Well, maybe you should call Garcia and let her know what happened."

Kenzie didn't like to come off as hysterical. She did her best to present herself as a level-headed, intelligent professional. Any time she had to present something that was out of the ordinary or sounded like a bizarre coincidence, it made her uncomfortable, like she had failed somehow.

"Do you think that it's related?"

"There was a threatening call, and then someone committed violence against you. I think you have to treat it as if it is related. Deal with it as a serious threat. What if whoever it was escalates the next time?"

Kenzie's stomach and chest tightened. She didn't want to think of the possibilities. She didn't want to think about the violence that they had been targeted with in the past.

Zachary was right. She needed to let Garcia know.

44

D r. Kirsch," Garcia's voice was sharp and irritated. "I was beginning to worry that something had happened to you. Where have you been?"

"Uh… I was in the hospital, actually. They always make you shut off your cell phone. What's going on?"

"I left you a message this morning about the therapy videos. I thought that you would call me right back."

"You did…?" Kenzie rubbed the bump on her head, wincing. "I think… did I listen to that message?" She tried to remember what she had been doing before the accident. "I might have, I'm sorry. It's all scrambled."

"What happened to you? Are you okay? Why were you in the hospital?"

"I was hit by a car."

She heard Garcia's sharp intake of breath and curse. "Are you okay? I had no idea."

"Yeah, I'm okay, just a bump. Well, a mild concussion, but I'm sure that will disappear within a few days. My dad always said I have a hard head."

"When you say you were hit by a car, do you mean that someone hit your car with their car, or…?"

"No. I was a pedestrian. The car had stopped or just about stopped when it hit me, so it wasn't too bad, but I was knocked out, and I'm having some trouble remembering everything that happened right before the accident. I forgot that you had left a message. I think I was supposed to call you, but I don't remember why."

"I called to tell you I had gotten video from Isah's latest therapy sessions. I sent them to you with a link, and there is a password to open them so no one else can except you. Try to outsmart our leak."

"I'll get out my laptop and take a look. I'm at home," Kenzie added lamely. Like Garcia couldn't figure that part out herself.

"Are you sure you should be? If you're injured, you need to wait until you've recovered…"

"It really isn't that bad. Just a small bump. Minor concussion. The thing is… I was talking to Zachary about it, and he asked whether I'd had any threats lately…"

It took Garcia only an instant to connect the accident and Zachary's comment with the telephone threat. "And you had received one. Do you think it's related?"

"It feels like it could be related, or it could be completely separate. The phone caller didn't make any threats of violence. If he had, then maybe I would say they are connected for sure. But he never said he was going to do anything to me. He didn't use my name and he didn't make any overt threats. The stuff that was vaguely threatening… was about my friends being able to get help. Which I still think was a weird thing to say in a phone threat."

"You thought the phone threat was related to Persons. Have you had any further thoughts on if there was someone at Persons that it might have related to? Anything anyone has said to you since to clarify the situation?"

"Not really."

"Okay… well, I don't think I need to tell you not to go there on your own. If you're going to go by there to talk to anyone, call me first. You are not a cop, and you shouldn't be acting like one. And even cops need backup."

"I'm not planning to go back… Well, that's not exactly true, because I plan to go back to visit with Rhys in a few days."

"Talk to me first. Even if you have a legitimate, non-threatening reason to be there, someone could still take it as snooping and decide to come after you."

"Okay. I'll let you know, I guess."

"You need to watch those videos," Garcia said grimly. "I wouldn't normally push it. I'd tell you to stay home and rest and relax. The videos will still be there when you get back and are ready to take on your usual workload. But in this case... I think you need to see them."

"Do you want me to call you back after I've viewed them?"

"You will," Garcia said, and disconnected.

Kenzie hung up, thinking that was an odd response. But she was concussed, so maybe she wasn't thinking straight or had missed some kind of signal.

Zachary looked at her as she stood up. "Are you okay? Can I get you something?"

"I don't need to be babied. I'm okay. Garcia had sent me some videos this morning that she wants me to look at."

"She can't wait?"

"No. She said I'll want to look at them right away." She looked at Zachary. "They're videos of one of my patients."

He nodded. "Okay. Well... let me know if I can help with something. I'm happy to do it."

"Anything?"

Zachary didn't balk and wonder what horrible task she might be about to assign him. "Anything," he repeated.

Kenzie smiled. "Just a Tylenol and a glass of water?"

"Your wish is my command. Is it bad? Do you need something stronger?"

"I think the Tylenol will be enough."

"Okay. I'll bring it in to you."

Kenzie retrieved her laptop and sat down on the bed with it. She had a home office, which she and Zachary shared but, more often, they chose to work elsewhere in the house where they felt more comfortable. Kenzie's preferred station was on the bed. Her posture was probably horrible, but it was comfortable for her.

As she opened her email and went to her phone to find the password Garcia had left in the voicemail message, Zachary brought in a couple of Tylenol tablets. He put them on Kenzie's bedside table with a glass of water. He nodded and left her alone without trying to engage her in conversation. She was working, and he knew what it was like to get distracted by someone else when he was trying to work.

It seemed to take forever to log in to the email server, find Garcia's email, download the video files, and then enter the password to open them. Kenzie didn't know if it was her perception of time that was messed up, or if she was having more trouble than she realized performing these simple tasks with a concussion. Maybe it was just slow.

Eventually, she pressed play on the first of the videos.

She saw Dr. Miller, one of the doctors who had been there the night when she picked up Leander's body. He welcomed Leander into the treatment room and had him sit on the couch. Leander appeared to be anxious and jittery as he watched Dr. Miller prepare an injection.

"You seem nervous," Dr. Miller said in a calm, even voice. "Is there anything particular that is bothering you?"

"I don't want to do this," Leander said.

"Well, we both know that this is what is best for you. You want to get better, don't you? This is how you're going to get better. With treatment. Sometimes treatment is difficult, like debriding a burn. But you need to clear the old, dead stuff out of the way so that new growth can occur. All the old trauma is like scar tissue that we need to remove so that you can heal properly."

Leander didn't argue the point. He sat there watching as Dr. Miller swabbed a spot on his arm, then injected him. Kenzie was anxious watching the doctor pushing the plunger slowly, smoothly injecting the clear fluid into Leander's vein. Her own heart started to race, and she watched Leander for signs that it was affecting him.

"That wasn't so bad, was it?" Dr. Miller asked.

Leander was staring off into space. "That's not the part that hurts."

They continued with small talk, though Leander didn't seem too engaged with the conversation. But gradually, his body language and behavior changed. He leaned toward Dr. Miller when he talked. He held his gaze longer and moved in closer. Dr. Miller began to guide the conversation toward Leander's traumatic past.

"Do you remember what we talked about last time?"

Leander shook his head. "No."

"We talked about when you were arrested back home in Africa. Do you remember that?"

"I don't want to talk about that."

"That's why we're here, Leander. It's time for you to think about these things and to talk about them so that you will be able to get better and move on. You don't want to spend your whole life in Persons, do you?"

"The rest of my life?"

"The rest of your life," Miller agreed.

"No. I don't want to be here the rest of my life."

Kenzie closed her eyes briefly. In fact, Leander would spend the rest of his life in Persons. He had probably assumed that his lifespan would be much longer.

Leander wiped his forehead, which was beading with sweat. His body temperature rising with the MDMA. Had Miller given him too much?

"Talk to me about when you were arrested. Do you remember?"

"Yes, of course I do."

"Tell me about what happened. You can look at it from the outside now. You don't need to worry about how it will impact you or anyone else. You can view it like a movie. As if it was something that happened to someone else."

"They took me away."

"Yes. They took you away from your home and family. Where did they take you?"

"The prison… it was a terrible, dark place."

Kenzie leaned forward, listening, as Leander described the prison in great detail. The cell where he had been confined, small and dirty, with no amenities, not even a mattress or blankets. He talked about the sound of water dripping constantly, the rats and the flies that afflicted them. She couldn't have imagined all the details, all the horrors that Leander had suffered through just by being confined in the prison. She knew that there was worse to come.

"They questioned me," Leander related in an emotion-filled voice. "They took me out of there and would take me to another room. Not always the same one. Different rooms for different… kinds of interrogations." He swallowed and looked around for a drink, licking his lips.

Dr. Miller got him a bottle of water, cracked the lid, and gave it to him.

"Water," Leander said, holding the bottle up to the light and turning it around so that it bent and reflected the light in different patterns. "They wouldn't give me water. Not until the end. Not until I was going back to my cell. I longed for my cell. Somewhere safe."

Kenzie shuddered at the thought of such a terrible place being his only asylum. The place that he looked forward to going back to. Leander chugged several gulps of water and wiped his mouth with the back of his arm.

"What else did they do to you?" Dr. Miller prompted, putting his hand on Leander's arm.

Leander had difficulty, but went on describing the horrors and torture that they had inflicted on him. It was hard to listen to. Kenzie took a break to take her Tylenol and water, considering leaving the video playing while she went and did something else for a few minutes. She didn't want to end up with PTSD from watching the video discussing the tortures.

But Garcia had told her to watch it, so there had to be something there that was relevant to Leander's death investigation. Kenzie glanced at the date of the therapy session she was watching and saw that it was a few days before Isah's death. She was not going to see him choke on his water and die on the screen in front of her.

Garcia had watched it. Kenzie could watch it, too. She could pause it whenever she needed to. Mute it. She had options. Unlike Leander, who was caught in the middle of it. Even when he resisted telling Dr. Miller something, Miller would continue to press and insist until Leander provided more detail about what he wanted. Kenzie watched the session, wondering whether Miller was even a licensed therapist. He seemed to be asking a lot of questions and pushing his patient a lot more than Dr. B ever would. But Kenzie didn't have a lot of experience with other therapists. They would, of course, all have different techniques and different levels of comfort with various techniques.

Miller was, Kenzie assumed, certified to deal with trauma patients and had probably been through all kinds of training to do with the administration of MDMA under the auspices of the pharmaceutical company that was running the trials. They would have a strict protocol about what was expected so that all the clinics they dealt with would have similar, reproducible results.

As Leander talked about what he had been through, Kenzie noticed that Dr. Miller was rubbing first Leander's arm and then his thigh, sitting closer to him on the couch, until their bodies were touching. She could barely breathe as she watched the therapist inflict more and more intimate positions and touches. Leander did not appear to object to the contact. There were a few times when he stopped the doctor or pushed him away briefly, but the man simply resumed, and Leander appeared to be responsive to the affections.

But that was due to the MDMA. As Garcia and Kenzie had discussed before, sexual arousal and sensitivity were commonly reported effects of MDMA. That didn't mean it was what Leander wanted or that he would have been okay with what Dr. Miller was doing if he had not been high.

Leander started hallucinating, describing auditory and visual hallucinations he perceived rather than the torture Miller was asking him about. He began to get agitated and afraid of the hallucinations, clutching at Miller and begging for his help and protection. Miller answered with calm reassurances, stroking Leander and giving him more physical affection.

Then they moved off camera. There was still audio, but not a lot of what Leander was saying made sense anymore, and it was punctuated by grunts and thumps and other noises Kenzie didn't care to identify.

It was clear that Miller had gone far past what was appropriate in the therapist-patient relationship. Kenzie was sickened by what she saw and heard. It was no wonder Leander had objected to the therapy and said that he wanted out. For someone who had been tortured while in prison in police custody, in various physical, psychological, and sexual ways, to then be re-traumatized in what was supposed to be a therapy session was unthinkable.

Even though she and Garcia had discussed Kenzie's findings that Isah had probably been sexually assaulted, Kenzie had not expected this. Had not been expecting to see and hear it with her own eyes and ears. Kenzie was used to dealing with bodies, grieving family members, and people who didn't know how to react to the death of a loved one. The violence her patients had been subjected to was over. They were past being hurt. She didn't have to see and hear it herself.

She did not watch the other two videos Garcia had sent.

45

Kenzie sat on the bed for a few minutes, thinking about what she had seen and what to do next. She didn't want to watch anything else. She didn't want to think about what she had observed. But Garcia was expecting her to call back, and she had been right that she and Kenzie would have to talk once Kenzie had seen what the videos showed of the therapy session.

Kenzie needed to analyze it clinically. Not to think about the man or the betrayal of the patient's trust. But to think about how it had impacted his health and may or may not have contributed to his death. Because that was all that was on her plate. She couldn't do anything about the regulation of the doctors at Persons or about criminal charges being laid. That was outside her purview.

She took a deep breath and hit the button on her phone to call Garcia back.

Garcia answered with a sigh. Not angry, as she had been the last couple of times that she and Kenzie had spoken on the phone. But resigned. Subdued.

"Kenzie."

"I wish you hadn't sent that to me," Kenzie told her.

"I can understand your feelings about them. Did you watch all three?"

Kenzie didn't try to cover up the fact that she had not. "No. One was all I could stomach. I assume they are all relatively the same."

"Yes. But with Isah's agitation level increasing each time and more drugs needing to be administered. I don't know if the doctor was giving him multiple doses of MDMA or if he was giving him something else to take the edge off. A sedative, benzos, something like that. I guess… we'll either find out from the doctor, or by whatever other medical professionals review those tapes."

"He had benzodiazepines in his blood. We were told that he had been sedated after the cafeteria incident and the visit from the police."

"Right. I guess at least one person knew exactly why he was getting so worked up."

Kenzie shook her head. "It's sickening."

"Yes. We were forewarned… but I still wasn't prepared for what I saw," Garcia admitted. She'd had longer to get used to it than Kenzie had. And she had probably watched them multiple times, talked to different people about them, and maybe passed them on to the special investigations unit, the medical board, and the management of Persons. It would be a lot of work.

"I don't know what else to say about it," Kenzie said. "It does not have a big impact on the death investigation. I could see that the MDMA was affecting him physically, not just psychologically. You saw him sweating?"

"Yes. Quite a bit, especially toward the end."

"That is the best evidence of your cause of death. The bloodwork I got back today shows that he was on SSRIs as well. His serotonin levels were astronomical. The combination of MDMA and an SSRI can cause Serotonin Syndrome, which can be lethal. His body was overheating and, at some point, his heart stopped. When I arrived there, some time after his death, the body was still too warm."

"What about the altercation before his death. Putting him prone and dogpiling on top of him. Did he smother?"

"He was still walking and breathing after that, though probably neither one very well. The surveillance pictures are too distant and low resolution to see if he was sweating or how dilated his eyes were. Using the session tapes you sent me as a reference point, he was probably still high after he came out of those sessions. MDMA can last for several hours. Janice said that sometimes his sessions were quite long. I guess Dr. Miller liked to take advantage of that nice long high."

Garcia grunted.

"The combination of the drugs, the PTSD and agitation, the altercation with the staff, and possibly having his breathing cut off briefly at that point... he would have been in bad shape. They took him back to his room. I don't know if he was in restraints when he died, but he had been restrained sometime before his death."

"Straitjacket? Padded room?"

"Wrist restraints at least. Maybe the police had him in cuffs while they talked to him to try to scare him straight. But he got so upset that they had to give him a sedative to calm him down. He wanted to go back to his room and go to sleep, so maybe that's what they let him do. I hope..." Kenzie's voice caught in her throat. She didn't know why she was getting so emotional about what Isah's last few moments had looked like. Did a few minutes of peace in his room before he died make up for everything else they had done to him?

"I hope so too," Garcia murmured. "I hope that for however long it was before he died, he had a little measure of peace. He didn't deserve to be treated that way."

Kenzie nodded and swallowed. She went on, holding herself as distant from it as she could and speaking around a lump in her throat.

"His heart gave out. I don't know whether they found him on his bed or on the floor. Whoever found him or someone who joined them shortly after that tried to do CPR. Broke his sternum and a couple of ribs. They probably thought that he had just recently stopped breathing because of how warm he was. But he'd already been gone for a while when CPR was attempted. There was no bleeding, bruising, or swelling around the ribs and sternum."

"And then they called the funeral home to pick him up," Garcia offered.

"Yeah. And almost got away with it. Would have if the nurse hadn't decided that the medical examiner needed to be involved."

"Thank goodness for that nurse."

. . .

There was a knock on the door, and Kenzie looked at it, reorienting herself to time and place. She had closed her eyes for a minute to try to set aside the disturbing images and information. It was stressful just knowing what had been happening to Isah, and she had found herself wanting to turn off the world and retreat into sleep. Apparently, that was exactly what she had done.

"Come on in," Kenzie told Zachary. "I'm off the phone."

He opened the door and poked his head in. "Everything okay? It's been a while and I just wanted to make sure you didn't need anything."

"I guess I fell asleep."

"Oh. I didn't mean to wake you up. You can go back to sleep if you want to. Do you want me to close the blinds?"

"I'd better not go to bed this early, or I'll wake up at two o'clock and won't be able to go back to sleep."

He grinned. "Then we can have a party together."

Zachary was frequently up in the early morning hours, either unable to get to sleep or, having slept a couple of hours, unable to go back to sleep.

Kenzie yawned, deciding to cover her mouth halfway through. "Sorry. How are *you* sleeping these days? Are you getting enough?"

"According to the experts, no, but it's enough for me to function during the day."

"And it's enough that it doesn't affect your mental health?"

"It doesn't make me more depressed. Just a little foggy sometimes if I'm really short on sleep."

"I remember that day last year when you hadn't slept for three days. That definitely affected you emotionally."

"That, yeah." Zachary waved it off with a motion of his hand. "I haven't had anything like that this year. I'm okay."

"You tell me and take a sleeping pill if that happens again."

He shrugged and nodded. "So you're getting up now?"

"Yeah. Let's have a late supper. I think I need something other than ice cream."

Zachary chuckled. "Heresy! You need some pizza to go with it?"

"Actually, I think I've got a frozen one. That might be a good idea."

Kenzie got up from the bed, her head throbbing a little but, all things considered, it wasn't too bad. The nap had probably done her good.

Putting a frozen pizza in the oven wasn't exactly a two-person job, so she did it herself, then joined Zachary again in the living room.

46

After a few minutes, Kenzie became aware that Zachary was studying her and wondered whether he had said something she had missed. She turned to face him directly.

"Are you okay?" Zachary asked. "Is it just the concussion? You seem... far away."

Zachary was usually the one dissociating, retreating from Kenzie when things got to be too much for him emotionally. Kenzie touched the bump on her head.

"No... I think..." She tried to think about what to tell him about what was on her mind. "I got some videos from Detective Garcia about what's going on at Persons. And... it's pretty disturbing stuff."

Zachary nodded seriously. "You want to tell me about it?"

"I really can't. It would be too inflammatory if it leaked out. Not that you would leak it. I'm just saying that I have to be really careful what I say. And honestly... you don't want to hear it. It would be too triggering."

"Okay." He touched the back of her neck and stroked a few tendrils of hair. "So what can I do to help?"

"I'm worried about Rhys." Kenzie swallowed. "He was supposed to have his first MDMA therapy today. I know that he's probably fine after just one session... just because something bad happened to another patient, that doesn't mean that the same thing would happen to Rhys. But… I just want to know he's okay."

"I can call Vera."

"I don't know if she'll even answer. She was not happy with me trying to talk her out of Rhys doing the MDMA therapy. She sees it as the only option, the only thing that might help him. She doesn't understand the risks and I couldn't tell her everything. I think we'd better stay out of it, or she'll say we can't see him. It might be worth it for me to be banned, if it gets her to reconsider the therapy. But I wouldn't want you to be blocked from seeing him too. I think he needs you."

Zachary frowned as he considered this. Kenzie knew he was going to argue the point.

But he tried a different direction instead. "How about Stanley? I could call him and see if he's heard anything."

"Yeah. That might work. He'll want to know how Rhys is doing too."

Zachary nodded his agreement. He took a minute to look at the contacts on his phone and find Stanley's number. It was late enough that Stanley would be off work, but not late enough for him to be in bed.

"Stanley, it's Zachary. I was just calling to see—"

He had put the phone on speaker, and Stanley cut in before he could even finish the explanation.

"He's not doing great," Stanley said. "The doctors say it will pass and they don't think it was enough to cause any damage. It was just a bad reaction, not an overdose."

Kenzie stopped breathing.

"What happened?" Zachary asked. "I knew he was supposed to have therapy this afternoon, but I didn't hear how things went. I was hoping you had heard."

"Vera didn't call you?" Stanley paused to consider this new information, then decided it was okay to give Zachary the information anyway. Rhys would have wanted his friend to know what was happening, so Kenzie thought it was the right choice.

"Well, like I said, he had a bad reaction to the drug. They're not saying that he was allergic or that it was an overdose. It's not life-threatening."

"What kind of reaction?" Kenzie asked, leaning toward the phone and hoping he would be able to hear her and wouldn't be put off by her involvement in the call.

"He's hallucinating... a bad trip, I guess, like on LSD. Seeing and hearing things. Not... not quite in this world."

Kenzie made a noise of understanding. "That can happen. Some people are quite sensitive to the hallucinogenic properties. Or it was a bad batch of MDMA, but that shouldn't be the case when we're talking about pharmaceutical grade."

"The doctors are telling Vera that it will wear off and he'll be fine and back to normal in a few hours."

"Okay, good. Is he still at Persons? Are they going to go ahead with another session right away?"

"No. They called for an ambulance. He's back in the city hospital. I don't know if he is still in emergency or in psych. But it's too late for visiting hours."

"They probably wouldn't let us see him anyway if he's in a crisis," Zachary said. "Unless he was asking for us and they thought it would help to calm him down."

Kenzie rubbed her eyes, thinking about it. "Do you know anything else about the session? How long it was? Who was leading it? Which doctor?"

Zachary's concerned gaze turned toward Kenzie, but she didn't meet his eyes.

"I don't know," Stanley confessed. "And I don't know whether Vera does either. Those kinds of things... aren't necessarily things they would tell us. It never occurred to me to ask, and I doubt she thought of any of those things. Does it make any difference?"

Kenzie tried to think of how to explain.

"Kenzie has been involved in an investigation at Persons," Zachary advised before she had a chance to get her thoughts in order. "So she knows some details about who is involved in what."

Stanley cleared his throat. "Vera told me that you didn't want him taking the therapy. I guess now we know why."

A bad trip was the least of Kenzie's concerns about Rhys. If it hadn't been caused by an overdose, Stanley was probably right and wouldn't cause any permanent or lasting damage. And might just be enough to convince Vera and Rhys not to continue with the drug therapy.

"You could try calling Persons to see if they would give you any details," Zachary suggested to Kenzie. "They could at least tell you who was treating him. You're a doctor, and you have the right to ask questions that are related to your investigation."

"It would be a stretch to connect Rhys with my investigations," Kenzie pointed out.

"I don't know what was in the stuff that Garcia sent you today, but Isah's death was related to the same kind of therapy as Rhys was being given, wasn't it? Seems like there's enough of a connection there."

Stanley spoke up again, his voice uncertain. "You think this therapy Rhys is doing is connected with a death?"

"I can't say anything about it," Kenzie told him. "I haven't released my findings to the public yet."

"I had no idea it was that dangerous."

"It shouldn't be," Kenzie said carefully. "Not in a controlled therapeutic setting."

"I'll tell Vera to give you a call," Stanley said. "If you know about this drug and this therapy, then she should talk to you about it before she does anything else."

"She doesn't *have* to call me," Kenzie said. "But I'd certainly be happy to talk to her about it. She should talk to someone who knows the real risks. Not just whatever Persons is telling her."

"I'll make sure she does," Stanley promised.

Kenzie was glad he was taking the line without any encouragement from her. She didn't want to push her advice on Vera, but she wanted to ensure that Rhys got the best possible treatment in a safe environment.

Persons was not safe, and Kenzie was glad he was out of there.

They said their goodbyes to Stanley and turned their attention to a call to Persons.

47

K enzie didn't have much hope that she would be able to find out anything by calling Persons. Even if they were open to talking to her about her investigations, they would be circling the wagons now. They wouldn't want to give her any more ammunition. They wouldn't admit any connection with Rhys or agree that she had the right to ask about him. In a world that was so strict about patient privacy regulations, she wasn't likely to get anywhere asking about him.

She spoke as officially as possible when she reached Persons's after-hours receptionist or answering service. She made her voice as pompous and confident as possible.

"I need to talk to Rhys Salter's treating physician."

"I'm sorry, we don't have access to that information," the woman protested. "You'll have to call back during office hours."

"Rhys was brought to the hospital after an overdose at your facility," Kenzie said sharply. "I think that you can find that information for me. I need to talk to the doctor who treated him."

"I... I'm not sure about that. Is it urgent? Dr. Richards can give you a call back in the morning..."

"Was Dr. Richards the treating physician?"

"Well, I don't know. She's one of the doctors over here, the one that manages treatment plans and patient records…"

"Do you have an after-hours number for her?"

The receptionist protested a bit, but clearly did have an after-hours number that could be given out in case of an emergency, and she reluctantly passed it on to Kenzie. Kenzie thanked her politely and tried the number.

After dialing it, she wondered whether she should have blocked her phone number so that Dr. Richards wouldn't know it was her. She didn't exactly have high expectations that Richards would want to hear from her. But the call was answered almost immediately, so maybe Dr. Richards hadn't even bothered to look at the caller ID before answering the call.

"Nancy Richards."

"Dr. Richards, it's Kenzie Kirsch. From—"

"From the medical examiner's office. Yes, of course, Dr. Kirsch. I couldn't exactly forget you, could I?"

Kenzie grimaced. It wasn't exactly a ringing endorsement. Dr. Richards did not sound terribly excited to be talking to her.

"I'm sorry for calling you at home, Dr. Richards—that is, are you at home?"

"Yes, I'm at home. What can I do for you, Dr. Kirsch? It must be urgent, or the service would not have given you my number."

"It's about Rhys Salter."

"Yes?"

"You know who he is?"

"Yes."

"I understand that he was rushed from Persons to the hospital today after an overdose or bad reaction to MDMA."

"Unless he died, and I was assured he was doing all right, I don't see how that is any of your business."

"Rhys is a personal friend. I was there to visit him on Saturday when Janice died."

"You were there, weren't you?" Dr. Richards said vaguely. "Yes, I remember that. But still, I am not sure I understand what you expect from me."

"Well, I want to know which doctor was treating him and what happened."

"As the medical examiner?" Dr. Richards challenged.

"As a representative of the medical examiner's office, I am sworn to protect the public good. After what I have seen of the therapy sessions conducted for Mr. Isah as part of my investigation into his death, I have to confess that I would not be happy to find out that Dr. Miller was allowed to treat anyone else, especially a vulnerable teen."

Dr. Richards didn't respond. A long silence drew out between them.

"I don't know what you're talking about," Dr. Richards said finally. "But Dr. Miller was not involved in Rhys's therapy. So if that answers your question…"

"Who was? I would like to talk to the person who treated him today to find out what happened."

"You are not entitled to that information. The family has not indicated they want anything to be conveyed to you."

Kenzie again let the silence speak for her. It had worked once; she hoped it would work a second time.

"I was the one who treated Rhys," Dr. Richards said finally. "Does that satisfy your questions?"

"You were the one who did therapy with him this afternoon?" Kenzie asked.

Even though she knew that Dr. Richards still had to be high on the list of people suspected of Janice's murder, Kenzie felt relieved for the first time since seeing the video of Dr. Miller and Isah. Her muscles loosened and her pounding heart slowed.

A woman could still be an abuser or even a murderer. She and Zachary had seen it in other cases. But she couldn't help feeling relief that Dr. Richards was the one who had treated Rhys. She could see the two of them together. She thought that Rhys would feel safe with Dr. Richards. The woman gave off a vibe of compassion and concern. Rhys would have been unlikely to have seen her as a threat, even considering that a beautiful young woman had committed murder in his own family. As she and Zachary had discussed previously, people were naturally drawn toward attractive women. It was hard to see them as unkind or predatory.

"Yes," Dr. Richards confirmed. "I gave him a low dose of the drug and we sat together to see how it would make him feel. Unfortunately, it did not give him a good feeling. He was agitated and began to experience very vivid hallucinations. Even though MDMA is a hallucinogenic, most of our patients do not have any negative experiences with a low, well-managed dose. It just makes them feel more open and accepting. It makes it easier for them to access their emotions and share them. To reach some of the old memories and traumas and actually address them for the first time."

"What happened with Rhys? How bad was it?"

"It was a safe dose, Dr. Kirsch. And I don't believe that the reaction he had to it was allergic. I think he is probably just hypersensitive. That those parts of his brain are just easily triggered."

"But you had him transported to the hospital."

"With everything that has happened lately... I wasn't taking any chances. I did not want anything to happen to the boy. I figured he was fine and would just come down naturally, but I wasn't going to gamble on it. I'm sure he'll be just fine, and he'll be able to come back tonight or tomorrow."

Not if Kenzie could help it.

"That's a big relief," she told Dr. Richards. "I appreciate you taking the time with me. I'll check on him in the morning. But for now... I can rest more easily, knowing that it isn't serious."

48

Kenzie was finished with phone calls. She could spend a little time with Zachary before bed, de-stressing and decompressing, and then she would be able to get to sleep. She would feel a lot better in the morning. At least, Kenzie hoped she would. She didn't want to think about how her bumps and bruises might feel the next day.

But her phone buzzed as she prepared to get up and find Zachary to tell him what she had been able to discover about Rhys. Kenzie looked down at it in irritation. She wasn't sure who was trying to catch her, but it was a little late in the day for any more work calls. If it was a callout to a site, she would have to decline and see if Dr. Cook could attend. She hoped that her concussion symptoms would recede enough by morning that she would be able to drive and do her job without any problems. A good night's sleep, and she would be feeling better.

But when she looked at the face of her phone, she saw her father looking back at her. A requested video call. Kenzie settled back down on the bed with her back against the pillows and answered the call.

"Dad. Hi."

"MacKenzie. I hope it isn't too late?"

"I'm up for a bit longer yet. How are you doing?"

"Just as good as ever. You? And... Zachary?"

Kenzie rubbed her forehead with a fist. "Just tired."

"You do too much. If you're tired, why don't you get ready for bed now?"

"I've been working. I need some time to unwind. You know how that is. If I tried to go to bed right now, I would just toss and turn and be too hyped up to sleep. I'll take the time to relax first so that I can get a good sleep when I'm ready to go to bed."

"Of course. And Zachary, how is he?"

"Umm... He's doing pretty well. As far as I can tell, he's still doing all right. That can change in short order, but it seems like he's in a good place right now."

Walter nodded, smiling pleasantly. Kenzie studied him, trying to figure out if he was playing with her. Why had he called? Just to ask how she was? She knew that smile, and it wasn't genuine. He had something on his mind, or he wanted something from her.

"What's up, Dad?"

"Nothing. I know I don't call often enough. Though part of that is on you... you don't either. The phone works both ways."

"Yeah." Kenzie knew she didn't call him as often as she should. "I know that. Sorry." She rubbed her eyes, trying to relax and enjoy the conversation with him. But she couldn't if she thought there was something else going on. Something else that he wasn't telling her. Seemed like the story of her life. The Kirsches, however close they were, tended to keep things from each other. They were reserved and tried not to let things get too emotional or personal.

"Are you still working on that case at Persons?"

Kenzie was surprised by the question. But it had been in the news. Of course Walter had found out about it. He was always up on the news that might impact him personally or professionally.

"I haven't been out there since Saturday. I don't expect to be. Unless it is to visit a friend of ours who is a patient there. I should be releasing my findings on the current cases shortly. Maybe tomorrow."

"Good to hear. They don't need all the negative publicity."

Kenzie raised a brow at this. She wasn't aware of any interest that Walter had in Persons. Not that he would tell her if he did. He might know someone on the board there, or be working on a campaign that affected them. Or have done so sometime in the past. Walter liked to stay aware of everything in his universe: past, present, and future.

"They are pioneering some important therapies," Walter offered. "Treatments that could change the face of psychiatric medicine. Do you know how many people in the world—even just in Vermont—would benefit from their trauma therapy?"

"I can't say I have been very impressed with what I have seen so far," she told Walter. "I know they are making some really big claims about how they will change the world, but you can't believe everything you hear."

Walter should know more than anyone about the way scammers worked. About the claims made and promise shown, which fell apart on close inspection.

"Really." Walter frowned. "I don't like to hear that. What's going on that concerns you?"

"I can't talk about it, since it's in connection with my work at the medical examiner's office. But you know you can't believe everything people tell you. Get the evidence to back it up. All the miracle cures claimed by Persons are just that. They are snake oil salesmen."

Walter leaned toward the phone as if it would help him understand Kenzie better.

"What is snake oil?"

"Anything about their trauma therapy. The hallucinogenic drug-mediated therapy. You have no idea how dangerous it is. You want to know why these are not authorized treatments? It is because of all the risks, with very little chance of success."

"In your opinion."

Kenzie scowled at the phone screen. "In my opinion," she agreed. "Whatever *that's* worth to you."

"MacKenzie!" Walter looked taken aback by her comment. Hurt.

But he really had no right to be upset. He was the one who had decided not to take his daughter's word for it. His highly trained medical examiner daughter. Why had he called her if he wasn't going to take her word for it when she answered him?

He peered at her through the camera. "Are you okay?" he asked. "You don't seem like yourself today."

Kenzie sighed. She smoothed her curls, trying to get herself together, but careful not to touch the painful bump. "I'm okay," she told him. "But I'm not quite myself today, you're right."

"Anything I can do? Is it just because you have too much work? I know they got a substitute for your careless Dr. Wiltshire, but is it enough? If you need more, you should tell them that."

"It isn't that. And Dr. Wiltshire isn't careless." She shook her head. "Where do you get that?"

He shrugged. "I hear things. If it isn't the job, then what is it? You said that Zachary was okay. Is that the truth?"

"Zachary is fine. It isn't work. It isn't Zachary. I... have a minor concussion. I had a small traffic accident and hit my head."

"What? Why didn't you tell me this? Does your mother know?"

"No, I didn't call her either. It just happened today. I got home not long ago. So I haven't been holding anything back..."

Although if he had not called, she'd had no intention of calling either of her parents to let them know that she had bonked her head.

"What happened?"

"I was..." Kenzie tried to think of how much to tell him. What to hold back. How she could minimize it as much as possible so that her parents didn't smother her with their concern. "I was crossing the street, and I was bumped by a car. It was stopping; it just... hadn't completely come to a halt. I fell, skinned my knee, bumped my head. That's all. Don't worry. I've had all the tests you could think of. Nothing broken, no brain bleeds or anything like that. The doctors have confirmed there is nothing to worry about and sent me home."

"Is Zachary there? He's not out on a stakeout, is he? You have someone there with you?"

"Yes. Zachary is here, and he's waiting on me hand and foot. He's doing everything that you would do if you were here."

Walter frowned, considering this. Like he was looking for something that he could do for Kenzie that Zachary couldn't. But all he could have done was throw money at her, and that wouldn't have made her more comfortable or taken away the bump on her head. Zachary would see to it that all her physical needs were met.

"And you're going to take it easy for a few days? Give your brain a chance to heal before you jump right back into things?"

"It's not that bad. It's a headache and a bit of fogginess. That's all. I'm sure that after a good night's sleep, it won't even be that bad."

"Call your mother."

"Dad… why don't you call her for me? I need to relax. My head is really hurting from having to talk on the phone. Just give her my love and tell her I'm taking care of myself and that I will spend the rest of the night relaxing with Zachary."

Walter brightened at being given an assignment. And it was probably what he would have done anyway. "I will do that," he confirmed. "But you need to call her tomorrow to tell her I wasn't just blowing smoke. She doesn't always believe me, you know."

"I wouldn't either," Kenzie agreed. "If she wants to text me to ask if I'm really okay, I'll text her back to confirm. But only once."

"I'll make sure she knows."

"Thanks, Dad. Thanks for looking after everything."

49

They would probably not have been able to get in to see Rhys, but the fact that Kenzie was a medical doctor meant that they could talk their way past the nurses who were trying to keep any unauthorized personnel away from the boy. Zachary had called Vera to ask to be added to Rhys's authorized visitor list. The combination of that permission and Kenzie being a doctor got them in when probably the only other person who would have been able to see him was Vera. She said that she would visit Rhys later in the day. She was obviously exhausted from what she had been through with him already, and she needed the extra sleep afforded her because she knew that Kenzie and Zachary would be by to see Rhys.

Kenzie didn't recognize the nurse who led them to Rhys's room. She didn't know whether or not she was one of the nurses that Zachary knew. She would have to ask him later. She paused before taking them in to see Rhys.

"We have someone sitting with him. He's quite agitated. We have him on something to counteract the MDMA and keep the symptoms to a minimum, but he's still in quite a bit of distress. I just want to warn you before you go in. It's not pretty. And there's not anything you can do about it. He'll get through it… eventually. As long as there is no permanent damage, and there *shouldn't* be with the dosage he was given."

"All of the MDMA should be out of his system by now, shouldn't it?" Kenzie asked.

"It lasts longer for some. We do have other examples of MDMA-induced psychopathy lasting several days, but it should gradually fade."

"You think it will?" Zachary asked, concerned.

"Yes. It just takes some time. I wouldn't recommend that he continue this therapy."

"Well, no!" Kenzie agreed. "That would be pretty stupid. I just hope Vera agrees. She was really hopeful that this would work. It might take several conversations to convince her to pull back again."

The nurse nodded and unlocked the door for them. Zachary and Kenzie entered the hospital room. Rhys was sitting on the bed, half reclined, and jumped up when he saw them. The male nurse sitting in a chair next to the bed stood up quickly, ready to insert himself between Rhys and the visitors.

"Zach!" Rhys exclaimed, reaching for him.

Zachary reached out both arms and Rhys embraced him and held him tightly, pounding on his back.

Kenzie didn't think she'd ever heard Rhys use Zachary's name aloud before. He didn't often use his voice and, when he did, it was often used to address Vera to express some need. Just a word or two as he could squeeze them out. Just one phrase seemed to exhaust him. Rhys pulled back from Zachary and held his arms apart slightly as if he didn't know whether Kenzie would want a hug or not. "Kenzie."

Kenzie raised a brow at Zachary, surprised. "Hey, Rhys, how are you doing?" Kenzie held her arms out and Rhys closed in and hugged her, too. Not a tight one like he had given Zachary, but softer, a gentle squeeze, and then he pulled back again quickly.

He headed toward the nurse, arms held out for a hug, and the man shook his head and pushed him back slightly. "No, Rhys. That's fine."

Rhys turned around again. There wasn't anywhere else in the tiny room to go, so he eventually sat on the edge of the bed, looking from Kenzie to Zachary, his eyes wide.

"Crazy," he said. "Everything crazy." He held up his hands to indicate the room around him, wiggling his fingers in a movement that suggested shimmering or magic.

Kenzie had never heard him use his voice so much. They were used to relying on gestures and text messages of GIFs to communicate with Rhys. It was strange to hear his voice.

"Are you seeing things on the walls?" Kenzie asked. It was a common hallucination.

Rhys nodded. He stood up, looked for somewhere to go, and sat again. "Time to go, time to go," he singsonged.

Kenzie looked at Zachary again in disbelief. They had not been expecting such wildly divergent behavior. Rhys was like a different person.

"How have you been doing, Rhys?" Zachary asked. "Are you okay?"

"The spiders," Rhys said nonsensically. "In the eighties. Pray for me. Pray for me." He pressed his hands together and bowed his head in mock prayer. Zachary put his hand on Rhys's arm, but the boy pulled away sharply. He started to bounce his head up and down, making loud shrieking noises and scratching his arms.

"It's okay," the nurse told him. "You're safe here. There are no spiders. We will protect you."

Rhys's cries subsided to whimpers. "The eighties," he repeated. "Why? Why?"

"You're safe," Kenzie repeated the nurse's words. "It's just from the drug, Rhys. It isn't real. It's from the drug."

Rhys rubbed at the tears on his face. He shook his head and made a pulsing sound in his throat that was half sob and half song. "They're hungry."

"Nothing is going to hurt you." Zachary held his arm gently. "You're in the hospital. Everything will be okay soon. This will all pass, and you'll feel like yourself again."

"He's hungry." Rhys switched suddenly to another voice. "Stop it. *Just stop it!*"

Kenzie was alarmed at the rapid changes. She wasn't used to dealing with psychiatric patients, but was sure that jumping from one disturbing thought to another so quickly wasn't usual. Did the second voice mean that Rhys was dealing with a separate personality? Or was he remembering something or someone from the past? She felt like they should be able to explain each thing that Rhys said, to find the logical reason behind it and deduce what he was seeing or hearing. But that wasn't the way it worked. The brain did not work logically when it was in this state.

"That's what Robin said," Zachary said in a low voice intended for Kenzie's ears rather than Rhys's. "When she would get overly upset by something, maybe a noise she didn't like, she would say that."

Zachary nodded toward Rhys and didn't repeat the words, "Just stop it."

"After Clarence's murder, that was the only thing Rhys would say. And then... he stopped saying anything at all."

Kenzie's heart squeezed when she pictured that little boy and the trauma he had been through. All that he'd had to suffer when he was young, bottled up inside him all through the years. Unable to talk about it or to share his pain.

Maybe there was something to the MDMA therapy. Even though Rhys had reacted badly to it, it had loosened his tongue, made it so that he could speak more than he'd ever been able to since he was a small child, made it so that he could tell them something about the trauma.

"Did you see Gloria kill Grandpa Clarence, Rhys?" Kenzie asked softly.

Zachary looked alarmed that she would suggest this to Rhys. To put it to him so baldly.

"Just stop it!" Rhys said it more loudly, a harpy's shriek. Then he cowered as if someone had shouted at him rather than his being the shouter.

"Is that what Gloria said?"

Rhys sniffled, the tears running down his face again.

"It wasn't your fault," Kenzie told Rhys. As a bystander, he was bound to feel guilty about what happened. That he hadn't been able to stop the murder of his grandfather, even if there had been nothing he could do about it.

For years, he had lived with that knowledge, knowing that Gloria had been the culprit and had never been caught and punished for her actions. And who knew how she had treated him, living in the same house? She might have abused and threatened him every night with all kinds of terrible things.

He stood up and went to Kenzie, hugging her again. Kenzie hugged him briefly, then separated herself from him, not wanting anything inappropriate to develop.

"What Gloria did wasn't your fault."

Rhys rocked back and forth on his heels. "Just stop it. Shut up. Just stop it now." His voice was thready, distressed.

"You're allowed to talk now. You can talk about it as much as you need to. No one is going to stop you."

"Just stop it."

"Were you doing something that Gloria didn't like?"

Rhys put his hands over his ears. "The spiders," he said, returning to the previous hallucination. He wiggled his fingers around his face, drawing the room as he looked around it, as if he'd been sprinkling magic pixie dust around. The spiders and other things he could see came and went over the next hour as they listened to him babble and watched him go from the frightening images around him, back to Grandpa Clarence's murder, and around and around.

It was exhausting. Eventually, they had to leave. Kenzie needed to get to work, and Zachary had his cases to work on, she was sure. In the space of an hour, Rhys had probably said more than he had in the previous ten years. Kenzie's heart ached for him. She didn't know what to expect. After the drugs wore off, would he go silent again? Would he be able to talk about the murder? Would it have done him any good to talk about it as he had?

It was no wonder Vera had needed the extra time to sleep.

Kenzie and Zachary just looked at each other, neither sure what to say.

50

It was strange to go to the office so late in the morning. But Kenzie hadn't wanted to leave the visit until the end of the day. She had wanted to see Rhys as early as possible to reassure herself that he was okay and everything would be all right with him.

She just hoped that it was true. She actually wasn't that reassured. Rhys was clearly still feeling the effects of the MDMA even after it should have fully cleared his system. She worried that he wouldn't go back to normal again as Richards had suggested. What if he was in that agitated, hallucinating state permanently? There was drug-induced psychosis. Drug-induced schizophrenia. People had been damaged by exposure to hallucinogens in the past, though usually LSD was identified as the culprit.

"I probably won't be able to get off for couple's therapy this afternoon," she warned Zachary. "Plan to just have an individual session. I'll probably need the time to catch up at the office after missing yesterday afternoon and again this morning."

"Okay," Zachary nodded, looking relieved by her words. Too often, he got wound up worrying whether she would make it to their session because she had missed it once. Since then, he had deemed her unreliable at getting to sessions, even though she had never missed again.

Since she had told him she would likely not be there, he didn't have to spend the whole day obsessing about it. He could just assume that she wouldn't be and that he would go on his own. Apparently, it was a relief for him to shed that burden.

"How are you doing?" Dr. Cook asked as soon as Kenzie walked in the door. He studied her face and then her body, looking for any sign of injury. He had probably expected her to be black and blue after hearing that she had been hit by a car, even though she had assured him on the phone that she was perfectly fine, aside from a skinned knee and very mild concussion.

"I'm fine. Still a little fuzzy today, so I'll need to be careful what I do, but I'm fine to put in a few hours." She decided not to build up his expectations either. She would offer a few hours and, if she were able to work beyond that, he would be impressed. If she had to go home to recuperate, then she had at least not promised a full day's work.

"Be careful," Cook warned. "You probably should have taken a few days off until you were clear of the concussion. Does it hurt?"

Kenzie nodded. "I've taken a Tylenol this morning but don't want to take anything that will just make me more foggy. So... a bit of a headache, especially if I get up too quickly or bend over to pick something up. And the bump itself is still tender." She reached up and touched the bump on her head, which she thought had already reduced in size. Even her own light touch made her wince. "But other than that, the worst injury is a skinned knee."

She didn't lift her pant leg to show him the large burn dressing that covered the skinned area and the bruise and swelling around it. It was such a minor issue compared to what could have happened with a car-on-pedestrian accident. She was lucky to be alive and so unscathed.

"Don't bend over to pick anything up then," Cook advised. "Call me and I'll pick it up."

Kenzie laughed. "How about I just don't drop anything?"

"Well, that works too. Do you want me to run you through the latest developments?"

Kenzie nodded her agreement and Cook detailed the latest arrivals and results, and anything else Kenzie needed to follow up on.

"Tox screens came back on your Janice Martin."

Kenzie nodded. "MDMA?"

"Among other things."

"Oh?" Kenzie clicked her mouse to navigate to the Janice Martin file and have a look.

"She had sedatives in her bloodstream. And the hair analysis was interesting."

Hair analysis showed what Janice had been using in the months prior to her death. A timeline of what she had taken when. "Oh?" Kenzie found the results and clicked on the report. She skimmed it as Cook summarized.

"Quite a history of LSD and PCP use as well as the MDMA. In about the same timeframe."

"So they weren't just using MDMA."

"Doesn't look that way. She has no history of using either before she started the MDMA."

Kenzie shook her head. "And those drugs were not approved for this trial." She had the trial protocols that Garcia had sent her close at hand. "MDMA was the only drug approved for the trial, and any other medications the patient was on had to be recorded and closely monitored to ensure that there were no contraindications."

"Sounds like they are playing pretty fast and loose over at that place,"

"Yeah. They really are. This trial seems like it was just a smoke-screen for all the abuses they could think of. This Dr. Miller was a real…" Kenzie paused, trying to think of a less offensive word than the one on the tip of her tongue. "A real low life. The guy knew he was on camera, and even that didn't stop him!"

Dr. Cook looked at Kenzie, one brow cocked questioningly. He hadn't watched the videos of the therapy sessions. She hadn't even given him the password to do so. Without knowing who had leaked the video of Isah's altercation with the staff, Kenzie wasn't about to trust Cook or anyone else with sensitive information.

She puffed out her cheeks and blew out a breath. "Unethical and abusive behavior," she summarized for him. "Detective Garcia is already looking at it, going to file criminal charges."

"Good. Don't need doctors like that giving the rest of the profession a bad name."

Dr. Cook eventually decided that he had caught Kenzie up on everything he needed to and was just hovering, and retreated to his office. Kenzie looked over the messages that had piled up in her inbox and voicemail and started reviewing and filing them as appropriate. Something niggled at the back of her mind. Something she had forgotten? Something that she was supposed to do?

She was partway through the processing when she realized she had not yet called Lisa. She had promised Walter that she would, and she had better follow through if she didn't want both of them on her case. Even forgetting something temporarily right now would be bad; they would think it was a symptom of her concussion and that she was being affected by the injury more than she was willing to admit.

Kenzie decided that a ten-minute break was in order. She got herself a fresh cup of coffee and dialed Lisa's number. She called from her desk phone, because it would signal to Lisa that she was at work. Which meant two things: that she could not talk for too long and that the injury was only minor, as evidenced by the fact that she could still work.

"MacKenzie," Lisa greeted, as though it had been months since they had talked, and she was amazed that Kenzie had finally taken the time. "How are you, my dear? Your father told me about your accident."

"Yes, I'm sorry I made him my errand boy rather than calling you myself, but I was tired, and he needed something to do."

Lisa laughed appreciatively. "That man does need to be kept busy."

Kenzie chuckled. "I hope you didn't mind too much."

"No, dear. I was glad to know what was happening so I didn't have to hear about it from another source. It doesn't look good when you don't know that your own daughter has been in a car accident."

"No, I guess not. I would have told you today anyway, but..."

"Would you?" Kenzie's mother's voice was teasing, yet a reprimand at the same time. How many times had Kenzie failed to report important developments to her in the past? There were probably too many to count. "Anyway, let's not worry about what could have happened. It didn't, and I am glad we found out immediately. Even if I can't do anything for you, I still appreciate knowing."

"Thanks, Mom." Kenzie was warmed by her mother's concern. They might not have the closest relationship that a mother and daughter could have, but they were both working on it. And as long as they were working on it, there was hope for a better, closer relationship in the future.

"And everything is okay with Zachary?" Lisa inquired. "How is he handling you being injured?"

Kenzie thought back to how he had shown up at the hospital— shoeless, hair sticking out like a porcupine, his wallet left at home.

"Well, he was pretty panicked when he heard about it, but he's been good. Once he saw that I was okay, he settled down. He's been spoiling me at home, you'll be happy to hear, and drove me in to work this morning. He's taking good care of me."

"Good. And it hasn't triggered his… issues?"

"No." Kenzie said it with assurance and then frowned, thinking about Zachary and wondering whether it were true. Just because she hadn't seen it, that didn't mean that Zachary hadn't been masking any evidence of his trauma. He wouldn't want her to know if he were having trouble, and wouldn't want to put that extra stress on her. But she needed to know. She needed to have some idea where his head was. "From what I can tell, he is still doing all right."

"Good. And… how is your young friend? Rhys?"

Kenzie frowned. She tried to remember what she had told Lisa about Rhys before. She must have told her about Rhys being admitted to the hospital. But so much had been going on that she couldn't recall their exact conversation.

"Rhys… well, that's a long story. He was transferred to Persons Residential Care and ended up back at the city hospital after a… reaction to a drug. We were just visiting him this morning before I came in to work, and… he's not in good shape. I was hoping that things would be a lot better than they were."

"I'm sorry to hear that. Is there anything that we can do?"

"No. I don't think so. It's just a matter of time. Seeing if everything goes back to normal after a few days. Some of these therapies can be very tricky. I don't know if... this one that is being offered at Persons is risky. I wasn't happy with it from the start."

"I thought..." Lisa trailed off for a moment. "I thought trauma therapy was what he needed."

"It is. But this is an experimental treatment, and I'm not convinced that the drugs they are trialing are the best solution. I think they are too risky."

"I see. He won't be going back to Persons, then?"

"I hope not. And if he does, I hope it will be for generally accepted, approved therapies, not anything experimental."

"You are comfortable with the staff there?"

"No... I am not." Kenzie rubbed her forehead. "Mom, this is really getting into stuff I can't discuss with you. Stuff that has come up with work and anything related to Rhys's care... I can't really share them with you. I'm ethically bound to keep them confidential."

"But you are not happy with Persons. You don't want Rhys to go back there?"

"No. I'm hoping to be able to talk his grandmother out of it. I didn't want him in this trial to start with, but she insisted because they offered her some kind of grant or scholarship and talked up this trauma recovery program like it was a miracle cure. But that isn't what it is. It's... playing with people's brains when we don't know what we're doing."

"I see." Kenzie got the feeling that Lisa was writing notes to herself in the pauses, but wasn't sure what she would be taking note of.

Kenzie looked at the timer on the phone to see how long the call had been. "Well, I need to get back to work now, Mom. But I wanted to make sure that you knew I am okay. You don't need to worry about anything."

Lisa said her goodbyes, and they terminated the call.

51

Once she had finished processing everything in her inbox and voicemail, Kenzie had a list of calls she needed to make. Results that needed to be passed on to various parties, calls to families of victims, some information to pass on to Dr. Wiltshire, and so on.

She dialed the number for Detective Garcia, wondering whether she would be able to reach her. Garcia might be out on another call or deeply embroiled in her investigations. But Garcia answered right away.

"Dr. Kirsch. Good to hear from you."

"I have some information for you on the Janice Martin file. I'll send it to you by email, but I thought I would give you a heads-up."

"Of course. Let me just grab a pen. Okay, what do you have?"

"At the same time as the MDMA trial was going on, Janice was taking—or being given—other psychedelics as well. Both LSD and PCP were being used as well."

"LSD and PCP? You're kidding me. Those were approved for use in these trials, were they?"

"No," Kenzie agreed. "They weren't. And any trials that they were approved for use in would be highly regulated."

"I am *not* impressed with the regulation of the trials at Persons.

Where was the oversight? Who was watching over these people? We expect our laws to protect the vulnerable, not leave them open to every kind of abuse."

"Yeah," Kenzie agreed. "I'm really not happy with what I have seen over at Persons. They don't seem to have any trouble operating completely outside of the law."

"And you expect that *your* voice would carry some weight with them."

"As a representative of the medical examiner?" Kenzie asked, a little confused. "Yes. I expect them to at least respect my authority. But they don't seem to take kindly to any kind of oversight, do they?"

"I meant your family name," Garcia said. "Boy, I'm really impressed with all the work your family does in the medical field. I see your name everywhere."

Kenzie nodded. She was used to that. People often recognized her name from the foundation's charitable works and Lisa Cole Kirsch herself.

"My parents do a lot in the state. It's mostly run by my mother. My dad and I watch in awe and sign where we are told to."

"You're involved in the family foundation?"

"Only peripherally."

"And you don't find that conflicts with your medical examiner work?"

"No. Why would it?"

Though Kenzie knew she had already run into conflicts once when she had, without realizing it, signed a document that made it look as though she had a bias or conflict of interest. She had to be careful not to let that happen again.

Garcia's voice was cautious. "Well, funding psychiatric stuff at the hospital and at Persons and then having to investigate them."

Kenzie stared at the screen of her phone as if that might enlighten her as to what Garcia was talking about. How much was the concussion muddying up her thinking? She couldn't even follow what Garcia was saying.

"Pardon me?"

"I'm talking about your family foundation being involved in the funding of Persons."

"I… no, I didn't realize they had anything to do with Persons."

"Well, I can tell you from the paperwork we have been processing over there the last couple of days that they are."

Kenzie's mind immediately returned to the discussion she had just had with Lisa. Kenzie had told her that she didn't trust the staff at Persons or the trial protocol. She had thought it was strange that Lisa should be so interested in Rhys's care or how he was doing. She had thought that it was just because Lisa wanted to keep up with what was going on in Kenzie's life and what was important to her. She'd had no idea that the foundation was involved with Persons.

"They have made a large donation quite recently," Garcia informed her.

Kenzie rubbed the space between her brows. "Oh, this is not good."

"I assumed that you already knew about it and that you had… recused yourself or whatever it is that you must do in a case like this. I assumed the medical examiner's office already knew all the details about your family's involvement. I mean," Garcia's voice was conciliatory, "you aren't directly involved. Just because your family has given Persons a donation, that doesn't mean they are involved in the drug trials or the abuses that are going on there."

"But it suggests that we support what they're doing, which isn't true. I don't want anyone to think that I am involved in this in any way. Why didn't they tell me the foundation was involved in Persons?"

"They wouldn't have known you had anything to do with it as a medical examiner."

"Not in the beginning, maybe. But they certainly would have as soon as that video was leaked. And when my mother talked to me about it this morning."

"Ah. Well. You might want to talk to them about it, then. But I assume stuff like this happens all the time. They put money into so many different causes—the hospital and everything too—that there might be points at which they discover that they have invested in something they don't want to be associated with in the future."

"She was just asking me a few minutes ago about the staff at Persons. If I trusted them."

"And I guess you told her no."

"You bet I did."

"So maybe now she's trying to figure out how to get out of it. There was a contract for ongoing funding. I guess they'll take that to their lawyer and figure out how to get out of it."

The thought of ongoing funding going from the Kirsch family foundation into Persons was untenable.

"I'd better call them and find out what's going on. Or drive out to see her. Only I've got a ton of work to get done here. Maybe I should insist that she come here to see me. They're the ones who put money into it without telling me about it. I'm supposed to know all the recipients."

But she had to admit that she would only have been able to name two or three of them off the top of her head. And she hadn't really looked very carefully at the lists she had been given of institutions and programs that had received money from the foundation. She had never done any kind of due diligence to ensure that none of them had ever been associated with investigations by the medical examiner's office, or any of the medical regulators that she should be aware of.

But how could she be sure that none of the institutions they had dealt with had been involved in any investigations in the past? Or wouldn't be in the future? Just because someone died at an institution and the medical examiner's office had to look into it, that didn't mean they had done anything wrong. People died, which wasn't necessarily the fault of the hospital or medical facility providing them care.

"I guess... I'm going to need to investigate this some more," Kenzie told Garcia, flummoxed. "Thanks for giving me a heads-up."

"You're welcome. And how are you doing? Everybody in the building must have heard about your accident. No one spreads gossip like the boys in blue."

"Yes... well... it was just one of those things. The cars that were coming saw me far enough ahead of time to stop before they reached me. Almost."

"You could have been flattened. You don't know who it was? You never saw?"

"I don't know. Like I said in my report, a guy was talking to me earlier, and it could have been him, but I don't think it was. I thought before I got hit that it wasn't him. It was someone else. But I don't remember if I saw or felt something that told me it was someone else. It happened so fast. I felt the shove, and then I was out in traffic, trying to stop myself from falling. It was only a few seconds, if that. And I guess… no one else saw him, could say what had happened?"

"The investigating officer questioned as many witnesses as possible, but some people had already left the scene. No one saw the shove."

"It figures. I think it was just one of those random things."

"You mean you don't think it was related to Persons."

"Right. I don't think they had anything to do with it. It was just a random thing. Why would anyone at Persons come out here, to where I work, to shove me into traffic? What good would that do anyone?"

"Well, you did get a threatening voicemail as well. Why would they leave that? It was before I got the video of the therapy sessions, so we can assume that they didn't want those recordings to be seen by anyone."

"But you were the one going after those recordings, not me. I needed them as part of my investigation but, if they wanted to stop someone, wouldn't it be you?"

"Maybe I don't go wandering close enough to the road. Maybe they came here to talk to me or put a stop to my investigation and then saw you. Thought they would take the opportunity."

"I suppose," Kenzie admitted. "But it's hard to imagine. If you were one of the doctors there, and had either been involved in the abuse or knew that it was going on, wouldn't you want to get away? Just hit the road and keep on running so no one could follow you? Why stay here? Where you could be caught?"

Garcia laughed. "People are stupid. Or they think that the police are stupid. They don't think that they will be caught. You can bet that Dr. Miller never thought he would be caught."

"When he knew that the therapy sessions were being recorded?" Kenzie demanded. "How stupid do you have to be to let yourself be recorded abusing a patient?"

"Pretty stupid. Isn't that what I just said?"

"So you've arrested him?" Kenzie asked. "He's behind bars?"

"He is for now. I imagine he will make bail, and then whether he stays around to see the trial through or not…"

"I'm glad you got him."

"Me too. As soon as we saw what was on those recordings, we were on our way to arrest him." Garcia waited a few beats. "But you were attacked before I got to him. Do you think that it could have been Dr. Miller?"

Kenzie considered. She pictured the worried-looking doctor she had seen at Persons. The predator she had seen on the recording. She hadn't seen her attacker. She had only talked to Dr. Miller once, and the attacker had been behind her. How could she be expected to be able to see what had happened behind her back?

"Aren't there any… traffic cams or storefront cams that caught it? I just didn't see him."

"Nothing that caught that part of the road, unfortunately. You hear how there are cameras everywhere, but sometimes they just aren't where you want them to be. But you keep saying *him*. How do you know it was a man?"

Kenzie shook her head impatiently. She was just saying "him" because it was easier than "him or her." She didn't really know. But when she thought about it, she was pretty sure that it had been a man. Was that just her bias? That she thought that anyone who performed that kind of violence would be a man? Was it the size of his hands? The strength of the push? She couldn't remember either one particularly well, but her subconscious mind might have been more aware of it than she was.

"I just… think it was a man."

"Why?"

"Because… I just do. I don't know why. But you can't assume that is true."

"Could it have been Dr. Richards?"

Kenzie's immediate reaction was laughter. Of course it had not been Dr. Richards. But why not? What was it that made her react that way? She pictured the lovely Dr. Richards. Her finely lined face, her large blond curls, all looking like she had just stepped out of a salon. Smelling like jasmine and roses.

Kenzie stubbed her finger down on the desk as if to pin this thought before it could get away from her.

"Dr. Richards wears perfume."

"Ah," Kenzie could hear Garcia's smile in her voice. "The other senses kick into gear. So your attacker was not wearing perfume."

"No… unless the wind was blowing it away from me. And even then… she uses a good amount. I think I would still be able to smell it."

"Good," Garcia approved. "What *did* your attacker smell like?"

Kenzie closed her eyes to immerse herself in the scene again, but her head was throbbing and it was hard to concentrate.

"I don't know. There were other people there. Other smells from the street and my lunch. I don't know what he smelled like, but I know it wasn't like Dr. Richards's perfume."

"Well, that's one person eliminated. Of course, it doesn't mean she couldn't send someone else, but at least we know she wasn't at the scene when it happened."

"Do you really think I was attacked by someone at Persons?"

"I don't know. It's a definite possibility."

"You're pulling all their records and looking at everyone else. So if there was anyone else there who was involved in the abuse of the patients or anything else, then you'll know about it."

"I hope so. We didn't warn them that we were coming for everything, but…"

"But they could have started destroying evidence as soon as Mr. Isah died and the ME's office refused to stay out of it."

Garcia chuckled. "Yes. That's right. They've had over a week now.

Hopefully, they don't know how to permanently delete anything from their computers. The electronics guys are looking at them."

"Are they still operating? Without their computers?"

"They can get by with clipboards and paper records if they have to for a few days. And computers are easy to buy. I doubt if we caused anything more than a hiccup interrupting their services."

"You don't think that anyone else was involved in the assaults, though, do you?"

"Where were they when the assaults were happening? When patients complained? Who was supervising Dr. Miller? What kind of background checks did they run? Does he even have a current medical license? There are lots of things to look at. At the very least, they failed to supervise Miller's work properly. They never reviewed the therapy recordings. What's the point in recording them if you never look at them? Or if they looked at them, then why didn't they do anything about it?"

Kenzie nodded her agreement. Somebody should have known what was going on. There should have been plenty of red flags.

52

O h, hi, Kenzie."
Kenzie looked up to see Julie, the young woman who often stood in for her at the front desk and phone reception when Kenzie had to be in autopsy or somewhere else.

"Hi, Julie." Kenzie looked at her desk and then at her calendar, trying to identify why Julie was there.

"I know I'm early. You usually don't need me until the afternoon. But I figured you might be behind or want to leave early because of…" Julie tapped her own head. "You might not be feeling very well. I had an open block, so if you want me to start now, I can."

"Actually…" Kenzie looked at the papers and notes she had scattered in front of her. Some written while she was reviewing her in boxes and some while talking to Detective Garcia. She had been tired before arriving at the office, and working through the rest of the day as planned seemed like an impossible task. "That would be so great, Julie. You're sure it's not a problem?"

"Would I be here if it was? I am at your disposal. Whether you want to stay here and get something else done, or go home or to your couple's therapy, whatever you want."

"Good. Yeah. I'm going to gather all of this up," Kenzie gathered the random notes into a pile, "And make sure that I process everything and get everything into my task list. Thank you. You're a lifesaver."

"Happy to help." Julie gave her a sunny smile.

Since Julie was there regularly, she already knew all the procedures and where everything was, and she was ready to slip into Kenzie's seat as soon as she vacated it. Kenzie took her papers to the boardroom and sat down to go through them.

She hadn't talked to Vera since they had been in to visit Rhys. She had expected Vera to call her by now to see how the visit had gone or to talk to her about what she thought the best approach would be to help Rhys.

Kenzie hoped that she hadn't gotten to the hospital to find Rhys in worse shape than he had been the day before. It was possible for a patient in an agitated state to have medical complications or to do something to harm himself when he didn't have the capacity to realize the damage that he could do. Kenzie's stomach knotted as she thought about all the things that could have happened to prevent Vera from calling her to chat briefly about Rhys's situation.

Of course, the other possibility was that even though she had given Kenzie and Zachary permission to visit Rhys, she still didn't want to talk to Kenzie about his treatment. It was, after all, her business and not Kenzie's, and they had differed on key points.

Only now Vera knew that Kenzie had been right about the risks of the MDMA therapy. That it might not be the miracle cure that she was hoping for, but had the potential to do permanent damage.

Kenzie called Vera's number, unsure whether she would answer the phone. If she were at the hospital with Rhys, as Kenzie expected her to be, then it might be turned off. Or she might just not want to talk.

"Hello?"

"Vera, it's Kenzie. How are you? I was just thinking about you and Rhys and wondering how things were going."

She didn't ask whether anything had changed, leaving it up to Vera to provide as much information as she wanted to.

"He's sleeping," Vera said. "He hasn't slept since the therapy session and was getting more agitated. The nurse thought it might be because he was too tired."

"That can certainly make things worse," Kenzie agreed. "Good sleep is really important for good mental health."

"I don't know when he slept last. I don't think that they were making sure that he was sleeping when he was at Persons. He went under pretty quickly once they gave him a sedative."

"Hopefully, he'll feel a lot better when he wakes up."

"Yes," Vera agreed. She blew out her breath. "Oh, my. I never thought that I would hear Rhys chatter on like that again. He talked when he was a little boy. He was a little chatterbox. But I've gotten so used to him being silent, except for the times he would get a word or two out. Having him talk like that..." she trailed off. "Did he talk the whole time you were visiting him?"

"Yes," Kenzie agreed with a laugh. "Yes, he did. And I know what you mean about it being disconcerting. Though it must be a hundred times more startling for you; you have lived with his silence for years. Zachary and I have only been occasional visitors."

"I don't think I realized... I knew that Clarence's death was traumatic for him. That was when he stopped talking. But I thought..." The seconds ticked by while Vera struggled to put her thoughts into words. "I thought that it had made a hole. That all those memories of what had happened around the time of his death were gone and that his brain was trying to reconstruct things in a way that was acceptable to him. I knew he had difficulty speaking and communicating, but I thought that was... because of the drugs and therapy he'd had when they sent him to the first place. That it had changed his brain chemistry. That *they* were the ones who had caused it, not us."

Kenzie didn't know what to say. She murmured something that sounded soothing but didn't make much sense. She was thinking along the same lines as Vera was. Whatever had happened that night had been far more damaging than anyone in Rhys's family or treatment team had ever thought.

It wasn't gone. It wasn't buried far under the surface. On the contrary, it was always in the forefront of Rhys's mind, bubbling up again and again. The feelings, sounds, and sensations of that day repeated over and over.

At least, they did when he was under the influence of MDMA. Whether that was how Rhys felt all the time, Kenzie couldn't be sure. But she knew now that what had happened that day long ago was not gone and forgotten, leaving a void behind. It was there in Rhys's brain, looming up, ever-present.

"I guess… it was long past time for Rhys to talk about it," Vera said finally. "I don't know why it took until now for me to realize. But he needs to talk about it. However we can get him to do that."

Hopefully, Rhys wouldn't stop trying to talk about it when he was no longer feeling the effects of the MDMA.

"I think you're right," Kenzie agreed. "I think it would be really good to get him into a situation where he's encouraged to talk about it."

"Yes," Vera sighed. Kenzie knew she probably didn't want to talk about Clarence's death and her own daughter's guilt.

"Vera… I wanted to ask you about something. This is sort of a change of topic, so I'm sorry. I don't mean to imply that this is unimportant. Just that there's something else I need to know, too."

"Yes?"

"You mentioned that Rhys had gotten some kind of grant to get into that program at Persons. Where did that come from? Was that something you had applied for?"

"Oh, no. We were approached by someone. They said that he had been specially selected for the program, that they thought he would benefit from it, and that there was a special bursary—like a scholarship—to cover it."

"Who was it? Was it someone from the hospital? From Persons?"

"No, a charity that handles things like this. But he said they preferred to stay anonymous in cases like this one. They didn't want to put undue attention on Rhys."

53

K enzie called both Lisa and Walter and got voicemail for both of them. It wasn't unusual for her to have to leave a message for Walter. He was often busy with his lobbying. In meetings, behind closed doors, wining and dining influencers; he kept pretty busy. He would call her back when he was free, probably in the evening when he finished his dinner appointment.

Lisa was usually more available during the day, only unavailable when she was out at evening fundraiser events. If she were at a ladies' luncheon, or out with friends, or organizing an event, she would usually pause to answer the phone when she saw that it was Kenzie calling. It was unusual, but not unheard of, for Kenzie not to be able to reach either one of them.

There was a tap at the boardroom door, and Dr. Cook stuck his head in. He peered at the papers spread out in front of Kenzie.

"Everything okay, Dr. Kirsch?"

"Yes... but I'm not sure I'm being very productive today. I'm distracted and this headache..."

"Why don't you go home? You already have someone covering reception. And you normally have this afternoon off, don't you?"

"Yes. But I figured I would work through today because I missed yesterday afternoon..."

"You didn't miss yesterday afternoon because you were taking a vacation or playing hooky. You missed because you were hit by a car. And I think you need to take a day or two to recover from it. We don't have anything that is so urgent that you need to work injured. You will recover faster if you take the time to heal than if you try to push through and wear yourself out."

Kenzie waffled on it. She had an ideal in her mind of what she wanted to do, and then the practicality of Dr. Cook's advice. She knew she wasn't at her best. Not just because of the head injury, but also because of her distraction with Rhys's problems and the questions running through her mind about the threads that connected the three cases—the deaths of Leander Isah and Janice Martin, and Rhys's therapy at Persons. It was all connected, and those connections worried her. Their implications pressed darkly on the back of her mind.

"Go home," Dr. Cook said firmly. "Julie and I will hold down the fort. But I won't start any postmortems without you. You won't be out of the loop. I'll catch up on signing reports and reviewing your work on the Isah and Martin deaths so that I'll be up to speed when you get back and are ready to discuss them."

Kenzie sighed. "Are you sure?"

"Why push it? If you try to work while you have a concussion, you will make mistakes. We don't want any mistakes. Better to wait."

"We'll get behind."

"We'll be fine. We can get someone else in if we need another pair of hands. But we don't have a brain to replace yours. You're the one who knows where everything is, the files, the procedures, the history. We'll need that when you get back. Nice and fresh and ready to go."

"Okay." Kenzie gathered her papers together. "But only because you insisted."

"I did," he agreed.

Zachary was surprised when he looked up to see who had arrived and saw that it was Kenzie. His face brightened, but he looked confused and concerned at the same time.

"Is everything okay? I didn't think you would be able to make it today? Don't get me wrong, I am glad you did, but… is everything okay?"

"Yes. Dr. Cook said to go home to recuperate. He would hold down the fort."

"And that worked?"

"He insisted."

"He insisted," Zachary repeated meditatively. "I'll have to remember to try that sometime."

Kenzie laughed. She knew that she was stubborn and didn't always listen to good advice when it was given to her, or listen to Zachary's cautions or other things that she didn't want to hear. She hadn't gotten into the position she was in by being a shy, retreating wallflower.

Kenzie took the chair next to Zachary's in the waiting room. He reached over and rubbed her back. "Glad you're here."

"Thanks. Me too."

In a few minutes, the receptionist, Elizabeth, called them forward and let them know Dr. Boyle was ready for them. Zachary and Kenzie made their way to her office and made a little small talk to get settled into the session. Dr. Boyle opened their file in front of her to review the last session's notes.

"Any new developments that you would like to discuss? How have things gone the last couple of weeks?"

Zachary looked at Kenzie, his expression and body language indicating she should take this one. Dr. Boyle looked at Kenzie as well, eyebrows lifted in expectation.

Kenzie glanced at Zachary, wondering how much he wanted revealed and what he wanted to focus on.

"Well, Zachary's friend—our friend—Rhys, he had a breakdown, and we don't know all the reasons for that. He was hospitalized and has been through some therapy since then, which has been… worrying for both of us."

Dr. B nodded. "I'm sorry to hear that. What has been the biggest impact of this?"

Kenzie looked at Zachary again to see if he wanted to jump in, but he did not take the initiative.

"It's been stressful. As well as not knowing what precipitated this breakdown, he's also been put into an experimental therapy program that I had significant concerns about. And I know that it's probably affecting Zachary as well. Making it more difficult to sleep..."

"Zachary?" Dr. B. prompted.

"Yeah. It's been... challenging," Zachary agreed.

They both waited for him to elaborate. Zachary looked at Kenzie and then away.

"I don't know much about the cases that Kenzie has been working on. But I know a little bit. Things that have made it to the news and certain discussion forums. And... things that I have overheard."

Kenzie cut a glance toward him. She didn't think that she had said anything within his hearing that was confidential, but she would have to be more aware of that in the future.

"I know that there were abuses at Persons," Zachary said. "The facility where Rhys was being treated. I know that Kenzie was investigating a death—two deaths—there. And so, knowing that Rhys was there, has been very... has made me very anxious."

Dr. B nodded. "That makes sense. How has Rhys been?"

Zachary scratched the back of his neck. "The drug therapy that they did—he reacted to it. He's been agitated, hallucinating, talking and crying about when his grandpa was killed. I'm afraid he's never going to come out of it. That's how he'll be for the rest of his life."

"He should come back down off of it," Kenzie tried to reassure Zachary. "In the case studies that I was able to find, they came back down after a few days and recovered. It's just a matter of keeping him calm and treating him while he's still reacting. They don't know why some people react that way."

"I know that's what the doctors are *saying*," Zachary agreed. "But I'm still afraid we've lost him for good."

Kenzie nodded. She knew better than to try to argue with a feeling. Feelings, as they had often discussed in their sessions, could not be argued down with logic or controlled by the person feeling them. Their reactions and responses could be controlled, and some situations could be reframed to make the person better understand what they were feeling or relieve some of the negative feelings. Still, there was no such thing as "turning off" a feeling. Only of hiding or repressing it, actions which could cause negative emotions to grow over time.

"That's scary," Kenzie acknowledged. "That thought really scares me too. I try to focus on the likely positive outcomes. But that doesn't mean there aren't possible negative outcomes either."

Zachary nodded. He stared down at the carpet in front of his feet. "I don't know how to turn the negative thoughts off."

"Have you tried any mindfulness activities?" Dr. B asked. "Any anxiety-releasing exercises?"

Zachary tended to scoff at things like controlled breathing and visualization. He didn't say that they didn't work this time, but it was clear that he didn't think they would and that was why he hadn't tried anything.

"How about your antianxiety meds?" Dr. B asked. "That's why you have them. To help to get through rough spots like this."

Kenzie shook her head, but Zachary nodded, surprising her. He pressed his lips together and looked away. "Yeah. I have a couple of nights over the last week."

Kenzie was stunned. Zachary always resisted taking the antianxiety meds, complaining about how they made him groggy in the morning and that he could manage better without them. He always pushed back when she suggested he take them, though sometimes he would eventually agree that it was a good idea.

She was shocked that not only had he taken the meds on his own without any encouragement from her, but also that he had done it without her knowledge.

He was a grown man and, of course, he was perfectly capable of taking care of his own health and had done it for years before meeting her and been stable most of the time. He didn't need her to tell him to take his meds, and he didn't need to report back to her whether he had taken something.

But she had thought that she would know. She would recognize that his anxiety was ramping up, and then she would recognize that he had taken something for it, the dampening effect of the drug on his panic or intrusive thoughts.

"I didn't even know," she told him. "You didn't tell me you were feeling so bad."

Zachary shrugged.

"You can share that with me," Kenzie told him firmly. "I want to be there for you. To help you. You don't have to hide it from me."

"I wasn't... you just had so much on your plate already. You were trying to do what you needed to so that you could issue your report on the two deaths. And you were just as worried about Rhys as I was. You need to get your sleep so that you can get up in the morning for work. You don't need me pulling you down and causing you extra worries."

54

Kenzie couldn't think of what to say. She looked to Dr. Boyle for help.

"Zachary recognizes that you have had a lot of stress this week as you have been trying to work through these issues as well," Dr. B stated.

"Yes. I know I've been stressed too. But I don't want that to stop him from sharing with me when he's feeling bad. Especially..."

"Especially what?" Dr. B prodded after a few seconds of silence.

"Especially... at this time of year when we know he is vulnerable to worsening depression. Any changes in his mental health could have a significant effect on how he makes it through the season..."

Dr. B looked at Zachary. "Do you think you might need some more support, which you're pulling away from? Do you not want Kenzie to see how you're feeling in case your depression is worsening?"

"I don't know. I thought I was doing the right thing. That I was helping her and being supportive of her needs."

"And you were. But let's talk about your needs too. How would you rate your depression this past week, as compared to the same time last month?"

Kenzie still had to learn to use these kinds of qualifiers and scales when asking Zachary about his depression. Not just asking him if he was feeling okay or whether he thought he might be slipping into depression again.

Zachary was silent for a few minutes, considering the question. Then he finally let out a sigh. "I guess... on a scale from one to ten, I was a four or five this time last month. And maybe a... six this week."

Still low enough that Kenzie wasn't too concerned about it, but trending in the wrong direction. As they had all known that it would.

"Good," Dr. B pronounced. She didn't say that he needed to evaluate his depression meds or that she wanted to immediately increase them. She just let that sit for a bit.

Zachary eventually looked at her. "Good?"

"Good. Thank you for giving me a nice firm evaluation. How do you feel about that?"

"Well..." Zachary took a peek at Kenzie before looking back at Dr. B again. "It's not much of a change. And we're both worried about Rhys. It's normal for it to be worse this time of year, but I think it's not too bad yet."

Dr. B made a couple of notes on the file in front of her. "You're not concerned about it."

"No. I don't think we need to make any changes."

"Okay. Kenzie, how do you feel about it?"

"Worried..." Kenzie looked at him, but he kept his face toward Dr. B, not looking at Kenzie. "But I'm more worried about you feeling like you need to hide what you feel from me than I am about a slight change in your depression."

Zachary nodded. He didn't voice any defense for this behavior. They both understood that he had been conditioned by society and the many families and social workers he had dealt with over the years to hide his negative feelings and pretend to be a strong, stalwart provider who didn't have tender feelings of his own. It took a lot of trust and reconditioning to confess how he was feeling to Kenzie. He had done well the previous year, when he'd had to be admitted to the hospital, of revealing to her the depth of his depression and self-destructive feelings.

With some more work, she thought they could get to the point where he would tell her about his slightly-worse feelings directly instead of having to share them in couple's therapy with Dr. Boyle mediating between them. They were making progress. They hadn't needed to pry out of Zachary the feelings he was having now.

"Is there anything that would make it easier to share these feelings with Kenzie?" Dr. Boyle asked.

Zachary shrugged. "I don't think so. I just... don't want to stress her out more than she already is."

"If she told you that she took a sleeping pill because she was having trouble putting the investigation aside and going to sleep, would you be upset by that?"

"No." Zachary shook his head. "I'd be glad to know she was taking care of herself."

"Kenzie," Dr. B turned her attention to Kenzie. "Do you think you would be upset if Zachary told you that he took an anxiety pill in order to calm down his racing thoughts?"

"No."

"Do you think you could accept it without worrying that he needed further intervention?"

Kenzie rolled her eyes. She didn't like being made to feel like she let her worry get out of control. Because that wasn't true at all. She worried about Zachary but didn't harass him to take other medications, call Dr. B, or admit himself to psych. At least, she didn't think she did. Not usually.

"Yes, I think I could do that." She looked at Zachary. "I will try not to assume that it means anything more than that you needed to take one antianxiety pill to settle down and get a good sleep."

Zachary nodded. "I'll try to... make it more natural to tell you."

Dr. B looked satisfied. "I think the two of you will find it helpful if you can share feelings and strategies without it having to be a big, life-changing event. You've come a long way in developing trust and sharing your feelings, but you are still both pretty sensitive about upsetting the other person by disclosing your true feelings. We'll keep working on that."

Kenzie and Zachary both nodded.

"And I hope that next week, I'll hear positive news about your friend Rhys."

They bought ice cream on the way home, as was their tradition. Kenzie was trying not to watch Zachary, assessing whether he was feeling stressed and anxious. He would let her know. She didn't need to analyze everything he did and said to evaluate his mental state. He had been quiet about his feelings while she'd been working on the Persons cases. But she had still known that he had been worried and anxious about Rhys, even if they hadn't talked about it at length and he hadn't mentioned taking anxiety pills during the week.

"Peanuts and chocolate?" Zachary asked, looking over the ice cream flavors.

"Mmm," Kenzie shook her head. She didn't like peanuts or peanut butter in ice cream. "Butterscotch ripple?"

"Is there one with butterscotch and chocolate ripples? I think you deserve both."

Kenzie laughed. "No, I don't think so... we could get a butterscotch ripple and a chocolate ripple and have a scoop of each."

"Ah, good thought," Zachary agreed. "Or we could do the butterscotch ripple and..." he gestured dramatically to the toppings section nearby, "chocolate sauce on top."

"Ooh. Yes, I think you've nailed it. Is that what you want too, or do you want something else?"

"I'm good with that. And what we've already got in the freezer."

There were several pints of other various flavors in the freezer already. Kenzie added a few bananas to their basket. That at least made it look like they weren't just binging on ice cream. Though, of course, they would be part of their banana splits.

After checking out, it wasn't long before they were home. They had just put their bowls of ice cream on the table when the doorbell rang. Kenzie looked at Zachary.

"Are you expecting a delivery?"

"No." Zachary took out his phone to check the doorbell cam. He raised his brows. "It's your parents."

"What?" Kenzie stared at him in disbelief.

"Walter and Lisa."

Her father had shown up at her house once or twice unannounced, but Lisa never would. She would always check with Kenzie before she showed up. Generally, she just invited Kenzie to come see her if she wanted to talk to her about something. Walter and Lisa were divorced and hadn't lived together for years. It made no sense that they would show up together.

Zachary could be mistaken. It could be Walter and some other woman that he had been dating. Zachary had only met Lisa once or twice. He might mistake someone else for her, especially if Walter were dating someone of similar physical appearance to Lisa. He probably had a "type."

Even though he was a PI and part of his business was recognizing faces. The man was not infallible, and he was looking at a small screen.

Kenzie went to the door anyway. If it was Walter, she should be the one to answer it and either welcome him in or turn him away if she thought he was up to no good. With her concussion and seeing Rhys and it being a therapy day, which always wrung out her emotions, she was exhausted and didn't want to have to see anyone.

Especially Walter, who she always had to be wary of and try to figure out his motivations and whether he were being upfront with her. Or more accurately, to figure out how he was not being upfront with her. Walter always held something back. As a lobbyist, constantly negotiating and exercising power plays, he always needed something in his back pocket that he could bring out when negotiations broke down and more pressure was needed. It was second nature, whether it was because he was a lobbyist or whether he was a good lobbyist because that was the way he was made.

Kenzie took a deep breath and let it out slowly. She didn't have to let him in. She could tell him that it was a bad time, and they would have to set up another time to meet. He had shown up without calling or making an appointment first, so she was well within her rights to tell him that it simply wouldn't work. She opened the door.

It *was* Walter and Lisa. Kenzie gaped at them. "Mom? Dad? What is this? What are you doing here?"

Lisa smiled. "I'm sorry to descend upon you like this without any warning. But since you called this morning, we figured we should handle this sooner rather than later. And better off face to face."

Kenzie opened her mouth to object.

She didn't have problems telling Walter it wasn't a good time and sending him on his way. But Lisa was another matter altogether. She wasn't used to telling her mother no about anything.

"If we could come in, MacKenzie. We'll keep it as brief as possible."

Kenzie stepped back and motioned them in. Zachary stood at the end of the hallway. He stepped out of the way, ducking back into the kitchen. Kenzie followed her parents toward the living room. They could see into the kitchen, where she and Zachary had been preparing their splits. Lisa followed her eyes.

"Oh, we're interrupting your dinner. I'm so sorry."

"Well, no, we were just having some ice cream…" Kenzie didn't bother explaining the post-therapy-session ice cream tradition to Lisa. Wasn't she the one who used to take Kenzie out for ice cream after a trip to the doctor or dentist? "Would you like to join us?" Kenzie offered, rather than telling Zachary to put the ice cream away and they would have it later.

"I wouldn't say no to ice cream," Walter said jovially, immediately stepping into the kitchen.

Lisa looked less certain. She smoothed her blouse and skirt down, as if checking to make sure that her stomach was still flat. She was remarkably svelte for someone who spent so much time at fancy fundraising dinners. She didn't eat very much of the steak and lobster.

"Come on in, Mom," Kenzie encouraged. "It won't hurt to have a spoonful of ice cream."

Lisa entered the little kitchen, looking around as if she weren't sure she belonged there. "Well, maybe half a banana," she suggested, looking at the small bunch that sat on the table awaiting the banana splits.

"It's not really a banana split if all you eat is half of a banana," she told Lisa.

But Lisa had already made up her mind, and her banana split *would* consist of half a banana. Kenzie might be able to talk her into a drizzle of chocolate syrup, but she wasn't counting on it.

For a few minutes, they were occupied with getting their splits ready. Walter had to look through all the flavors of ice cream, weighing the merits of each one. Always one to make a careful, discerning choice. Kenzie and Zachary had already decided what they wanted, and Lisa was going with half a banana. Eventually, they were all finished dishing up and sat down at the table with their bowls, looking at each other.

Kenzie wanted to know what they were doing there.

55

You called and left messages for both of us this morning," Lisa said briskly. "So I assume you have at least some idea of what this is about."

Kenzie looked down at her ice cream and had a few spoonfuls, making sure to get lots of chocolate sauce in each one, before answering.

"I was calling you about Rhys."

Lisa nodded.

Zachary looked back and forth at them. "Why would you be calling her—them—about Rhys?" he asked. "They don't even know Rhys."

"No," Kenzie agreed. "But I mentioned the first day when Rhys was admitted to the hospital, talked about what had happened and how worried I was about him."

"We both were," Zachary agreed seriously, looking at Walter and Lisa. "And we still are."

Kenzie nodded. "But I think... well, I guess maybe I should have figured it out sooner. Where the grant for Rhys to get into Persons and into the trauma therapy study there came from."

"I did try to talk to you about it," Lisa said, "but you were so busy with everything else. You won't just stop and read an email. You get caught up in everything else and think that any of the family stuff is a lower priority. I don't know how to change that."

Kenzie rubbed her eyes and wished her head weren't pounding so much. Zachary looked at her, but wasn't following the conversation. Kenzie knew what was coming, but she had already been thinking about it for a few days, and Zachary was coming into it late in the game.

"Mom… it isn't that I don't think it is important. It's just that… other people can handle it. Before I started getting more involved in the foundation, you had other people to handle it. So I know you can do it without me."

"But we don't want to do it without you. It is *your* legacy. You need to step up and help run it and decide what you want to finance and what you do not. And you're a doctor. You have a much better understanding of the different causes than any of the non-professionals on the board."

"It isn't for me to run. Not yet, anyway."

"We don't want you to just take it over when we are gone," Lisa said. "What kind of parents would we be if we just dumped it on you at the end of the day? You need to learn the business and how to run it gradually so that you're ready for it when it is your turn to take over. You need to be trained and taught what to do and how to direct it."

"Okay. Yes," Kenzie agreed. "I agree with all of that. But I can't run it at the same time as I'm running the medical examiner's office. It's too much for me to take everything on."

"But you need to take more. You need to have a say in what is being financed and how. Otherwise…" Lisa sighed and shook her head.

Walter took up the conversational torch. "Otherwise, you end up in a mess like we find ourselves in now."

Zachary shook his head. "Should I even be here? It sounds like you're talking about family foundation stuff, and I am not part of that. I can work on other things while the three of you talk." He picked up his bowl as if to leave.

"No," Lisa and Kenzie said together.

They exchanged a look.

"This is about you too, Zachary," Lisa said firmly. "Not as a director of the foundation, but as someone who has an interest in how the foundation runs and the parties that it benefits."

Zachary shook his head. "That's for you and Kenzie to decide."

"If we are focusing our efforts on a mental health project, then shouldn't you have some say in it?" Walter asked. "You are the one who is most interested in and invested in deciding what mental health projects are the most viable and helpful programs. For the rest of us... it's just academic. We can look at numbers and talk about what has been funded in the past, but *you* are the one who knows the bones of the business. Which programs really need funding and are doing the most good."

Zachary had been happy to sit by while Kenzie and her parents discussed mental health issues in a general way. And while Tyrrell, his brother, helped to pick out the companies and programs that he thought would make the most difference, based on his experience with abuse, addiction, and family issues. Zachary had been happy to let them all do their thing and cheer them from the sidelines.

But Lisa was right; he was the one who had the most experience and the most insight into what programs would be the most impactful.

He looked uncomfortable. "I'm not part of the foundation..."

"What did you think of the program we put Rhys into?" Walter asked.

Zachary opened his mouth and then sudden understanding entered his expression. Until then, he had not guessed what Kenzie had—that the Kirsch family foundation was the anonymous donor who had reached out to Vera to sponsor Rhys's admission to the trauma program.

"That *you* put Rhys into?" he repeated.

"Well," Walter shrugged. "It was his grandmother who put him into the program, of course, but we are the ones who approached her with the idea and funded his admission to Persons. She would not have been able to afford to put him into the program herself. And he needed a trauma treatment program, didn't he?"

"Well, yes," Zachary agreed cautiously.

"But you wouldn't have put him into that one."

Zachary shook his head slowly. He shot a look at Kenzie, worrying about whether he was doing something wrong by admitting this. He didn't want to alienate her parents and cause some kind of rift between them and Kenzie. Kenzie nodded, trying to convey that it was okay to express his opinion on the matter. And of course, he already knew how she felt about the program. They had discussed it repeatedly. He had been right behind her in trying to dissuade Vera from putting Rhys into it.

"No," he admitted. "I wouldn't have put him into it. These drug trials are... controversial. Untested. And there have been some very negative experiences around them. Even if they show good results overall, they have to be properly regulated and supervised and some patients will react very badly to the medications. Like Rhys did."

"You anticipated that he might have a reaction to it?"

"The risks are too high. Especially with a teenager. They often have paradoxical reactions to psychiatric meds."

"Why?" Lisa asked.

"I don't know." Zachary looked at Kenzie. "Your daughter can tell you the whys better than I can. I just know that it's true. Kids don't react the same way as adults. They are the ones who start hearing voices or having suicidal thoughts even though it works just fine for most adults."

"Changing hormones," Kenzie shrugged. "The brain is rewiring itself. They metabolize drugs differently. They are more likely to be heavy drinkers or into recreational drugs and not tell their parents or doctor. We don't know all the factors."

"When Kenzie said that Rhys was in crisis and needed some kind of treatment soon, we acted," Lisa explained. "Maybe before checking things out carefully enough. Persons was strongly promoting this new trauma therapy program they were working on. It was being touted as the most revolutionary and successful trauma program, and they were the only ones in the state authorized to offer it to teens. It just seemed like the natural choice. It was close to his family. It was trauma therapy. It was something he hadn't tried before. It was the only one open to teens. All his family needed was the money to get into the program."

Zachary nodded. He kept his eyes down, not letting Lisa look at them. Kenzie put her hand briefly over his, not wanting him to feel badly for admitting that he wasn't impressed with the drug program and would have recommended against it. There was nothing wrong with revealing that he would not have recommended a program that they now knew had been all wrong for Rhys. Run by people who were, at the very least, looking the other way and ignoring the problems within the program.

"There are things that I can't tell you, Mom," Kenzie told them. "You'll hear some of them in the news over the next week or two. But I can't tell you myself. If you had approached me about this program and about funding it for Rhys, I would have told you no."

"But we couldn't approach you on a program at a facility you were already dealing with on another matter," Lisa pointed out. "You would have had to recuse yourself and not say anything about it, just like you can't say anything now. We knew you were investigating a death at the facility, and we couldn't talk to you about this."

Kenzie turned her palms upward in a pleading gesture. "If you knew I was investigating a death at Persons, then why would you think that Rhys going there for a program was a good idea?"

"People die in hospitals," Walter said baldly. "And from what we saw in the news, it was the result of an altercation with the staff, not anything to do with the therapy program. And there wasn't anything to suggest that the patient was part of that trial. The trial was not even mentioned, so we assumed it had nothing to do with his death."

"I don't get this," Kenzie said. "You just decided unilaterally that you would take Rhys and put him into this trauma program because you figured it was the best thing for him. You knew there might be a problem at that institution and that I was investigating it. Still, you didn't let that affect your decision. You didn't even bother to *tell* me that you had made this decision."

"It was… meant to be a nice surprise for you," Walter said lamely. "Later on down the line, when you found out about it and you were no longer involved in any investigation at Persons. You would find out that we were the ones who had put Rhys through this program, and would be impressed with how well Rhys did in the program, and you would be grateful that we had taken the initiative and put him into it."

"But it didn't work out that way," Lisa said, her eyes sad. "Clearly."

And if Rhys hadn't reacted so badly to the MDMA, maybe things would have worked out how her parents had planned. But there was always the concern that he would be abused in the program as Isah had been. Or that he would be given non-approved drugs, as Janice had been. Kenzie's parents hadn't stopped to thoroughly investigate the program and whether it was being run properly. Maybe they wouldn't have found out anything even if they had looked, but they had not taken any time to investigate it. Not when Rhys had gotten into the program the day after Kenzie had told Lisa about him.

"I think it's best," Kenzie said slowly, "if you don't pick out individuals you think will benefit from specific treatments. If you are going to fund mental health initiatives, then pick the study or the company doing it, or a special media campaign or whatever. Don't pick a person and interfere with their treatment."

"Interfere?" Lisa challenged. "You wanted to get him out of the hospital and into a program. That family would not have had the money to do that. They didn't have any options available to them."

It was true. Kenzie had been desperate to get Rhys out of the hospital, where he had not been getting any effective treatment as far as she could tell, and into a program where he could try something new, something that would lead to success. Lisa had responded to that urgency, but things had not worked out the way she had hoped.

56

"W e should go out to dinner," Walter suggested jovially, now that the serious business was complete.

Kenzie looked down at the remnants of the ice cream melted in the bottom of her bowl. "After ice cream?"

"Well, why not? You could eat again in a couple of hours, couldn't you? I never knew you to have a poor appetite. And your mother..." Walter shrugged. "She only ate half a banana. She can eat dinner."

Walter looked expectantly at Zachary, waiting for him to chime in that he could eat in a couple of hours.

"No," Kenzie said firmly. "I do not want to go out anywhere else today. And I don't want to make something at home or entertain you for the next few hours until everyone is hungry again, either. This has all been... it's been a really tough day, and I can't deal with any more stress. We'll have to take a rain check on dinner."

"Tomorrow?" Walter suggested. "My calendar is miraculously clear for dinner tomorrow. I was going to call around to set up a business dinner, but if I could eat with my daughter and her family, that would be much better."

Kenzie turned tired eyes toward her mother, waiting for her to announce that she had a fundraiser that she needed to be at. Lisa always had some kind of event that she needed to attend. If Kenzie wanted to get onto her social calendar, she needed to schedule it weeks in advance.

"I need to speak at a girls' empowerment evening in Montpelier," Lisa said. "But I am free after that. I don't have to stay to eat at that one. They're just having pizza or some kind of fast food afterward."

Lisa wouldn't stay for that. She would never have planned to in the first place, so she wouldn't have to talk her way out of it now. She had probably planned to go home for a home-cooked—or at least, home-warmed—dinner of chicken and rice or salad and a quiet evening.

"Well?" Walter looked at Kenzie expectantly. "What are the odds of both of us being available for supper at a moment's notice? If you tried, you probably couldn't find another night that we were both free between now and Christmas."

That was probably true. And even if they did find an evening that they could both make work, there was no guarantee that Zachary would be in any shape to go to it. Who knew how he would feel as they got closer to Christmas Eve. She looked at him, trying to read his expression and anticipate what he would want to do. He shrugged at her, indicating that she could agree to it if she wanted to. If not, she could use him as an excuse. He would follow her lead.

"Well, I suppose," Kenzie agreed, trying not to sound too reluctant. "If it works for both of you, that has to be some kind of a sign. When and where do you want to meet?"

Kenzie was eager to hit the sack, even though it was earlier than their usual bedtime. "I hope you don't mind," she told Zachary. "I'm exhausted. It's been such a busy day, and my brain is just wrung out. Even watching TV would be pointless."

"Then let's get to bed," Zachary agreed. No argument. Kenzie knew that getting to sleep early would be a problem for him. He might not even be able to get to sleep for a few more hours. It might screw up his sleep schedule for the rest of the night. And screwing up his sleep schedule was something that she didn't really want to do.

"Are you sure?" Kenzie checked. "You probably don't want to."

"If I don't fall asleep with you, I'll just get back up. Watch TV or work on some photographs until my body decides that it is ready for sleep. Then I'll come back in."

She was glad he didn't say he would just sleep on the couch. She was comforted by the fact that he would be at her side for the few hours that he slept. She could reach out in her sleep and touch him, warm and solid, in the bed beside her.

"Okay. Then I'm going to sleep."

Whether it was the concussion or just her general exhaustion, Kenzie fell asleep quickly and slept through the night, not even aware of whether Zachary had gotten up during the night. The next morning, she found him in the living room working on his computer, the smell of fresh coffee rich in the air. They had a pleasant breakfast, both quiet and thinking their own thoughts about Rhys and work and the planned dinner with Kenzie's parents that evening. Kenzie's head was not hurting as much as it had the previous day, so she hoped to put in a full day of work and fulfill all her usual responsibilities.

She parked her car in its usual spot in the parking garage attached to the building. As she walked from her car toward the elevator, she heard the hollow echo of heels hitting the concrete, which was matched in time to hers, off just a fraction of a second so that it was jarring to Kenzie's ears. She turned her head to see who was there, as the police station wouldn't open to the public for another hour. There wasn't anyone else who usually parked on the same level as Kenzie at the same time. She could hear the woman's shoes behind her, but couldn't turn her head far enough to see who it was without being obvious. She didn't want to look anxious or snoopy, so she didn't.

Not at first.

But the sound kept following her, and Kenzie's chest tightened. It set off all her jangly nerves. The ones that had become much more sensitive since her kidnapping. Something was wrong, and she didn't want this woman, whoever she was, anywhere near her. She stopped and turned around to confront her. She didn't care how paranoid she looked.

The woman following her, closing the gap between them with each step, was Dr. Richards.

57

"What are you doing here?" Kenzie demanded.

There was absolutely no good reason for her to be in the building. Richards didn't have anything to do there. Even if she were a member of the public wanting to file a police report, that didn't give her access to a parking space in the garage. It didn't give her a security pass. And the police department complaints desk would not open for another hour.

"You come to my place of work uninvited," Dr. Richards challenged. "Why shouldn't I come to yours?"

"Actually, I was invited to your workplace," Kenzie pointed out. "I was invited there to review a death scene and retrieve a dead body."

"And then you were told that there was no reason for you to be there. That you didn't need to investigate it. And you still did. And you kept coming back, even after you were warned."

Kenzie narrowed her eyes at Dr. Richards. "You were the one who called in that threat that was left on my voicemail?"

"I don't know what threat you're talking about," Dr. Richards said unconvincingly. "Why couldn't you just stay out of it and mind your own business? Why did you have to come in and screw everything up for everyone? Do you know how many people rely on us? How many people we are providing an essential service for? And what do you think will happen to all those people if we have to close down?"

"I'm not closing you down," Kenzie told her. She looked around for a security guard. There was always a guard close by, someone who saw her to and from her car. Where was he today? Out to pick up a coffee or donut for breakfast? Taking a bathroom break? Why wasn't he there when Kenzie actually needed him? "I don't have the authority to shut you down, so I don't know what you're talking about. If you're dealing with problems with the police or other regulators, you need to talk to them, not me. I don't have anything to do with it."

"It's because of you and your inquiries. You snooping where you are not wanted or needed."

"I'm required by law to investigate every death that occurs at a mental institution," Kenzie pointed out. "I didn't write the law. I'm just following it. Did you think that all the abuses would never come to light? That you could just continue operating in the dark like you were doing forever, and no one would ever be the wiser?" She couldn't understand how anyone could think they could allow illegal human experimentation and physical and sexual abuse to run rampant in the institution and believe it would never get out to the authorities. Sooner or later, they were bound to be investigated for something. Then the dominoes would start to tumble, one after another, all in a row.

"I didn't know anything about any abuse," Dr. Richards snapped. "Do you think I would allow that to continue if I had known about it? Once I found out, I would have shut it down. And we would have been able to continue our efforts to help those who have been so terribly abused in the past, to help them to confront their demons and enjoy life again. To give them back their childhoods, their teens, the years they suffered in silence."

Kenzie thought about Rhys's silence and swallowed.

Your friends will benefit by you staying out of the way.

Of course Dr. Richards had been talking about Rhys. She knew he was a friend of Kenzie's because of the Kirsch family foundation.

She knew that the foundation had sponsored his registration in the program. The donor might have been anonymous to Vera, but had to be properly accounted for on Persons's books.

"I did what I was required to do by law," Kenzie said. "It's not my fault you and the other doctors broke the law. You had to know there were problems with how the program was being run."

Dr. Richards's lovely face twisted into an angry scowl. "I'm supposed to know everything the other doctors are doing? Everything was set up the way it was supposed to be. We got all the approvals and ran it the way we were supposed to. What they did on their own is not my fault."

Kenzie watched Dr. Richards's hands warily. She didn't want to end up on the business end of a scalpel. She'd seen that movie before.

"Look. I'm sorry things turned out badly for you. I hope it all works out and you can continue running your facility. But people died." She met the woman's clear blue eyes. "Not just Leander and Janice. Others too. And who knows how many of the patients were abused by Dr. Miller? All of them? Just some of them? You're supposed to be healing people; instead, they're being put through additional traumas. Incapacitated by drugs and abused. How do you think they felt?"

Dr. Richards's lips pressed together. Despite her salon-fresh appearance, she wasn't looking so beautiful anymore. "I know how they felt!" she growled. "And I would have put a stop to it. I never had the chance. You just swept in and destroyed everything I built."

"Everything okay over here?"

Kenzie breathed a sigh of relief at the husky male voice that interrupted their conversation. A security guard in uniform moved toward them. "Bert."

He nodded. He recognized her, of course, and turned his gaze on Dr. Richards. Kenzie held her breath, worried that the guard would melt at the sight of her. Would assume, as they all did, that a beautiful, vulnerable-looking woman could not be a threat. That she was a friend of Kenzie's or someone who had wandered in by mistake or who needed help.

"What's going on here?" Bert demanded, taking a couple more steps toward Richards, his hand on his taser. "Are you causing trouble for Dr. Kirsch?"

He must have heard them arguing, heard the tone of Dr. Richards's accusations and complaints, even if he hadn't been able to discern the words.

"We're just having a conversation," Dr. Richards told him, giving him a warm smile. She was very good at what she did. Using her body to get what she wanted. Kenzie wondered fleetingly how often she herself used her feminine wiles without even realizing it. Harmless flirting to get out of a traffic ticket, to get into a show after the ticket booth had closed, or to explain her presence somewhere she hadn't been invited. It wasn't something she even thought of, just something inside her that turned on when the circumstances demanded it. How much of that had been ingrained by society? And how much by her mother, telling her how to always be gracious and still get what she wanted under every circumstance?

"You are not authorized to be in here," Bert said flatly, ignoring the smile and the charm. "Dr. Kirsch? You want me to call the police?"

"No." Kenzie gave Dr. Richards a look. "If she'll just leave on her own and not come back…"

Dr. Richards took a step back. No scalpel appeared. No attack seemed imminent. She was just a frustrated woman who had come to express her grievances. Not someone Kenzie needed to fear.

Still, she was relieved when Bert stepped forward to escort Dr. Richards off the property, not trusting her to leave voluntarily. He said a few words into his shoulder mike, alerting the other guards that he was dealing with a trespasser and calling for Pratt to check in with Dr. Kirsch.

Kenzie let her breath out slowly as she watched Bert escort Dr. Richards away. Pratt was there by the time Bert was out of sight.

"Everything okay, Dr. Kirsch? Another wacko?"

Kenzie chuckled. "Yeah," she agreed. "Escaped from a mental institution."

He shook his head. "Let me walk you to the door."

He escorted her in the other direction, watched her swipe her card to enter the corridor to the medical examiner's office, and waved a hand in farewell. "Don't you worry about anything, Dr. Kirsch. We'll keep our eyes open."

58

Kenzie would not have suggested Old Joe's as the restaurant to meet with her parents. She would have looked for something more sophisticated, more likely to satisfy Lisa's particular tastes. Probably something in the city, since Roxboro didn't have anything that fancy. But Zachary had gone ahead and set it up and, despite the image that Kenzie had built up in her head of socialites who would never lower themselves to eat at a mere steakhouse, they both seemed comfortable and happy to be there. Neither dithered over the menu and complained that they didn't have the right cuts or a world-class chef. Kenzie started to relax and feel more comfortable having Zachary and her parents at the same table.

She had built up the differences between them so much in her mind, creating a schism between them and the feeling that it would be impossible for them to break bread together and enjoy it. Which was silly because no matter how much money her parents had or how embroiled they were in their charities and politics, they had raised Kenzie. And they had raised Amanda, and she hadn't been a snob either. They had both always been down-to-earth people at home, expecting her to do her homework and chores, to have friends over, and to make messes and break things. Because that's what kids did. Kenzie had been allowed to play at the playground and to ride her bike around, to explore her independence and to fall and skin her knees. Parents like that were not the type who would refuse to go to a steakhouse or put on a show of not enjoying it.

"So, how are things going with your investigations?" Walter asked. "Are you still working on those deaths at Persons?"

It had only been a day since they last spoke, so Kenzie could be forgiven if she snapped and told him nothing had changed in the last twenty-four hours. But of course, it had. She had reviewed all the details with Dr. Cook and Dr. Wiltshire and published her findings on both Leander Isah's death and Janice Martin's.

"I finished with them today. Filed my reports. So they are now public, or will be whenever they get posted."

"Was Janice Martin a suicide?" Zachary asked, his head cocked slightly.

Kenzie studied him. His question suggested that he'd had doubts about it, but Kenzie had never told him about the inconsistent bruising she had found. She had kept it all to herself to ensure that nothing could leak to the press, even though she knew that Zachary was not the source of the leak.

"No," she said slowly. "Janice Martin did not commit suicide. She was strangled."

"Homicide." Zachary nodded, seeming unsurprised by this.

"How did *you* know?" Kenzie demanded.

He shrugged and sipped his water. "It was... a little too convenient. And in a place like that... we should not have been the ones who found her. They should have had her on a watch. And she said they were not allowed to be in their rooms alone during the day. Her door should have been wide open so that they could see if anyone was inside. And they should have had someone walking by there every fifteen minutes. She shouldn't have had the opportunity and, if she had, they should have discovered her immediately."

"So you figured that someone had staged it."

Zachary nodded. "Not easy, but if patients are not supposed to be in their rooms, they shouldn't be in the corridor where they could see something going down. They should be in the common areas, visiting like they were supposed to."

Kenzie let out a breath. "Yeah. Things just didn't add up. People *do* find ways to commit suicide in places like that. But... it didn't really fit."

"You could prove it?" he asked.

Kenzie nodded. "The bruises on her neck went the wrong direction."

"I don't know if this is really dinnertime conversation," Lisa protested.

Kenzie rolled her eyes. "Dad asked. Get after him."

"And the other one?" Walter asked, ignoring his ex-wife's objection. "Was it also homicide?"

"Not that I could prove definitively. It could have been, and certainly the things that they did to him contributed to his death, but I believe it was actually the MDMA. Accidental death. A reaction to the drug, whether they gave him too much or if together with the SSRI it triggered Serotonin Syndrome. His body was overheating, he was very agitated, and, in the end, his heart just gave out. Sudden cardiac death due to MDMA ingestion."

"How sad," Lisa observed. "They were trying to help him."

"Well... some of them were," Kenzie agreed. "But there were a lot of abuses going on there too. A lot of things that should never have happened. There was supposed to be oversight. Controls in place. But it didn't work out that way."

"You're talking about that doctor they arrested?" Walter asked. "Disgusting that a predator like him should be able to operate in a facility with such vulnerable patients."

Kenzie nodded. "And other things that they are still building cases for. He isn't the only one responsible for what happened to Isah."

"And you think he is the one who killed this woman too?"

"That would be my guess. But it's not up to me to build a case against him. Just to give the police whatever I can. I suspect... Janice Martin was talking too much. She told me Isah wanted out of the program before he died. And she had been talking about missing time and other issues she had with the program. I suspect he wanted to shut her up before she said too much to the wrong person."

Zachary and Kenzie's parents all nodded, looking appropriately shocked at what had happened. Zachary was looking at Kenzie, a frown of concentration on his face. Kenzie wasn't sure what he was thinking. Maybe it was about her cases or about something completely separate that he was working on. Or perhaps just trying to think of another conversational segue to keep her parents engaged.

"Do you know for sure that it was the drug that killed Isah?" Zachary asked.

He had worked enough cases where it had turned out that the ME's findings were wrong. He knew that they could make mistakes as easily as anyone else. Or not have been provided with the information they needed to make the right ruling.

"Sudden cardiac death can be caused by other things," Kenzie said slowly. "He could have been experiencing heart or respiratory problems when they walked him out of the room after the altercation in the cafeteria, or when he was faced with the police, who he feared. He could have had a sudden, devastating allergic reaction. To what, I don't know, but it is possible. They might have placed him in restraints when they took him back to his room or to an isolation room. Someone might have waited until everyone was asleep and then smothered him."

"If it was an allergic reaction, he would have had hives and a swollen throat," Walter said, "And if he was smothered, he would have had those red dots. Those petechiae."

"If this was a TV show, yes," Kenzie agreed. "Because they always have enough clues on TV to nail everything down beyond a reasonable doubt. But in real life… someone with an allergic reaction severe enough to stop their heart may have no other physical signs, even microscopic ones. It happens so quickly that there is no sign on the body. They are dead in seconds. And not all asphyxiation cases show petechial hemorrhaging. Seventy to eighty percent do, but not all of them. A medical examiner gathers all the information he or she can from all different sources: the body, the scene, the trace evidence, the witnesses. But sometimes, it is still not enough to make a final determination. We just give it the best shot we can, and then…" Kenzie shrugged. "Move on to the next case."

"It could have been a toxin," Zachary suggested. "Something rare that paralyzes all the muscles of the body so that he can't breathe. Or that stops his heart."

"And some of the tox screens may still come back with more information. But the preliminary testing doesn't show anything, and we can't test for everything in the world. We can test for things that seem likely based on the signs in the body. But there is no way to test for every substance in the world."

He stared off into space, clearly thinking of all the different things it could be.

"He was on MDMA," Kenzie said. "MDMA kills. Occam's Razor."

"When you see hoof prints, think horses, not zebras."

"Exactly," Kenzie agreed. "And speaking of nature, I need to answer a certain call... back in a minute."

59

Kenzie stepped into the back hallway of Old Joe's and paused to let her eyes adjust to the dim light before proceeding past the kitchen and toward the ladies' room. When she returned from the bathroom, she stepped to the side for a tall, distinguished-looking patron headed toward the men's room. He barreled directly into her, smashing her into the wall.

"Hey!" Kenzie protested, outraged, "Look where you're—"

"Shut up." His hand closed over her mouth and pinned her head back against the wall tightly to prevent her from moving or speaking. Kenzie struggled to escape him and then realized who it was. She had only seen him once, on the occasion of Isah's death. One of the other doctors from Persons. Dr. Alvarez. But what was he doing there? And what did he think he was doing?

She tried to tell him to let her go but, with his hold on her, she couldn't. His eyes darted around, and he changed his grip to pull her away from the wall. He swept her toward the back emergency exit before she could even formulate the idea to fight back. She was out into the chilly night. The emergency door slammed back into place, and he pressed her against the outside wall, the rough red bricks biting into her head and back. His hand was still over her mouth, preventing her from saying anything.

"You should have listened!" he growled. "You should have minded your own business and just walked away! But you wouldn't listen. And you didn't die!" He shook his head and pressed her even more tightly against the wall, nearly smothering her.

Kenzie tried to fight back, but he was much bigger than she was, much stronger. Her mind went a mile a minute, adding up the things she hadn't accounted for.

Alvarez had been there when Kenzie went to pick up Isah's body. But why had he been there at night? It wasn't like with an emergency room, where they needed doctors there all the time. Everyone was asleep at night. There might have been a doctor on call if a patient was sick or needed something, but he would just give the nursing staff instructions over the phone.

Instead, he had told Nurse Craig to stay away from Isah in breach of their own protocols. And when they had discovered that he was dead, he had instructed the nurse to call a funeral home rather than the medical examiner's office. Alvarez, not Miller.

Had Isah already been dead when Alvarez told Nurse Craig that he was sedated and was not to be disturbed? He must have planned to obscure the time of death, giving his body longer to cool down to a normal temperature. Did he know about the problems Isah's hyperthermic state would cause in identifying his actual time of death?

Kenzie again tried to escape Alvarez's grip. What did he think he was going to do? Kidnap her? Kill her? She hadn't seen any weapon. He didn't take her to a car or van, which was good because she already felt nauseated and her head was throbbing. If she had to add a kidnapping to the horror of what was happening to her, she didn't know how she could handle it.

He had already tried pushing her out into traffic. That had failed and now here he was ready to try again, and who knew what he would do this time. A more direct approach?

Alvarez started to look around. Maybe it had just occurred to him that he hadn't really planned things out. What was he going to do now? Leave once he'd aired his grievances? Kill her? With what? His bare hands? A makeshift weapon? Kenzie tried again to squirm free of his grip. She tried to use her voice, even though he was not letting her speak. She could still get a noise out. A pleading sound. Something to remind him that she was human; he was holding a human life in his hands.

He looked at her, his eyes meeting hers for the first time. Kenzie stared into his dark eyes pleadingly. She tried to reach out to that hurt part of him that was causing him to lash out. He was frustrated. Disappointed. Like Dr. Richards, he'd had his dream pulled out from under him. The fact that it had happened because of his own choices made no difference. Not to him. He still felt the loss of his job and the nice set-up he'd had there. He blamed Kenzie for it but, if she could make him see her as a person, an individual, maybe he would let her go. Maybe it would make a difference.

She made another noise under his hand. Soft. Questioning. Like she was asking him if he was okay. If she could help him.

"It's *your* fault," Alvarez growled, clearly not getting the message she was trying to send him. "If you hadn't shown up, sticking your nose into something that was none of your business, it would all have been different. We could have kept Persons going. You've ruined everything."

Kenzie tried to make a sorrowful, apologetic noise. Her mind slid to Rhys. How he'd been silenced for so many years. How hard he had to try to make himself heard when he couldn't speak. She'd never appreciated how difficult that was. How lucky they were to communicate using words when Rhys was left with pointing, gesturing, sending them pictures and the occasional text to convey his feelings, questions, and needs. She wanted to help Rhys if she could. She didn't think they were done yet. They could still help Rhys. Just because the MDMA trial had not worked out well for him, that didn't mean it was the end of the road.

Alvarez gave Kenzie a little shake, bringing her thoughts back to him. It was as if he had sensed her drifting away from him. Maybe he was restricting the flow of air into her lungs and she was experiencing symptoms of oxygen deprivation.

"You're going to pay for this," Alvarez shouted, furious not to have her full attention. He wanted her to be afraid, terrified. He fed off of fear. That must have been one of the perks he got from working at Persons. Lots of traumatized people. Lots of anxiety and fear to go around. Especially if he were part of the abuse, either as a partner or an observer.

"Julio Alvarez!" a loud woman's voice called out. "Put your hands in the air and back toward me."

Dr. Alvarez stared into Kenzie's eyes. He didn't turn around to look at the cop who had called his name. He wasn't willing to give up his position of power, to have to relax, let Kenzie go, and hand himself over to someone else's authority. He was in a position of strength, threatening her, frightening her, and he was not going to let go.

Physically, Kenzie had no way of breaking free from him. He was too strong and none of her attempts to break free had been successful. None of them had even made him budge.

Kenzie could only think of one way to escape his power.

She closed her eyes.

60

L ook at me!" Alvarez's grip on Kenzie tightened, and she could feel his face get closer to hers. She could feel the proximity of his body, its warmth, his damp breath on her face.

She didn't open her eyes. She tried to relax her body as much as she could. Like when she was at the dentist and realized that she was holding her whole body rigid during a procedure and would force herself to relax all her muscles. To pretend that she was at a spa for some pleasant treatment, the buzzing of the drill or cleaning tool just white noise, drifting toward sleep.

Alvarez could feel her relax and started to panic. "No! No, come back here!" He shook her, grinding the back of her head into the rough brick wall. "No! That wasn't long enough!"

Kenzie refused to open her eyes again. She decided it would be good if he thought she had completely blacked out and loosened her knees, letting her body fall away from his, slipping down and to the side, so that he was trying to hold her up instead of just pinning her in place.

She heard a shout. Knew that Zachary was there with Garcia, too. He believed she was hurt, unconscious or dead. But she couldn't respond to the anxiety in his voice. She needed to do her part to get away from Alvarez and let the police do their jobs. The concrete below her feet was hard and studded with gravel and possibly broken glass. Not the best place to land in an unconscious state. She did the best she could to cushion her fall, but couldn't be obvious about it.

Alvarez turned away from her. The police were yelling at him, giving him instructions. Eventually, they managed to put him under arrest, search him, and cuff him without incident. He carried no gun. Or scalpel. But that didn't mean he couldn't have killed her. Kenzie watched the latter part of this process through her lids, cracked just slightly open, not moving. Not until they had him in cuffs.

Garcia hurried over to check on Kenzie as she sat up and started to brush the gravel from her arms and legs.

"Dr. Kirsch! Are you all right?" she asked earnestly, her accent stronger than usual, reaching out to take Kenzie's hand and to check her pulse.

Zachary was telling the other cops to let him through to go see Kenzie, and Garcia turned around and told them to let him. Zachary hurried over, crouching over to hug Kenzie and reassure himself that she was alive.

"Don't get up," he told her as she tried to get to her feet. "You passed out. Let the paramedics check you out—"

"I didn't faint," Kenzie told him. "I was shamming."

"What?"

"It was an act. He was getting off on my fear, on connecting with me and terrorizing me. So I shut him off."

Zachary blinked, considering this. "But I saw your eyes close. I saw you collapse."

"Just acting." Kenzie brushed gravel from her palms and looked down at her pants, which looked pretty bad after landing on the grimy sidewalk. There were specks of blood on her hands from the sharp gravel and glass. A tear in the knee of her pants and another graze. The opposite one from the one she'd hurt when he had pushed her into traffic. A matched set now.

Zachary put his hands out to steady her, but didn't touch her, watching to make sure that she was stable and then pulling back to let her have some space.

"Go tell Walter and Lisa I'm okay," Kenzie instructed him. "How did you know where I was and what was going on?"

"You're never long in the bathroom," he said with a shrug. "Not like some women. I could see you on my friends app. See that you weren't in the restaurant anymore. You didn't have any good reason to be in the back lane. GPS can be off, but... I couldn't see you in the back hall. And I knew it wasn't just one man."

"You knew...?"

"At Persons. One man couldn't have gotten Janice hung up in that position. The set-up would need at least two."

"Well... you might have mentioned that."

He smiled. "I was going to." He touched her cheek briefly, comforting her and confirming to himself that she was okay. "I'll go tell them you're all right. I'll get our bill, unless you want to stay for dessert."

Kenzie laughed. "No. I had ice cream yesterday. I think that will have to count for today, too. I don't think I could sit down at a table again tonight."

He left to go talk to her parents. Garcia shook her head slowly. "Are you sure you're okay? What did he say to you? Anything incriminating?"

"I don't know... it all happened so fast. It was more about blaming me for ending all the good stuff than admitting anything he had done."

"Oh, well. We've got plenty we can charge him with now, while we look at the situation and see what else we can prove."

"I guess he and Miller must have been working together."

Garcia nodded. "We'll play them off each other. See if we can get them to implicate each other."

"Dr. Richards showed up at work today. I was going to call you and tell you about it... and then I got distracted by other things."

"Oh? Is she part of this too? I was beginning to think she was just a dupe."

"I don't think she did anything. Just looked the other way. Played ignorant. I can't see her not knowing any of what was going on. Especially when those therapy sessions were being taped. She must have watched a few of them back in the beginning. Maybe before things got so advanced. But she must have known that the trial wasn't running the way it was supposed to."

"Why did *she* come to see you?"

"I don't know if she intended to do anything more than just complain about me screwing everything up for her. I was a little anxious she might be carrying a scalpel with my name on it. But security came along and got rid of her."

"I'll have a chat with her. Make sure it doesn't happen again."

"Thanks. I really don't want to have to keep worrying about people showing up and threatening me!"

"No, that's probably enough for one week." Garcia smiled. "I'm glad you're all right."

"And glad that Zachary called you instead of playing cowboy?"

"Good for him," Garcia agreed. "If Alvarez had been armed, holding you at gunpoint or knife point, he could really have put you in danger. But I suspect if we hadn't gotten here pretty quickly, Zachary would have been around back in that alley within a few minutes."

"Probably." Zachary didn't have the best impulse control. The fact that he had called Garcia and not run directly toward trouble surprised Kenzie. Maybe he was learning. Or maybe he had trusted her to take care of herself for a few minutes.

"What do you need from me?" Kenzie asked. "Can I give a statement tomorrow? I've got my parents here, and there is only so much drama I can deal with at once."

"Sure. Come by the office, and you can make a report tomorrow. We have enough to start proceedings based on what we saw."

61

W e were just hoping for an update on Rhys," Zachary said to Vera, his phone lying on the table with speakerphone enabled. "Has there been… any change?"

"He's doing better," Vera said cautiously. "The doctors say that the effects of the MDMA are wearing off. That his brain is… healing. Returning to the way that it was before the break. They hope… that there won't be any permanent damage."

"That's good news," Zachary told her.

Kenzie was glad to hear it. She felt terrible that her family had been part of the cause of what had happened to Rhys. If he'd been permanently damaged by that initial therapy session, she didn't know how she could handle it. Even though she had begged Vera to take Rhys out of the program. It was still partially her fault that he had been in it. Her family money. Her worry about Rhys expressed to her mother. She hadn't wanted it, but she still felt like it was her fault.

"Could we visit him again?" Zachary asked Vera, "Are they letting him see people?"

"I don't know…" Vera hesitated, and Kenzie didn't think it had anything to do with the hospital and whether they would allow Kenzie and Zachary in. "I suppose it would be good for him to see someone other than me. He always enjoys his visits with you."

Except for maybe the last one.

"Are we still on his approved visitor list?"

"Yes, of course. You can go see him anytime, if the hospital approves it. And I'm sure they will unless he is in therapy when you want to visit."

"We'll pick a time when he isn't in therapy. Maybe call ahead to be sure. Has he… said anything about what happened? Before, I mean. When Stanley found him."

Vera didn't answer right away. "I've been afraid to ask," she admitted eventually. "He's been through so much; I don't want to traumatize him more by bringing it up. I'm hoping that… maybe it was just one of those things. A virus. Sleepwalking. And that he'll just go on like normal."

As before, her first reaction was to ignore that there was a problem. To cover it up, forget that it ever happened.

"Do you mind if we ask him?" Kenzie asked. She didn't want to do something that was strictly against Vera's wishes. But she also didn't want Rhys to be left to deal with it himself, swimming in whatever sorrow or trauma might have triggered him again.

"Well… maybe that would be a good idea," Vera conceded. "And if you think it is something that I need to know about… or that his doctor does…"

"We'll let you know," Zachary agreed.

They were able to get in to see Rhys at the hospital. He was not in his room this time, but was well enough to be in the common areas without getting too agitated or disturbing the other patients. An orderly hovered nearby, keeping an eye on things, ready to step in if the situation became too much for Rhys. Kenzie tried to ignore him and to focus on the boy and how he was doing.

Rhys shook hands with Zachary, slapping him on the shoulder with his free hand. He didn't have the big smile he usually did when greeting Zachary, but at least he knew who they were and wasn't opposed to seeing them. He looked at Kenzie and hesitated, unsure how to greet her. Kenzie offered her hand, and when he took it tentatively, she leaned in and gave him a brief hug around the shoulders too. She often greeted him with a kiss on the cheek, but she didn't this time, worried it might be too much for him. She released his hand and motioned to the table where they could sit. Rhys looked at Zachary, and when he sat, Rhys did as well.

"How are you feeling?" Zachary asked. "You've been through a pretty tough time."

Rhys shrugged and nodded. He raised one hand and wobbled it back and forth. *So-so.*

"That drug therapy really affected you," Kenzie suggested. "Do you remember everything that happened?"

He shook his head.

"Boy, were you ever talkative," Zachary told him. "You just went on and on and on."

Rhys thought about that for a minute. He pointed tentatively at his head, then made a "blowing up" gesture, spreading his fingers apart to signify an explosion.

"Some people have a feeling of being opened up," Kenzie said. "Or of being able to see and experience things they couldn't before."

He pointed at her and nodded slightly. Maybe not a fully accurate description of his experience, but close enough.

"You talked a lot about when Grandpa Clarence was killed," Zachary told him.

Rhys looked at Zachary, but made no response.

"Do you remember that?" Kenzie asked him. "Vera didn't think you remembered anything about when your grandpa died. Or at least, not clearly."

Rhys pointed at himself and gave an emphatic nod.

"You remember what happened that day?"

He nodded again.

"Do you want to talk about it? To us, or your grandma, or a therapist? It might help to be able to talk about it instead of keeping it hidden all the time."

Rhys made a horizontal slicing motion with his hand. A definite *no,* and yet, there was something else behind it. As if Rhys were saying, *No, not about that.*

"You want to talk?" Kenzie tried.

He nodded. He looked at Zachary.

"Do you just want to talk to Zachary? I can give you guys some space. Go check out the gift shop and pick up some snacks."

The corner of his mouth twitched in a slight smile, but he shook his head.

"You want to talk to both of us?" Zachary asked. "Or just to Kenzie?"

He pointed to them each in turn.

"Okay." Zachary nodded. "We're both staying, then. Did you just want to visit, or was there something particular?"

A nod. Zachary rolled his eyes, recognizing that he'd trapped himself again, asking two questions and then not sure which Rhys was responding to.

"You don't want to talk to us about when Clarence was killed," Kenzie said.

He shook his head, agreeing with the statement.

"About the therapy?" Zachary asked.

He shook his head again.

"Did anyone hurt you when you were at Persons?" Kenzie asked. "Or… get inappropriate with you? Some of the doctors there were… doing a lot of things they shouldn't."

Rhys grimaced and shook his head again, adding a negating hand gesture as well. But there *was* something he wanted to talk to them about.

"Before that?" Kenzie suggested.

He nodded. Kenzie looked over at Zachary. Maybe Rhys wanted to talk to them about whatever had been on his mind lately. What might have triggered his fugue state, his inability to communicate with them at all.

"Something happened that upset you," Kenzie suggested. "Was it something going on at school? Were you being bullied?"

He pointed at her, then hesitated and shook his head. Kenzie was doing what she had just observed in Zachary. Peppering Rhys with too many questions, not giving him a chance to answer one at a time, which confused the process. She tried to slow down.

"Something happened that upset you," she repeated, making it a statement of fact. Something had sent him way off the rails. It was possible that it was just a virus or a hormone surge, or some developing psychosis, but she didn't think so.

Rhys nodded his agreement.

Something had upset him. It had sent him out on the streets looking for Stanley Green, a strong male role model. Someone who could help him. Only whatever bothered him was too much for him to handle, even with Stanley's help. By the time he got there, things were spinning out of control.

"Something going on at school?" Zachary asked, trying to pick up where the disconnect had been. Rhys had started out with yes, and then drawn back.

Rhys shrugged and wobbled his hand back and forth. *Sort of.*

"Did someone at school threaten you?"

Rhys shook his head.

"Are they bullying you? Causing you problems?"

He shook his head.

Kenzie and Zachary looked at each other. Kenzie tried to fathom what would have upset Rhys enough that it had sent him into a fugue state. If not someone targeting Rhys, then maybe he had witnessed someone else being hurt? That could also be very traumatic. Especially given his history with his grandfather being killed, and then his aunt, and then Bridget being kidnapped. Rhys had shown himself to be a protector. Someone who had stepped forward when Madison had needed help, and Luke and Aster. And who had insisted that Zachary take care of himself and admit himself to the hospital when things had gotten too bad for him. Rhys was someone who cared deeply about other people. That had to be it.

"Is someone else being hurt or bullied?" Kenzie asked.

He didn't respond immediately, then nodded slowly.

"We want to help too," Zachary said. "I don't want to see any kids being hurt."

Rhys shook his head.

Another misstep. Kenzie wasn't sure how they had lost the thread. "Can you tell us who is being hurt or bullied?"

He looked around him, seeming unsure what to do. He pointed at himself and then made a phone gesture.

"Oh. Of course," Zachary dug his phone out of his pocket and slid it across the table toward Rhys. Rhys frequently communicated by messaging on his phone. His communications were severely curtailed if he wasn't allowed to have his phone during his stay in the psych ward.

Rhys shook his head and pushed the phone back, pointing insistently at himself. Then he turned his head to look at the orderly, nodding to indicate him.

"You want *your* phone."

Rhys nodded.

Zachary waved the orderly over. "Can you get Rhys his phone?"

The man looked stern. "Patients are not allowed to have their phones without supervision. We've had a number of incidents with… misuse. And then there is the issue of trying to work with someone on their mental health when all they will do is stare at the screen."

"Rhys's phone is an assistive communication device," Kenzie said firmly. "He needs it now to communicate with us. Please go get it."

The orderly opened his mouth to argue.

"I'm sure you wouldn't want to be accused of abusing the rights of a disabled person," Kenzie suggested. "Denying accommodations for communications under the *Americans with Disabilities Act—*"

"Okay, okay," the orderly held up his hand. "As long as you will be responsible for its use. If there are any issues…"

"There aren't going to be any issues," Zachary said. "He wants to be able to talk to us."

The orderly looked at Rhys for a moment, then nodded. "I'll bring it to you in a minute. I just need to sign it out."

Rhys nodded.

The orderly walked away. Rhys rolled his eyes. He pointed to Kenzie and with his brows raised, made a fingernail-polishing gesture against his chest.

"I can be pretty tough," Kenzie said with a laugh. "Just try bullying someone around me."

Zachary looked at Rhys and nodded his agreement. "She's not kidding."

Rhys grinned, the first genuine smile they'd seen from him since arriving. After a week of not seeing him smile, it was a relief. Kenzie felt a flood of warmth and, for the first time, she felt like Rhys would be okay. They hadn't done irreparable harm. He was on his way back, and he would be okay.

It was a few minutes before the orderly returned with Rhys's phone. He handed it to the boy with a nod, then retreated to his previous position.

Rhys held the phone close to him, then turned it on. The screen didn't light up. Kenzie closed her eyes in frustration. Had they let the battery drain in the time since Rhys had been admitted?

Frowning, Rhys held down the power button and, in a moment, the screen lit up as it rebooted. It still had juice. It had just been powered down.

They waited while the phone restarted, and all the texts and messages sent while the phone was off were delivered. A lot of messages. Kenzie was glad at the evidence that people had been concerned about Rhys. His absence had not gone unnoticed. Rhys waited, but didn't read through all the new messages. Eventually, the phone stopped flashing and buzzing and settled down again. Rhys tapped and swiped his way through his phone and then stopped. He held the phone against his chest for a minute and looked at Kenzie as if reconsidering whatever he had planned to show her.

"It's okay," Kenzie said. "We want to help you. It doesn't matter what it is."

Zachary nodded his agreement. "We're here for you, bud."

Rhys held it away from them for a moment longer, and then put the phone down on the table and slid it across to them.

Kenzie looked down at a photograph. The picture of a man's face. The pallid blue-gray skin was a tip-off even before Kenzie focused on the round, dark red hole in the man's forehead. Kenzie looked more closely. A lot could be accomplished with a little stage makeup. There were some experts in the business who were very good at what they did. Thrillers and zombie movies were a big thing. Realistic blood and gore. But she knew, looking at the man, that he was dead.

She looked back at Rhys. He knew it, too.

"Where did you get this?" Kenzie asked.

He shrugged.

"A friend? Someone at school?"

He nodded.

"And where did they get it?"

He shrugged and made a round, circulating gesture. He mimed sending messages out several times.

"It's going around school," Zachary interpreted. "Everybody's sending it around."

Rhys nodded.

"Do you know who it is?" Kenzie asked. "Where they got it?"

He shook his head. He pointed firmly at Kenzie, and then at the picture.

"You want me to find out."

Rhys nodded his agreement.

Kenzie looked at Zachary, and then stared down at the man in the picture. "Well then... I guess I'll look into it."

Did you enjoy this book? Reviews and recommendations are vital to making a book successful.

Please leave a review at your favorite book store or review site and share it with your friends.

Don't miss the following bonus material:
Sign up for mailing list to get a free ebook
Read a sneak preview chapter
Other books by P.D. Workman
Learn more about the author

DON'T MISS A THING! GET THE LATEST NEWS AND A FREE EBOOK

Your First Taste

PDWORKMAN.COM/SIGNUP

PREVIEW OF CAPTURED IN DEATH

I t wasn't the way Kenzie's cases normally came to her.
As an assistant to the medical examiner, she was used to
bodies being brought in by van, laid out on the table and
cleaned, ready for her to begin her post-mortem. She would have
some scene notes to peruse, or if she had gone out to the scene
herself, she would have dictated the notes. Maybe she would be by
herself, or maybe with Dr. Cook, who was substituting for Dr. Wiltshire while his broken hand was healing.

A very different scenario than the one she currently found herself
in, sitting in the visiting area of the psych ward with Rhys sitting
across and Zachary next to her. Kenzie pulled her eyes away from the
photograph on the phone she held in her hand to the serious Black
teen who had handed it to her and was waiting for her to say
something.

"Rhys, this needs to go to the police. They need to investigate. Do
you even know who this is?"

Rhys, non-speaking as usual, spread his hands apart, palms up, in
a gesture of helplessness. *Don't know.*

Zachary leaned in to look at the picture again, his face close to
Kenzie's so she could smell his shaving cream. He usually sported a
three or four-day growth of beard, which made him look like a home-

less person or at least someone down on their luck. Someone people didn't want to make eye contact with and would forget as soon as they walked away. As a private investigator, he didn't want people to remember him. But today, he happened to be clean-shaven. His dark eyes were intense as he stared at the photograph. He ran a hand over his close-cropped dark hair.

"We don't even know if it is real," he pointed out. "It could be... stage makeup."

Kenzie didn't have to look again at the grayish skin or the bullet hole in the man's forehead to know that this was no makeup job. She had seen enough corpses in the course of her work to recognize one when she saw it, even in a picture.

"He's dead," she told Zachary with certainty. "It's real."

Rhys nodded his agreement. His dark skin kept him from looking pale, but his expression was pinched and worried. His frown deeper than usual. He had been through an ordeal, a mental collapse apparently triggered by this very picture, followed by a reaction to the drug used in the experimental treatment program he had been placed in, and then finally sedated to let him catch up on the sleep he needed and get back on track again.

It had been over a week since Stanley Green had found him wandering in the street in a fugue state. And if that fugue state had been triggered by viewing this picture, then the man in the picture had been dead for over a week and still hadn't shown up in the morgue.

Maybe he never would. Maybe his body had been dumped somewhere no one would find it.

Rhys held out his hand for his phone. Kenzie shook her head, not giving it back to him. "This is evidence. The police will want to look at the photograph's metadata and any other evidence on your phone. Where you got it from." Kenzie raised her eyebrows, asking again for Rhys to tell her where he had gotten the picture. How did a teenager end up with the picture of a murdered man on his phone? Who had sent it to him and why?

Rhys looked frustrated. Maybe he wanted to text her something on his messaging app. He relied on his phone for communication. He couldn't tell his story to her in gestures and facial expressions. Some things could be communicated that way, but he needed something more.

Kenzie slid her own phone across the table to him. "Send messages to Zachary's phone," she prompted.

Rhys picked up her phone with long, slender fingers and operated it quickly. He found the messaging app he wanted, swiped and tapped rapidly with his thumbs, and the first message popped up on Zachary's phone in a few seconds. Zachary held it so that he and Kenzie could see it at the same time, their heads close together.

Rhys had sent a picture of a dog, a recurring theme in his messages. This one was a cartoon picture of a basset hound dressed in a Sherlock Holmes deerstalker hat and peering into a magnifying glass.

Kenzie nodded. "I know you want me to look into it. To find out what I can. And I will... but this is a police matter. They will have to figure out where the picture came from and who it is. Until I actually see the body, there's not much that I can tell just by looking at a picture."

Rhys pointed at the picture of the dead man, rolling his eyes. What other information did Kenzie need than the fact that the man had been shot in the head? Wasn't that enough to determine cause and manner of death? It was glaringly obvious.

Then what was he expecting her to find out in her investigation? Was she supposed to be able to tell from the photograph who did it? Why?

"Okay, yes," she said as patiently as she could. "I can see that he was shot. Cause of death. I can't issue a medical examiner's report based on a photo. I don't know who it is or the circumstances surrounding his death. I mean, I do issue reports on John Does, but it still needs to go through the official channels for me to do that. I need human remains. Who did you get this from?"

He shrugged and made the ASL sign for "friend," both index fingers hooked together. A well-known sign, even though he did not generally use ASL to communicate, but relied on his own gestures and the phone pictures and short texts to get his message across.

"A friend from school?" Zachary asked.

Rhys nodded.

"And do you know where *he* got it from?"

Rhys shrugged. He had already communicated to them that it was something that had been circulating the school. His friend had gotten it from another friend, who had gotten it from another friend.

"What are they saying about it?" Kenzie asked. "They're not just sending it around by itself with no explanation."

He pointed at the phone and made a gun shape with his hand, complete with a jerk showing the gun had been fired.

"What?" Zachary asked. "'Here is a picture of a man who was shot.' That's it?"

Rhys nodded. Kenzie wanted to search through his phone to see who it had come from and exactly what the attached text had said. But she didn't want to touch anything that the police would want to look at. It had probably been sent through an app where the message self-destructed, and all of that information was gone. But maybe the police techs could pull off information that had been deleted but not overwritten.

There was just one thing that she needed to do. If Rhys wanted her to investigate the man's death, she needed a copy of the picture. She didn't know what she could do for Rhys, but he needed to see that she was doing everything she could. He had trusted them with this information that he hadn't shown anyone else, and he was counting on her being able to make everything right.

She didn't know if she could do that, but she would do everything she could for him.

PREVIEW CHAPTER 2

"I'm going to send this to your phone," she told Zachary.

It might make more sense to forward it to her own phone. She would need it there eventually. But Rhys didn't need it popping up in his face again while he was holding her phone in his hands. It had been traumatic enough the first time.

And she would probably get Zachary to look at the photo's metadata to see if he could tell her anything about its origin.

Zachary nodded his agreement. Kenzie sent it to him, then slid Rhys's phone into her pocket. It would need to go to the police as evidence. Kenzie would get Rhys another phone. His grandmother, Vera, could probably not afford it. Kenzie didn't think she had much disposable income. But Kenzie didn't want Rhys to be left without a means to communicate beyond gestures.

"This whole thing," Kenzie motioned to the phone in her pocket. "I'm so sorry you had to deal with it. It must be really difficult after what happened to your grandpa."

Rhys nodded. His eyes dropped to the phone in his hand, but he didn't type anything immediately.

Until the drug therapy that Rhys had reacted to, they had all assumed that what had happened to Grandpa Clarence when Rhys was just five was long forgotten, or at least very murky in Rhys's memory. But the MDMA had made Rhys voluble, overcoming his usual mutism, and he had related the images to them over and over again.

His grandfather murdered before his eyes. Shot in the head, like the man in the picture.

It wasn't that Rhys was afraid that the same murderer might have come back, that she had killed a second time and he might be in danger.

Because Rhys knew who the murderer was. He had always known, and he had lived with her for years after Grandpa Clarence's death. Because it had been his aunt Robin. She had since passed. so they all knew that it wasn't the same killer. Just the same cause of death.

Kenzie saw Rhys's lips moving. The same mantra repeated over and over again. Even though he didn't voice the words, she still recognized them.

Stop it. Just stop it.

Robin's words, the night she had killed her father.

"I know," Kenzie said softly. She leaned forward and put her hand over Rhys's briefly, unsure how he would respond to the physical contact. "This is terrible for you. Are you having a lot of flashbacks?"

After remaining unfocused for a few long seconds, Rhys's gaze finally returned to Kenzie's face. He cocked his head slightly as if he knew that Kenzie had said something but wasn't sure what it was or what she meant.

"I asked if you're having flashbacks," Kenzie said slowly, "if you keep remembering what you saw and felt the night that your grandpa was killed, there are things that you can do to try to reduce the impact of the flashbacks, to… get back to the present."

He held out one hand, palm out, inviting her to go on, eyebrows raised curiously.

"One method that helps Zachary is called anchoring." Kenzie looked at Zachary.

He nodded but didn't explain. His flashbacks were better than they had been, but he wasn't over them. The fire that had destroyed his childhood home and precipitated the rift in his family was still ever-present in his mind. Even if he wasn't having flashbacks, he was still aware of it. And although he could stand to be around a lit candle or small campfire now without being thrown back to that experience, other things still triggered flashbacks for him.

"You concentrate on your senses," she told Rhys, since Zachary didn't seem inclined to explain. "You name five things that you see, five things that you hear, five things that you smell or feel. Focusing on those things, on your senses and surroundings, helps minimize the flashback and help you to anchor to the present."

Rhys nodded slowly. He couldn't name the things he saw out loud and probably couldn't type them on his phone when he was in the throes of a flashback, but he could still focus on them and hopefully get himself out of a flashback faster.

"Maybe you could tell Vera about anchoring, too," Zachary suggested. "She can help talk Rhys through it."

Kenzie nodded. "*You* should probably talk to her rather than me."

Kenzie wasn't exactly in Vera's good books these days. Kenzie had been vocal about Rhys not going to Persons, the private psychiatric facility that had done the experimental drug protocol, for treatment. Kenzie had tried to tell Vera that it was too dangerous, that what they were doing there was not ethical, and that MDMA therapy was too risky for Rhys.

But Vera had been desperate. After years of not hearing Rhys's voice more than just a word or two here and there, and then him falling into the fugue state where he was completely uncommunicative, not even acknowledging that they were speaking to him, let alone trying to respond, she had been willing to risk anything for the miracle cure Persons had dangled in front of her.

Kenzie had been right. The fact did not endear her to Vera. Kenzie was sure Vera would feel awkward and embarrassed that she had gone ahead and done what Kenzie had warned her about and that the result had been negative, just as Kenzie had afraid it would be. Kenzie being right about the therapy would be harder for Vera to forgive than being wrong would have been.

Zachary looked at Kenzie for a few seconds, reading this in her face, and eventually nodded. "I'll talk to her about anchoring," he agreed. "Walk her through how to do it." He looked at Rhys. "It does help. It doesn't make them go away completely, but it helps you to… not drown in the flashbacks."

Rhys gave a thumbs-up. He was all for anything that might help.

Kenzie wondered how he felt about the treatment that Vera had put him through. Did he understand that she had just been trying to help him? Did he resent being treated like an animal or a child with no understanding, with no choice in how she decided he should be treated? He hadn't been able to talk to her at the time, hadn't been able to understand or to express his wishes one way or the other, but that understanding wouldn't necessarily change his feelings about what had happened.

Feelings were not always logical. Kenzie sometimes found herself feeling completely opposite from what she wanted to sometimes. No matter how much she tried to talk herself into feeling a certain way, she couldn't control her primitive brain.

"So…" Kenzie took a deep breath and let it go.

They had asked him whether he wanted to talk about Grandpa Clarence and what he remembered. He had shown them the picture of the stranger and asked Kenzie to look into it. Kenzie didn't know how much success she would have in her assignment.

Rhys was looking tired and strained around the eyes. It was bound to be taking a lot of effort for him to act as normal as possible and socialize with them. He had been through a lot in the last couple of weeks, and it would take time for him to recover.

"So, I guess we should probably be going," Kenzie said, standing up and looking at Zachary to encourage him to do the same. "You're looking pretty tired," she told Rhys. "I don't want to wear you out. I'll talk to the police and get started on this… and one of us will bring you a new phone by the end of the day so you can use it to communicate. I don't know how long it will be before you get this one back. I assume they'll need it for a day or two to get all the information they need."

Rhys shrugged, looking unconcerned about whether he got the

phone back or not. Kenzie supposed that if he got a new phone in the deal, he wouldn't be too upset about it, as long as he could still log back into all of his accounts and not lose any information.

Captured in Death, Book #10 of the *Kenzie Kirsch Medical Thriller* series by P.D. Workman can be purchased at pdworkman.com

ABOUT THE AUTHOR

P.D. Workman is a USA Today Bestselling author, winner of several awards from Library Services for Youth in Custody and the InD'tale Magazine's Crowned Heart award, and has published over 100 mystery/suspense/thriller and young adult books, including stand alones and these series: Auntie Clem's Bakery cozy mysteries, Reg Rawlins Psychic Investigator paranormal mysteries, Zachary Goldman Mysteries (PI), Kenzie Kirsch Medical Thrillers, Parks Pat Mysteries (police procedural), and YA series: Tamara's Teardrops, Between the Cracks, and Breaking the Pattern.

Workman loves writing about the underdog, who the reader may love or hate. She has been praised for her realistic details, deep characterization, and sensitive handling of the serious social issues that appear in all of her stories, from light cozy mysteries through to darker, grittier young adult and mystery/suspense books.

> P. D. Workman, does not shy from probing the deep psychological scars of childhood trauma, mental illness, and addiction. Also characteristic of this author, these extremely sensitive issues are explored with extensive empathy, described with incredible clarity, and portrayed with profound insight.
>
> — —KIM, GOODREADS REVIEWER

Some of Workman's titles have been translated into Spanish, French, Portuguese, German, and Italian.

Workman began writing at an early age and is a prolific reader as well as writer. She is also passionate about teaching and learning, expresses her creativity through art and cooking, and loves exploring the Calgary parks and green spaces where the Parks Pat Mysteries are set. She was a legal assistant for many years and has done extensive charitable work.

Workman was born and raised in Alberta, Canada, and is married with one adult son.

———————

Please visit P.D. Workman at pdworkman.com to see what else she is working on, to join her mailing list, and to link to her social networks.

———————

If you enjoyed this book, please take the time to recommend it to other purchasers with a review or star rating and share it with your friends!

tiktok.com/@pdworkmanauthor

facebook.com/pdworkmanauthor

x.com/pdworkmanauthor

instagram.com/pdworkmanauthor

amazon.com/author/pdworkman

bookbub.com/authors/p-d-workman

goodreads.com/pdworkman

linkedin.com/in/pdworkman

pinterest.com/pdworkmanauthor

youtube.com/pdworkman

Find P.D. Workman's books at

PDWORKMAN.COM

Scan the QR code below